D0812236

78518
7140

GREEN HILLS PUBLIC LIBRARY DISTRICT
8611 WEST 103RD STREET
PALOS HILLS, IL 60465

DEMCO

# ONLY THE DEAD
# KNOW BROOKLYN

MANHATTAN

Greenpoint

Williamsburg

Map of
Brooklyn

Brooklyn
Heights

Fort
Greene

Bushwick

Cobble
Hill

Red
Hook

Carroll
Gardens

Downtown

Bedford-Stuyvesant

Cypress
Hills

ATLANTIC AVE.

Park
Slope

Crown Heights

New Lots

GOWANUS BAY

Prospect
Park

Browns-
ville

East New York

Greenwood
Cemetery

Windsor Terrace

FLATBUSH AVE.

Flatbush

Sunset
Park

Borough Park

Canarsie

Bay Ridge

Flatlands

Bensonhurst

Midwood

JAMAICA BAY

Gravesend

Sheepshead Bay

GRAVESEND BAY

Coney Island

# ONLY THE DEAD KNOW BROOKLYN

A NOVEL BY
## Thomas Boyle

DAVID R. GODINE, PUBLISHER · BOSTON

GREEN HILLS PUB. LIB. DIST.

BOY
c1

First published in 1985 by
David R. Godine, Publisher, Inc.
306 Dartmouth Street
Boston, Massachusetts 02116

Copyright ©1985 by Thomas Boyle

All rights reserved. No part of this book may be used or repro-
duced in any manner whatsoever without written permission except in the case of brief quotations embodied in critical articles
and reviews.

Excerpt from "The White Negro" from *Advertisements for Myself*
by Norman Mailer reprinted by permission of the Putnam Publishing Group. Copyright ©1959 by Norman Mailer.

Thomas Wolfe, excerpt from "Only the Dead Know Brooklyn" in
*From Death to Morning*. Copyright ©1935 F.R. Publishing Corp.;
copyright © renewed 1963 Paul Gitlin. Copyright ©1935 Charles
Scribners Sons; copyright renewed ©1963 Paul Gitlin. First ap-
peared in *The New Yorker*. Reprinted with the permission of
Charles Scribners Sons.

**Library of Congress Cataloging in Publication Data**
Boyle, Thomas, 1939–
Only the dead know Brooklyn.
I. Title.
PS3552.093305     1985     813'.54     84-48753
ISBN 0-87923-565-9

First edition
Printed in the United States of America

*To Peggy and William, Mother and Ken,
and, of course, Aunt Gertrude*

"Listen," I says. "You gotta get dat idea outa yoeh head right now," I says. "You ain't nevah gonna get to know Brooklyn," I says. "Not in a hundred yeahs. I been livin' heah all my life," I says, "an' I don't even know all deh is to know about, so how do you expect to know duh town," I says, "when you don't even live heah?"

"Yes," he says, "but I got a map to help me find my way about."

"Map or no map," I says, "yuh ain't gonna get to know Brooklyn wit no map," I says.

"Can you swim?" he says, just like dat. Jesus, by dat time, y'know, I begun to see dat duh guy was some kind of nut. . . ."

—Thomas Wolfe, *"Only the Dead Know Brooklyn"* (1935)

# CHAPTER I

FLETCHER CARRUTHERS III had a habit of picking up the phone between his index finger and thumb, and holding it an inch or two from his ear; then he would pause, while breathing quite audibly into the mouthpiece, before answering. This had the effect not only of discomposing his callers—tilting, as it were, the balance of power his way—but of discouraging those whose messages he judged to be trivial from venturing to approach him so audaciously again. On this particular eleven P.M. he could imagine no possible good coming his way from any telephonic intrusion, so his silence was, even for him, perversely long.

The caller cracked first: "Hello," she more or less shouted, "Are you there?"

"Mmm. Indeed."

"I'm trying to reach Professor Carruthers." When there was no immediate answer, she went on, tentatively, as if she had already begun to question her own motives for dialing: "Of the Institute? The Institute for Urban Studies?"

"Speaking."

"Professor! I hate to bother you . . ."

Carruthers snorted, thinking: But you *are*.

"But I've made a discovery which may be quite valuable, valuable to the world of letters. And of course valuable to you as an eminent scholar."

Carruthers sighed. "Go on," he said, resignedly. He would *have* to give a listen. The bluestocking type, of which this one seemed a prime specimen, *did* tend to go *on* so. But one never knew what gems might turn up on one's doorstep under such circumstances. After all, it had been just such an unsolicited call that had introduced him many years ago to the idea that Edgar Allan Poe had used a street-naming code in his "Dupin" stories, a suggestion that had led directly to three published papers, not to mention tenure and promotion to Associate. So he settled in for a while, wriggling his tiny rear end into the leather cushions, pushing the "reject" button on the stereo control board that had been built into the arm of his Eames chair. With Pachelbel's Canon in D Major, it was preferable to start over from the beginning. It was not a piece into which one walked, voluntarily at any rate, *in media res*.

Still, he was edgy: "And I suppose you expect to be paid for revealing this discovery of yours."

"Why, that's not fair at all." She sounded truly hurt, then testy. He realized she had an overlay of British accent, a certain aristocratic dignity. Admirable. "You don't even know what *it* is. If it's legally mine, of course I'll expect to be paid for it, if it is sold or used for profit. If, that is, I don't decide to keep it for myself."

Carruthers scrambled to maintain his superior air: "It is not my profession to be *fair*. Surely you must understand that I am consistently harassed by individuals looking for their own profit, with publishing schemes of dubious value. *Do* be succinct."

"I'm not sure where to begin, when you put it that way."

"Try the beginning."

There was no sound for a moment, except distant street noises. Fifteen floors beneath him, Washington Square Park was reaching the shank of another of its undesirable evenings, ringed by policemen and unwary tourists. Carruthers had recently considered writing a letter to the *Times* suggesting that the park, and its habitués, be enclosed in steel-mesh caging, and that admission be charged to those who wanted to observe the goings-on therein. The proceeds could be used to rehabilitate the South Bronx. The park people would then be sent *there* as pioneer settlers, much as English criminals had been "transported" to Australia in the eighteenth century.

The woman finally replied. Her tone was still defiant: "The beginning, sir, is often rather difficult to pinpoint—as you yourself have pointed out in your recent essay on Victorian railway cars as signifiers of cultural dismemberment."

Carruthers was taken aback. This one was not only plucky, she was downright well-read. "The one in *Charing Cross Review*?"

"Yes. Now let me get to the point. Which is hardly the *beginning*. I think I've found the original holograph manuscript of *Leaves of Grass.*"

Carruthers sat upright. The earpiece touched his flesh for the first time: "The 1855?"

"Yes."

"Nonsense. That was lost in a fire. In a printer's shop in Brooklyn. Before the Civil War."

"At Cranberry and Fulton, in fact. In 1858. I looked it up in your book on Whitman. But here I am, renovating an old house, and I've broken through a wall and found these sheets of foolscap folded into a small green notebook. There are twelve poems, in scratchy old-fashioned ink."

"How do you *know* it's authentic?"

"Obviously, I don't. That's why I'm calling you. I need an expert like yourself, and I have a need, a *great* need, to place this in hands like yours. If I've sounded demanding, you must understand. What would something like this be worth? A hundred thousand?"

"I think you could name your own price." The thought induced a great sense of ease in Carruthers. Even if he did not get a commission from the sale, he would be washed over by a river of awards and honoraria. But this was no time to appear eager. He affected indifference: "Could you hold on a moment. My secretary has a call on another line." Carruthers waved soundlessly and pointed at a red and black chinoiserie chest. From a corner emerged a young man wearing a caftan. "Neville," he hissed, "the Fonsecca '55." He turned back to the phone: "And this house of yours is on Cranberry Street?" he asked smoothly.

"No, it isn't. I think we'd better not continue this on the phone any longer. I'm in a booth; I'm out of change, and I'm going to be missed at home. We must meet privately, face to face."

"I'm sure I can fit you in within the week," he continued, struggling to suppress his enthusiasm. "Give me your name and address. I can hire a car . . ."

"Sorry, no. Be on the D train heading to Brooklyn tomorrow. As close to nine A.M. as a train arrives. You should get on at West Fourth about eight-forty-five. I'll be on the platform at DeKalb. First stop after you cross the river."

The recording came on informing them that their time was up, that another dime had to be inserted. There would be only a few seconds before they were cut off.

"But I don't know you! What *is* your name? You don't know me. This is ridiculous."

"Your picture is on the dust cover of your book, *The Cities of Walt Whitman*. I'll know you."

"But that was fifteen years ago!"

"Wear a white ribbon in your buttonhole, then. . . ."

There was a click, and the line was dead. Neville stood at attention, having poured two fingers of dark liquid from the broad-shouldered black bottle into the glass. Carruthers hung up the receiver, took the glass by the stem, swirled the port in the glass, drank, moved it from cheek to cheek in his mouth, ventilated it dramatically, and swallowed. The heady bouquet and deep flavor saturated him for a moment with sensual calm.

He raised the glass to Neville: "Bin Twenty-seven. Magnificent. How many bottles do we have left?"

"Four or five." Neville's eyes were limpid, credulous, inviting; but there was a nasty twist to his half-smile. He ran his fingers slowly over his crew cut.

"If this woman isn't mad, Neville, we'll be able to buy this ambrosial nectar, if I may be so vulgar, by the pipe. We'll need a warehouse to store it." He pushed a button, starting the Pachelbel over again. "And Neville?"

"Yes, Massa?"

"Get out the Whitman file for me. Whitman, Walt. 1819 to 1892. It's in the old cabinet. Lord, I haven't looked at that stuff in years."

# CHAPTER 2

THE HELICOPTER HOVERED over the Long Island Expressway, made an abrupt vertical ascent, and accelerated laterally, at a rakish tilt, south along the Brooklyn-Queens Expressway. The co-pilot held his stomach and groaned.

"Big night on the town, Artie?" asked the pilot. "You look a little green around the gills."

Artie nodded, glumly: "My tongue feels like the Kosciusko Bridge." He pointed downward: "Rust, Kielbasa, soot, potholes . . ."

The pilot silenced him by waving his hand. A red light had gone on on the control panel. "We'll be live in thirty seconds," he said.

The anchorman's deep, rotund tones reverberated through the headsets: ". . . April One, eight-fifty-five A.M. And now we have the WVBA traffic report from the chopper. . . ."

The pilot spoke into the mike: "Nothing unusual, Fred. It's business as usual on the Long Island Distressway. Looks like it's backed up all the way to the Hamptons. And there are two trucks down on the left lane of the Kosciusko, southbound, so you'd better hug to the right. And there's a real *mess* at Humboldt Street. Don't even try to get into Greenpoint or Williamsburg. All of North Brooklyn is in a severe state of grid-lock. . . ."

The anchor interrupted: "And *dead*lock, Mel. There's been a bizarre graveyard killing out there. We're going to have a report from Megan Moore in the Brooklyn Mobile Unit shortly. How does the rest of the borough look?"

"Good news, Fred. Below the Manhattan Bridge things are easing up. The East River crossings are in good shape. Gowanus and Prospect expressways are clear, so if you're head-ing into the city from the Verrazano, or Flatbush, or Benson-*hoist*, head for the Battery Tunnel or the Brooklyn Bridge."

The tape of a beer commercial took over the airwaves. Mel switched off the mike. Artie said:

"Graveyards, look at 'em! The entire northern border of Brooklyn is one long graveyard. And they got 'em everywhere else too. And you know what's happening. These Caribbeans. The you-know-whos. Do voodoo! Chicken bones and blood all over the tombstones. When I was growin' up we used to be known in Brooklyn for the Navy Yard and the Dodgers. Now it's graveyards and voodoo. So my mother, she moves out to Star-rett City, which is built on the old Canarsie dump, to get away from the chicken bones and the you-know-whos. The planes from Kennedy buzz her roof every ninety seconds or so, and the you-know-whos are takin' over Starrett City, and she sleeps with a loaded shotgun . . ."

The pilot hushed him again, switching on the mike and buzz-ing for air-time. The anchor was just finishing a pitch for a New Jersey used-car dealer.

"Now back to the chopper," he intoned, not missing a beat.

"Forget what I said about the Gowanus and so forth. There's a thick smoke or mist rising from the Brooklyn end of the Battery Tunnel. It's no patch of fog, Freddie. Maybe the Gowanus Canal has finally exploded. Seriously, if this smoke, or fog, or smog, keeps spreading, all of South Brooklyn, from Sunset Park, Bush Terminal, Red Hook, up to the Bridge, will be down to zero visibility. . . ."

The light on the panel went out. The two fliers heard over their earphones:

"Hate to break in on you from the old anchor-desk, Mel, but Megan Moore is actually in that bit of pea soup you're describing. Here's a live report from the Mobile Unit. Go ahead, Meg."

"I'm on the Gowanus, Fred. The expressway, not the canal, of course."

"If you were in the canal, the Mobile Unit would have dissolved by now, ha ha."

"Well, it's incredible here on the expressway anyway. I'm in the middle of . . . well, it's just *darkness*, sudden *darkness*. It's not a fire. The air is clear of smoke. It's easy to breathe, but the traffic is *not* moving. Whoops, there's a fender-bender. And another. I can't see a thing. I'll put my mike out the window. Do you hear the sound-effects? It's like a boiler factory out there."

The anchor emitted his jolly Santa Claus laugh: "Terrific, Meg, that's real *live* coverage. The Voice of the Big Apple plays heavy metal. . . ."

The pilot threw his headphone onto the floor of the cabin. He pulled back the stick, and the whirlybird veered out over the river, hovering at the edge of the fog. "That fancy broad," he said, "she's supposed to be at the Cemetery of the Evergreens. She gets stuck in traffic, going the *wrong* way, and she comes out with an exclusive, smelling like a rose."

Artie closed his eyes briefly. He rubbed his temples with the tips of his index fingers: "Give her some time on the Brooklyn Crime Beat, Mel. Consumer reports, mayor's conferences, she does fine. Leave her out *there* for a while," he indicated the sprawling borough by pointing his thumbs forward, "and she's gonna step in shit and not come out smelling like any rose. She's gonna smell like everybody else on this fleabag of a station does. Like shit."

# CHAPTER 3

FINALLY, THE D TRAIN had begun to move again, up the approach to the Manhattan Bridge, passing over the encroachment of Chinatown on the Lower East Side. On the sides of the few remaining old-law tenements, revolutionary murals—a Puerto Rican Grandma Moses working in Da-Glo—were juxtaposed to the vestigial remains of billboards touting long-forgotten cigar and clothing manufacturers. Carruthers snapped off the Sony Walkman headset and returned it to his briefcase. He had had enough blather of fender-benders and tabloid crime. There were bigger things on his horizon.

Never before had he so looked forward to crossing the bridge. If the Whitman manuscript were the real thing, it was the chance of a lifetime, a buried treasure worth a career. *Ten* careers.

The train again screeched to a halt.

Carruthers's patience was beginning to wear thin. He sprang from his seat and quick-stepped, a study in short-legged agitation, up and down before his co-passengers. Most of them seemed to have been frozen into a state of diminished responsibility—by the *News*, or the *Post*, or the pieties of some evangelical tract. This was certainly not his milieu.

It was all the woman's fault, subjecting him to the indignity of a meeting on an unsavory subway platform in downtown Brooklyn. It was cloak-and-dagger hogwash of the most reprehensibly female sort; no wonder the etymology of "hysteria" led back to the Greek *hystera*—uterus, womb.

How about "wombat"?

He wrinkled his nose and squinted, a characteristic expression of his that communicated self-pleasuring. There was no point in allowing the D Train and its attendant miseries to deflate his buoyancy for one moment. Carruthers had ascertained the night before while going over his papers that the source for the story about the 1855 manuscript burning had been Whitman himself. The poet had made an offhand remark to that effect to an interviewer when he was a crotchety, possibly senile old man in Camden, N.J. So any suggestion that this, the poet's, version of the story was untrue could not be overlooked. It was worth, as the young people said, *a shot*. So the woman could be forgiven a little excitability, and he could bear a little discomfort.

Carruthers's fingers itched at the thought of holding the priceless holograph. Were the pages yellowed? Had Walt's ink faded?

He stopped pacing, took a vacant seat among the rabble. He removed, more or less by habit, pen and notebook from his breast pocket, retreating thereby into his own ordered world, one conspicuously free of either women or wombats, in which he discovered his own meanings. Now he attempted to focus his attention, taking notes, exclusively on the inside of the car, looking for a signifier to salvage from these lost minutes, something to interpret and convert into publishable matter. But there was nothing to observe except the dated and patently unsellable message that he was surrounded by the detritus of a civilization on the skids. It seemed only yesterday that the Transit Authority had introduced with pride its spanking-new cars, with orange and blue decor, but the one he now sat in had taken on the devastated air of a Beirut or Belfast outpost of Howard Johnson's. The posters heralded Preparation H, Roach Motels, the

Spanish Yellow Pages. Graffiti covererd the walls and windows; even this (a dead issue, from a publishing standpoint anyway, since its period of fashionability as a popular art-form had passed away a decade before) yielded nothing to the imaginative inference. It was meaningless, a discontinuum of mad swirls, Cyrillic crossed with Arabic, the work perhaps of a schizophrenic Armenian immigrant, deluded that he sat astride the Caucasus Range rather than the East River.

Then the train was moving, full speed ahead. Brooklyn came into view: the Navy Yard, smokestacks of industry, *The Watchtower*, the Heights:

"THERE'S NEW LIFE IN BROOKLYN—
IN OLD BROWNSTONE NEIGHBORHOODS.
BROOKLYN UNION GAS."

The billboard's sentiment infected Carruthers and obliterated all other hints of Brooklyn's essence. A potent phrase had entered his consciousness, triggering a reverie. He was plunged into the nineteenth century: a brownstone façade, stained-glass windows, overstuffed furniture, glistening mahogany from newel post to pier mirror, the gaslit ceiling frieze, *Leaves of Grass* hidden behind the plasterwork. And the phrase! In such a form would his name be entrusted to posterity: *The Carruthers Whitman!* Carruthers would establish its authenticity. Carruthers would uncover the palimpsests. Carruthers would speculate on signs of stress in Whitman's hand at the more suggestive passages. An entire panel at next year's MLA convention would be devoted to Carruthers's triumph. There would be a new facsimile edition, of course (Oxford? Yale?), amply footnoted by Carruthers, and he would have the Chair of his own choosing. Perhaps best of all, he would never again have to encounter, let alone teach, an undergraduate.

Thus engrossed, he failed to notice that the fog had now enveloped South Brooklyn, as predicted by the Voice of the Big Apple, and had begun to extend wispy fingers over the river. The train reentered the earth on the Brooklyn side. DeKalb

Avenue, his point of rendezvous with destiny, was the next
stop.

*The Carruthers Whitman.*

On the platform at DeKalb, Carruthers slowly adjusted the
white ribbon in his buttonhole and then touched it expectantly,
looked over the crowd, waiting for the woman to show herself.
He had anticipated a buxom matron, well dressed, in sensible
shoes. Instead two nuns detached themselves from the others
and approached him. One of them was a Negro, coffee-colored,
with plump cheeks. The other was pale, with blond eyebrows,
and seemed a couple of sizes too small for her habit. The black
one engulfed Carruthers's hand in a hearty grip. She was quite
tall. She spoke, and her British-inflected voice was the same
one he had heard on the phone the night before.

"Professor Carruthers? How thrilling it is to meet you. I'm
Sister Eusebia. This is my colleague, Sister Regina."

Carruthers was surprised, but pleased in a way. As part of his
Victorian fantasy, he had assumed that there would be one
woman, wealthy and well-born, and he would have to tolerate
from her the tiresome minutiae of the genealogist or house-
restorer. He remembered the tone of the conversation of the
night before; however well-informed, she would be a handful.
The appearance of these two young nuns suggested that he
could dominate them from the start. He cleared his throat with
authority:

"You've taken me well out of my way here. I am driven, in
an automobile, to the Institute once a week. I want you to know
this is a distinct aggravation for a man in my position. So now,
Sister, will you please produce the document in question? I'm
sure there is some reasonably private place nearby. . . ."

While he was speaking, another train pulled up, across the
platform. With short, mincing steps, the smaller nun edged
toward it. Sister Eusebia took his arm with a sort of maternal
force and stage-whispered in his ear, while pulling him along,
"Precisely, Professor. Believe me, we would not have put you

out for a moment if it had not been in the interest of keeping our
. . . document . . . *our* own." Her smile, so near, was toothy,
her breath redolent of the Near East: currants, mint, coriander.
"We are in the process of renovating a new convent for our
order. Many of us are involved. Some would, in a case like
this, balk at approaching a secular authority. Others might insist
that certain profits go to charitable causes. There are contractor's men in the house. Who knows what they see. Or pick up.
Do I make myself clear?"

Carruthers saw the picture, indeed. He understood what she
meant. He knew the trouble he had attempting to get his way
with his so-called "colleagues" at the Institute. He nodded his
assent as she led him, preceded by Sister Regina, who had been
standing in the sliding door to prevent it from closing, into the
other train.

Sister Eusebia continued, just above the roar of the trains:
"So we couldn't have a visiting dignitary—yourself—pulling
up at the curb in a hired limo, could we?"

Carruthers shook his head with vehemence.

"Nor could we take a chance on appointing any particular
time for you to quietly knock on the door, or stand on a nearby
corner for that matter, could we? And what if one of the others
suspected something? And followed us?" Carruthers half-
shook, half-nodded his head this time. He had indeed recently
read a British thriller in which a monastery was a nest of in-
trigue and distrust. One assumed the same sort of thing occurred in convents. She continued, "And we couldn't very well
remove the goods from the premises, since others were present
when it was discovered—they *are*, however, quite ignorant of
its significance. So, I put it to you: what were we to do except
what we have done? First, meet in a place where we couldn't be
followed. Second, take you to the house our *own* way, at a time
when it should be empty. The rest of the sisters are at Mass right
now, and the contractor is on another job today. We are but a
few stops from our destination."

The complete logic of her thinking had escaped him, but he

had already stopped listening with undiverted attention. He had come this far, why not see the thing through? The worst that could happen would be the loss of a morning's writing.

The train began to pull out of the station. The roar abated somewhat, and Carruthers began to frame a question. As he had gone over his files, he had realized that almost all of Whitman's homes and contacts in those days had been in the neighborhood east of the old Fulton Ferry Landing, particularly in the high land above the Navy Yard: now called Fort Greene and Clinton Hill. He was about to ask whether that was where they were headed. This would suggest to the nun that he was a step ahead of her, that he had already anticipated the first move. But she hushed him kindly, a finger to her lips. What did it matter? It was a lost cause.

"Not to say anything until we're within our own four walls, eh?" she hissed.

Dutifully, he sat between the two nuns. It was too god-awful noisy for conversation anyway. He took out his notebook, now trying to remember a line of Whitman's that had flashed across his mind as he had been listening to the radio, something about grass being "the uncut hair of graves." The train roared through the tunnel.

Looking up, he realized he was disoriented. This was no longer the D Train. Of course, they had had to cross the platform. He tried to picture Brooklyn, its enormity, and think of DeKalb as a sort of hub. In which direction were they going? North and east, he would bet. But what line ran that way, in the direction of Queens?

The nuns sat rigid on each side of him. He thought of the lions flanking the steps to the public library. This would make him the pathway to knowledge. He wrinkled his nose again, this time showing his dentures under the Guards' moustache he had affected since his sabbatical year at Oxford.

He strained his eyes to read the panel identifying the train, but all he could make out was an upside down "9" in one panel, and a "Q" in the other. He had never heard of such a line. He shuffled through his briefcase looking for the map of Brooklyn, but realized that he had left it at home on his desk. In any case, it was an antique, or a facsimile of one, made while Whitman still lived there.

There was a sign for the Long Island Railroad. This suggested that they must be running parallel to the D track, about to climb Park Slope to Prospect Park. That was gratifying. His earlier visions of a perfectly restored mansion returned. A convent in Park Slope, on the right block, could be quite grand indeed.

"Next stop," said Sister Regina, and the two nuns rose as one, hanging from straps. The taller one leaned over to whisper into her colleague's ear. The train hit a curve and the nuns swayed almost into Carruthers's lap. For a moment, he felt swallowed up in their skirts, lost—in the olfactory sense—in a Levantine bazaar, veiled from the world. . . .

Things then passed quickly. Too quickly.

He saw the words *Pacific Union*, or was it *Union Pacific*? Then *Astoria*. He was rushed out of the car into another underground station, with blue-and-white-tiled signs. They moved quickly up the stairs. There was a corridor reeking of urine; another, of airplane glue. They emerged onto an outdoor platform, the air thick with haze.

Through the mist he could barely make out a silent, empty train waiting on the track. They entered this train. It began to hum. They sat down. Through the haze he could see nothing but a hint of green walls. Before he was quite conscious of the train moving, they were leaving it. There was the sound of metal crashing on metal, somewhere out in the fog. The platform that they now hurried across was identical to the one they had just ascended. Had the train moved at all?

Then he noticed that he no longer had his notebook. There was no time to check his briefcase or go back to the train, for now they were descending a steep wooden escalator. Sister Eusebia's broad shoulders pressed back against his knees. Suddenly he had an irrational urge to break and run, but at that moment

Sister Regina, from behind, touched the back of his neck, then his earlobe. "I really like your writing," she said, speaking, for the first time, in a flat urban nasality. "It's so . . . you know. . . *together.*" Her fingernails were very long. That didn't seem right, but now nothing did. He was frightened, but could see no way to dislodge himself from the path he had chosen. Or had accepted. "We'll be there in just a minute. I can't wait to hear what you think of . . . our find." Then, she asked, "Where do you think this smoke is coming from?"

She began to hum a Beatles tune—"Eleanor Rigby"—obviously not expecting an answer.

There was another down-escalator, murderously slow. How high had they been? Where could they be? The incomplete map of Brooklyn that Carruthers carried in his mind had become useless.

They were in the street, in what appeared through the mist to be a barren intersection on a road to nowhere. Choking dust swirled under the fog. Trucks filled the narrow thoroughfare, frozen into motionless rage. There was a brief cessation of their honking, and he heard a foghorn so close he felt as if he were drifting on water. Then, in the void beneath the elevated track, voices, arguing in Italian, drifted down to him. It was as if he had found himself at the center of the deepest circle of an Inferno created by a collaboration of Fellini and Godard.

Urged by the nuns, he stumbled along. There was a vacant lot; cobblestones; a low disused institutional edifice, old enough to suggest a connection with Whitman after all. He felt a touch of relief. They turned into an alley, and all his tension dissipated. The short narrow block was a perfectly preserved example of workers' housing of the middle years of the nineteenth century, neat narrow houses all of a kind. He could have kicked himself. It was just such a project as this that Whitman would have been involved in during his period as a contractor and real-estate speculator.

Now his mind was consumed with the need not only to touch the manuscript but to get into a house that perhaps no one had written of, that Walt had built, or lived in, or sold, a discovery in itself worth a monograph or two. The alley was packed with fog. His step picked up. Sister Regina had to run to stay abreast of him. Sister Eusebia lifted her skirts and loped past, turning him into a stoop under which there was a door no more than five feet high. She produced a key, turned it, and shoved the door open. Carruthers could not hold back his eagerness. Crouching, he scuttled out of the gray mist, through the door, into almost total darkness.

"Sorry," said the British accent from the outside, "there's no light yet in the vestibule. Can you feel the other door? It's got a very low knob."

Carruthers felt around until he found it.

"It's not locked. Turn it. The light switch is inside, about three feet to the left. Thank you."

Obediently, he shoved open the heavy door, was greeted by a musty odor, and put one foot into the pitch-black cellar. He groped along the rugged stone wall until his entire body was inside the room.

There was a sound like an intake of breath, and the door swept closed behind him with a soft click.

With the sliver of light from the door gone, he could see absolutely nothing. Desperately, he moved further along the wall, but found no switch. He made his way back to the door. It wouldn't budge. He hammered on it.

Nothing.

He called out tentatively. When nothing answered, he screamed.

By the time the echoes died down, he had realized from the acoustic reverberations that he was sealed off from the world by the stone walls and thick hardwood door. No one could hear him.

He began to stumble across the room, hoping to find another way out. He heard a scuffling sound nearby, and, as his eyes began to adjust to the dark, made out a looming figure just on his right. The flesh on the back of his neck tingled. A flashlight snapped on, directed into his eyes, and he was blinded again. Powerful hands gripped him from behind, toppled him to the floor, and held him down. The flashlight found his arm, and he watched, immobile, as his sleeve was pulled back roughly. A hypodermic syringe appeared in the circle of light. A hairless, gnarled hand squeezed his arm until a vein popped out.

The needle was slipped expertly into the vein.

# CHAPTER 4

THE BLUE CAR moved past the Lincoln-Mercury dealer, came abreast of the Burger King, and abruptly, almost as an after thought, cut hard across Bushwick Avenue through the gates of the Cemetery of the Evergreens.

"That was close," said DeSales sardonically.

Kavanaugh was wheezing from the effort. The steering wheel dug into his ample girth. He wiped his brow: "Christ, it's thick today, Frankie, and the seat's broke. I can't get it to go back any further. Where now?"

"You put on any more weight, you'll have to drive from the back seat. Look for signs. We want Beacon Hill, then Sumachs."

Kavanaugh slowed the car to a crawl on the narrow incline of macadam. There was open sloping lawn on the right, then a line of mausoleums on the left.

"Howdya like to get laid to rest in one of these little houses, Frankie? Marble, probably. Must of cost a bundle."

Lieutenant Francis DeSales, NYPD, did not answer; expressionless, intent, he scanned the roadside for directions: "There's something."

Kavanaugh braked, squinting at the signpost: "Lookit the

fuckin' names: Ascension, Bethany, Nazareth, Mount of Olives. Just right for Holy Week, huh? And the place ain't even Catholic. Or Protestant. Non-denominational, it says. I looked it up at the office before we left."

"It says turn right here."

Kavanaugh started up again, climbing the sharp curve. "I always forget. Was you an altar boy? Sure. Boy did they shove that shit into us at Immaculate Conception! Somebody gets his ear cut off and they stick it right back on; Judas gets his piece of the action: twelve silver big ones; Jesus confronts his afflicted freaking mother; the Garden of, what was it? Gastronomy? How about Guesstimate? That's what the Jews in City Hall would call it. And then they'd have the Last Supper. At the Russian Tea Room maybe: blintzes, sour cream, that shit." He wheezed again, now with a note of triumphant good humor, making a halfhearted attempt to swerve from the path of a brightly-colored pheasant cock. At the last moment, the bird skittered out of the road. "Then they pull the rock back. On Easter morning, right? You guessed it, *zero*! 'The Case of the Missing Messiah,' my cousin Eddie called it. You remember Eddie, Frank, in the D.A.'s office?"

DeSales's blue eyes remained cold and unsmiling, but there was a flicker of humor at the corner of his mouth.

"The one they got in the Knapp Commission, right?"

Kavanaugh raised both eyebrows and half-smirked, "They claim he sold half the heroin take from the French Connection, but all he copped to was a technicality. So he had to resign." He shrugged his shoulders and winked. "He invested his 'savings' in real estate, and now he's making a bigger bundle. He buys old houses on the downtown fringes of Bed-Stuy, clears the spades out—the city gives him what they call a 'tax abatement' to help him with the removal process—does a little plastering and painting, puts in a kitchen with a trash compactor, and sells them to white white-collar types from Manhattan. For a fortune. The people who live there now call it Fort Greene. In the real-estate ads, Eddie calls it 'Brooklyn Heights Vicinity.' After dark and when the weather gets hot, it's still Bed-Stuy to me. Hey, lookit the view. You can see all the way down there. That's the Williamsburg Bank Building."

DeSales shuffled through the papers on the seat: "The graveyard map says this is Beacon Hill. They had the antiaircraft center here during the war. I remember my old man talking about it."

"And look at the fog. Past downtown. I never seen that before. Looks like a picture I seen once of L.A."

"Yeh. And Crown Heights will soon be Beverly Hills, right?" DeSales held the map up close. "I still don't see any Sumachs."

Kavanaugh was still thinking about the general prospect. He pointed down the hill, just past Bushwick Avenue. "Lookit the car yards there. They gotta have razor ribbon on the fences to keep out the vandals and the graffiti artists. Antiaircraft, bullshit! These people—our dark-skinned brothers in Brownsville and Bushwick and East New York—could do more damage than the whole fuckin' Luftwaffe. New Lots Avenue would make the Siegfried Line look like the Chorus Line. . . ."

"You got your wars mixed up," snapped DeSales, now impatient, looking up from the map. "We missed a turn. Keep going and we can double back at the section called Eastern Slope."

They passed, on their left, platoons of sarcophagi, obelisks, winged figures. On their right all of Brooklyn was laid out, flat, tedious, uninviting, just as DeSales always imagined it. Just as he wanted it. The fog was nothing he had seen before, but it didn't surprise him. It seemed appropriate. They entered a newer section of the cemetery. Tall hemlocks now obscured the view to the south. The gravestones were plain, shiny, and symmetrical. On most of them, names were engraved in both Oriental ideograph and Latin script.

"Eastern *Slope*," shouted Kavanaugh, "that *is* a laugh. They're all Chinks. Look! Hong Wing, Ding Dong, Long Wong. I didn't know the slopes buried their dead. Honest."

Following DeSales's finger, he turned left. Ahead were the

unmistakable earmarks of a Scene of Crime: ambulance, video truck, uniformed patrolmen, sawhorses, cluster of press.

DeSales settled back comfortably, as if knowing that his grim objective was now within reach had made his day. His chiseled olive features relaxed. He fished a Benson & Hedges regular from a box and pushed in the lighter on the dashboard.

"Maybe you thought they hung them in windows on Mott Street, Bernie, like Peking Duck?" Kavanaugh wrinkled his brow. Before he could answer, DeSales was saying, "Pull over there. Make sure the media is herded up, and move those sawhorses further back up the road."

"Maybe we should seal off the entrances?"

"This place is as big as Hoboken, Bernie, and even a fat detective could climb the fences. Forget it." He lighted up and was out of the car, smoothing his gray French-cut suit down over his trim figure. As he made his way through the damp dark leaves toward the area which had been cordoned off, he heard Kavanaugh beginning his patented banter with the media:

"Hey Rosemary, where's your girfriend Megan? I wouldn't' a taken this case if I thought she wasn't covering it."

"She's stuck in the fog down by the Battery Tunnel. Just heard her on the radio." Rosemary had orange hair, heavy legs, and a man's trench coat. She held an earphone to one ear.

"No shit? Now let's move over behind the mausoleum, ladies and gentlemen of the press. G.A.R. That's Grand Army of the Republic, right! Anyways, this here Civil War monument will be your headquarters for the duration, okay? I'd like to get stuck in the fog with Megan Moore, Rosemary. You let her know, huh?"

"I'm sure you're right at the top of her list," said Rosemary dryly, restationing herself with her colleagues.

DeSales skirted a sawhorse and shook hands with the sergeant from the local precinct who had taken charge.

"I only got here a minute before the vultures," said Sergeant Lurtsema, nodding toward the media people. "Somebody called them before we were notified. So I've spent most of my time keeping them off the grass, so to speak. I got here at eight-thirty. The call was at eight-oh-five. There was a gravedigger here and the boss undertaker, or whatever he is, who looked like he'd just tossed his cookies. So he probably *isn't* an undertaker. They've seen everything. The gravedigger is a Dominican and he didn't seem too bothered at all, except his English isn't too good, so who's to say? All I could get was that he, this gravedigger, showed up for work just before eight, and found *her*," he shook his head in the direction behind him without taking his eyes off DeSales's, "and ran up to the office." He pointed further into the cemetery. "He found the boss—his name is Keefe and he's a real peach . . . that's right, calls himself Director—and they called us and came down here to meet us. *El Señor* was digging a new grave over there just on the fringe of the circle, so he couldn't miss her. He swears he didn't touch nothing. Just ran for the boss."

"Did *he* call the papers?"

"Says not. And there ain't any pay-phones in the mausoleums, you know. So he would have had to do it at the office with Keefe's knowledge, and I don't think Keefe is happy that the press knows about this at all. Anyway, I sent them back up to the office to wait for you to question them. One of my men is with them."

"Anybody else around?"

"Oh yeah. The digger had a partner that never showed up today. Another Dominican. I guess we could say that's suspicious, or figure the partner showed up late, saw the body, took fright and is right now hoofing it across the Williamsburg Bridge."

DeSales nodded. He stubbed out the cigarette on his shoe and field-stripped it. He bared his teeth, not unpleasantly: "*If* he stopped on the way to call the *Post*. If he didn't he's probably in New Jersey by now." He bared his teeth again, making his way past the sergeant. "Usual orders, Wally. Don't let anyone up here except Kavanaugh. And the M . E .'s men, of course. What circle were you talking about?"

"You'll see. The firemen's circle."

His back turned to everyone, DeSales closed his eyes momentarily, attempting to shut everything else out of his mind. It was the way he approached a crime scene. He wanted to encounter it fresh, in a logical progression. He did not want to think about the woman until he had envisioned the scene at the moment before her presence had diminished the comparative significance of everything else in sight, living or dead.

What Lurtsema had meant by "the firemen's circle" was indeed obvious. Two stone fire-fighting hats, nineteenth-century style, marked an opening in a circular formation of modest flat gravestones that, in turn, was surrounded by a larger circle, incomplete, of larger upright stones of a later date. A tarpaulin covered an open excavation in this outer circle, presumably the one being dug by the Dominican who had discovered the body. DeSales methodically scoured the soft earth on the periphery and found nothing remarkable. He noted that the monuments were actually quite new, dated within the last ten years. Most were cheap, even gaudy. A few of the names were Spanish. There was no apparent connection between them and the firemen's hats.

The older stones in the inner circle, on the other hand, belonged only to firemen. They were simple, and faded.

There were two large statues within this inner circle that dominated the entire area with their presence. Or at least they *had* dominated it before the woman arrived. The second, and larger, was a fifteen-foot-high representation of Victorian Virtue in fire-fighting costume. The man carried a torch in his right hand, and bore a child, whom presumably he had saved from death, on his left shoulder. Over the right arm someone, recently, very recently, had draped a towel. The towel was badly stained with what DeSales took to be blood. The engraving at the base announced that the statue was dedicated to all the firemen of Brooklyn, E.D.

"E.D." would be the Eastern District.

The stone face of the fireman had been painted black, coal-black, with distinct unpainted circles left around the eyes. Like Al Jolson singing "Mammy."

The statue in front was smaller, perhaps ten feet from plinth to the top of its fire hat. This, also in blackface, was dedicated to a man named Baldwin who had died in the line of duty in 1880, age 36 years, 8 months, and 27 days, on Montrose Avenue.

Just about two years younger than DeSales would be in another couple of months. He felt for a moment the pull of his old love-hate relationship with mortality, the fear tinged with titillation that made him a likely candidate for a homicide dick from the beginning.

When he squatted, keeping low to the ground, inspecting inscriptions, dead flowers, ravages of winterkill, he knew he was now teasing himself, holding off the *pièce de résistance* until the last possible second.

Abruptly, he stood and looked up. In life, the woman had been voluptuous, with full breasts, pinched waist, rounded hips, and long legs. Now, although these general contours remained, she was most striking for other reasons. There was the contrast between her waxen pallor and raven hair; there were the sunken cheeks, the flaking dried lips, and the eyes that seemed to have receded into her head. There was the metal stake that protruded from her left breast. There was the odd purplish-black color at her shoulder blade, running along her spine to her buttocks. There was the fact that her wrists had been tied around the neck of the statue of Baldwin, and her ankles around his waist, in a grotesque parody of upright copulation.

DeSales stepped forward, tentatively touching the hair that hung plumb to Baldwin's belt like a used mop. He leaned forward to inspect the wound and the stake. On the shaft of the weapon a blue-and-white sticker had been affixed. It bore a familiar slogan:

"Another Cinderella Project From Brooklyn Union Gas."

Kavanaugh came up behind him and leaned over to read the

sticker. He whistled: "This guy must be a lot of laughs, a real wacko!"

"Or he's been reading too many billboards."

Kavanaugh pinched his arm: "That's a gas, Lieutenant."

DeSales pushed his hand away: "Find an evidence bag, and get that towel down from the other statue."

Kavanaugh pulled a large, transparent, three-mil plastic bag from under his coat: "I'm never without, Frankie. Bernie the K's Kondoms: no ribs, no lubrication, no sensitivity. Instant penance for all Catholics who still think birth control is a sin."

"Enough with the Catholic jokes. Shut up and get that thing down. I want it laid out on a flat surface. Then into the bag for the M.E."

The fat man began to try to get a foothold on the monument.

"Not that way, dummy. You'll screw up any prints he may have left."

Kavanaugh stopped, looked about, and finally spotted a branch lying outside the enclosure, next to a tombstone adorned by an angel with a broken wing and a tribute to someone called "Old Joe." Gingerly, he fished the towel down with the branch, placed the bag across one of the flat stones near Old Joe, and laid the towel across the bag.

The stain on the towel had the outline of a human face.

DeSales heard the crippled rumble of the A Train running above Fulton Street, beyond the razor ribbon, and the car yards, above the inevitable Pentecostal storefront churches. Crows cawed, circling in the sky.

"It's like in the Stations of the Cross. Which Station?"

"Jesus Meets His Afflicted Mother?"

"No," said DeSales, "not Jesus Meets His Afflicted Mother. The lady who gave him the towel. Veronica. Jesus Meets Veronica."

"Maybe this guy was an altar boy too," said Kavanaugh.

# CHAPTER 5

THE INTERCOM BUZZED. Timothy Desmond pushed the button and picked up the receiver.

His secretary's voice was almost gloating:

"Tim? I know your office hours don't start until twelve-thirty but I thought you should know. Carruthers didn't show up for his class today, didn't call in with an excuse, and his students, all twenty of them, are out here. They want to register a complaint."

Desmond swore to himself, then responded levelly: "Come on, Helen. We've got to give *everybody* the benefit of the doubt. He hasn't missed before this term; he's probably stuck in the subway."

"He refuses to *take* the subway."

"Or in traffic. Or," he smiled guiltily, "an accident." Even the most fanatically humane secretary or administrator at the Institute would be at least tempted to smile at the prospect of Fletcher Carruthers III having an accident.

"Tell them there's no sense complaining when it might not be his fault," he added.

"They don't want to just complain about his absence," she

went on, her tone of vindictive pleasure growing. "They just want to complain about *him*. In general. He's,"—now she was scrupulously quoting what was being said to her—"he's insulting, he refuses to accept late work, *even* if there's a good excuse; he doesn't teach, just talks about himself; he won't make appointments for conferences because he's too busy; he's . . . what was that, honey? . . . He's racist, sexist, cruel . . . "

"And unusual punishment," Desmond finished for her. He had heard enough. The worst part was that a full professor with tenure would have to do a lot more than miss some classes and alienate his students for any action to be taken against him. "Helen, you know the drill. Tell them to write up the complaints, get as many signatures as possible, and send one or two representatives over tomorrow. I'll give them all the time they want. But nothing can be done until something is in writing. Assure them I'm sympathetic."

"Okay, Tim. Will do. And," she lowered her voice, "there's another one here, not one of Carruthers's. He's, well, *upset*, to say the least. Frankly, I'm a little scared of him. The other girls are at lunch, and . . . "

"Say no more, Helen. Clear out the Carruthers bunch and send the other guy in right away. Keep smiling."

Desmond took a last bite out of his egg-salad sandwich, gulped some coffee, and threw the papers and containers into the wastebasket. He crammed the *Times* he had been reading into his shoulder bag and hurriedly rearranged the papers on his desk, forms on the left, printouts on the right. He put the grant application he had been filling out on top of the pile in his "In" tray. He sat back, prepared for anything.

"I'm Juan Cruz," said the man standing in the doorway of the inner office. "I got problems."

"Tim Desmond. I try to solve problems."

"I been fucked over. Royal."

Cruz was a stocky man, about thirty. He had brown, pockmarked skin and a thick drooping black moustache, and his hair was long, combed straight back like a Hollywood Indian. He wore an Army fatigue jacket with his name over the left breast pocket. If the stripes were real, he had been a sergeant first class. He was missing two fingers on his right hand. His dark eyes smoldered.

Desmond swung his chair around and tilted it up, putting his feet on the typewriter stand. He faced Cruz by turning his head to the right: "I'm sorry to hear that, Mr. Cruz, but you've got to be more specific." He folded his hands on his chest and waited.

Cruz removed a white paper, badly wrinkled, from his pocket, and tossed it onto Desmond's desk. Desmond picked it up, unfolded it, and, although he already recognized the form and suspected its meaning, gave it a semblance of intense scrutiny. He looked up:

"It says here that you have to pass Communications One before you graduate." He turned up his palms. "That *is* the rule. For everybody."

"But I awready pass it."

"When?"

"I don' remember."

"Got a transcript?"

Cruz produced a billfold from a hip pocket. From this he fished out, with two of the remaining fingers on his injured hand, the transcript. Hand quivering, and with a distinct air of resentment, he threw it after the other form.

"It says here you passed Communications One in 1975 and failed the writing proficiency test in 1976. It's a clearly stated rule, I'm sorry for your sake, that anyone who failed the test is required to take the course over again, pass the *course,* and also pass another proficiency test. Like the one you failed in 1976."

"Nobody tole me."

"It's in the bulletin. And, as I remember, we had at least two riots over that rule. One in '76 and one in '77. You can't very well claim ignorance."

"They . . . riots . . . was because the test was racist. It was prejudice against blacks and Hispanics. But I got a better escuse." He held up the damaged hand. "This. I got it in 'Nam. A week before they was sendin' me home. I can't write in a test situation. I need *time*, man."

Desmond stood, took a deep breath, and gazed out the window, his back to Cruz. His view looked across the sand of Coney Island beach to the Atlantic, and down the boardwalk to West Thirty-Seventh St., where barbed wire and armed guards separated the private community of Seagate from the rubble of broken tenements and vacant lots that much of the former Pleasure Capital of America had become. It was a view that Fletcher Carruthers III, for example, refused to tolerate, demanding instead an office looking back to the city and the Verrazano Bridge, where the sunsets were picturesque. In much the same way, Carruthers would not tolerate the likes of Cruz. The very presence of a Cruz in his class, as far as Carruthers was concerned, justified his indifference to his students. They didn't deserve to be in college in the first place. Desmond tried not to think about Carruthers for a while. Cruz was saying:

"What kinda right they got to do this? I pass the course. Ask Professor . . . I forget his name. Tall white guy with bushy hair on the sides, bald on top."

"Greenstein," said Desmond, not turning. "Greenstein is no longer with us." Two black children were throwing whiskey bottles at one another in a lot adjacent to the boardwalk. A gleaming ocean liner made its way to Europe against the dim stunted horizon of New Jersey. Or Staten Island? Desmond could never remember which his window faced. On Surf Avenue, two hookers were accosting a man pushing a baby in a stroller. The day had started out foggy, but it had burnt off now and the ocean, under the bright sky, seemed full of tinsel. Greenstein had once been one of his best friends. Greenstein gave A's for effort, B's for deprivation, and C's for body language. No D's, no F's. To give D's or F's to the culturally disadvantaged was to perpetuate the fascist infrastructure of American society. Just about the time the writing proficiency test had been instituted—as an antidote to Greenstein's grading practices as much as anything else—Greenstein had departed for California to devote himself to what he called the "Human Potential Movement." Thus he would avail his services to all of humankind, not merely the oppressed minorities. He was now, Desmond had heard, running an EST center on the fringes of Malibu. Cruz was one of Greenstein's leftovers. Cruz, like the memory of Greenstein, symbolized a past that had been full of hope, a foolish hope perhaps, which had gone sour.

Like a lot of other things.

"When did you get out of the service, Mr. Cruz?"

"I toldya, '72."

"And you started here? At the Institute?"

"I think '73."

"Fall or spring?"

"What is this shit? How should I know? You got the transcript; check it out."

"Of course." Desmond's tone remained one of polite concern. He carried it back to the window, as if the job of interpretation he had to do required direct sunlight.

"You came here in spring, '73."

Cruz was burning again: "So, who cares? Fall, spring, I got fucked. 'Cause I'm a Vet and 'cause I'm PR."

"When you entered in spring '73, there was a rule that you couldn't register unless you took Communications One your first term."

"I did."

"And? It says here you didn't pass."

"I din't. I was sick. I got malaria in 'Nam."

"That's irrelevant unless you continued to have malaria through the four subsequent terms when you didn't take Communications One again and *didn't* sign up for tutoring. . . ."

Cruz was out of his seat, pressing Desmond's back. Desmond turned. At 6'3" he had to look down at the other man who, at close quarters, reeked of cheap wine. Night Train, Desmond said to himself. Their eyes locked. Unblinking, Desmond took off his glasses.

"*Irrelevant*," Cruz was screaming. "*Irrelevant*! I got my

fucking hand shot off for this fucking country!" He waved the crippled part feebly, but the rest of him was rigid with hatred, intimidating. "And I ain't gonna let no chickenshit Communications Department or asshole schoolteacher ruin the rest of my fucking life. I gotta get a job. I gotta get a degree. So what if I can't write nothing about no poems or that shit? I wanna work with my own people—social work, I'm a major in. I don't need no fucking writing, no poems, no essay shit. I wanna work with the *people, comprende?*"

At this point he backed off a step, as if he had unwittingly revealed a secret part of his own personality. He made an ineffectual shoving gesture at Desmond without touching him. He sat down again in the chair. His shoulders shook; he was almost in tears: "You ever turn you back on me again when I'm talkin' you, you go out that fucking window!"

Desmond waited a moment, patted Cruz's bad hand gently, and returned to his desk. He sat on the blotter. "You better calm down, Cruz. You're in a mess, and if you don't want to get in any deeper, if you do want to get a degree and work with your people, *ever*, you better listen. Now I'm going to review your case from *my* perspective. Okay? Which is, for better or worse, the perspective of authority around here."

Cruz crossed his legs and fixed his hurt, brimming eyes on the map of Literary England—left over from some previous, higher-minded administrator—that hung on the wall behind Desmond's chair. Desmond's voice took on a tough, uncompromising tone:

"When you entered here, as I'm sure you well know, this school was a breeze, a pipe, a gut. There was open admissions, and even then there was the need for the senior colleges—Brooklyn, City, Queens, Hunter, for example—to dump the people they couldn't handle somewhere else. These students they didn't want, of course, were minority students with no background or a weak background; often, like you, somebody with," he looked at the transcript, "a high-school equivalency diploma from the Army. You'd all been shafted by the system and needed a helping hand to get through. Somebody up there," Desmond gestured vaguely to the ceiling, "meaning somebody in the BHE or the mayor's office, decided that something called 'Urban Studies' would be, well, relevant, which, as you and I know, Mr. Cruz, in 1970 meant *easy*, right? Without too much effort on your part, or too strict an enforcement of Basic Skills requirements on our part, guys like you would get to work for your people, join the middle class, even run for President someday. Working for revolutionary goals within the system, right?"

Desmond stood again, put his hands in his pockets, loomed over Cruz for a moment, walked around him, then settled his shoulder blades against the map. His eyes were level with Wordsworth's cottage at Nether Stowey. Cruz held his head in his hands.

"You had it handed to you on a platter, Cruz, and you fucked up. Your first term you flunked the only course you *had* to pass to graduate. And in those days it wasn't easy to flunk. When Freshman English is euphemized as *Communications One*, or Two *thousand* one, you have to work hard to flunk. Then, instead of simply taking the course again, and trying, or getting into one of the free tutorial programs, you just *evaded* doing anything. Finally you heard about Greenstein, were assured that, with your general social *relevance*, you could pass just by having your name on the roster and your image indelibly engraved in Greenstein's raised consciousness. You played a game, but you got caught; you got caught because you waited so long that someone had gotten wise to what was happening, and the rules were changed. Up there," he pointed to the ceiling again, "somebody finally figured out that college graduates who couldn't read or write or do long division weren't worth any more to their people than grade-school dropouts who couldn't read or write or do long division. So they put on the proficiency tests in 1975 so no one could sneak through and get a degree until he could prove that he had mastered his basic skills. And you got caught in the pinch. Of course, you flunked the proficiency test because your English was lousy in the first place and you'd never done anything to improve it. And then," he moved over to the window again, careful not to turn his back, rapping on the glass with his knuckle for emphasis, "then you tried the ultimate ploy; you'd just not do anything, just hang out for five more years, and then come back, hoping everybody had forgotten, and pick up your diploma. You assumed that the guy in this office might be Greenstein or the Pope handing out dispensations. . . ." He was out of breath: "Just don't give me any more of the *indignant* bullshit. Now, let's start over. What *can* I do for you?" He dropped back into the chair.

"I want a chance," Cruz said in a child's voice.

"Okay, good. First of all, you'd better see the Veterans' Counselor. We have one now, since last year we decided to recognize the conflict in Southeast Asia as legitimate. He'll make sure your benefits are straight and arrange for a re-admit. Then go to see Professor Smith in the Writing Center. Tell her I sent you. She'll give you a diagnostic essay assignment. You'll be placed at the appropriate remedial level. She'll go over it with you word by word, show you why you didn't pass the proficiency test, and arrange for tutoring before you do take the test. All you have to do is commit yourself to the effort. *I'll* do the tutoring if you want, but you might be better off with an E S L tutor if Spanish was your first language. If it's true that your injury prevents you from completing examinations on time, we'll accommodate you. There are special typewriters, or we could just give you extra time, okay?"

Cruz nodded. His eyes were suddenly clear and he smiled tentatively, as if all he had been asking for in the first place was a good cathartic chewing-out. Followed, of course, by a reprieve. He shook Desmond's right hand with his left. *"Gracias, amigo."* The door closed behind him.

Desmond watched the door for a long time. For a bad moment there he had imagined himself as a statistic on a police report, part of a headline in the *Post*: "Crazed Viet Vet Knifes

College Prof." And for what was he taking such risks, any risk? To display his mastery of the role of brave administrator who, having browbeaten his threatening adversary into submission, reveals a heart of gold beneath the crusty exterior, a fund of benevolence from which he bestows his patronizing largesse? So Cruz could do a couple of weeks of tutoring and then return frustrated to the streetcorner *bodega* where he would smoke reefer, drinking his Night Train and Colt 45 out of brown paper bags, and bitch about *Los Estados Unidos*, vowing revenge?

Maybe, Desmond thought, he did it because he felt some weird kinship with Cruz, some shared wound, some common emotional emasculation that had been converted into aimless anger.

This brought to mind his wife. He did not want to think about his wife any more than he wanted to think about Fletcher Carruthers III. But he had to address himself to both. There was a weekend planned in the country; if Carruthers did not show up soon, he would have to find a replacement for him. If this took time, he would have to leave for the country house late, and this would disrupt his wife's plans.

His mind drifted, probing without real direction for something more comfortable to contemplate. The Institute stood on the original site of a nineteenth-century amusement park called Dreamland. That was appropriate. Dreamland had been torn down in the thirties and, in the flush of post-war prosperity, a luxury home for the aged—five stories high—had been built there. It was called The Sea-Breeze. That, considering the origins of the Institute, was also appropriate, if you liked cheap vernacular puns. The blacks had then moved into Coney Island, and the old Jews in The Sea-Breeze had fled to Long Island and Florida. The city had bought the building in the late sixties and founded the Institute there to accommodate the minorities who had driven out the elderly whites. Now Coney Island was mostly rubble, buildings burned down and abandoned, it was rumored, by landlords who were the children of the people who had fled The Sea-Breeze. So the blacks were now being driven back out of town, to Long Island and Florida, and the new city projects seemed to cater to Russian and Oriental immigrants. The Institute had raised its standards, and grew whiter—and yellower—every term.

That was progress.

It was certainly good for Brooklyn real estate.

It probably even pleased Carruthers.

The intercom buzzed. Helen said: "I don't believe you, Tim. That guy looked like he had a machete, and meant to use it, and you send him out smiling. You're wonderful!"

"Thanks, Helen." He didn't bother to tell her that he didn't feel particularly wonderful.

"And there's a call for you on line Three. I think it's a student."

"Okay. Could you get Roseanna Bova to meet Carruthers's other class if he doesn't show?"

"Sure."

He pressed the appropriate button. The voice was muffled, somewhat more feminine than masculine, vaguely British:

"Professor Desmond? Get this straight. I'm just saying it once. We've got Carruthers. Don't bother to call the police. We've already called them for you. You may, however, call the senile imbecile in the White House if you choose. Carruthers is to be tried by a People's Revolutionary Tribunal. For crimes against the People. For being emblematic of the city's elevation of style over content. Of irrelevant scholarship over social progress. The dispensation of his case will be much influenced by the willingness of your institution, and the entire university, to submit itself to radical change. There is a death penalty, by the way. More explicit directions will follow."

Desmond found himself listening to the dial tone. He cradled the phone slowly. He leaned back in his chair, repeating with disbelief, "We've got Carruthers . . . We've got Carruthers."

Carruthers kidnapped? Who the fuck would *want* him?

The intercom buzzed again.

"Tim, it's the police. A Lieutenant DeSales."

# CHAPTER 6

DESALES THUMBED THROUGH the Medical Examiner's preliminary report. Kavanaugh, subdued, as always in the office, listened while scraping at a stain on the knee of his polyester trousers.

"Discoloration on back and ass . . . sunken eyeballs . . . loss of fluid . . . means the body's been lying in one position for a long time. Weeks, maybe. . . ."

Kavanaugh looked up: "But there wasn't hardly any decomposition. Relatively speaking, she hardly stunk. Relatively speaking."

After repeating the phrase, he pursed his lips. It was something he did after uttering anything that a listener might take to sound educated or pretentious.

"No buildup of insect ova anywhere . . . suggests that she's been in a protected environment. A deep-freeze, maybe, for a few weeks before she's hung up there to hump the fireman."

"Check the morgue. See if any of the residents took a walk lately."

"That's not necessarily a bad idea, Bernie. *You* do it. Write it down in your little assignment book."

"Does he know *what* killed her?"

"'Nothing conclusive.'"

"That Friedman's an asshole."

"Doesn't think it was the shaft. Maybe she was choked or suffocated. You can't always tell. If the guy has a sure touch, the bruises don't stick."

"Don't *always* stick."

"Don't *always* stick. You know, Bernie, I can't help but think about that hooker we found in the Gowanus last winter."

"The Christmas Present? Forget it. What about the blood?"

"On the towel or the ground?"

"Both. Either."

"Same type. It's hers. Came when the stake was stuck in. Penetrated one of the places where it had collected, like a sac. That happens when they're dead for a while."

"It came out the back, then. 'Cause she was lying on her back wherever he had her."

Kavanaugh stood and removed his jacket. There were half-moons of perspiration under his arms. He poured coffee from a pot on a hot plate, offered it to DeSales, who shook his head. He tasted it, and made a face. He sat down heavily, still holding the cup in his right hand. Two desks away an old woman was screaming at another detective that her son was trying to murder her. Her voice was swallowed in the din of the cavernous, dilapidated room.

"Let's run this one through," said DeSales, taking his feet off the desk, "step by step."

"He kills her."

"Where and when and how we don't know." DeSales's cheek twitched.

"He puts her in cold storage."

"He takes her to the cemetery, presumably motorized transport. Say she's in the trunk of his car. The gates over there open at seven A.M. He has an hour before the gravediggers show up . . ."

"Or he brings her in the night before . . ."

"Or he has a key to the gate and brings her in whenever he goddamn pleases. We've gotta assume morning because of the absence of decomposition. If she'd been there all night, she would have got a little ripe."

"From the road up," said DeSales, scribbling on a notepad, "there were no tire-tracks on the turf."

"A strong mother."

"You bet. And then he had to attach her to the statue. That took *some* lifting, and then get the stake in. He did it after she was hung up, the blood's right underneath the place the stake comes out."

"Could he have brought her in over the fence?"

"That's *too* much. Let's let that one ride."

"And the towel. He dips it in the blood . . ."

"Wrong!" DeSales became emphatic. He stood up, pretending he was trying to lift a great weight against his chest. "For the face to come out the way it did, it had to be just like in Bible History. The blood came from Christ's face. The blood had to be *on* the perp's face already. . . ."

Kavanaugh was uncharacteristically disturbed: "You mean you think he dipped his *face* in . . ."

DeSales was still bearing his great burden: "How's this? He's got her up there, see, and he's got to get the stake in, so he gets behind her, plunges it in like a mugger might, from behind. It gives leverage; his weight behind and beneath her gives a solid backing, and," he looked almost triumphant, "he pushes too hard with the stake, hits the sac and breaks through the skin on the other side, and . . ." He looked toward Kavanaugh like a teacher prompting an inattentive student.

"And . . ."

"And he gets a faceful of blood."

Kavanaugh attended to the stain on his pants.

"Are you suggesting this was all an accident, Frank?"

"No. Just the Veronica."

"Why?"

"Because whoever did this is walking the streets; anybody'd

dip his face in a blood-puddle to leave a message for us is too crackers to stay out long enough to pull the rest of this. That's the point. He also had to paint on the blackface. He had to have picked the right spot. . . ."

Kavanaugh rolled his eyes: "There's lots of them like to get blood on them. Maybe it's one of these Haitian voodoo blood-drinkers. He's just trying to quaff one—from her back, see—and he misses."

DeSales ignored him. "The rest of it is a message; it's deliberate, a signature. The towel was just another opportunity. This guy can sustain logical thought; he's got a theme he's trying to get across."

"Which is?"

"I don't know. But there's a lot more to read into here than the Christmas Present."

"Which we never really figured out. And we knew who she was almost immediately from the prints. This one don't have prints on record anywhere. In New York, anyway. But you're crazy, Frankie. Mention that there's a lunatic on the loose wasting white broads with big tits and then recycling them as holiday greetings, and the mayor will either bury you or forbid you to sleep until the guy's brought in on a silver platter. There's a primary in June, remember?"

"So we wait a while before we say anything. Meantime, we wait for the national Missing Persons line to come in, circulate a glossy in the neighborhood, be prepared to go to the media with a sketch. Until we know who she is, where she came from, when it happened, there's not much sense speculating anything about this guy."

"Right!" Kavanaugh licked his pencil with mock enthusiasm, "We're looking for a woman who had the misfortune to be murdered by a 'rational' killer who managed to get away with spending an hour in broad daylight in a public cemetery hanging the nude corpse on a ten-foot-high statue of a fireman, whose face, by the way, our perp has just taken the time to paint black all over."

DeSales made a dismissive gesture with his hand, and stood up and stretched. He lighted a Benson & Hedges. In his mind's eye, he saw not blackfaces nor bloody towels nor tombstones, but the large, gaily wrapped Christmas package standing on the Carroll Street Bridge, where it had been fished from the Gowanus, on Christmas afternoon. The bells from Our Lady of Peace Church were playing "Adeste Fideles." The wind was cold and mean, the junk lining the banks of the canal covered with a light dusting of snow. He peeked in the box. The woman's body was curled up like a hibernating squirrel or chipmunk he had seen in a grammar school textbook. At Our Lady of Peace School. Or like a baby in a womb. Behind the police lines he could see the Italian grandmothers in babushkas, their lined faces set in silent screams. The young wiseguys from the neighborhood leered. This is not just a killer, DeSales had thought; this guy is trying to take Christmas from these people. People who don't have much left.

And take something from DeSales. He had grown up on these ravaged banks of the Gowanus himself, in a row house behind the church, a house too mean and rickety to ever be called a "brownstone" or to be "gentrified." Christmas to him had meant shooting at the bottles that floated down the canal with someone's new BB gun; taking aim at a rat; teetering while playing tag on the icy edges; trying to urge his sled down the hill of Park Slope across Fourth Avenue—traffic screeching— and as far as the canal. Then playing photoelectric football or Monopoly at John Rizzo's house with the smell of lasagna and turkey competing from the oven, and tinsel dripping from the tree. The Christmas Present, as the press had called it, broke into the sanctity of those images, and for a moment he had felt as though the church bells were ringing for the last time.

DeSales shook his head, trying to clear it. Sentiment was something he had given up on long ago. Sentiment, and nostalgia, and credulousness. He looked about his fiefdom, as if for the first time. Just as he had never really believed in Santa Claus, he had never really believed that his Task Force headquarters would be restored to "their former grandeur," as he had been promised by the mayor's aide before he had taken the job as chief detective. And he had been right. The room he stood in was the same dingy loft it had been for fifty years. Since the Depression.

Cigarette dangling from his mouth, hands on his hips, he moved to the wall and inspected the map of Brooklyn he had taped there. The outlines of the borough looked like a man's head. A very low-browed, primitive, screwed-up man. The Cemetery of the Evergreens was located near what brains the creature might possess. The Carroll Street Bridge over the Gowanus was in the left nostril. He moved his pushpins about, dropping ash to the floor, looking for a pattern. From the nose to the brain. From Christmas to Easter time—or April Fools' Day. Santa's helpers. A & S wrapping paper. An old Frigidaire box. Minstrel men. Brooklyn Union Gas. Cinderella.

"You still trying to link these things up?"

"Only in my gut, Bernie, only in my gut."

"The guy from the Urban Institute is still waiting downstairs. On this disappearing professor thing."

"Christ, I forgot. How did we ever get assigned to this one? Don't answer that. Just get outa here," DeSales flashed his Bogart smile, with sad sincerity this time, "you bum. Send this guy up and go have a beer or four, then home to the old lady."

"Thanks, Frank. There's one more thing."

"Yeh?"

"Megan Moore. From W V B A ? She missed the press conference this morning. She'd like to interview you. A short one."

"I got no time tonight for a fluff with a tape recorder."

"But I promised. Just this once?"

"And you'd give up your pension to have her sit on your face. Just this once. You're pathetic, Bernie. Tell her I don't know. Let her wait and take her chances."

# CHAPTER 7

CARRUTHERS FINALLY MANAGED to open his eyes. For a long time, he had lingered on the edge of consciousness, but his eyes, stuck together, had resisted. There was a dull chronic ache in his arm where the needle had been so rudely plunged. Now he could see that he had entered—visually—another, lesser, pitch of darkness. He moved his head, and a circle of pain traversed the back of his skull from ear to ear. As he winced, it came to him that he was now lying on a lumpy mattress, still in the basement where he had been attacked. He tried to sit up, in spite of the pain, and found himself chained to the bedstead.

He tried to take things in from his prone position on the bed as his eyes adjusted to the new light. From some point up to his left there was a glow and the murmur of voices. He tried to call out, but only a croak came from his throat. His tongue was dry and his palate sour. He strained his neck a bit and guessed that the sound and light came from the top of a stairwell.

A door opened. The crack of light now expanded to flood the stairs and reach with straining fingers across an oil burner, falling just short of the bed. Instinctively, he closed his eyes again. He had been crazy to try to call out in the first place, before he had taken time to try to size things up, to work out some strategy. Realizing that he had been kidnapped, he also realized that, beneath the pain, he was weary, as if he had drunk himself into a world-class hangover. One of the voices belonged to Sister Eusebia:

She whispered: "I think this is the best I've felt since I was in SDS at Madison in 1969. Fanfuckingtastic. Blowing up buildings. Making war on the war machine."

"Madison?"

"Wisconsin, you nit. What were you in '69? Nine or ten years old? Hey, shouldn't he be awake by now?"

Sister Regina answered: "*He* said it would be eight to twelve hours; it's been just eight."

"What does *he* know anyway? *He* can hardly lace his bloody shoes in the morning."

"*Tyrone* knows." There was a suggestion of fear underlying her calloused Brooklynese.

"He *would*, wouldn't he?"

"Shall we wake him up?" The fear—if indeed it had been that in the first place—was overtaken by enthusiastic anticipation. One of the two women began to descend the stairs. Carruthers peeked through a half-closed eye. It was Sister Regina. Or a facsimile of the nun he remembered. The light from the doorway caught the back of her head and shoulders, revealing a scrawny girl, shoulder blades protruding under the straps of her gaudy tank-top; her hair, hideously ruffled like the feathers of a baby chick, was dyed a medley of colors, the most predominant being a grotesque orange. The percussion of her feet on the stairs suggested spike heels.

Carruthers now saw again the long crimson fingernails, heard replayed her humming of "Eleanor Rigby." It seemed like months ago that he had descended the escalator. With a grimace he remembered that he had lost his notebook.

"Let sleeping dogs lie, luv," intoned Eusebia from the top of the stairs. "You can be sure we'll have our fill of his lot before this thing is finished."

"I think he's cute," murmured the orange-haired girl. "Can we keep him for very long?"

Carruthers felt, rather than saw, Eusebia shrug. He braved opening his eye a bit further. From this squint he could just make out in the doorway the gloss from the woman's brown cheek, and a flash of baubles hanging from the ends of long tight braids of ebony hair. "It's entirely in the hands of 'The Man Upstairs,'" she pronounced sardonically. She pointed above her, and shook her head with slow precision, as if to gather momentum before rising through the ceiling. The trinkets at the ends of the corn-curls tinkled softly. Regina, with a reluctance in the incline of her neck, went back up the stairs.

"Why does *he* make all the decisions?" she whined.

Eusebia let out a laugh that was a kind of bray: "But he *doesn't* really, does he? Because he owns the house, we let him think he's calling the shots." She repeated the sound, "If there ever was a crypto-bourgeois, he's it," she scoffed.

"Do you think he's smart?"

"The Man Upstairs?"

"No. Him!" Regina pointed into the darkness where Carruthers lay. She was very young, barely out of her teens.

"What do you care?"

"I care."

"He's got all the proper degrees and titles, if that's the sort of rot you mean; I fancy he thinks himself a genius. But all it means is that he's exploited the system; or, rather, the system has exploited the masses in such a way that the privileged few, such as our good Doctor Carruthers, can live off the proletariat like leeches."

Regina appeared to be impervious to this sort of analysis. She persisted: "What do you think his IQ is?"

"Who *cares*?" Eusebia had become irritable, impatient. "You know all about the bias of IQ tests. What a stupid question! Now, let's go back up and let him finish his little nappy."

"You see," continued the scrawny girl, "I have an idea. I'd like to, before we're finished with him, I'd like . . ."

The door closed. The voices of the women were once again reduced to a murmur. Then there was a shout and the sound of a sharp percussion. Eusebia was laughing uncontrollably. The door inched open a bit, and, with the crack of light, he heard Eusebia, convulsed with glee, manage: "You nit, he's a faggot, a bloody queen if I ever . . ."

"Does that matter?"

Eusebia's only response was more laughter. Carruthers heard their feet moving away from the door on the floor above him.

Carruthers was in bondage, and his vocal cords were so tight from what he assumed must be terror that he could not cry out. Yet there was a distinctly sensual edge to his predicament. He strained against the shackles, now oblivious to the earlier, trivial aches, and moved his hips from side to side in a pathetic bump-and-grind, abrading his buttocks on his own tweed trousers and on the exposed buttons of the moldy mattress. This in turn evoked a series of Proustian images: his mother's delicate, ivory hands . . . a porcelain chamberpot, decorated with hand-painted wildflowers glistening with morning dew . . . hands again, less refined . . . a towering marble urinal in a cafe in Barcelona . . . the street called *Las Ramblas* . . . an American Marine with a spit-shined belt . . . a beating. . . .

# CHAPTER 8

DESALES RESENTED Desmond at first sight.

He resented his rumpled corduroy jacket, his chinos, his jogging shoes, his shaggy hair that had the appearance of having been recently washed but not combed, his old-fashioned round tortoise-shell spectacles, his loosely knotted club tie, his air of bemused indifference, his height. He reminded the detective of the army of youngish men who had cluttered the city administration during the tenure of John Lindsay as mayor. Limousine liberals, Abe Beame had called them. Or had it been Mario first? Mario Procaccino. How could he forget Mario! In any case, Desmond was another of the same breed, now closing in on middle age. And passing himself off, presumably, as an expert on something. That was what they did. If they weren't running the government.

Uninvited, Desmond sat in the chair facing DeSales and crossed his legs.

DeSales resisted the impulse to rudeness. He would be short and to the point and get the guy out of there before he exploded. He wanted nothing to do with this case. Tomorrow he would farm it out to the Political Crimes Unit. Or Missing Persons. Or the FBI. At that thought, he smiled. Desmond smiled in return. Slightly gap-toothed, his smile was too engaging by half.

"You Carruthers's boss?" DeSales heard the guttural accents of the Gowanus Basin creep back into his voice, an aggressive defense.

Desmond raised an eyebrow: "Hardly. He outranks me, but I'm doing my obligatory tour of administrative work, and one of my dirty responsibilities is making sure the staff shows up for classes."

"You do keep track of him, then. Does he usually miss any days?"

"Not really. But he only comes in one day a week, so he hasn't much opportunity to be AWOL."

"How does he get a deal like that?"

"It's a long story. . . ."

"I'll take a rain check. Are you surprised by this . . . kidnapping?"

"Yes."

The two men stared at one another for a while. DeSales touched the knot on his gray silk tie and imagined that the other man was sizing *him* up as flashy, vulgar.

"Let me put it another way, Professor . . ."

"Call me Tim, okay?"

"You got any idea who could've done this? Or why?"

Desmond shrugged his shoulders: "I've asked myself the same question since the woman called. The answer was no. Still is."

"What was said?"

Desmond told him. Kavanaugh took notes. DeSales nodded.

"And I suppose you didn't recognize the voice?"

"No. It was English, though. Or transatlantic."

"West Indian?"

Desmond shook his head vigorously. As he leaned forward, the glasses slid down his nose a bit. "Not at all enough lilt, music. No. *English*. Upper-middle-class. No regional traces of accent or dialect, is what I mean. Southern England, if anything, which is more standard."

"You're an expert on this?"

"Not at all. Just took the linguistics course in grad school. Like everyone else. And I've spent a number of summers in Britain."

"Like everyone else."

DeSales struggled to keep the sarcasm out of his voice. Kavanaugh snickered. During the lull, Desmond looked around the room, as if he expected to see someone he knew.

"I'm beginning to feel, Professor . . ."

"Tim."

"Tim. That we're wasting your time. You got nothing to tell us about this Carruthers, right, his disappearance is a bolt from the blue for which you got no explanation? He's just a regular nice guy who only works one day a week and doesn't have an enemy in the world."

Desmond laughed, heartily. "On the contrary: he was generally hated. By the students, by the Dean, by me, by the entire Sociology Department, to give some minor examples."

"Then why are you surprised that he's been lifted?"

Desmond ran his upper lip back and forth over his teeth. As if he had resigned himself to a formal but unnecessary explanation. He began, "*I'm* sorry. I was assuming that somebody like you, working," he looked about the room, "with something like this at least forty hours a week, would have an even lower opinion of my profession than I do. There's no one among Carruthers's dozens of sworn enemies at the Institute who has either the aptitude or the courage to actually pull off anything so daring."

"How about students?"

A shadow fell across Desmond's face. The image of Cruz screaming at him returned. He shook his head slowly. "Maybe a shotgun in the classroom. Or a knife in the back. But nothing premeditated. Organized. No Revolutionary Tribunals. I

haven't even heard such rhetoric in years." He shook his head
again, more emphatically, but part of the shadow remained.
Something was gnawing at his memory; something at once
more distant and intimate than the likes of Cruz. Cruz, he realized in an instant, hadn't really touched him. That was why his
secretary had thought he'd done the job so well: he was just
walking his way through a part. Untouched by misery, ignorance, injustice, sleet, snow, rain. Like the postman.

"You don't seem so sure of that one."

Desmond pushed the glasses back up to the bridge of his
nose. "I'm sure of that. I was just thinking how different things
were. When the Institute started, it was all Black Panthers,
Revolutionary Justice, Kent State. When *I* was in school, it was
the Free Speech Movement, Bay of Pigs, 'Blowin' in the
Wind,' 'The Times They Are A-Changing.' Sure. All of our
students today want to be CPAs and buy houses in Bay Ridge
or Westchester before they're twenty-five." He pronounced the
place-names with distaste.

DeSales leaned back, running a fingernail along the neat part
in his black hair. There was a perverse twinkle in his eye.

"Bernie here," he said, tilting a shoulder toward Kavanaugh,
"lives in a house in Bay Ridge. You like it down there, don't
you, Bernie?"

Kavanaugh was deadpan: "Neighborhood's goin' down,
Frank. The wife wants we should get out. Westchester, maybe
Mahopac."

"I'm sorry," said Desmond, "I wasn't being clear." He now
appeared sincere in his apology, but managed to deflect his
concern to a lack of clarity rather than any social *faux pas* or
any feelings he might have hurt. Being clear, he was trying to
make clear, was very important to him. "I was trying to make a
point: the students at the Institute may hate Carruthers, but
they're so bound up in normal middle-class pursuits that they
wouldn't jeopardize their careers just to get at him. As opposed
to the old days, when the students might at least have *talked* a
revolutionary game. But it's Carruthers you're interested in,

and, see, Carruthers has nothing to do with either position. He has disdain for the house in Bay Ridge," he nodded empathically to Kavanaugh, apparently hoping that *that* wound was healed, "and for social activism too. He wanted nothing to do with either position and he made that abundantly clear to faculty and students alike, which is why everyone hated him, and also why no one would bother to stick out their necks to get back at him."

DeSales smiled evilly, touching the point of his Roman nose with the finger that had been tracing and retracing the part in his hair: "You shoulda been a lawyer, Professor."

"Tim. Thanks. Or no thanks . . . I didn't mean to offend. Whatever, what I just said isn't bullshit."

DeSales nodded: "So what *did* matter to this Carruthers then? What could he get involved in that would be important enough to . . ."

"He wanted everything. Hey, we're already referring to him in the past tense. Isn't that the way you catch murderers? Get them to make a slip of the tongue? Admit that they *know* the victim is dead?" He adjusted his glasses with mock suspicion. "Carruthers *wants* everything. For Number One. He's published two books and two hundred and ninety-three articles, and I guess he expects at least the Nobel Prize: something that will relieve him from teaching or any other such onerous tasks. A Distinguished Professorship which will be distinguished by his general absence from the campus."

"And what does he write about?"

"Whatever's fashionable. These days, it's hermeneutics and semiotics; when he did his book on Whitman—*Walt* Whitman," he said to Kavanaugh, who was scribbling madly, "it was homosexuality and pantheism. That's a good story, you know, Carruthers was hired at the Institute because they needed a well-published literary scholar with a specialty in urban writing. Carruthers had published a book called *The Cities of Walt Whitman* or some such, so they hired him as a full professor with tenure, and the sweetheart teaching deal I mentioned . . .

This was also because by then he'd published a hundred and seventy-nine articles which *no* serious administrator would stoop to actually *read* . . . but the Whitman book had *nothing* to do with cities or with Urban Studies. It merely pointed out that it didn't matter where Whitman was living or working, it was other things that drove him, not Brooklyn, or Washington, D.C., or Camden, New Jersey."

"Like homosexuality and pantheism?"

"Right." Desmond laughed humorlessly. "So the highest-paid teacher at the Institute for Urban Studies doesn't believe in Urban Studies."

Kavanaugh raised his pencil: "Who's this guy Herman?"

Desmond looked puzzled. DeSales intervened, "It wasn't a name, Bernie." He looked to Desmond, "You said 'semi-something and Herman-something.'"

"Oh. Nothing worth knowing about. Just new fads in literary criticism. Or *old* fads. Semiotics is finding meaningful signs in cultural artifacts; hermeneutics is, generally, the interpretation of texts. In Carruthers's case, it means he would look at things like graffiti, street signs, architectural frills, clothing styles, and interpret them as 'signifiers.'"

"Meaning?"

"Anything. That, say, the new ticky-tacky towns on Long Island or in California have streets named 'Honeysuckle Lane' precisely because there aren't any honeysuckles left. Which in turn says something about the state of the Union. Don't ask me what."

"And no more Whitman."

"Indeed. No more Whitman."

Kavanaugh raised his eyebrows at DeSales, who was shuffling papers. DeSales looked up suddenly:

"Was Carruthers a homosexual?"

Desmond was thoughtful. "I guess I've always assumed so, but who's to know? I once heard he had a pretty strange roommate. Straight out of a Tangier movie, if you know what I mean. *Come to the Casbah.* Let's just say it's a pretty sure bet he isn't an active heterosexual, number one; and number two, I can't imagine a man who would admit going to bed with him."

DeSales was looking through his papers again. He put another cigarette in his mouth, patted down his pockets. Kavanaugh produced a match. Puffing, DeSales stood and leaned over Desmond:

"What if I told you this 'Tangier roommate'"—he lifted an eyebrow at Kavanaugh—"says that Carruthers left his house this morning to work on a project concerning Walt Whitman? Something about his life in the nineteenth century. There was a phone call last night about some discovery which Carruthers thought was going to fix him for life."

"I'd say you were crazy. Nobody cares about writers anymore, or their lives. Just texts." Desmond stroked his chin, uncrossed his legs, and inspected the letters on his jogging shoes: N-I-K-E. He was beginning to feel like an unguided missile. "And everything's been done on Whitman anyway." He took off his glasses and wiped them on his shirttail, which he then carefully retucked in his pants. He wrinkled his brow. "But *Whitman*? Why Carruthers? How would he find out about any special project? He'd be the next-to-last person I'd call if I found something like that."

"Who'd be the last?"

"Me. You've heard of 'publish or perish'? I've already perished."

"But you still have a job. With tenure, right?"

"Right. It's hard to believe, isn't it?"

# CHAPTER 9

DESMOND HAD TO FIGHT his way onto the West Side IRT at Borough Hall, parting a sea of black faces. He straphung for five stops, pressed on three sides by a young Rastafarian wearing a green-suede pillbox hat, an elderly, tiny Chinese couple, and a coffee-colored nurse who was literally asleep on her feet. In one corner of the car a man with very black skin and a blacker beard was twisting the arm of an equally black woman who screamed periodically. No one paid them any attention.

At Grand Army Plaza, he joined the exodus of most of the remaining whites from underground to Park Slope. Wall-Streeters, artists, professors. Brain Drain. On the stairs, he turned and watched the #3 disappear into the tunnel, penetrating more deeply the heart of Brooklyn. He imagined emblazoned on the dusky foreheads of the weary workers who remained on the train the names of destinations for which he had no objective correlatives: Franklin, Utica, Van Siclen, New Lots Avenue. Nor could he conjure up any concrete image of these places, no smell or sound or sight, beyond their essential Negritude.

At the kiosk he bought a *Post*. The front page of the tabloid was a riot of banner type: TOMBSTONE TERROR AND PROFNAP IN FOG CITY! He tucked the paper under his arm and turned into Eighth Avenue, walking south. Indian heads, facing outward, were embossed on the heavy cast-iron railing that enclosed the Venetian grandeur of the Montauk Club. Death-masks of an extinct race. Long Island. Whitman. The Noble Savage. He was passing now the restored mansions built by the nineteenth-century merchants who had first "settled" the high land near the new Prospect Park. He felt again the tickle of the guilty inarticulate memory that had assailed him in DeSales's office.

Damp evening had begun to sink into the gray day. Pockets of mist hung about the tops of budding oaks and maples that stood, sentry-like, before the stately brownstones. The parlor-floor windows were a festival of hanging plants, hardwood shutters, sparkling chandeliers. This too had been one of Timothy Desmond's dreams: an archaic backlot version of social history, something gleaned from *Dr. Jekyll and Mr. Hyde* and *The Barretts of Wimpole Street.*

He turned down Berkeley Place. "'This too,'" he muttered half-aloud, self-mocking, "'has been one of the dark places of the earth.'"

But still he couldn't make the connection, get to the tip of the tongue of his memory.

He ground his teeth. Maybe it was nothing at all, except the certainty that the detective had disliked him, which had stirred up the anxiety. But *why* should that bother him so? He had been disliked before. Indeed, DeSales was exactly the type from whom he expected animosity. No, it was something at once external to his dim neuroses and buried in his equally dim past.

His own house was part of a well-preserved row of tidy neo-Grecs. He climbed the stoop and turned keys in four locks, two to each door. As he slid the bolts back in place, he felt a rush of relief blowing from the empty silence of the old house. He opened the shiny new refrigerator in the shiny new kitchen and lifted out a jug of Soave. He found a long-stemmed goblet in a cupboard and filled it almost to the brim. He drank heartily. Then his special moment, almost autoerotic in its intensity, was broken in mid-swallow by the phone.

Mona. Of course.

"It's me," she announced, definitely on an up.

He finished too quickly and coughed, "Yeh?"

Her animation dissipated: "You sound your usual cheery, vigorous self."

"I was holding a private tasting of plaster dust. The 1885 vintage. Some went down the wrong way."

"You made your bed, as they say . . ."

He didn't want to start *that* again. "How's the country?" he cut in.

"Muddy as hell, but at least it *smells* nice. And no plaster. Just the wood fire. That was a good idea of yours last fall, putting a little spruce in with the hardwood. Aromatic. And I like the snap, crackle, and pop." She sounded sincere. He hadn't yet forgiven her for her ugliness about his selection when he had cut and stacked the wood the year before. It was not the way her father would have done it.

"Nice. Lucky you."

"Look, Tim, I'm sorry about last night. I *was* tired. And upset. I can't turn it on and off like a faucet, you know."

"Forget it." He drained the glass, poured some more.

"And I knew, thought I knew, you'd be coming up here tonight. We could talk . . . away from the dust. Maybe I could make you understand, make it up to you."

He couldn't handle the open pitch for intimacy. He held desperately on to his anger. He changed the subject, trying to sound totally exasperated by events beyond his control: "You won't believe this, but someone has kidnapped Fletcher Carruthers."

"I do believe it. I just heard it on the news. But what has that got to do with you coming up here?"

He could see her now. She would be looking for a cigarette. Her mouth would be half open, her flecked brown eyes wide, smudged windows on a generous heart that was easily twisted by hurt, imagined or real. When they had first met, new kids in the big city, the hurts were all ignored; or perhaps they didn't even happen. Tim and Mona Desmond were as excitement-prone as a couple could be, sharing enthusiasms, one or both always airborne with happy anticipation. Now their existence had become encrusted with a tissue of criticism and nay-saying. He lied:

"I've been placed in charge of his absence, as it were. The police want me to stay within reach. In case anything breaks. So I have to stay in Brooklyn." He realized he did not sound as if even *he* were convinced. He fished: "And I could try to start stripping those shutters for the bedroom, and I got the name of a mason who might point up the back of the house before the rains come. . . ."

He heard a sharp intake of breath. She had found the ciga-rette. She exhaled slowly.

She said, "Okay, Tim. You're a good little boy."

He had nothing to answer. He listened to the quiver in her voice. It was something she did after lighting up. It meant she felt vulnerable. It also meant she was contemplating attack.

Finally, she said, "When I heard about Carruthers, I thought of that creepy friend of yours."

"What creepy friend?"

"Back when you were singlehandedly carrying the burdens of poverty and educational deprivation around on your sleeve. Oh, forgive me, I mixed up my metaphors. The one who got canned so they could hire Carruthers. He had a funny name, ROTC shoes, and looked like he'd just been discharged from Ellis Island."

"Joe Verb?" Desmond had difficulty adding the question mark. She had rung the bell of recognition.

"I thought," she drawled, "well, maybe old Joe's finally got his licks in."

As usual, she was right. It had been Joe Verb whose exis-tence Desmond had been trying to recall. And he knew immediately why it had been so difficult. Guilt. It was typical of Mona that she could unerringly find the appropriate rock, turn it over. For a moment he hated her. Desmond looked through the tall parlor windows. Across the street, Ian and Patti Griswold and their four children were eating peanut butter and jelly sandwiches under a crystal chandelier. He looked up at his own thirteen-foot ceiling. Paint had flaked off the moldings; the elaborate wreathlike frieze was one-third missing; and where there should have been a chandelier, a naked bulb hung from a gaping hole in the plaster.

It took all of his concentration to maintain a level tone: "Look, Mona, honest, I'm going to take advantage of being around here for the cops to get some contractors lined up. If I get my promotion, we'll afford it easily. . . ."

There was now only contempt in her voice. "Enough. You're the Best Little Boy. And I'll be goddamned if I'm going to play Bad Mother in *your* fucking scenario!" She hung up.

Desmond went up the stairs with a purpose. Above the ground floor, the house was a warren of cubicles left over from the decrepit rooming house the Desmonds had bought and been unable, or unwilling, to restore totally. In a file cabinet, he found an old Institute address-list. He dialed Joe Verb's number. It was busy. Suddenly the weight of the quandary returned. How was he to know whether this was still Joe's number, or whether he was still living with his wife if it was? What would he say to him—"Joe, I think you kidnapped Carruthers. Give yourself up."? This was really something to be passed on, for which he had no responsibility, in which he had no right to meddle. He began to dial the number for the Violence Task Force that DeSales had given him. Halfway through, he faltered and eased the receiver into the cradle.

How could he call the police on the basis of a wild hunch? About Joe Verb, of all people? Joe Verb in particular? Desmond *owed* Verb, owed him rather badly, and it was this sense of obligation that had in effect buried his memory until Mona resurrected it.

He looked at the telephone with distaste, an instrument of distancing, of passivity. He had to *see* Verb. He had to do something besides sit around the house drinking himself into a wine stupor because, among other things, his wife seemed disinclined to sleep with him. Maybe if he found Joe, they could talk, rebuild some bridges. If, on some odd chance, Joe *had* been involved in the Carruthers thing, maybe Desmond could disentangle him from the foolishness, get Carruthers back where, sadly, he *belonged*. Something productive had to come from an assertive venture into the Brooklyn night; and anything was better than spending one's evenings tripping over the floorboards of the past. And the present.

He got the car keys and a map of Brooklyn and headed back out into the mist.

# CHAPTER 10

DESALES TRIED TO avoid Megan Moore as he was leaving headquarters, but she caught him at the door.

"Lieutenant? Bernie—Detective Kavanaugh—said you might be able to give me a minute. I missed the briefing this morning, so I don't have any tape . . . on you . . . to file."

DeSales leaned against a doorway molding, cast his eyes briefly heavenward, then met her steady, almost quizzical gaze head on. He said nothing. Her eyes were green. Finally, she cast them down. She scuffed a low-heeled Gucci pump on the wide boards of the floor.

"I was stuck in the fog. The one caused by the malfunction of the asphalt plant." She worked the corners of her mouth into the approximation of a hopeful smile. "So you *could* say it was the city's fault. They own the plant, so then I would deserve. . ."

DeSales grunted, beginning to push open the door to the street. "I'm sorry, Ma'am, but I don't think I can be held accountable for every traffic jam the city causes. And I'm working on more than one case, you know. I've got a long . . ."

Megan Moore reached out to touch his shoulder, but he

turned abruptly and she found herself running her fingers across his torso. He was wiry and muscular. Hard. It was clear she would get nowhere joking or playing on his sympathy, as she did with Kavanaugh. She had to make her play now, without preliminaries. She chuckled self-consciously, removing her hand, feeling the cold silk of his tie.

"Okay, Lieutenant DeSales. I know the story: you're a no-nonsense guy. So no screwing around. Tit for tat. You give me a short interview that I can put on the air, and I'll tell you why there will be a piece running on my station in . . ."—she looked at her watch—". . . the next half hour or so, hinting that there's a connection between today's corpse in the Cemetery of the Evergreens and the Gowanus Christmas Present last winter. That poor woman with the pathetic name—Jerry Jacuzzi, she called herself."

DeSales looked to see if there was any indication that she was bluffing. She was a small woman, fine-boned and delicate, with light-brown hair that gathered itself in tight curls. He tried to figure what it was he liked about her: her voice wasn't phony like most of the rest of the broadcast media, who tended to sound as if they had acquired their timbre and diction by sending a cereal boxtop to Battle Creek, Michigan. Her clothes were quiet, discreetly expensive. She had spunk. And there was something about the way she plucked her eyebrows. Something kinky. Which he liked. The pretty green eyes were steady. He decided she had something. Or believed she had something. So her coercion was sincere.

He pushed the door open, holding it at arm's length so she could pass through without bumping him with the cumbersome bags of tape equipment she carried on one shoulder.

"What are you drinking?" he asked in a tone of good-humored resignation.

"Wine." Her voice grew smaller as she stepped into the noisy street. "White. Chilled and dry."

"Good," he said, slitting his eyes at her back. "I know just the place. They serve Gallo Sauternes. On the rocks. In high-ball glasses."

Megan Moore threw her head back and laughed.

The cop put his left hand into the small of her back and guided her to the corner on the right.

The white van eased itself from the curb and tracked them slowly. They turned the corner, and the man in the driver's seat cursed, clutching the wheel. *One Way. Do Not Enter.* Then he could see them go into the saloon with the letters missing from the neon sign outside; he relaxed. A bit. He could circle the block and wait for them again. He drove as fast as he could without attracting attention, slowing only to check if there were any back or side exits that they could slip out without being seen from the front.

Settled in again, the van idling at a fireplug, the driver disengaged himself from behind the steering wheel and stepped, crouching, into the back of the vehicle. He lighted two sticks of incense, myrrh and strawberry, and inserted them into the soft clay of the holder next to the sleeping bag. Then he reached into the Coca-Cola cooler, withdrew a dripping sixteen-ounce can of Budweiser from beneath the layers of ice, popped the cap, and sucked off the head. With the other hand, he withdrew a joint from the pocket of his facsimile Brooklyn Dodgers jacket, flicked a kitchen-match against the cooler, and lighted up. He took two long tokes and then extinguished the roach with his wet index finger. He maneuvered his heavily muscled body and can of Bud back into his seat, turning on W V B A - F M at low volume.

Maybe he would hear *her* voice, coming on tape from some fancy fortieth-floor studio in the city or something, while he simultaneously had her cornered in O'N_i_s T_vern on the ground floor of an old factory building three blocks from the Brooklyn House of Detention. That was the kind of thing a guy could really get off on.

So he rested his preternaturally large head against the top of the seat, lowered his amphibian lids until they were almost closed, assuming an attitude of somnambulistic vigilance. There, against the low rumble of the exhaust, the almost-in-audible-but-still-clearly-feverish chatter of the Voice of the Big Apple, the 69¢ Stores, Sneaker Circuses, and disused Movie Palaces of downtown Brooklyn, all yellowing in the twilight, he attempted to reproduce the technique he had been learning all those years ago at the Divine Light Mission in the Village before he had ripped all the pictures of the fat little brown-skinned fucker with the shit-eating grin off the walls and they had asked him not to come back.

That was no good, to think of the Maharaji at a time like this; counterproductive. You were supposed to be able to turn it on, like a bathtub tap, let it all fill up. Until it was empty.

That was what they called a paradox.

The table in the booth had a black formica top and an overflow-ing bronze tinfoil ashtray. DeSales rattled the cubes in his Dew-ar's-on-the-rocks, then sipped. He looked up, across the table, with a kind of bored disbelief.

"Wet? So she was wet. So what? And how do you know? You weren't even *there*."

"I can't name names, but one of my colleagues who got there before you did noticed it. They said, 'It was really funny. The corpse was wet.'"

"And you've already mentioned this on the radio?"

"Not exactly. I was discreet. I just said there was evidence which established a potential link between the two cases."

DeSales put his back against the wall and his legs up on the bench. The toes of his expensive shiny black shoes jutted into the room. He gestured to the barman for a refill. Megan Moore's wine was still untouched. It had a brownish tinge to it and, contrary to her order, had been served straight-up and warm.

"Some evidence," DeSales said. "It's really funny, you know. The vast majority of persons we fish from the water tend to be wet. And not only from the Gowanus Canal. You name it: Gravesend Bay, Coney Island Creek, the East River. All *wet!*" He shook his head.

Megan Moore tasted the wine. Cautiously. Through bee-stung lips. She made a moue, a gesture more of self-control than distaste, then, finally, swallowed. She said, "The Cemetery of the Evergreens is not under water."

"True enough. But it has lakes. At least one." DeSales managed not to blink.

Megan Moore sounded mildly incredulous: "You mean you think she was drowned there, or dumped in a lake there, and then taken out and strapped to the statue?"

The Scotch arrived. DeSales disengaged from eye contact. After cradling the drink on his chest, he continued to look toward the bar. "I didn't say that. But she could have been in the water. You want another?"

She pushed aside her drink, leaning eagerly across the table. "Lieutenant, listen! Don't you remember? The girl in the Gowanus wasn't wet because she was in the canal! She was in a box, and the box hadn't sunk! It was floating. And her hair was still wet!"

"We assumed she'd been tipped over, or dropped in the canal at some point. Why, under those circumstances, wouldn't her hair be wet?"

"Did you ever check?"

"Check what?"

"Whether the water on her hair was from the canal. Had it frozen? I can't remember. Does the canal freeze?"

"This is ridiculous. I don't want to talk about it anymore."

"Okay, but I think you should check. The water. On her hair, in her lungs, see where it comes from."

DeSales shrugged his shoulders.

Megan Moore put her hand across the table and touched his elbow: "You know what I think? I think you're scrambling pretty hard to prove that there's no relationship between the two cases, which suggests that you're afraid there *is* one. Maybe you're trying to persuade yourself."

"We don't even have ID or sure cause of death; I'm not trying to eliminate anything." He knew he sounded stupid, defensive about being defensive.

For a moment, she was silent, sizing him up. "Okay," she finally breathed, "let's *not* talk about these cases anymore. Let's talk about *you*. Since you won't let me tape you anyway, Lieutenant . . . May I call you Frank?"

"Sure."

"Thanks. You know, Frank, you have a cherubic smile—no, it's the smile of a guilty choirboy. Is that why they call you 'The Saint'?"

DeSales laughed, good humor ignited by a sense of relief. "You want me to answer that? To be quoted on your lousy *News Update*?"

"I want you to answer that. So I can understand you better."

He turned to face her, feet flat on the floor, elbows on the table. He lighted a cigarette and almost immediately laid it down to smolder in the overflowing ashtray. He sipped his Scotch. "Nothing to do with my cherubic smile, thanks. It's my name. I assume you're a WASP. Any self-respecting Catholic would have heard of Saint Francis de Sales. I'm named after a saint. Saint Francis de Sales. He was a Frenchman who was Bishop of Geneva and wrote about how we should love God as a friend rather than fear him as a judge. Lived about the same time as Shakespeare."

"Your parents were interested in the Renaissance . . . ?"

DeSales slapped the table. His cigarette rolled out of the tray. He picked it up, grinning, and inhaled smoke: "My father was a Canuck, a French Canadian who worked on the docks and shipped out every now and then. He could barely speak English, and he certainly never heard of the Renaissance. My mother was an Italian Catholic, the most devout. From Red Hook. I think she married my father because of his name."

Megan Moore raised the finely etched eyebrows.

"How many guys with real saints' names you find in Red

Hook? If she'd found an Aquinas wandering around there, she would have married *him*; then I'd be Thomas, see. A Seton, maybe I'd be *Mother*, except I don't think the lady had been canonized yet. Beatified, maybe. But that wasn't enough for my mother."

Megan Moore's body convulsed with silent mirth. She pulled at one of the tight little curls. Her eyes glistened. Then she threw back her head. It was the way she showed she was really enjoying herself. The top button on her high-necked dress had come undone, revealing ivory flesh and delicate bone structure. Her breasts rose and fell, and DeSales realized for the first time that she had a voluptuous figure and dressed in such a way as to tone it down, cut short the curves. Big boobs were not All Business.

"Nobody told me you were *funny*," she said.

DeSales had forgotten himself for a moment. He had pleased her; he had felt the correspondent stirring of desire; he had been wondering what she was like under the Bergdorf-Goodman clothes, who or what had been inside her, how she had felt about it. He caught himself; or, rather, the recurring images of wet female corpses, like inflatable dolls, forcing their way to the surfaces of murky liquids, brought him up short. He had been stupid, missing the hair. He must have been in a daze. All day long. And now here he was, getting hot pants for a broad reporter. He needed a little R & R, and quick. He stood up.

The disappointment on Megan Moore's face was palpable. She had raised her glass toward the bar, prepared to order something else, stay a while.

"It's over? Just like that?"

"Sorry," he muttered, "I just remembered another case. Phone call."

The booth was in an alcove near the men's room. DeSales dropped a dime in the slot and dialed a number. He let it ring four times and hung up. He reinserted the coin and dialed again. This time it was picked up on the first ring. The voice was thick and sultry, a marked contrast to Megan Moore's. DeSales was already breathing more easily.

"Yeah. This is four-five-nine-eight."

"How about a number three in the eighth, Roz?"

"Saint! Where you been?"

"Working. I thought I'd lost the urge."

"Too many stiffs to get stiff."

"Some people say they turn me on."

"Don't you believe it. I know the man behind the badge."

"You able to fit me in tonight?"

"I'm free the whole night after ten."

"How free? I'm a poor civil servant, remember."

"I'll turn off the meter when things get too rich."

"Your place or mine?"

"Yours. I'm tired of lookin' at the Twin Towers, and the waterbed is gettin' me down. Give me your busted springs any day."

Megan Moore looked up expectantly, her head tilted, one hand touching an ear. The nails were bitten. DeSales, everything back in its place, now felt emanating from her little more than a neurotic fussiness. The nails, the voice, the facade of liberated independence; a sense that underneath, behind the chance of a few good times, there lay a demander, a whiner in the missionary position. Complications he didn't need. He shook his head: "Gotta go."

She rose reluctantly, bundling up her equipment. DeSales was already at the door.

"Did it occur to you," she asked, scrambling, "that there could be more than one killer? That it probably took more than one person to get that woman up on that statue, and it could have taken different people to leave such different kinds of clues, or messages, like graffiti artists or something?"

"No, it didn't," he said. "Where's your car? I'll take you there, and then I gotta hustle."

Hustle is right, he thought. He felt as if he had been sleep-walking. He had a good three hours before Roz would get to his place. He had to get the M.E. on the horn; he had to pull the files on the two other cases from last year. He remembered vaguely that there had been an eyewitness in one of them, an eyewitness who had bummed out. Roz could help with that.

Roz could help with a lot of things. He had forgotten that a date with her made him feel like a man who was holding good cards.

The man with the big head was still trying to let it flow. He had gotten tired of that Indian shit before, and now it was coming back again. Indians! The Man Upstairs called them Native Americans and said they had founded Brooklyn, been there before everyone else, and then been slaughtered or driven out by white men. Whiteskins, Redskins. The Redskins were in the Super Bowl, and the act of driving the Indians out of Brooklyn had been an Early Manifestation of American Imperialism. Or Colonialism. It was sometimes hard to tell them apart. And now, these days, there were Indians pushing out the Puerto Ricans down by where he was sleeping in the van, where the book said the PRs had driven out the Norwegians. Among others. These were Indians from India. *East* Indians. Some were as black as the ace of spades, and a lot were heavy into big business. Doctors, lawyers, lots of newsstands. No Maharaji shit for them, no sharing the wealth. And there were Puerto Rican Indians too; he knew some heavy PR dudes had a Spanish name for them, and treated them like dirt. And how about the *West* Indians? They were taking over Brooklyn. And they *were* niggers. Deprived at home by British Colonialism, just as our niggers were the victims of American Racism and Imperialism. So what were they doing *here*, then? It was like 'Nam, another connection he couldn't make. The gooks had taken the heat in 'Nam, not the GIs, not really. So why did he have to think about some Dutch farmer driving the Canarsee tribe out to the Hamptons in sixteen hundred or seventeen hundred and something, when right now, today, all over Brooklyn, good people were being driven out, out, out, until they came to the water maybe. And drowned. . . .

He tried to conjure up Megan Moore's skin, so pale it could glow in the dark, feel her soft curls bunched in his fingers, hear the voice with the money in it . . . and just then he heard her come on the air and saw her step out of the saloon behind the cop. She had her head down now and dragged her feet. The cop looked up at the streetlights. They hadn't hit it off. But her voice on the radio was bright and clear and sure of itself. It was like at one moment she was two persons. Or three. And as he released the clutch he felt together with her in that he also was at least two persons. She held sway over him for a moment, the mastery of the airwaves, the driving out toward the water. She was up to her pretty neck in it. Drowning.

> *Mobile Unit*: There are now unconfirmed reports flying around the municipal buildings that there is a connection between today's ghoulish homicide and the so-called Gowanus Christmas Present of last year, the prostitute Selma Goldblum, a.k.a. Jerry Jacuzzi, of nearby Pacific Street. . . .

> *Anchor*: Wasn't there something unique about that package, the one the corpse was found in?

> *Mobile Unit*: Yes, as a matter of fact, it was gold and red and had a Magi scene.

> *Anchor*: Right.

> *Mobile Unit*: There's a second connection, Larry. The fact that these bodies were discovered on holidays. This is April Fools' Day.

> *Anchor*: So we may have a serial killer on our hands, a homicidal sexual psychopath stalking the streets for the young women of Fun City. Another Son of Sam. Only with a sense of gallows humor.

> *Mobile Unit*: I wouldn't want to state it so baldly, but

it should serve as a grim reminder to us what holidays are coming up next: Good Friday and Easter. Crucifixion, burial . . . and *Resurrection*. Hey, forget I said that. Cut the line about Resurrection. . . .

But the technician had missed her directive. The foolish conjecture stood. Made her sound like *The National Enquirer*. It was typical of W V B A.

Megan Moore turned off the radio, turned off *herself*, with disgust. Why was she doing it? The money, the independence, the chance to make it someday on a legitimate station or network? It was the old litany: she wasn't going to give up, that was all there was to it.

She crossed Atlantic Avenue, into the fringe area between Boerum Hill and Cobble Hill, turned right on Bergen, then a left and another right. The street was, as usual, dark and dignified, like a funeral. She was relieved to see a parking place under the streetlight across from the carriage-house she rented for almost half her salary. Cobble Hill. Brooklyn Heights *vicinity*. Not even Brooklyn Heights. Not long ago, she would never have dreamed of living in Brooklyn, let alone in a residential backwater fed by an avenue of Arab shopkeepers. Shish kebab and barrels of spice. But Sam had needed a big place to put up his kids on custodial weekends. And she had wanted Sam, badly. She knew now that she had wanted his kids—or the *idea* of his kids—even more. But Sam, like so many others, had not worked out, and he had taken his Canoe aftershave and six-packs of St. Pauli Girl and bearlike sexual ineptitude and every-other-weekend parental responsibilities back to Manhattan, to a woman with a white loft in Tribeca; Megan hoped, for the woman's sake, that she possessed a monumental indifference to Sam's drinking and inability to tell the truth.

She stood under the light, attempting to sort out her keys. The car keys fell in the gutter. She swore. The two bald gay guys with the dachshund who lived on the corner passed, clucking tongues at her in mock disapproval. She forced a smile.

Finally she got the car locked and found the key to the house. She turned the key; the door, heavy mahogany with stained-glass lights, swung inward. She had left her bags in the car. She threw the house key down in the vestibule, and stalked back out to the car with the car keys. She had to go to the bathroom.

She jerked the leather bags out of the car. One fell with a thud on the cobbled pavement. She imagined tape rolling loose, realized she was doing something foolish, un-street-smart, diddling about on a dark street with her front door hanging open and thousands of dollars of equipment in her hands; and she scurried into the house.

In the tiny W.C. with the clever wallpaper made of old *New Yorker* covers, she got up her skirt and pulled down her pantyhose, sat heavily on the cold seat, and thought about Frank DeSales as she relieved herself. There was something hard and sexy about him: a man-sized erection. But that something was also a bit frightening. Also like an erection. She wiped herself hastily and grinned into Sam's leftover shaving mirror. That could be a problem, couldn't it? Hard, sexy, frightening. *Always was a problem.* But what did it matter? She still had her sense of humor even if she had scared him off. Somehow. He had been interested, looking her over, turning on the charm. And then, just like that, he was a wet towel. The shit. She was glad she hadn't mentioned the holiday angle to him. She would develop that on her own.

The phone rang.

She had a new number, unlisted. It had to be someone from work or someone she had given the number to in the past couple of days. Maybe it was DeSales. She rushed into the kitchen, pantyhose only partially adjusted, W.C. door ajar, and toilet unflushed. The white phone with the long spiral of cord and the dial in the mouthpiece almost tumbled off the hook.

"Hello," she gasped.

There was the sound of traffic, heavy traffic. For a moment or two, no one said anything.

Oh Gawd, she thought, not another breather. *Already.*

Then he spoke. She heard his voice for the first time. For a moment she thought it was someone who could barely speak English, then she realized that she was hearing someone with a voice that was the essence of proletariat Brooklyn who was trying to elevate his diction by speaking like a foreigner, slow, tentative: over-enunciating, for example, his *r*'s. His voice was deep and had a kind of rumbling indifference (as if "dese," "dem," and "dose" were just beneath the surface, struggling to get out) that was bizarre in juxtaposition to the exaggerated attempt at genteel speech.

"Megan, baby," he said. "You the smartest."

"Who is this?"

"A lissenah . . . *lisst-enn-errr*. You give me funny ideas, you know?"

"Now just wait a minute. How did you get this number? I've just had it changed to fend off sickos like . . ."

"Don't say it. This is somebody very important to you. I wanted first to compliment you on being the first to see that the hooker in the Gowanus and the woman today were the work of one and the same . . . *criminal*." He said the last word with pride. "And as a reward for your brainpower, I'm gonna give you a scoop. No. Two scoops."

Suddenly she felt giddy. Fear, loathing, ambition? She almost giggled, almost punctured the mood by saying foolishly: "Scoops? Of ice cream?" But she remained silent.

It was fear. She had never been so frightened, but she had to stay with him, bring him out.

She heard horns honking. The first part of his speech was obliterated. If she had only hooked her recorder to the phone!

". . . Good Friday a good idea, maybe Easter even better. An artist needs his materials to work with, you know. Maybe you'd like to volunteer."

She mumbled, incoherent.

"Ha. That's okay. I wouldn't use you *yet*. I like to hear you talk about me on the radio. That's a nice station you're on, y'know."

"Yes," she said. She stared at her collection of Cuisinart blades. "Thank you."

"So you have given to me short notice. But I'll be on the alert, y'know? I aim to please. Another gift for the holidays."

He was waiting for a response.

"Of course," she said. "And you were going to give me another scoop?"

He seemed for a moment to have forgotten, to have lost track. Then he rumbled: "The girl today? At the Evergreens? Her name was Samantha. And another holiday, y'know. She disappeared on Lincoln's Birthday. You're the only one who knows *that*. Besides me. And one more thing. Megan. I value hearing you. Don't fuck around in the street with your keys so long. You could get hurt. Ripped off." He chuckled. "G'bye."

The line was dead. She sat on the barstool she kept by her counter and picked up a *Gourmet* magazine. There was a picture of a raspberry tart on the cover, a feature on a "gourmet holiday" in Strasbourg.

The man with the big head began to leave the phone booth on Atlantic Avenue, but his attention was riveted by a poster; South Slope House Tour. Easter weekend. House tours were just about the best place to find new talent. He smiled, hopping into the van. He cracked another Bud and pointed himself south. When he was on Third Avenue, under the expressway, with the roar from above in his ears, and surrounded by abandoned storefronts with broken windows and boys on the corners in gang jackets with names like "Homicidal Maniacs," he felt cozy, at home, after a hard day's work well done. He threw the beer can out the window into the street and almost heard it clattering along as he turned down toward the docks.

# CHAPTER 11

TIMOTHY DESMOND maneuvered the ten-year-old BMW 2002tii around Grand Army Plaza and through the gates into Prospect Park. Weaving in and out of the late-rush-hour traffic, he downshifted and accelerated noisily through yellow lights on the circular park drive. He passed the Sheep Meadow, where Mona's father and all the other nice respectable little WASP kids from the neighborhood had once performed the annual Maypole Dance in white suits and dresses. That had been around 1910, just before the family had joined the first exodus of the Brooklyn bourgeoisie to the suburbs. Now Desmond had brought the family back. Downward mobility. He passed the Picnic House, whose red-brick exterior was being restored by the city at great expense so the new gentry could hold fundraisers there for their private schools. He passed the forested knoll where, the real-estate woman who had sold them the house on Berkeley Place had proudly noted, Montgomery Clift was buried in a Quaker cemetery. Then he was rounding a long curve and approaching on his left the broad expanse of water where two ghetto children had fallen through the ice and drowned during the winter. A red-and-white sign warned, belat-

edly, *Peligro! Helado!* Desmond, vaguely aware that he was
now on the "other" side of the park, might easily have taken the
sign to be an all-seasons bulletin, a warning that uncharted,
potentially dangerous terrain was approaching, and caution
should be exerted. Instead he stepped on the gas. He was on an
up, his first of the day, and he had not only cast off the oppres-
siveness of his own house, his personal responsibilities, but had
also remembered that he had once before visited the Verb apartment on Ocean Avenue and had no need for the map he had
brought with him, a final encumbrance discarded. None of William Blake's "chartered streets" for him; he was on automatic
pilot.

Besides, on the radio, WCBS-FM, it was 1969, which
wasn't at all bad. Creedence Clearwater filled the car:

> *Rollin', rollin',*
> *Rollin' down the riv*uh . . .

He sang along, moving in his seat.

The Ocean Avenue exit was closed—permanently, it appeared (another sign someone might interpret as ominous)—but
he decided to go with the flow. He would circle the park once
more, get off at Coney Island Avenue, and follow Prospect Park
South, parallel to the drive, to Ocean. The other exits on the
wrong side of the park—Lincoln, Empire—were mysteries to
him, would drive him back to the map. And that, he didn't need
right now.

The music stopped, as if it had hit a wall. The DJ's voice
intoned: "This should bring a chill," and the weird wavering
opening of "Gimme Shelter" came on. The Stones. The sitar
sound, something like gravel on a gourd, a big lead guitar, a
ghostly "Whoooo" vocal backdrop that suggested temporal sta-
sis, relief from change:

> *Somewhere the storm is threatening*
> *Louder and louder today*
> *If I don't get some shelter*
> *Oh yea I'm gonna fade away*

He dropped into second gear, and let the engine whine as the odometer climbed past 5000 rpm. He was taken back completely into the nonfiction novel of his own past. He was a guitarist, a biracial fantasy of a fantasy, swaybacked, foot-stomping, turning a long saturnine face slowly from side to side, an amalgam of Chuck Berry and Keith Richards under hot lights. He remembered 1969. Reality. The Village. He was strutting into Callahan's, having smoked a joint of Panama Red on the walk across Eleventh Street from University Place to Seventh Avenue South. He passed through the dark tinted entry, adjusting his flesh to the air-conditioning. He wore a drooping moustache, a badge of sensuality.

> *I gotta get some shelter . . .*
> *It's just a shot away*
> *It's just a shot away.*

He was camel-walking along the backs of the crowd at the bar to the far corner, *his* corner: there was Jerry Juice, Sheila, Long Tall Sally, Krump the Lawyer, Black Jason (always with the V-sign, the knowing smile over the glass of Stolichnaya). Desmond could see himself in the long saloon mirror. There was electricity in his stance, charged by the certainty that the night promised tequila shooters, more dope, a choice of strange beds to wake up in.

He missed the *strange* of it. The absence of dread.

> *It's just a shot away*
> *It's just a shot away . . .*

He wheeled out of the park, along the Parade Grounds. Ocean Avenue brought him down. Fast. There was a McDonald's on the corner where once one had been able to exit from the park. That was the only immediately perceptible sign of life in the falling darkness. This had been a thriving middle-class Jewish district, solid and dismally reassuring. That had been not so long ago. *After* the sixties, which seemed closer. Now the brick apartment buildings that lined the avenue had windows shattered or boarded up. Sheets of metal covered the storefronts that had formerly housed Kosher delis and dry-cleaners. Under a working streetlight down the block, there was a shabby *bodega*. As he drove closer, he saw that the doorway was clustered with black men drinking from brown paper bags. Instinctively, he checked the locks on his doors.

He pulled in without enthusiasm in front of the building where he had visited the Verbs, remembering how they had lived. Half the apartment told you about Sherry Verb's dreams: a blond wedding-present suite of furniture, *tchatchkas* on every available counter or table top, a Princess phone. Hot pink. Joe's litter hid everything else; layers of mimeographed manifestoes covered even the heavy Marxist tomes on which he was supposedly working to complete his thesis. Now Desmond squinted through his car window, down the dimly-lit, once-grand entranceway into the cavernous lobby of the building, and was hard put to imagine that any of it, porcelain puppies or propaganda, remained. The mood of the radio switched as well, further back into the sixties, when things had been just beginning, around the time Bob Dylan went electric:

> *When you're lost in the rain in Juarez*
> *And it's Eastertime too*
> *And your gravity fails*
> *And negativity don't pull you through . . .*

The old Jews who had occupied the benches in the long walkway were gone; so were the benches, literally ripped from the concrete. Along the walls, where once there had been flowerbeds, stood groups of adolescents, all dark-skinned, in sleeveless leather jackets, strap undershirts, old sweatpants. Many of the young men wore high-topped sneakers with the laces meticulously undone, tongues protruding, an orchestrated statement of defiance.

Defiance of what?

Desmond knew better than to ask such questions. He also knew better than to try to run this gauntlet of hostile kids. His confrontation with Cruz that morning had more than filled his quota for the year, for the decade. Besides, since there was no way the Verbs would still be living here, why bother?

> *Don't put on any airs*
> *When you're down on Rue Morgue Avenue*
> *They got some hungry women there*
> *And they really make a mess out of you.*

He mistrusted the shrug of his shoulders implicit in the words, in the "why bother?" There was cowardice there that was not all that different from the cowardice of sitting home with the jug of Soave, perhaps watching Joe Verb self-destruct on TV. Like Patty Hearst watching her pals from the Symbionese Liberation Army. That was something that had happened in the seventies. Sometimes it seemed to him that nothing had happened in the seventies, that he had aged from thirty to forty watching TV with a jug of wine nearby, while nothing changed enough to be interesting. That was somewhere near the heart of his problem with Mona. So he had to tell himself for the thousandth time, "You've got to start somewhere," when every ounce of his being resisted starting at all. He was embarrassed.

He opened the car door. There would be a super he could talk to, someone who remembered when, and where, the Verbs had gone. Inertia carried him out of the car. He was just doing his job.

The powerful scent of marijuana in the air seemed sadly inevitable; the "Weed of Love" had become another commonplace of despair. Oversized portable radios gave off noisy vibrations, impenetrable acts of aggression. Desmond saw cold dark eyes turn on him, incipient moustaches, thick lips parted in scorn, facial scars that suggested tribal rituals. He looked at the pavement while he strode forward, as if, like Carruthers, he intended to squeeze the significance out of the graffiti. In his mind, the Dylan disc spun on.

*I cannot move*
*My fingers are all in a knot*
*I don't have the strength*
*To get up and take another shot*
*And my best friend the Doctor*
*Won't even say what it is that I've got*

Desmond imagined footsteps behind him, decided it would be uncool to look around. A girl in short shorts with heavy thighs and a Michael Jackson hairdo stepped in his way. He sidestepped her, muttering, "Excuse me." A cigarette lighter flared on his right. The cement beneath his feet, where it was not shattered, said FUCK PUTA FUCK PUTA.

For some reason, at that moment, with his palms sweating and the spasms in the muscles at the small of his back coming on, he remembered his first visit to Bennington College in Vermont, many years before. The entrance to the campus was flanked by elegant stone columns. Then there was a drive that swept through what seemed like miles of empty silent meadows. Acres and acres of Wordsworthian revelation. Splendor in the grass. A true high mowing. When he finally reached any sign of civilization, the buildings more closely resembled stately homes gone to seed than classroom space or dormitories. It was midmorning, the last week of classes for the spring term, a time of bustle on any campus. Yet there was only one person in sight: a sinewy, deeply tanned young woman, with hair like cornsilk, played volleyball alone on the lawn in front of the administration building. On her T-shirt was lettered: THE YEAR OF THE COCK.

Bennington was the most expensive college in the United States. He guessed the girl had something to do with the reason why.

Now, back in Brooklyn, he heard a boy's voice spit, "Asshole," and he knew he was going to be okay. It was going to be name-calling, shadow-boxing; no one was going to put a hurt on him. He turned. Someone *was* walking behind him: a twelve-year-old followed his footsteps, mocking his long-legged gait. Derisive laughter rang in his ears, but he managed a wave in return.

He was through the door, into a lobby stripped of furniture. Broken parquet tiles were piled randomly in the corners. The floor was littered with brown bags, gum wrappers, nacho crumbs, broken glass. No one pursued him.

But once inside, he felt no real relief, no sense of escape. He had undergone the trial by fire and now confronted the mirror image of himself at the other end. Why, at such a moment, had he begun to think of Bennington? It was another one of your core problems. And he knew the answer: why not? It was the same as with Cruz. It was easy enough to make a career of poverty, of *studying* urban reality from a distance, of even *helping* alleviate some problems, as long as there was always a Bennington at the back of your mind. Desmond knew that somewhere in his gut was a perverse reassurance that city grit wasn't really there, that it didn't really have to be dealt with. Riding in your BMW, you just rolled up the windows and locked the doors at the sight of the first group of black faces.

Joe Verb was the one who knew better, of course, but Joe had flipped his lid. Wasn't craziness in the eye of the beholder?

The contradiction gave him some ease. He passed across the lobby to the bank of doorbells and mailboxes. J. Verb's name was still there. But the bells were out of order. So was the elevator. He could walk to the third floor. He had been deflecting reality, hiding out when J. Verb had been fired, too. So here he was, trying to reverse the flow. But, like Bennington, Bob Dylan had stayed with him until the end:

> *I started out on Burgundy*
> *But soon I hit the harder stuff*
> *Everybody said they'd stand behind me*
> *When the game got rough*
> *But the joke was on me:*
> *There was nobody even there to bluff.*
> *I'm goin' back to New York City;*
> *I do believe I've had enough.*

He climbed the darkened stairs. He was no longer frightened, only numb. The door to the third-floor corridor had been defaced by a neat feminine script: "Jesus Say." That was all, as if the writer had been molested in midsentence.

The hall was empty, had once been painted green, had once been carpeted. The doors were closed. Still, it was very noisy, as if he had walked into the midst of an invisible international bazaar. He heard jazz, the box radio boom-boom, someone singing passionately and off-key in Spanish, a curse in muddled French. He smelled curry, dogshit, hambone pea soup, human sweat. From 3-E there emanated a pungently fishy odor, the like of which he had never encountered before. He rang the doorbell. For a moment he heard a high keening sound, like summer insects at twilight, underscored by a rhythmical low moan, a dirge played at fast forward. There was a squawk, then silence.

He put his ear to the door and thought he heard the padding of feet. He rang the doorbell again. Still no answer. He hammered on the door until his fist hurt. Suddenly he was very angry with Joe Verb. Just as he was about to turn away, a powerful hand gripped his arm.

Desmond completed his turn to confront a cocoa-skinned man, who was dressed pretty much like the boys in the entranceway. He wore motorcycle boots, Levis, a leather vest, and a bandanna tied around his bushy hair. The same hair covered his chest and stomach in a thickly-matted graying jungle. He was probably about Desmond's age, over thirty-five at any rate. He was sweating profusely. Probably he had run up the stairs.

"Looking for somebody, mahn?"

Desmond had to look up to answer; the man was at least 6'5", with shoulders as wide as a doorway.

"Verb," Desmond said, composed, "an old friend and colleague of mine. At City University. Name's on the mailbox downstairs."

The man let go of Desmond's arm and put a friendly yet forceful hand on his shoulder, as if he intended to lead him back to the stairs. "Sorry," he said. "I thought you were trying to hassle somebody. They's lots of people up here don't need has-slin'." He raised his eyebrows, as if they were sharing an irony: "Verbs are long gone."

"Maybe you know where."

"Hey, mahn, I only been super here since the building went colored. I *pre*-sume your friend is white?"

Desmond nodded quickly.

"And there are no records left? Forwarding addresses? Look, this is important. Not only to me, but to him. He's owed something. Like an old debt. I want to pay it off."

The super shrugged his shoulders, then gave Desmond a once-over. He rubbed his chin: "What this Verb look like?"

"Short, black oily hair, pointy nose. White." He pictured Joe Verb's pallor. "*Very* white."

"In 3-E? Maybe I *saw* him once. When the church brought the Boat People."

"Church? Boat People?"

"You know. From Vietnam. Or over there somewhere." He jerked his head as if Southeast Asia were just on the other side of Coney Island Avenue. "There was a white lady here with two kids just a few days after I took the job. They moved out, and this funny little dude showed up, said he was the husband. Had his name on the lease. Which the old lady had jumped. Man could *talk* some shit." The super emitted an odd laugh, joyous yet subdued, like something you might hear in the background of a rhythm-and-blues record. Another version of "Night Train," thought Desmond. "All about equality and justice and illegal wars and Imperialism. Shit from the sixties, you dig. And he introduced me to this guy who said he was from a church that was placing refugees." He laughed again. "Wanted to place 'em *here*, sign the lease over to the church, in a building his wife couldn't handle, not one bit. I suggest that if I was a refugee I might not *want* to be stuck here, but they pooh-poohed me. And who'm I to argue with a man could put down such ed*oo*cated shit?"

"Which church?"

"Can't remember. Protestant? Quaker maybe. I just told the church guy to call the management. Management was mostly interested in decontrolling the rents. Verb's was still controlled. So a deal was worked out. Church agreed to pay top dollar. They was in a hurry. Had these people waitin' on the dock, I think. Wanna see 'em?"

"Who?"

"The Boat People."

Before Desmond could answer, the man had pulled out the elastic keychain from his belt loop, inserted a key in the lock of 3-E, and opened the door. The room that had been Joe and Sherry Verb's living room was now more or less bare, with the exception of some rattan mats on the floor and a cot in the corner. Sitting, or rather cowering, on the cot were three adults and two children. Orientals.

"Here they are," said the super, as if he were a used-car salesman showing off a most interesting buy.

The brown-yellow faces all laughed silently, and then the keening sound began again.

"Means they're scared," said the super. "Both the laugh and the noise. 'Course, they always scared. Don't belong here. Folks laugh at 'em, rip 'em off, rape 'em." He shook his head, "And they don't even fight back. Not part of their thing. This the third or fourth family we had. One gives up, runs away, the church sends another. This bunch likes me. They like it when I just walk in on 'em. Makes 'em feel someone cares." He spoke rapidly in a language Desmond did not recognize. The man of the family answered solemnly. The super said something else. The women tittered, then the children. The older woman and the man wore black pyjamas. The younger woman wore cheap jeans, high heels, and a garish tank-top. The children, a boy and girl about nine and ten, wore underwear, Flintstones jockey shorts, and T-shirts. Used.

Desmond looked puzzled. The super winked at him: "You surprise a nigger super in Flatbush can speak Gook? Mahn, I was *over* there. Got out just before things got hot. Had a little slant-eye sweetie. Our own hootch. Didn't bring her back, though. I was just kiddin' *them* about wantin' more of that fish sauce. They's afraid to go out since the sister-in-law," he nodded at the younger woman, "got gang-banged up at Parade Grounds couple days after they move in. Not rape. Call it a cultural misunderstanding. She give in easy enough but she don't like it. It's what they do. Maybe that's why I don't bring my woman back. Wouldn't fit in over here. So I give the boys up the Parade Grounds a little seminar," he clenched his massive fist, "on cultural differences, but these here Boat People still don't go out. I get 'em their groceries when the welfare come. Even the fish sauce. The smell make me *sick*; you?"

Desmond nodded. It wasn't the only thing that was making him sick.

"Maybe that was another reason I don't bring my woman back. After a while I couldn't look at her without smellin' the fish sauce." He held up his pink palms and smiled foolishly. "Oh, right, you wanted to find out about this guy Verb." He barked some directions at the Boat People. The sister-in-law got up and strutted clumsily into the other room. She returned with a sheet of paper and handed it to the super, giving him a shyly seductive look. He handed the paper to Desmond and patted her buttocks with the other. Desmond hurriedly scribbled two addresses, that of the church and that left by Joe Verb, on a card from his wallet. He returned the slip. The super gave it to the sister-in-law, then kissed her on the nose, bending over precariously. Desmond saw that the parents and children watched this exchange gloomily, each with short legs pulled up to their chests, arms hugging their knees, their bare toes digging into the cot. The super let him out the door.

"Thanks," said Desmond. "What's your name? I'm Tim Desmond."

"Call me Sarge, everybody does."

"If you can remember anything else about Verb, let me know.

Okay? You can get me at the Institute for Urban Studies. Here, I'll write it down."

"I don't gotta write nothin' down, mahn. You can find me here. I work all the buildings on this block. Everybody knows me." He made a show of clenching his fists again, giving the sly smile.

"I appreciate what you're doing for those people. It's sinful to drop people like that . . . they're rural peasants, aren't they, not even familiar with their own cities . . . in a place like this."

Sarge gave the background laugh this time. "A place like this," he mused, "a place like *this*. Listen, bro, you don't have to be a foreign Boat People to get dropped in a place like *this*. They's sharks around here, sure. Bad boys. Psychos." He laughed again, louder. "We even got psycho *litterbugs*. But they's more nice folks, Americans, here, than sharks, and the nice folks don't deserve it no more than the Boat People." He gripped Desmond's arm, even more tightly than their first contact. "Remember that, bro. It's the key to understandin' what goes on in a place like this. After a while, some of the nice people can't take it no more. The raped starts rapin'; the Mr. Clean turns into the litterbug, you dig?" Now he laughed loud, abrasively, giving Desmond's arm one last squeeze. "Give them Boat People a little more time, and they'll get the beat. Just so long as the Quakers keep sendin' in fresh troops."

# CHAPTER 12

LT. FRANCIS DESALES returned to the office to find a new mound of paper on his desk. He scanned the daily crime-sheet: Flatbush rapist, black, soft-spoken, six feet, two hundred pounds, works quiet streets late at night. . . . Marcia Rodriguez, eighteen, charged with possession of stolen box radio and firearm, Sunset Park. . . . Gaspar Voltaire, New Lots Avenue, charged with assault and criminal use of firearms by Brooklyn North Narcotics. Defendant shot victim in back nine times. . . .

He tossed the new paper on top of the Carruthers pile, looked at it a moment, and then heaped the lot on a side table. He had already bracketed Carruthers the professor as something that didn't belong to his office. Tomorrow he would farm it out. Nothing had been heard from the Revolutionary Tribunal, in any case. It was their move. If they had one. He could only concentrate on one thing at a time.

He picked up the phone and dialed the M.E.'s office. After a wait, the man he wanted came on.

"This is DeSales."

"I suppose you're in a hurry about this Evergreens lady."

"Right. What's the story?"

"It's a bit strange. First of all, she's been dead at least a month. You can tell by the blood having shifted . . ."

"I noticed. How do you pinpoint the time?"

"The usual. Organ analysis. Liver was . . ."

"And how did she die?"

"Tossup. She had enough downers in her to do it."

"Barbiturate?"

"Probably Quaalude. But she was also submerged underwater for a while, so it's hard to say whether she was knocked out and then drowned or if she was already dead, or moribund, when she went under. There's enough water in the lungs. From a purely investigative point of view—wanting to make a collar—I suppose it doesn't make much difference. She was knocked out and then put underwater. If we'd found her alone in her bathtub, I'd be inclined to attribute it to suicide or accidental causes. But, under the circumstances, we can only conclude . . ."

"Listen, Doc, I've got one problem with this hypothesis. She's been dead at least a month, she was submerged, yet she didn't look anything like someone who'd been under the water for any length of time at all."

"I don't think she was."

DeSales lighted up a cigarette: "But when we saw her this morning she was *wet*! I touched her hair . . ."

"It looks as if she was submerged *twice*. First, over a month ago, about the same time she'd ingested the overdose. Then last night, say, for a couple of hours."

"So she was under cold storage in the meantime."

"I assume. Remarkably well-preserved for not having been embalmed. On the outside, at any rate. Innards are always another story."

DeSales inhaled and shuffled some more papers. He nudged the Carruthers pile with his toe. The M.E.'s man went on:

"She was also, I'm sure you noticed, remarkably free of bruises. This suggests, as does the placement of the body, a person of remarkable strength carrying her around. I would have dropped her a dozen times." He paused. "And the stake was inserted *after* the body was elevated."

"And the blood?"

"Hers."

DeSales butted the cigarette, began to extract another from the pack, and then instead reached for a Rolaid. Chewing noisily, he said, "And the water, Doc? What kind of water was found in her lungs?"

The coroner sounded sullen, a man who has done his job to his own satisfaction and now finds another external demand awaiting: "No results on that."

"And the water in her hair? Whatever she was in last night."

"Same. No results."

"You mean you didn't run the test. So, Doc, I hate to overwork you, but I need that info. And I want to resurrect an old case. The Gowanus thing last winter. A hooker named Jerry Jacuzzi. You still got any parts of her left to analyze?"

"Unsolved?"

"Yes."

"Probably. What do you want?"

"The same as this one. She had some water in her lungs too. We assumed it was from the Gowanus. Can you check that out?"

"Maybe. It's chancy."

"Thanks, Doc. Call me in two hours?"

"I'll try. You working a short day?"

DeSales chortled. The M.E.'s man hung up.

Next, DeSales began a rough sketch of the scene in the Cemetery of the Evergreens. There was no question in his mind that the selection of the site and the application of blackface and the Brooklyn Union sticker were not at all random. They were quite deliberate acts of communication.

And, he realized, thinking of the Medical Examiner's report, it was now likely that the killer had killed first, then preserved the body while scouting for an ideal place for its next-to-last repose.

So the message was more important than the murder.

What was the meaning of the site? Old-fashioned, traditional heroism was being mocked, or subverted in some more general way. Perhaps. Was the blackface meant to recall laughter, minstrel shows, nineteenth-century entertainment?

Or was it a racial statement? The Cinderella Project sticker had lots of racial implications. Brooklyn Union Gas was underwriting the renovation of many of the old neighborhoods downtown that the banks wouldn't touch with a ten-foot pole. Banks called it red-lining. But, as often as not, the so-designated "Cinderella Projects" tended to benefit the white investors rather than the blacks who had been living in the old houses and to whom, ostensibly, the Gas Company intended to give a leg up. The nasty stepsisters, as was usually the case, ended up wearing the glass slippers after all.

He drew a picture of the circle of new graves that surrounded the firemen's place. The firemen had been, presumably, white Anglo-Saxon Protestants: Baldwin, Smith, Weeks. Or perhaps an Irishman here or there. The establishment. The new graves, on the other hand, had names that suggested the majority population of 1980s Brooklyn: Hispanic and black. And the gravestones were, by conventional standards, cheap and vulgar.

But what was more cheap and vulgar than erecting a ten-foot-high statue to oneself—or one's organization—in a completely heroic mode?

He was allowing his questions to get abstract, imposing his education on his profession. A cop does not need to read books or have a good vocabulary, was a truism he often uttered.

Someone was clearing his throat. The desk sergeant from downstairs was standing before him.

"Here's a present from the Transit cops, Lieutenant. Murphy dropped it off."

He handed DeSales a five- by eight-inch spiral notebook.

"What's this?"

"Something to do with the Carruthers guy. The hostage? Obviously Murphy didn't see any profit in it or he would have taken it up the Transit ladder instead of laying it on us."

The desk sergeant had a moustache and long sideburns. DeSales remembered a time when people who called cops "Pigs" and threw rocks at them wore moustaches and long sideburns. Now when you saw a guy with a moustache and long sideburns, it was a good bet he *was* a cop.

"I'll take it, Fred. Thanks."

He dropped the notebook on the rest of the discarded pile. He went back to his drawing. Suppose someone didn't like blacks? And was laughing at the notion of their pumpkins being converted to fancy carriages? But what did that have to do with firemen? Of all the city's civil servants, the fire department had most successfully resisted integration. And the woman was *white*. Maybe they would find out she had a black boyfriend or something. That rang a bell.

He had gone far enough. He would try to hold that thought, let it ripen overnight. Now, his brain was turning to jelly.

And he had to sit it out waiting for the M.E. If the doc called back and found he'd gone home, he'd never get an express job done again.

And this Carruthers shit! The same day. No wonder he had missed the wetness factor!

Against his better instincts, he picked up the spiral notebook. He opened it. Inside the front cover, in neatly lettered script, it said:

> F. Carruthers III
> Institute for Urban Studies
> Professor of Humanities

There were four or five entries, precisely dated at the top, written in the same neat script. The last was the only one that interested him. It bore the date April 1, today, and was less legible, more of a scrawl, than the others. DeSales guessed that it had been written either in haste or on a moving vehicle. The sense of haste or movement was reinforced by the sketchy, impressionistic nature of the phrases contained therein:

Sundown Poem

D Moses

Beirut HoJo Cyrillic

Roach Motel Prep H

New Life B KL N!

Carruthers Whitman Brooklyn Union Gas

Convent queens?   9Q

Union Pacific?   Manifest Destiny?

Astoria.   Wrong.   9.   Blue and white tiles.   Up and out

New Train

FOGCRASHLEFT

DeSales shook his head, dialing the phone.

"Transit? This is DeSales, chief of Violence Task Force. Is Murphy there?" After a while there was an answer. Then he said, "Is anyone there who knows about this package Murphy dropped here tonight? A notebook. Where was it picked up? When? Goddammit. Call him at home. I want that information before I get in here tomorrow morning—I don't *care* if it's Good Friday. Tell Murphy *he'll* be crucified."

Then he called the desk sergeant.

"Get that professor who was here today. Desmond. Tell him I want to see him before tomorrow afternoon. I want him to practice some hermeneutics for me. If you can't get him tonight, have the man on duty at eight A.M. tomorrow call him first thing. At home if necessary." He gave the numbers.

"Herman who, Lieutenant?"

"Just write 'Herman.' He'll figure it out."

"Okay. Hold on. There's a call from the M.E. For you."

DeSales punched the button that was blinking.

"Hello, Dr. Friedman."

"I have a tentative answer to your questions, DeSales."

"Shoot."

"The Evergreens Lady was never near anything but plain tap water. God knows, maybe she did die in her bath."

"The hair, also?"

"The hair, also."

"So she had a hair-wash, maybe, before she was put on display. And the hooker?"

"Well, it's hard to say after all this time, but it certainly looks like tap water for her too. Nothing as toxic as the Gowanus canal, certainly."

"How about that," said DeSales. "Shit."

# CHAPTER 13

DESMOND FOUND THE blond furniture and Sherry Verb in a semi-detached frame house with an address in the East Twenties, some distance further into Flatbush. To find her, he had needed the map after all. Not only was his knowledge of the area, besides a few main avenues, sketchy, but the layout and numbering of the streets themselves made little sense. How could something in the middle of Brooklyn be "East" when Coney Island, as far southeast of Manhattan as one could go, had streets numbered in the *West* Twenties? And he had a vague notion as well that there were streets in the Twenties, without geographical prefixes, no North, South, East, or West, in the neighborhood just south of his own house, which had to be pretty far *west* of Coney Island.

"You," she said.

She opened the chain.

"I'm looking for Joe."

"Last place you'll find him." She put a burning cigarette in her mouth and squinted. Her hair had a pink tinge where it had once been blond. She was draped in a shapeless muu-muu. She looked as if she had been hired to do an impression of Shelley Winters.

"You've split up?"

She laughed crudely: "That's one way to put it. Joe would probably say, 'Humanity beckoned,' or some such garbage. One day I say to him, 'Joe, you spend day and night trying to help the poor and downtrodden, so how about us, we're not humanity? Charity begins at home, right? Wrong?' And he looks me over for a long time. I get the feeling I'm not passing the test because my skin isn't dark enough. You ever get that feeling?"

"Sometimes," said Desmond. "I was just over at your old building on Ocean Avenue." Sherry Verb appeared to not have heard him.

"So Joe's eyes begin to glaze over. I figure, 'I've lost him,' but I didn't know it was for keeps." She did a kind of glide around the living room, fingering her *tchatchkas*. Sherry fell into the sofa heavily. Desmond sat on the edge of a chair. "So what did I expect?" she went on. "He was a wildman. My mother said it ran in the family. Did you know about Joe's father? Abraham. Had a candy store in Brownsville, when it was still a Jewish ghetto. Kept a tab for the neighborhood kids, on a tab he had them." She shrugged her shoulders. "Some were bad, some were good. Some made Murder Inc. and some became scientists, writers, millionaires. They all paid their tabs. Then Brownsville turned blacker. Old Abraham Verb still kept tabs for his customers. Only the new kids didn't pay up. And when they got a little too old for free candy, the *schwartzes* burned the store down. All Joe, *my* poor bewildered Joe, learned from that number was that you should keep a tab for the poor kids. He forgot about the second half of the lesson. . . ."

Desmond broke in, hoping to bring her a little closer to present matters: "So you must be relieved to be off Ocean Avenue. It's changed, like that."

She looked at him incredulously and lighted another cigarette. She lowered her eyelids: "Have you checked out *this* neighborhood?"

"Not really. It seems quiet. And the houses look comfortable. It's . . . well . . . suburban."

She snorted. "They *followed* us here. Sometimes I think Joe knew it and it was part of his plan. The Great Integrater! Didn't you see them on the porches? They can't stay inside. Probably can't stand the smell of the food. They eat *goat*, you know. And the music! What do they call it? Something to do with Haile Selassie?"

"Rastafarian?"

"I know that much. That's the religion. The music?"

"Reggae."

"Right. *Reggie.*" She pronounced it like the man's first name.

She stubbed out the cigarette in her coffee cup. The cup had a picture of a little Dutch boy, wooden shoes and all, on the side. The cigarette continued to smolder. She cocked an eyebrow: "So, ya wanna see Joe?"

"Old business."

"The Institute? You should be ashamed." She stood up, crouched, and hastily turned the dial on the blond console TV. She had been watching a show that featured a profile of a former movie starlet named Claudine Longet who had once been married to a singer named Andy Williams, a man of such success and significance that he had his own golf tournament. Claudine, it seemed, after splitting up with Andy had taken on as her lover a professional skier named Spider something. Claudine had shot Spider. To death. All this had taken place in a glamorous part of the Rockies. You could tell it was glamorous because people spent a lot of time in hot tubs. Now Sherry had switched to an educational show on how apes and whales communicate. She swore; she had hit the wrong station. She stood again and turned the dial more methodically. She lingered over the opening credits of a TV movie based on Bulwer-Lytton's

*Last Days of Pompeii*, which suggested that Lord Lytton had written the steamiest of pageturners, a sort of *Scruples* in mini-togas. Finally she found the program she wanted: "The A-Team."

Desmond was beginning to feel sorry for Joe Verb. Verb had always had that effect on him: one couldn't stay mad at him long, no matter how infuriating he was. Still, when Verb had left the Institute, Desmond realized, he had experienced a sense of relief (even if one tangential consequence of Joe being fired was the advent of Fletcher Carruthers III), relief from the emotional roller coaster: even if you weren't on it, it was always *there*, noisy and distracting. A lot of people had felt that way about him.

"Coffee?" she asked, back in her seat again, behind the smoking cup. The offer was halfhearted. She obviously had little inclination to rise again.

"No thanks," said Desmond. He noticed the dim glow of another TV from a darkened adjoining room. He could just make out the scrawny form of a human being lying on a couch. One of the younger Verbs. He wondered what the *next* generation was watching for edification.

Sherry had summoned up her energy: "You want I should help you with *anything* after what you did to Joe? So he's a *schmuck*, a first-class *schmuck*, he still didn't deserve the screwing he got from the Institute. He's a human being. Or he *was*. That maybe was what finished him. So he justified his existence that he had a job helping underprivileged people. So without the job, he had to become an underprivileged himself. Live with them. Like an animal. Abandon his family."

"I had nothing to do with his firing, Sherry. I was lucky to hang on to my own job. It was the year of the city budget crisis. I had finished my doctorate, Joe hadn't. It was as simple as that."

"Did you *protest*? Did any of his so-called friends? You were all coming all over yourselves a couple of years before to run all the way down to Washington to impeach Nixon or protest the oppression of some Mississippi *schwartzes* you'd never even seen before, but you didn't make a peep when a friend was in trouble, getting screwed over, right here in Brooklyn. No, not when *your* asses were on the line."

"Sherry, Joe *knew* when the crunch came he would be first to go. He wouldn't finish his dissertation. He wouldn't play by the rules. He knew the system."

"System, *shmystem*. I thought that was what you were all trying to overthrow."

She made a kind of spitting gesture with her lips, then reached for the coffee cup. She remembered the cigarette butt, got up slowly, headed for the kitchen where she poured herself a new cup. She picked up a pack of Virginia Slims from the counter, lighted one on the stove, and began to waddle back to the couch. On the TV, a very large black man with a Mohawk haircut, dressed—or, rather, undressed—like someone from *The Last Days of Pompeii*, was helping a peace-loving cult use nonviolence to defeat a corrupt sheriff. He was doing this by throwing one of the sheriff's deputies repeatedly against a concrete wall. The black man was called Mr. T. Desmond knew that from the tabloid covers he inspected while on supermarket lines. Mr. T wore a lot of jewelry, which flew about, flashing, as he worked up the sweat that made his bare bulging muscles gleam under the hot studio lights. Sherry Verb stopped at the coffee table, momentarily entranced with the spectacle.

Desmond decided to try another tack.

"Okay, Sherry, say I was a coward, I sold Joe out. That's history. I'm trying to live in the present. Something's come up that makes me think I can help him. Make it up to him."

Now she slit her eyes. Her face, he realized, was never in repose. Maybe it was the coffee. "You think he lifted this guy Carruthers, right? I heard it on the news. Right before 'Entertainment Tonight.'"

"Do *you*? Think he did it?"

She shrugged her shoulders: "Three, four years ago he didn't have it in him. Now, who knows?" Her high, almost oriental cheekbones seemed to quiver. For a moment, it looked like she would cry. Then a dark cloud suffused the features, radiating out from the close-set eyes. She had been almost pretty; now she was pure ugliness. "Who knows who he's been living with? Who gives him his ideas? I always thought this whole thing was about sex anyway. They're supposed to be better at it, aren't they?" She lighted another Virginia Slim. Her neck had broken out in splotches. She looked Desmond directly in the eye: "Was that it? When you were carrying the signs around the White House, you were getting black pussy on the side, right?"

Desmond reached out to touch her hand, he had no idea why. She pulled back.

"No, Sherry, I wasn't getting *anything* on the side. Look, can you help me find Joe?"

She shrugged her shoulders.

Desmond went on: "The super over on Ocean said there was some church group Joe was involved with. That was placing the refugees over there."

"Forget it. I tried them the last time the child-support check didn't come. They haven't heard from him in a year."

"Does he work? Where's he been living?"

"That's the joke. An uncle left him some real estate in his will. Houses around the borough. So the great socialist is into owning private property."

"And he's a landlord?"

"Your guess is as good as mine. He lives in one, rents the rest, maybe."

"Where?"

She shrugged her shoulders again. "The uncle's name was Neffsky, Nevsky? Old Brownsville connection. I never met him. Joe disapproved. I think the old bastard left him the houses as some kind of test."

"So I can look up Nevsky . . ."

"Sol."

"And find the houses."

Sherry laughed. Her jowls shook. "A joke. I tried that too.

Then I remembered Joe ranting and raving once about his slum-lord uncle. Too clever. Never owned a house under his own name. Might want to abandon it rather than pay for violations. Wanted to make the profits disappear so the tax man didn't find him. He owned the houses under corporate names. Who knows? The A-Team? The S.U.C.K. Company?" She laughed again, more briefly. "Maybe Joe Verb's got himself registered in the Bahamas or something. Maybe he's a Liberian freighter or something. The Flying African Jew?"

She went into the kitchen and coughed phlegm into the sink.

"You better go," she said.

Desmond peeked into the other room as he was leaving. Verb's teenage son was watching a basketball game. The Knicks and the Celtics. An enduring cultural artifact.

# CHAPTER 14

"I WILL ASSUME, Professor Carruthers, that by now you can see the connection between your farcical appointment to *teach* at a *public* university, and the hypocrisy of instituting an Anti-Harassment Unit at the so-called Department of Housing Preservation and Development!"

A telephone rang in the distance. The heavy, plodding step of the man called Tyrone crossed the room. It was the step of an unenthusiastic but determined executioner. A door opened and closed, a flimsy door, a door rather too small for its frame, shrunk perhaps by the cold dry winter. Or by years of minimal heating.

Carruthers marveled at how little of his highly-developed aural and tactile senses he had heretofore utilized in his writing. He had formerly concentrated almost exclusively on what he *saw*. But now, blindfolded and damned near bare-assed in a hospital gown tied loosely at the back, he had become intensely aware of how his perceptions were influenced, even altered, by what he heard or felt. For example, his interrogator, a man who had apparently preceded him at the Institute and who was called Joe but was referred to by his comrades in his absence as "The

Man Upstairs," had a plebeian other-boroughs intonation that—aided and abetted by Houston Street delicatessen breath—tended to underline the emptiness of his speciously erudite text. Then there was Carruthers's own sense of vulnerability. The sense he had, in the gown, of wearing a woman's skirt without underwear—an unpleasant sensation that had always discouraged him from going in for drag—enhanced the feeling of dislocation that he was fighting every moment, which in turn intensified his impatience with his surroundings, with the speaker, and, once again of course, with the speaker's text. There was a critical vein here that had barely been touched outside, perhaps, cognitive psychology. Mining it, he could double his publishing output.

Joe, undeterred by Carruthers's silence, answered his own question:

"The connection is painfully simple. You are provided with a salary on the pretense that you are educating and uplifting the *people,* while you are instead devoting yourself to self-promotion and self-gratification. Housing and Preservation has created its Anti-Harassment Unit ostensibly to provide a medium via which the poor can protest ill-treatment on the part of the landlords. Instead it solicits input through the *Times,* which the needy can neither read nor afford. In both cases, institutions created in the interests of social progress have opted instead for self-preservation through elitist window-dressing. . . ."

"Right on," said Sister Eusebia, whom Carruthers had come to know as "Yoo-Hoo." Sister Regina, a.k.a. "Birdie," giggled.

"Bullroar," shouted Carruthers, still hoarse. There was a muffled silence. The thud of Tyrone's footfalls could be heard returning down the hallway. Carruthers was determined not to be intimidated. He felt convinced that these people would hurt him only through their own ineptitude. Sassing back would keep them on their toes, which would, in turn, advance his prospects for survival. He continued, "You know as well as I do that the city is almost broke—and powerless—because of the immense sums it has wasted on the criminal and indigent segments of the population. And"—he exhaled loudly, then smirked—"a scholar is *created* and *educated* to do scholarship, not to teach the unteachable; just as a property-owner has nothing if not the right to do as he wishes with that which is rightfully . . ."

"Rights," screamed Joe. "*Rights*! What about the rights of the people? All over the city poor minority folks are being driven from their homes by unscrupulous landlords, mostly white, so that the landlord can convert his housing, *gentrify* it, in order to make an immoral profit. He hires thugs to intimidate the poor, the weak, and the aged. He turns off their heat and water. He drives them into the streets so that he can repopulate his brownstone—around here, at any rate—with white or upscale quiche-eaters. And *you* are the thug the Institute hires to drive the educationally disadvantaged back into the streets with your elitist 'standards'. . . ."

"Tsk, tsk, tsk," Carruthers was saying, almost flinching at the possibility of being hit while still telling himself that these were not hitters, when the door slammed open. Tyrone whispered to Joe. Joe whistled, then let out a little shriek. He ran softly down the hall.

Tyrone said, "That'll be all for this guy t'night. Put him back in the closet." For that was where they had moved him.

Carruthers's wrists were bound again, then his ankles. He was half-pushed, half-carried back into the darkness. Just as the door was closing he felt a distinct and deliberate fondling of his genitals. His testicles were briefly cupped. A finger traced the length of his penis. Two fingers scissored the organ gently and stroked it for a moment. The caress was not without its effect. It occurred to Carruthers, in line with his earlier revelations about neglect of the tactile sense, that one could not tell the gender of one's contacts by their hands—particularly on the genitals. The genitals, while sensate, were not particularly discriminating. Certainly Tyrone's hands were larger and more calloused than

Yoo-Hoo's, and Birdie's would be skinny and fragile. Yet he couldn't tell. The eyes, the ears, or one's own hands did the discriminating.

He wondered, almost disbelieving, whether that wonderful muscular hunk of a rumbly-voiced man—as he imagined him—had indeed just been *groping* him.

Desmond lay in his bed, exhausted but unable to sleep. The images of his nightmarish ride home kept running through his brain, like film at fast forward. He had decided not to retrace his steps but to simply find Flatbush Avenue, which he knew ran back through the park to Grand Army Plaza. Instead, he came up against a dead end at Brooklyn College, and was spun into a maze of one-way streets where he noted, among other things, two black men washing a new Mercedes in pitch darkness. When he hit Flatbush, he turned the wrong way and found himself on Kings Highway. For a while Kings Highway hypnotized him with contrast: it was a broad suburban avenue of single-family homes, traversing a dozen dark narrow-streeted mazes. But then he passed under an elevated track, through the looking glass, and found himself in the heart of a rubble of devastation that made Coney Island look like Malibu. There was a sign proclaiming a firebombed building as part of a Brownsville Reclamation Project. Tattered men lounged in doorways that had lost most of their buildings.

So this was Brownsville, where Joe Verb had not learned the lessons his ex-wife thought he should have learned. Desmond, within moments, felt claustrophobic, as if he would never get out. He felt a sense of urgency too great to allow him to pause and check the map, so he reversed direction at the first familiar name: Eastern Parkway. That led back to the Plaza, to *white* civilization. He drove for a very long time, beginning to doubt his choice, and then, suddenly, there was the Museum, the triumphal arch at the Soldiers and Sailors Monument, and he was home. All he could remember of this last leg of the journey was a sense of social tumult, as if Jerusalem, the Caribbean, and the Upper West Side had been jumbled together and turned inside out.

Now he tried to play an old game of his to induce sleep. He imagined himself as a TV pundit or columnist or celebrated scholar asked to give pithy articulation to his experience of the evening. He tried for a long time and could come up with nothing. Nothing appropriate for himself, that is, for he was having a rough time imagining himself, where he fit in. So he pretended that he was a Carruthers, role-played, and came up with something immediately: "Brooklyn is not a mystery; it is merely a series of anomalies." A phrase sufficiently meaningless to appear profound. Perhaps he had found that his true voice lay in mimicking the voices of others. He said it aloud in the darkened spacious bedroom: "Brooklyn is not a mystery; it is merely a series of anomalies."

The phone rang. Mona. Checking up. Still, he welcomed the approach of the familiar. Any known quantity would do. He picked it up.

Instead of Mona's boarding-school accent, he heard Joe Verb's, 1940s Brownsville lurking in each phoneme.

"I hear you're looking for me, old buddy."

Desmond regretted that this was indeed true.

"Right," he finally answered. "How's it going, Joe?"

"Fine, fine. Fine." Joe sounded excited, even manic in his eagerness. "I'm glad you are. Looking for me. We got a lot to talk about, don't we? Old times. New times."

Desmond tried to make an agreeable noise. Verb cut in:

"Listen, Tim, I don't have a lot of time right now. To stay on the phone, if you know what I mean. *So.* Meet me, uh, Sunday dawn. There's a tour after a sunrise service. Easter, right. Nice Christian endeavor. Just join up. I'll fall in along the way."

"Where, Joe?"

"Oh, forgot. Greenwood Cemetery, main gates."

"Where's that?"

There was muttering on the other end of the line. Verb appeared to be consulting with someone. Then he said: "Twenty-fifth and Fifth."

"That's Madison Square, Joe."

Verb's tone was momentarily superior, as if some political issue were involved. Joe only took on a superior tone if political issues were involved. "You'll always be a Manhattan type, won't you, Tim? Hard to bring your heart over the bridge? There's a Twenty-fifth and Fifth in Brooklyn too. And Tim, I'm sure you know the rules: don't bring anyone along, right? We just keep this between old buddies, right?"

Joe Verb came running back into the room. His eyes were shiny. He took off his cap and scratched his shiny, spiky black hair: "I don't believe it," he said. "They've finally bitten. We're in business."

Yoo-Hoo stretched languidly, her cut-off tank-top rising to expose the bottoms of her breasts: "*Who's* bitten, Joe? And how hard?"

"Hook, line, and sinker. And I might add, with no further threats of violence or adventurism." His look said *I told you so.* "They sent Desmond. From the Institute. To make a private contact. I guess they want to negotiate."

"Don't trust them," said Yoo-Hoo. "It could be a setup."

"He's a friend," said Joe. "He wouldn't willingly . . ."

"How does *he* know? They could be using him."

Joe drew himself up, defensive. "Don't worry about that. I know what I'm doing."

The door opened behind him, and Tyrone stood in the doorway, a looming, heavy presence.

"So what's the next move?" asked Birdic. "I'd like some action."

"I meet Desmond Sunday. We hammer out some ground rules, get the mayor and the chancellor of the City University directly involved. Issue a formal statement regarding changes in the structure of the university and the Department of Housing. Acknowledge the racist, elitist nature of the government.

And give Brooklyn back to the people it belongs to." His passionate intensity seemed to run out of steam as he articulated his goal.

Yoo-Hoo's eyes flashed. "Sounds chickenshit to me, Joe. Let's get the media in right away. And Carruthers's trial? And justice. When do we get justice?" With her braids and skimpy costume, there was something Polynesian about her. She was a bloodthirsty savage princess. "And Carruthers? What do we do with him?"

Joe made a farting sound with his mouth: "Carruthers is merely a cog in a larger system. We used him as a tool to wake up the establishment. We can drop him on a streetcorner and disappear, further underground, after we get what we want."

"Pipe dreams, Joe. Bloody wish-fulfillment fantasy. It's too easy. *They* don't give up their privilege so easily. They have to be put up against the wall, the motherfuckers. We *try* Carruthers, execute him, with regular communiqués to the press, and then they'll be willing to go beyond signing a meaningless piece of paper."

"Let's keep things going a *while*," said Birdie. "Nobody's going to find us *here*. And there's a kind of . . ."

"There's legitimate ecstasy in fucking with the establishment and keeping them fucked," Yoo-Hoo finished for her. Almond eyes still seething, she glared at Joe: "And where is this wonderful *detente* to occur, pray tell?"

"Greenwood Cemetery."

Now *she* was cool and superior. "And why there?"

"There's a tour. We can watch him from a distance first. Do an eye-frisk. Make sure he's not followed. The streets will be empty. I've been planning on doing maneuvers there anyhow. It's so big we can get lost easily. We could conduct a guerrilla war from the place. And it's symbolically right for our political purposes."

"*Why*, Joe?"

"And Tyrone thinks it's the best place possible."

"Fuckin' right," said Tyrone.

Yoo-Hoo stared at Tyrone for a long time. He met her gaze unflinching. Finally, she seemed to wilt before him. She uncrossed her legs, rose, and left the room. Birdie followed her.

# CHAPTER 15

DESALES ROLLED OVER and found himself alone in bed.

"Hey," he shouted without opening his eyes.

"Keep on gropin', blind man."

He peeked. She was leaning into the refrigerator in the kitchenette of the long, narrow studio apartment. Even from the distance, her flesh was so alive, such a deep vibrant brown, that it appeared to have been polished by a company of Marines preparing for inspection. When she stood erect, her buttocks thrust themselves out, high and prominent.

"What're you into?"

"Checkin' the place out. Anybody ever tell you you need a woman in your life? This cupboard is bare. Not to mention the furnishings." She swept her arm across the rest of the room. Her nipples were purple and sat pertly on the top half of her heavy breasts; they jiggled on a horizontal plane as she turned. There was no sag.

"So're you. Bare. The only difference is, the rest of this place has been exactly the same for twenty years. Since I was walking a beat. Before the Colombo family made Ocean Parkway a neighborhood of choice. Before the Syrian Jews bought out the Don Capos and made it mandatory to have two Mercedeses, one in the garage and one out front. And this apartment is going to stay the same for another twenty. Now get your sepia ass over here!"

"*Sepia*? Cops shouldn't be allowed to be English majors." She patted one cheek affectionately, sassily putting her butt further into relief. "*I'd* call it *mahogany*."

"And you've seen too many Diana Ross movies."

"Anyway, you sure do like to give orders."

"The customer is always right, Roz."

She sauntered to him, catlike. She sat on the bed. She resisted a moment, then allowed him to rub her short Afro. The long Donna Summer fall she wore when the trick required it hung over a chair.

DeSales pulled back the covers: "Look."

"I see. Already. Hmmm. Impressive."

"Yes. Touch me that way. And now . . . right, do it."

For a long time, it seemed, he heard only the soft rhythmic breathing through her nose, punctuated by the beating of his heart. His mind drifted for a moment and he pictured the firemen in blackface, then the three Wise Men on the Christmas package. Their faces were also black, he now remembered, and they seemed to be grinning at him. He said: "Enough, terrific, turn over."

"You wanna get the K - Y?"

"No need. Just taking a different angle on my favorite shot."

Once inside her, he reached around with both hands, one caressing a nipple, the other probing the top of her thighs. He found the spot. Then it was a dance of nuance, a quiver here, a stretch there, but no overt movement. Then there was a perceptible spasm and they finished almost together, her jerks and moans setting him off. After a while, she rolled on her back, pulled him to her, wrapped her legs around him, and kissed his eyes, his nose, his lips.

"Y'know, Saint," she said. "I never know about you. You don't want nothing too tricky. You don't want nothing too simple either. You don't want to get tied up. You don't want to hurt me; you don't even want me to *pre*-tend you're hurting me. You actually spend a lot of time turning *me* on. You know what I think? I think you just want to be able to call the shots. 'The customer is always right' shit. If I say 'Yes,' without an argument, that's enough. We could probably even forget the fucking and you'd still call me up from time to time just to have me around saying, 'Yessir!'"

"The customer is always right."

"I saw some white bread in there. Maybe I can have some toast?" She began to disentangle herself.

He held onto her. She squirmed. He held tighter: "I want to call a couple more shots."

"Who you think you are, Cuban Superman?"

"Not sex. Just some questions. You supply the answers."

She rested her elbow on the bed and her head on her fist. Her teeth were predictably ivory-white, but one of the front ones was crooked and this made her grin wicked: "I know what it is. You're still working out the power-struggle with your mother. Something pre-Oedipal maybe."

"Psychology majors, Roz, can really be a pain in the ass."

"Can't major in English, like you did. Man says my language skills ain't good enough. In Psych we got multiple-choice tests."

"You can take off that ghetto talk just like your wig, and you know it."

"Flattery gets you nowhere. If I was majoring in computers I'd still say you got a hangup about your mother."

"Maybe you noticed. I'm trying to change the subject."

"This hurts. It's gonna turn out you got me over here as a stoolie, not for my body. Think what *that* does to my ego. *My* momma raised me up to be a sex object."

"When they found the hooker in the Gowanus last winter, we talked about it. Remember?"

"Sure. You say, 'Roz, you know this broad?' I say, 'Yeh, but not well.' You say, 'That house she was usin' for her tricks, was it dangerous?' I say, 'She streetwalks Third and Fourth Avenue, where they run the Marathon, and the house is around the corner. Whaddayou think? Is the Pope Polish?' It was left like that, right? You went along with the commonly held belief that she got a homicidal john in that house on Pacific Street, that he either killed her or knocked her out in the room, because there was blood on the floor, and that he put her in the box as a way to get her out of the house unnoticed, and that he then threw the box into the nearest body of water, which was the Gowanus, but she only partially submerged, so somebody found her the next morning still afloat." She shook her head as if she were shooing away a fly, rolled over on her back, lifted her hips with her hands and, legs extended, began to pedal in the air. Her toes were long, the bottoms of her feet pink. She went on: "That was the conversation. It was at my place. Afterwards we made it. Twice. And I gave you breakfast, ham and eggs, in the morning, and you paid me at half my going rate. It was between Christmas and New Year's. December twenty-eighth, to be exact."

"I'm impressed with your memory. Now I'd like to prod it a little more. You did know her personally, right?"

"Ships that pass. I was workin' my way up in the world; she was on her way down. A house a little closer to the Heights. *Mixed* clientele."

"I'm thinking about a racial motivation here. On Pacific Street. A white woman working in a house that catered to a lot of black men."

"What is this, Sunday funnies? The major part of the industry is interracial. What say? Miscegenation. Speak for yourself, Saint Francis. Ain't nobody hereabouts bothered by it. Black dudes pay top dollar for the *ugliest* white trash. Everybody knows, nobody cares."

DeSales began to pull on his pants: "It's true I don't ever remember a case of a pross getting hurt because somebody thought he was a racial vigilante, but I thought, well, maybe a guy from out of town. A Southerner. A Ku Klux Klan. A South African. A Mormon. . . ."

Her laugh was high-pitched and derisive: "I haven't been to South Africa, but I *been* down south and I've *known* some Mormons and I repeat, it's just business; nobody cares when it's business."

DeSales paused in the middle of sweeping the contents of an ashtray into an empty glass he was taking to the kitchen. "Okay, you've just confirmed my instinct. Now, what *else* did you know about Jerry Jacuzzi?"

"Hmmm. Let's see. She was pretty boring. Had been in a couple of porn films and she was proud of that, but she was getting too old and that made her sad. Didn't drink, do drugs, no sadistic pimps around. Bragged about how she used to do all house calls. When she was in the flicks. Hey, house calls, that's right."

"House calls what?" He moved back and sat on the edge of the bed.

"What she *mostly* talked about, in the three or four conversations I had with her, which was why she was so boring, was . . ."

"What? C'mon."

"Houses."

"Whorehouses?"

"No. Brownstone houses. In Brooklyn. How she was saving up to buy an old brownstone and renovate it. Spent all her free time looking at real-estate ads and decorators' magazines. Magazines. Boy, I've heard old whores with dumb pipe dreams, but . . ." She began to pull on her body stocking. "I said, 'Listen, sister. I grew up in one of those houses. In Bed-Stuy. On Gates. They're dark, narrow, spooky places, and the neighbors is on top of you all the time. And the pipes burst all the time and that shit. Give me a penthouse, or a loft with a manager and a super—like I got downtown now—any old time.' In the city, for sure. I don't get why everybody's nuts for Brooklyn brownstones these days. Or Brooklyn, for that matter. Send the whole borough out to L.A. with the Dodgers. Only reason I cross that bridge is to see you. . . ."

She moved over to embrace him, but he was already dialing the phone.

# CHAPTER 16

BACK AT THE OFFICE, some hours later, DeSales was speaking into another mouthpiece. "But, Sam," he pleaded, "I've got every man available hustling on the Evergreens Murder. We're canvassing the neighborhoods. There are several solid leads. I'm working on it myself night and day. How can you stick me with this Carruthers thing?"

The connection was bad and the District Attorney sounded as if he were speaking from underwater: "You're the best we got, Frank. And we gave you the best supporting cast, precisely because we wanted somebody available to handle potentially volatile cases like this one."

"But *violence*, Sam, violence. We've got no evidence there was violence involved. We don't have any evidence he's really being held hostage."

"The presumption is, there's a kidnapping. Kidnapping constitutes a violent crime against one's person. If he was kidnapped and *isn't* being held hostage, we've probably got Murder One. So . . ."

DeSales sighed. He swiveled in his chair. He looked at the cuffless bottoms of his sharply creased brown flannel slacks.

He had miscalculated the weather. The heat had become punishing, for April, and the air-conditioning was broken: "So you want me. But I'm *Brooklyn*. This guy was last seen in Manhattan. It's *their* baby. There's no *proof* he was in Brooklyn."

"You're making me impatient, Frank. His boyfriend assumed he was headed for Brooklyn. The kidnappers made two calls, to you and to his place of employment, both in *Brooklyn*."

DeSales put his head back, cradling the phone with his chin. The phone began to slip. He sat up, scrambled, caught it at the last minute. He decided to play his final card, a long shot: "I'll level with you, Sam. I didn't want to say anything prematurely, but . . . well, I'm afraid this Evergreens thing is going to mushroom, blow up maybe. I think there've been more than one of these by the same perp. As bad as Son of Sam, maybe. And I think there's a racial angle. It could get very ugly. . . ."

"It's already very ugly, Frank. Have you been listening to the radio lately? Now get back to work. You're wasting your time, and I don't think you can afford it."

DeSales held the receiver with distaste, then dropped it with a thud on the desk. Bernie Kavanaugh hung it up for him. In his other hand was a transistor radio.

"I called the station, Frank. She's going to be on in about thirty seconds."

DeSales grabbed the radio and turned up the volume: "You and your fucking girlfriends," he said.

> *Anchor*: Welcome to "Drive Time." It's Good Friday. And here's Megan Moore with the holiday body count.
>
> *Moore*: I'm broadcasting live and on tape from the studio today, a midtown studio which has taken on the appearance of Crime Central USA. Item One: What is being done with the notorious "Profnap" case by the so-called authorities? I have it from a reliable source that, although one of the city's most eminent scholars and distinguished citizens languishes in the hands of terrorists today, the police are reluctant to act in the

case. Police Public-Relations Director Ellen Spielberg claims that this is not true, that the sensitivity of the negotiations and concern for Professor Carruthers's safety dictate caution. However, it is more likely that a disturbing behind-the-scenes scenario is occurring. At least one prominent Task Force officer is reportedly trying to drop the case like a hot potato, and there are rumors that the FBI is considering forcing the issue by taking jurisdiction. When will New York's Finest act? Where is Fletcher Carruthers the Third? Is he the victim of revolutionaries, or police indifference? Or ineptitude?

*Anchor*: We care, Megan, we care. But the entire Big Apple is waiting for your latest report on your direct contacts with the alleged "Graveyard Grim Reaper."

*Moore*: That's Item Two. I can only say now that I am keeping a line open for him at all times if he wants to talk again. And we repeat our bulletin: the woman found yesterday unspeakably assaulted and murdered in Evergreens Cemetery was named Samantha and disappeared from her home on Lincoln's Birthday, Monday, February twelfth. If you recognize her name, date of departure, or description, please call *immediately* the Violence Task Force at 522-2727. Please help Lieutenant DeSales's Violence Task Force. They need it.

*Anchor*: When—if—he calls again, Megan? Will you ask him to turn himself in? Will you reason with him?

*Moore*: I'll do anything my responsibility to the citizens of New York requires.

*Anchor*: Do you expect to be placed under surveillance or protective custody by the police?

*Moore*: I'm not sure they even know we're out here, or that they would have the capability of hearing or understanding someone else's point of view if they did. Here's the description: Samantha, five-eight, a hundred and thirty pounds, early thirties, long dark hair, Caucasian. . . .

DeSales put his head in his hands. Kavanaugh switched off the radio. "You must really have turned the charm on her, *Lieutenant* DeSales. Is that why they call you the Saint?"

DeSales rubbed his eyes. "How many calls have we had? How many Samanthas?"

"At last count, seventy-three. A lot of cranks, as you can imagine. One seems pretty solid. About five people say they missed her. A Samantha Lawrence. In Fort Greene. Right on one of the blocks my cousin Eddie's invested in. She and her husband bought a building, renovated it, and then split up."

"A not-unusual occurrence these days, I understand."

"Anyway, they lived in the garden duplex and rented the other two floors. Part of the separation agreement was she could stay there until the divorce was final, but the husband had to collect the rents and pay the mortgage. She didn't have a job. So when she disappeared, everybody—tenants, husband, and so forth—assumed she'd gone to the Bahamas or something. Seems she'd taken up with a skin-diver down there last fall. It was the long weekend. Lincoln's Birthday. I just sent Kurtz and Rios over to check it out."

DeSales stood up and walked to the window. Out of the subway stop below, lawyers and other white males bustled toward Borough Hall and Brooklyn Heights. Another group, predominantly black and female, headed for A & S and the Albee mall. He cracked his knuckles for a while. Finally, he said, "I've got an idea, Bernie. Get the D.A. back on the line. Tell him we'll willingly . . . no, *enthusiastically* commit ourselves to the Carruthers case, but that we need the Feds in on it. He must agree to cooperate with them. The next condition is that the FBI has to send that black guy over here. Whatsisname. Allen. The one they sent up to the New York office from the Behavioral Science Unit at Quantico. No one else is acceptable.

Maybe, just maybe, we can kill two birds with one stone."

"And also," he rapped the window with a fingertip and turned back to his desk, "we better do something about Megan Moore. So she doesn't have to do her next broadcast impaled on Gil Hodges' first base mitt over in Holy Cross. Put a tail on her. Discreet. I just don't want to have to talk to her—or look at her—right now."

Kavanaugh handed out the xeroxed sheets. Desmond skimmed his first, then read it again, more deliberately:

Sundown Poem
D Moses
Beirut HoJo Cyrillic
Roach Motel Prep H
   New Life BKLN!
Carruthers Whitman Brooklyn Union Gas
Convent queens?   9Q
Union Pacific?   Manifest Destiny?
Astoria.   Wrong.   9.   Blue and white tiles.   Up and out
New Train
FOGCRASHLEFT

He looked up. DeSales was on his left. A heavyset black man in a blue pinstriped suit sat on his right. The man's name was Maceo Allen, and he was from the FBI. Kavanaugh hovered in the background, making coffee, humming "Danny Boy."

DeSales fingered the knot on his tie, then cleared his throat before speaking. His voice was nevertheless hoarse. He said:

"This is from Carruthers' notebook. Written yesterday morning before the mysterious rendezvous. We wanted to see if we were missing anything. We thought you might pick up anything that has to do with the Institute or this Whitman business maybe."

"So that was why you left the message about 'Herman'?"

DeSales nodded, but was otherwise unresponsive. He appeared to have fallen out of his joking mood. That was all right with Desmond. He wasn't feeling particularly lighthearted himself. He looked back at the collage of phrases. "Where was this found? Should I know?"

"Why not? Bernie?"

Kavanaugh continued to lean over the coffee, watching the black liquid drip through the paper cone into the pot. "On an F Train. In Queens. Middle car. It had gone out of service at Forest Hills and was towed into the IND yard, Corona Park. It had left Coney Island heading north, uptown, at eight-fifteen. Got to Forest Hills at ten-fifteen, way behind schedule. Surprise."

DeSales added, "We started out going with the roommate's testimony that he *thought* Carruthers said he was going to Brooklyn to 'make a killing' on Walt Whitman at eight-thirty yesterday. Finding the notebook in Queens kind of goes against the hypothesis, so we spoke to this guy Neville again and now he says he's not sure *where* Carruthers was going. Just knows he was meeting a woman about Whitman."

"Sounded to me like he'd got into the booze cabinet," said Kavanaugh. "Neville, I mean."

"So we're beginning to think maybe we should try to narrow this down to where we assume that Carruthers dropped or deliberately *left* the notebook on the train between West Fourth in the Village and Forest Hills. Say, between nine-thirty, when the train finally got to West Fourth, and ten-fifteen, when it broke down in Forest Hills."

Desmond shook his head. "It doesn't fit, not with what's written here."

"Why?"

"Sundown Poem."

"You *know* it? Christ, I had two men over in the library this morning trying to look it up. No soap, anywhere."

"That's because it's called something else in the texts. Whitman originally called it 'Sundown Poem.' But officially it's 'Crossing Brooklyn Ferry.' It's about contemplating Manhattan and Brooklyn from a ferryboat in the East River at the end of the day. I shouldn't say it's *about* that. I mean that is the setting, the premise, of the poem."

"How's this, then?" Allen leaned forward. He was a handsome man with an open, rather sensitive face, except for his nose, which had been broken at least once and was as flat as a boxer's. "Maybe he's already coming *back* from Brooklyn. That would fit better with the timetable anyway. If he's waited until this train got to West Fourth heading uptown, he would have been sitting in the station for almost an hour."

"And the roommate said he was in a hurry to catch a train."

"No." Desmond shook his head. "Look at the text. The movement is from Manhattan to Brooklyn. The poem has the same sense, although it isn't explicit: going home from the city after work. I remember it pretty well. I had to memorize it for a dramatic reading in high school."

Allen was querulous: "But you can't be that literal; it wasn't even *sunset*—it was nine A.M."

"It's corroborated by what follows," Desmond went on. "'D' for D Train. How about that? I used to take the D to work when I lived in the Village. It goes over the Manhattan Bridge. That's the sense I get from some of the lines that follow: Moses? Grandma? There are plenty of primitive murals as you come out from underground and go up on the bridge, for example."

DeSales made notes on a pad, muttering to himself. Desmond continued:

"And the 'New Life B K L N' line. Isn't there a billboard somewhere?"

"Also the Manhattan Bridge, our side." Kavanaugh closed his eyes and intoned, a mock-Gregorian chant:

> "There's new life in
> Brooklyn Brownstone Neighborhoods
> Brooklyn Union Gas
> *Dona nobis pacem.*"

"Yeh, but Convent Avenue? In Queens?"

"Only in Upper Manhattan," said DeSales with certainty. "Near Columbia. No help."

Desmond ran his finger down another line, then across: "'Manifest Destiny.' Well, you certainly could identify *that* with Whitman, I guess. The sense of the country moving, expanding west. Further and further until we'd dislodged all the Indians and started a few wars. I don't know that Old Walt went for wars or massacres, but," he closed his eyes and knit his brow, "I can't really say for sure. You'd have to ask somebody closer to the subject. Like Carruthers." He smiled feebly. None of his interlocutors responded. "You know, time plays funny tricks on politics. Maybe imperialism and poetic humanism were synonymous in those days. Anyway, 'manifest destiny' was kind of a nineteenth-century euphemism, like 'pacification' in Vietnam."

"What subject are *you* particularly close to, Mr. Desmond?" asked Allen, out of the blue.

Desmond found himself speechless. He had barely heard the question. The subject of imperialism, coming up as it had, had brought Joe Verb's image uncomfortably close; imperialism was one of Joe's favorite topics. American imperialism, particularly. For the tenth time, Desmond felt the urge to give in, to report his contact with Verb to DeSales, but he couldn't bring himself to play Judas. And all there was going against Joe that was vaguely concrete was his excited, conspiratorial air on the phone. It was still entirely possible that all he wanted to talk to Desmond about was old times. More likely, he had found out that Desmond was now an administrator, and wanted to get his old job back. In any case, *he* had started this thing about contacting Joe, not the other way around. If he were to turn him in, it would be the worst form of entrapment.

Now he worried that his eyes were betraying his two-edged guilt. Allen's question finally caught up with his brain:

"*My* specialty? 'The Literature of Urban Crime in Eighteenth-Century England.' That's the theory. In fact, I spend most of my time functioning as the complaint department, chief cook and bottle-washer for the Institute. An ennobling experience."

DeSales made a gesture with his hand that, in effect, waved away the digression, both the question and the sardonic answer. "Is there anything else here?" He seemed genuinely eager to hear Desmond's opinions. Respectful, even.

"What I was saying was, the Whitman that they used to teach in survey courses, the one I knew, spent a lot of time getting high on the vastness of America, the space, and the endless migration of populations." He looked at the sheet again, warming to the task. "You know, I have a peculiar sense that something changed here for Carruthers."

"How so?"

"Everything up to this point, where it says 'Manifest Destiny,' is typical Carruthers. Even if you don't get the specific reference, you can feel him straining to make connections. Flashy ones. Like 'Roach Motel' is probably an ad he saw on the subway, but he wrote it down because he could use it somewhere as a portent of filth or bad taste, or doom for that matter. But below 'Manifest Destiny,' the lines are strikingly literal."

How academic he sounded, thought Desmond. How funny that was. And he did it well, too. It was what he had been trained for.

"They're just straightforward transcriptions of what is actually, phenomenologically, happening to him, rather than doodling notions maybe based on reality but really twisted and stretched by his creative imagination. He sees a sign he thinks is wrong. He gets off that train, goes 'up and out' to another train. There he finds himself in fog and hears some kind of crash." He took a breath, "There *was* a fog yesterday morning, wasn't there?"

"Red Hook, South Brooklyn in general," said Kavanaugh.

"So maybe this indicates that he got lost. In any case he feels threatened. So, consciously or unconsciously, he's sending out an SOS. He's been brought back down to earth. He's got to deal with the real world. And," he crossed his legs and began to wipe his glasses, "the real world is another country to that guy."

Although he was wearing only light chinos and a tennis shirt, Desmond was suddenly conscious of the heat. He realized that Kavanaugh and Allen, both stout men, were sweating profusely in their suits. Even DeSales, who usually projected a cool, almost serpentlike affect, was visibly uncomfortable, wearing flannel pants and an oyster-gray shirt with a starched collar, shifting about in his seat. But Desmond knew that what he was feeling had little to do with the humidity. What he had been saying about Carruthers could just as easily be applied to himself, the growing tenuousness of his relation to reality. Moreover, the suspicion had crept into his brain that this entire bravado act of interpretation was no more than the wanton smothering of the real intent of Fletcher Carruthers's words by Timothy Desmond's subjectivity; he was forcing the text to conform to his own state of mind. Perhaps the reader was more important than the writer after all.

So he reached down into the bag of his critical being and came up with something external, easily observable, arguably "objective," to assure himself and his listeners that he was not merely off-the-wall. He replaced his glasses on the bridge of his nose and spread his palms, as if displaying some incontrovertible truth:

"And the HoJo. How about Howard Johnson's? Orange and blue? Those are the colors in the D Train, right?"

"Right," said Kavanaugh.

"And the F Train too," said Allen. "No help."

DeSales got up, appeared to wander aimlessly, and then headed for the map on the wall. He looked it over for a while, chin in hand.

"You got that new subway map, Bernie? Pin it up over here. Next to the regular one." Then he appeared to register for the first time that Desmond was still in his chair. "Listen, Desmond. Tim. Thanks a lot. You gave me more than I thought I could get. And no bullshit either. That's a rarity around here."

Desmond began to rise as DeSales continued the friendly dismissal. "Y'know, you don't have to put down your work so much, complaint department, no publishing, all that stuff. Seems to me you're clear, efficient, get the job done. That's what's important, not *what* you do. You wanna be a cop, God help you, call me up anytime." He reached out to shake hands.

"I'll take that as a compliment." Desmond gripped the offered hand briefly and turned to leave, feeling even worse now about withholding information.

"Listen," piped Allen suddenly. His voice was high-pitched, almost preadolescent, although his temples were gray. "Why should he leave? If we're going to continue brainstorming on this," he indicated Kavanaugh and the map, "maybe he can provide additional insights."

Desmond caught DeSales's eye. There was a beginning of a tic at the corner of the shorter, swarthy man's mouth; the usual metallic glint in his eye seemed to have intensified. Desmond was sure that the detective had an inkling that he was not telling the entire truth. So, although he had little inclination to stay with these men, he decided to play it bright-eyed and eager. He seemed to have earned their respect with his professional demeanor and intelligence; now he had only to stifle any lingering suspicions about his integrity and enthusiasm. By the time DeSales began to say, "If it's okay with him," he was sitting down again, entrenched for the duration.

"Don't pin that up, Bernie. I changed my mind. Get a card table and lay it out."

When the map was spread out and the three men leaned over it, Kavanaugh peeking around Allen's arm, DeSales began to trace with his manicured index finger the route of the D Train from West Fourth Street, past Houston Street, into Chinatown, over the bridge to DeKalb. He paused to contemplate the ceiling, then went back to the map.

"What we've got so far, thanks to Tim, is that maybe Carruthers was on the downtown D crossing the bridge. He sees the Brooklyn Union sign, goes back underground to DeKalb. If he'd stayed on the D, he'd have gone Atlantic, Seventh Avenue, across the park to the Zoo and Botanical Gardens at Empire, then Parkside-Ocean and into Flatbush. There's no sense of any of those places in the notebook. Besides, if Carruthers is anything like what I've heard, he might not willingly go above the surface on the other side of the park. And I can't see anyone visibly *forcing* him. We'd have heard about it by now."

Desmond opened his mouth to speak. He was about to say that he had been between Parkside and Church the night before and that DeSales's estimate of Carruthers's reaction was accurate. But he swallowed his words; that would bring up the subject of his own private search for Joe Verb. But Allen had noticed the movement. His raised eyebrows silently questioned him. Desmond had to say something, so he offered, lamely: "It would figure he'd get off at DcKalb. That's near where Whitman lived and worked."

Allen nodded. He seemed to have a one-train mind: "Besides, taking the D as far as Flatbush eliminates the F, which doesn't connect with the D until Coney Island."

DeSales got back in on it. "At DeKalb, he could have switched to a lot of other trains. Let's put everything else aside, and see how he could have got on the F from DeKalb. Let's forget the 'Convent queens' and '9Q.' They don't seem to fit with anything." He pressed his thumb into the map, as if he were trying to force something out of it. "The IND runs a couple of trains due south from DeKalb. The B and the N. . . ."

"I know the N from Bay Ridge," said Kavanaugh. "It skips DeKalb during rush hours. Crazy motherfuckers at the TA."

"How about the B?"

"In rush hour, the B skips DeKalb too. Would you believe it? Anyways, at all times it runs express, all the way from DeKalb to Thirty-sixth Street in Sunset Park before it turns away from Bay Ridge to Borough Park. Full of Hasids. Wouldn't Carruthers have mentioned them?" He looked at Desmond, saying off-handedly, "In the old days Sunset Park was Lower Bay Ridge."

DeSales snapped his fingers. His voice rose: "I've got it. The BMT. The RR Train. It connects at DeKalb, runs local, and see this 'Astoria wrong' here in Carruthers' notebook? That's the northern terminal for the RR. We all know that the motorman is as likely as not to leave the same destination sign in the train when he turns around at the terminal. Why change it? Let the riders guess where they're going, right? So he takes an RR south. Where does it stop? Look: Pacific, then Union. So Carruthers turned them around." He looked at Desmond conspiratorially: "This goes with what you were saying. Union Pacific sounds like the railroad to California. Thus 'Manifest Destiny.' Carruthers was bending the facts to fit the image he wanted to create. And then . . ."

He folded his arms and tapped a foot: "There's two 9s. The RR stops at Ninth Street after Union. Then what happens?"

The only response was a silent shaking of heads. DeSales smugly answered his own question. "What happens is you get off in an underground station with the old-fashioned tiles, climb up to street level, then you can climb up another level to an el that heads back to Manhattan."

"Which train?" asked Allen. "I was in Virginia too long. And now that I'm back I take the bus when I can't afford a cab."

"The F Train, of course! The one I always took from down there when I was a kid and wanted to go into the city."

"Back to Gowanus, South Brooklyn, Frankie. Maybe we can run *both* these investigations from a command post on a barge in the canal."

"Hey, wait a minute," protested Allen. He picked the map up off the table, arms spread wide, and adjusted it so he could get a better angle of vision. With the tip of his nose he followed the route that DeSales had traced with his finger. He threw the map back onto the table. "Look, you guys, all you've done logically is expand the area, not cut it down. If you can *prove* that Carruthers got on that train at Ninth Street in Brooklyn, say just before nine-thirty A.M., then that means that he could have got off the train anytime between then and ten-fifteen and anywhere in the many miles between South Brooklyn and Forest Hills. Christ, he could have gone right back home to Washington Square. Maybe he made a pickup and was attacked on the way home." He looked at the map again, again adjusting it until he was leaning sideways and the map was turned almost upside down. "South Brooklyn? Why the hell is it called South Brooklyn? It looks like three-quarters of the borough is further south than *South* Brooklyn."

DeSales shrugged off the questions. Trivial. "I've got to follow my instinct, Maceo. And the fact that the last writing occurred in the fog. The F Train goes underground after Smith Street, so he wouldn't *see* the weather after that. It looks like we should focus on the area between two stops: Ninth Street and Smith Street, the area where the F Train comes above ground at Ninth Street, goes across an elevated trestle over the Gowanus Canal, and is a stone's throw from the Gowanus Expressway where they had the big chain car-crash yesterday in the traffic approaching the Battery Tunnel."

Allen cocked his head to the other side, lowered his eyelids, and finally nodded assent.

Desmond said, "It's South Brooklyn because the borough was originally composed of six towns. Brooklyn—or Breuckelen—was only one of them. That area was the southern extreme of the old town of Brooklyn, but north of some of the other towns, like New Utrecht, Flatbush, Gravesend, Flatlands. I can't remember the other one."

"How d'*you* know that?" Kavanaugh appeared incensed. "I thought you didn't know your way around. I lived here all my life and never heard that one."

Desmond remained deadpan, but allowed his eyes to twinkle, one of DeSales's mannerisms. "I've never been in South Brooklyn in my life, except to pass over it on the expressway, going to the Verrazzano Bridge to go to Pennsylvania. But I'm the professor, remember. I'm paid to read books. One time I had to teach a course on 'Brooklyn in Literature'; in the course of doing it I picked up a lot of little nuggets of information. That's one of them."

"The sixth town was Bushwick," said DeSales, not looking up. "Where the Cemetery of the Evergreens is. Where the firemen came from. Now, Bernie, we've got to call the TA and make sure that this little trip we've imagined for Carruthers—D to R R to F—was possible yesterday morning."

Desmond had left. Kavanaugh was now fixing the subway map onto the wall. DeSales was neatly filing the Carruthers material into an accordion folder, at the same time barking orders on the phone to one of his underlings to establish a canvass and patrol in the areas accessible by foot from the Ninth and Smith Street subway stops. He promised a photo of Carruthers within the hour. When DeSales hung up, Allen leaned forward, smoothing the thighs of his trousers, then folded his hands: "Okay, Frank," he said. "I've done my part playing straight man in this poetry-interpretation and geography seminar. Now, why did you have the D.A. pull me over here? You know I only deal with motiveless stuff, the rapists and serial murderers. Political kidnappings are as far from my bailiwick as you can get. So is Brooklyn, for that matter."

DeSales pulled another accordion file from under the desk. "I presume you've heard about the guy the media is calling 'The Graveyard Grim Reaper'?"

"With interest."

"Here he is." He thrust the folder into Allen's hands. "Or rather, here's what he's done. Pictures, transcripts, the works. It's all in triplicate: one for me, one for you, and one for you to send to your Behavioral Science boys at Quantico."

"Right on."

"And Mace?"

"Yeh?"

"Remember that lecture you gave at John Jay?"

"Yeh."

"One of your lines was something like, 'The more bizarre the crime, the easier it is to tell what kind of person did it'?"

"Yeh."

"This one should be *real* easy, then."

# CHAPTER 17

"IT WORKED OUT SO *conveniently*," the man in the paisley silk bow tie and red blazer was saying. "May is *absolutely* closed out, you know. The Heights has the first week. The Slope has the second. Cobble Hill has the third. Clinton Hill–Fort Green has the fourth. June is a definite loser—everyone's started going to the beach. And Lefferts Gardens and even Flatbush were jostling for the dates in late April. So we decided to go for it. Why not try a house tour early April, Easter weekend? And so here we are, the weather and turnout are *fabulous*. Of course the article in the *Times* real-estate section didn't . . ." The man in the bow tie finally realized someone was waiting. He smiled insincerely at the man with the big head. "And how many will that be, sir? One? Five dollars, please. Remember, next year you save a dollar if you buy your ticket in advance. And don't forget the program! And don't miss number nine; it's *fabulous*."

It had worked out conveniently for the man with the big head also. The First Annual South Slope–North Sunset House Tour was being held close to the cemetery, and it was a neighborhood he knew well. Too well. It was the first of many he had grown up in. And, with his mom, been driven out of. He knew it so well that he had not even bothered to turn to take in the panoramic view of the Upper Bay, all the way across to Bayonne, which the house-tourists were *ooh*ing and *ahh*ing over. Instead he merely watched with his own twisted smile as the gawkers turned from the freshening breeze to the mixed block of neat modest row houses, a tenement or two, and a red-brick factory. There were clusters of Puerto Ricans in the street, oblivious to the stream of visitors. They wore dirty undershirts and drank from seven-ounce bottles of Miller High Life. They swung plastic bats at whiffle balls, laughing loudly when the balls careened near the strangers on the block. One of the houses was on a rent strike. Above the banner proclaiming the liberation of the building from a greedy, unscrupulous landlord, fat whorish women with roses in their hair leaned out the windows. They pressed their tits against their arms in such a way that they swelled out like balloons. Out of the dark rooms behind them, radios blared songs in which the phrase "*mi corazón*" echoed again and again. You could tell by the expressions on their faces that they would be moving on pretty soon; he had a good idea where.

This reminded him of Boys' Town, Nuevo Laredo, 1967. He was stationed in San Antonio that summer, waiting for his "Unadaptable" discharge from the service. Just before they sent the rest of the company to 'Nam. The wetback women were nice. In Boys' Town they didn't give two shits what you looked like or how you came on to them. There was a joke he used to tell. That summer, when he was nineteen, he got two discharges: one from the Army at Fort Sam, the other from a broad named Carmelita in Boys' Town—only that discharge came out of his cock.

"It's beautiful," he heard a youngish, balding man exclaim. "Big Sky Country!" The man was carrying an infant against his chest in a kind of sling, Indian-style. His wife was short, flat as a pancake in front, and wore Bermuda shorts over her chunky thighs. She reminded him of the kind of women they had in the Divine Light Mission. Or was it the War Resisters' League?

Sometimes it was hard to separate those experiences out. Boys' Town was easy to remember; but the years he was crashing in the Village after the Army were not so easy. One of the doctors said he had blown his mind on speed. So what the fuck did *he* know? The wife patted the only part of the baby that stuck out of the sling, a wispy blond head, and almost purred, "Maybe we'll find something. Let's go right through, one to ten, I want to see them *all*." The baby began to scream. A bottle was shoved in its mouth.

The man with the big head skimmed the program as quickly as he could. He was not a particularly good reader, but he knew what he was looking for. Thus he was able to eliminate seven out of ten places immediately, about average. These were houses or co-ops which the program said were owned by husband-and-wife teams. Husbands could get in the way. The remaining three, he knew, were chancy, but there was no specific mention of a man in residence. One referred to "the owner," another to a "Page Zelenik," who could have been a man or woman; and the last to "the occupant." There was usually a single woman around, one of these house-freaks, who couldn't resist showing off; sometimes they were trying to prove something, that they could do what men could do. There were all kinds of fucked-up people around.

He remembered how he had found that one, Samantha, at the seminar he'd seen in the personals section of the *Voice*. For "Victims of House Restoration Divorce Syndrome." There was another joke: restoration had killed her, but she'd *preserved* real good.

The problem was, he had nobody to tell it to.

So he would have to choose among the robust brownstone with the L-shaped stoop, Eastlake woodwork, and gas chandelier; the former drugstore with ceramic floor-tiles and Art Deco features; and the old factory that had been converted to co-ops, one of which was on display, in which the "occupant" had opened up the floors to create a triplex with a loft aerie bedroom overhanging a three-story living room, the windows created in part from the original garage doors.

He decided to see the last first, not because of any particular intuition, but because his mother had once worked there, sewing life-preservers.

He walked briskly up the hill, joining the line outside the building, holding his ticket out to be stamped while averting his eyes from the volunteer at the entry. He didn't like to look at them.

Directly in front of him in line was a woman with hennaed hair, an "East Village" T-shirt, and high-topped black sneakers. When he was around the East Village, they didn't have T-shirts for it. And only the spades from Avenue C had worn high-topped black sneakers. That was when they came over to beat in the brains of the flower children who were sleeping off their trips in doorways on St. Mark's Place and Second Avenue. The woman was conducting a monologue with her companion, a very short man with a hairdo identical to hers:

"What was that thing in the parlor at the last house? What was it for? Originally? I never saw such a thing. Why didn't they have the kitchen in the basement? What did they use that little room next to the baby's room for? A laundry? Maybe it was a *servant's* room. But *so small*. Maybe a bigger room was broken up. I'm not sure I go for this remuddling. You think all those fireplaces work? The parquet was certainly damaged; that's why they had the rug in the back parlor. . . ."

They moved forward. He felt a little edgy. He had a lot to accomplish before he was due at the cemetery. At least he didn't feel so conspicuous. This was a funkier crowd than usual, and all the spics in the street helped. And he'd put on a long-sleeved shirt. These people had a real problem with the tattoos.

They went through the door. "Oh, Gawd!" exclaimed the woman in front.

It was not the place for him. He knew immediately. He had to resist two urges. The first was to just turn around and push his way out. But he couldn't afford to call attention to himself in even the smallest way. The second was to just trash the fucking place. The loft aerie bedroom was a kind of open balcony at the top of some very steep stairs leading down into the open living area. The bed looked like a kind of space module. There were shiny handcuffs attached to the chrome headboard, and a snakeskin whip hung from the globular side. Down below, the only things identifiable as furniture were a big piano and a couple of wooden pallets. On each landing of the stairway, there were eye-level photographs, black-and-white, of bare asses, most quite hairy. At the bottom, the largest photo was a frontal study of a sweaty Spanish type with no shirt, a prominent bellybutton, and a swirl of pubic hair peeking over the waist of his jeans, where the model had deeply hooked his thumb. The jeans were very tight, and there was a considerable bulge at the crotch.

Faggots.

"Well," the redheaded man said, "They say when *they* discover a neighborhood, you know it's turning around. Realestatewise."

The woman nodded her head, grinning: "You think two of them go up in the *aerie* to ball, and a third plays "Bolero" on the piano?"

"Wearing a rug, of course."

She groaned.

Outside, the couple with the baby was not happy.

"So it's for sale," she said.

"That's why they had the hot tub and paddle-bladed ceiling fan turned on in the bathroom. Wanted to make it seem sexy."

"I'm sweating like a pig. How's Jessica doing in the Snugli?"

"Okay. You believe the price? For a Jacuzzi, a fan, some exposed brick, and a lot of unusable space? In *this* neighborhood?"

"The *Times* says it's turning around. I say, give me the old Landmarks Preservation Districts."

The man adjusted the baby's sleeping head, then ran a comb through his own thinning hair.

"Darling," he hissed, "we can't *afford* a Landmarks Preservation District. We got in the market too late."

"You were the one with the slow sperm," she countered.

The two couples went on up the street, in the direction of number nine, the bow-fronted limestone whose garden floor, with its exposed beams and whitewashed walls, provided an exquisite setting for Gary and Prudence Fenstermacher's white bamboo furniture and mementoes of their many visits to the South Pacific. The man with the big head backtracked for the robust brownstone, preserving his anonymity. As soon as he was through the iron security gate under the L-shaped stoop, he knew he had struck a vein. He could smell it, like an animal. And some people thought he had burnt himself out on speed.

An attractive thirtyish woman wearing pyjama trousers with an organdy ribbon tied around the waist was holding forth to an assemblage of listeners: "This *is* a bigger house," she enunciated slowly. "It was built at the turn of the century by some Finns who were a bit more prosperous than the Irish, Poles, and Italians who first settled here." She raised her arms as if upping the tempo. "So lucky *me*! One of the things I love, besides my house, is that at the newsstand down on the corner you can still get a Finnish language paper alongside *El Diario* and *The Irish Echo*. Anyway, someone asked about these panels . . . ."

He lingered at the rear of the audience until he was sure they were captive and that no one else would imminently enter the house. As she began listing available wood-stripping devices, he slipped away and up the stairs. He ignored the kitchen and living room. Quickly, he checked the door to the deck. A large window had been converted into a glass door in a heavy wooden frame. Cast-iron security gates stood outside. These would be tough to crack. Then he saw that she had secreted a key to each of the inside locks, for ready availability in case someone was trapped in the house, by hanging them on a string alongside the paneling of the inside door. He made two quick impressions in the wax he carried in a tin, hoping he would not have to use them. He didn't feel like climbing backyard fences. But if he *did* find a convenient place to wait inside, he would have to remember to remove the keys *entirely* so she could not get *out*.

He went back to the open stairwell. New arrivals were bunching still at the bottom of the stairs. "There were at least *thirteen* layers of paint, and *seven* of wallpaper," she was saying. "All *ugly*." There was polite laughter.

He hoofed it up the stairs to the next floor. There was a bright studio in the rear, catching the afternoon sun from the west. She did weaving; there was a loom. An easel stood in the far corner. The front room was for sleeping. The bed was kingsize, with a quilt woven with a representation of what looked like Noah's Ark. He wasn't interested. He remarked the absence, on the bureau tops, of pictures of children or of men her age, and then, aware that time was running out, had a choice: inspect the drawers or closets, or give the adjoining bath a going-over. He chose the latter; it would be quicker to cover comprehensively. There was no razor in the medicine chest, only a Lady Bic on the soap rack in the shower. All the soap was scented, and the shampoos the feminine type with hair conditioner. He was especially pleased to see that the shower curtain was a thick brown vinyl. She would be easy to approach. Transparent curtains were only good for the movies. There was a bidet and lots of thick fluffy towels hanging neatly folded from gold-tinted plastic racks. He was convinced; there were no men living here. Everything was falling into place. He had one more prayer, as he heard the crowd move into the kitchen area on the floor below.

It was there: a neatly knotted yellow ribbon cordoned off the top floor from the rest of the house. A hand-lettered sign hanging from the ribbon said, "Tour stops here; top floor off-limits." He stepped over the cord and scurried up and into the room over her bedroom. As he had expected, the renovation had been arrested on the floor below, and this floor was occupied by only a rooming-house lavatory and a couple of rooms stacked with builders' materials and bric-a-brac. In the front room she had piled odd bits of furniture and books, stuff with which, he would bet, she littered the rest of the house when it was not being shown off. He spat, quite deliberately, into a corner. There was a large closet, almost as large as the one they were keeping the professor in, above her bathroom. The door hung on loose nails. He entered, closed it carefully behind him, and sat cross-legged on the floor. Perfectly still. It would be at least a couple of hours. The tour didn't end until four, and then there was usually some kind of party to entertain the committee and the people who had volunteered their houses. This, of course, would be at someone else's house. He could get her then, while she was getting washed and dressed to go out.

He thought of the various bottles of fancy perfume and cologne and body lotion arrayed on her marble washstand. He remembered the day he had come home from school and asked his mother what kind of perfume she wore. "Four Roses," she had said. When he took this information back to the nun at school, she had rapped him across the knuckles with the pointer, and all of the girls had laughed.

He thought of the painting of lilies that had been ostentatiously displayed on the easel in the studio downstairs. Lilies. It was the day before Easter. One Easter he was supposed to have been a lily boy in the procession, but his mother had neglected to get him the white shorts-suit, and the nuns had refused to allow him to carry the lilies without the proper costume. Then his mother had gone to the school and not long after that they had had to move to Bushwick. Where they had the fire.

What was it that the Protestants, the Scandinavians, had carried around at Eastertime? Pussy willows? Cattails? Had he ever seen colored people carrying such stuff?

No, that was the Greeks.

Faggots.

He decided to take a nap on the hardwood floor. He would need the sleep. He could be up all night.

# CHAPTER 18

"DO YOU LOVE IT, Mace," chortled Kavanaugh, "not only was it possible for Carruthers to switch from the D to the R R at DeKalb, but there was a screwup and the R R was running on the I N D track, so he only had to step across the platform to do it; didn't even have to walk over to the other line."

Laughing, Maceo Allen sat in the chair next to DeSales's desk. "I do love it," he said. Then he became solemn. He lowered his attaché case to the floor. He hitched up his pants— gray pinstripes this day—from the knees. He reached into the case and removed a sheaf of papers held together at the top with a metal clamp. He glanced at the top sheet, then spoke slowly:

"The computer says your murderer is a white male, about thirty-five years old, comes from a broken home and can't form a lasting relationship with a woman, didn't know his victims, and either works or lives—or worked or lived—in the immediate vicinity of the Cemetery of the Evergreens. He probably has a criminal record for violent behavior, and we shouldn't be surprised if he also has been placed under institutional psychiatric care at some point in the past. Just the same, there's no reason to expect that he killed anyone before Jerry Jacuzzi. So his organization profile will tell us a lot more than a prolonged search through the files of unsolved homicides."

A muffled grunt came from Kavanaugh's throat. His mouth was full of cheese Danish.

Allen bowed. "Elementary, my dear Watson."

DeSales looked wary: "I know you guys, Mace. The computer gives some direction, but you've got to *read* it. What do *you* think?"

Allen rolled his eyes: "Okay, I'll give you chapter and verse. But you guys know most of this stuff as well as I do. We're just a little more scientific in our approach." He chortled. "There's no question, I don't think, about the age or gender. Men, and men only, commit crimes like this. And the age can be pretty well tied down by two elements: his post-offense behavior, and the fact that he's walking the streets."

"If he is."

"Right. If he is. Let's stick with the assumption that he is, that he's not in some nutbin or halfway house with lax security, or that he hasn't been paroled by some soft-headed judge after serving a few months for mass homicide."

"Sorry," said DeSales, "I knocked you off track."

"No problem. I got all day. You got any more of that Danish?"

Kavanaugh served him a piece on a paper plate. He took a large bite. "First, he's too organized to be a kid, even in his twenties. There's no suggestion that either killing was the act of a frightened or enraged kid. It was fairly cold-blooded, no frenzied attack or anything. I personally haven't ever seen bodies taken care of as nicely as these except by someone confident, over thirty. And the messages—body language, one of the guys at Quantico called it—" he chortled again, "is post-offense behavior I'd only associate with a mature man. Yet he's probably not as old as forty either, because that's a basic cutoff point for the beginning of this sort of sexual violence. . . . I say sexual not because there was an outright rape but because of circumstances, nudity, bondage, positioning of the bodies.

Anybody over forty who has this kind of urge started younger and is, in all likelihood, either dead or deep in the slammer. So, thirty-five is a good assumption."

"And white?" DeSales was thinking about the blackface.

Allen read his mind. "White, but *not* because of the black-face. That's the problematical part, but I'll get to that later. White because the vast percentage of killings like this—motiveless, as we call 'em—are *intra*-racial. White men kill white women. Black men kill black women. The only exception to this, as you're well aware, are these black teenagers who murder and rape elderly white women. But that's another kettle of fish: they're overcome with intolerable childish rage, impotence; they're getting back at the grandmothers who, in black culture, often raise them—too sternly, the kids think. And also the fact that there's a robbery element involved, and these old, apparently rich white women—defenseless—become surrogates for the grandmothers of whom the kids are still afraid. So, wham! Anyway . . ."

He chewed some more Danish.

"The post-offense behavior also suggests some other things. He had to spend a lot of time at the Evergreens that morning, yet he didn't seem to let that hurry him. He knew the place well. He picked the appropriate site for his message; it happened to be on a knoll that can't be seen from any of the main roads or the offices. He must have also known the work-schedules. In short, he felt at home."

"At Gowanus, too?"

"Let me get to that. Got Sanka, Bernie?" He held his stomach. "Pre-ulceral condition. Caffeine's a killer. Especially if you don't want to give up the vodka martinis."

He stirred the packet into the cup of steaming water. The weather had let up. It had rained during the night, and there was a breeze off the harbor.

"Weapons," said Allen, sipping tentatively. "We don't know yet. But we do know that he didn't slash them with a kitchen knife or club them to death with a two-by-four. Also suggests organization. In any case, heavy facial beatings usually indicate some familiarity. . . . In fact, the degree of familiarity is proportionate to the degree of beating. So we can say he's not familiar with them, since he's handled them with kid gloves, as it were. I guess that's the gloss, except the broken home and women problem thing. You know, it's a truism." He shook his head. "Yet I still can't get used to it. My old man split when I was ten. My ma raised me and times were tough. Yet here I am." He held out his large rough hands, "Not hurting anybody. Married twenty-four years. Yet you look at the guys in the headlines the years I've been in law-enforcement—DeSalvo, Speck, Manson, Coral Eugene Watts in Texas, the Atlanta guy, Wayne Williams—they all came from backgrounds which are, on paper at least, similar to mine in one way or another."

"What do you think makes the difference?" asked DeSales laconically.

"You know better than to ask a Quantico man, Frank. We're sworn to never play psychiatrist. We want to know what happened and whodunnit, *not* why. Just feed the patterns into the computers and follow the statistical probability. Just the same, I think I can go as far as to say that it has to do with how they worked out the relationship with their mothers."

"I get the sense the statistics aren't enough in this case."

"Put it this way. One of our primary indicators is based on personality type: disorganized, organized, mixed. You find 'mixed' in some cases where a guy is a bit flaky, like someone on a job who's seventy-five percent efficient. But this guy—in the second killing, he's ninety-five percent organized, but in the first one he's much less so. The shaft in the second case, the tossing the box in the canal in the first, where it could have disappeared or floated out to sea. It's like he's got mixed feelings, or last-minute ambivalence about what he's doing, or . . ."

"Or what?"

"Or as if he's two different people. That's also evident in the messages. He's clever and ironic on the one hand and literal-minded, even single-minded, on the other."

"Jekyll and Hyde?"

Allen shrugged. "Maybe. Maybe he's two different people. We've had cases like that. There was a murder victim in Ohio beaten to death in her kitchen with a skillet—messy and impulsive, you bet—and then she's neatly raped posthumously and deposited in the perfect hiding place, nicely covered from the elements. Turned out it was brothers. One had a terrible temper and he killed her in a rage. The other was a cool-headed sadist. And he was the one who raped her and got rid of her. I'm against that in this case, though."

"Why?"

"I can't really answer that, except that there's a single-mindedness here, *one* message, which the computer tells us is uncharacteristic of a team. The team would either be formed like the brothers in Ohio, on the spur of the moment to accommodate an unpremeditated situation, or it would be a pair of thrill-killers, torturers, like Bianchi and Bono on the West Coast."

"And the message?"

Allen took the paper plate off his lap and carried that and the coffee cup over to the table. He came back swallowing the last crumbs of Danish, then licking his fingers. He wiped off the fingers with a fresh white handkerchief, sat down, and hiked up his trousers again. He smiled, raising one eyebrow.

"First I want to ask you a question, Frank."

"Shoot."

"Did you request me on this case because of my expertise or because I was black?"

DeSales looked him straight in the eye, then he responded solemnly: "First, because you're black, obviously; second, because I knew that you would come over and eat all the Danish, which would cause Bernie to lose some weight; and third, because I'd like to be the next Attorney General of the United States, and I need you guys on my side for that. Right?"

"I just knew you'd give me a straight answer, Frank."

"Good. Now you tell me how you figured out that I only love you for the color of your skin."

Allen flipped over some more sheets. He looked solemn. "That's what I was holding off on. The most mixed signal I'm getting here is this racial angle. First a white hooker is murdered who has a black clientele, and she's found packaged in a box with the Magi scene on the wrapping paper composed of three *black* Wise Men. Then. Have you established positive ID on the Samantha woman?"

"Yes. We got prints and dental work. The same. Samantha Lawrence of South Oxford Street."

"Then, you have a middle-class housewife, newly separated, who was a white 'pioneer' on a previously black block, which has, since she moved in, 'turned around,' as they say. Which translates into 'going white.' She's found in a previously all-*white* cemetery location, which is being encroached upon by graves of minorities. The monuments to white men thereabouts are painted in blackface. She's placed in a compromising position with one of these fellows. Statuary rape, huh?" He winked.

DeSales groaned: "Spare me, Mace. Bernie's bad enough, with his sacrilegious riffs. And how could your being black help me with what you just said? A dumb Canuck Italian like myself can figure that out."

Allen held out his palm: "Give me time. You're more devious than that. . . . So the most superficial interpretation could be that we've got someone who's against integration. Black men around white women." He looked off into space for a moment. "You know, the Wise Men *were* supposed to be black . . . or brown. They would have been Egyptians or Indians probably . . . but there are problems with that: the Brooklyn Union Gas Cinderella Project line. A wit. The Christmas gift-wrapping on Christmas Day, and the bloody face on the towel . . . definitely a Catholic, don't you think? Then the Lincoln's Birthday bit—the day she disappeared. Freeing the slaves? More anti-integration again. But, and this is a big but . . . "

"What, Mace?"

"These were not cases of blacks moving into white neighborhoods, the conventional racist objection. It's white women soliciting blacks or moving into *black* neighborhoods. . . ."

"And here comes the part where the color of your skin comes into this."

"Say what?"

"How do you feel about it all, as a black man?"

"What do I know from hookers, any color? I've been boringly faithful these twenty-some years."

"Jerry Jacuzzi wasn't just a hooker, Mace. Her hobby was house-renovation. Her ambition was to buy a brownstone in a neighborhood like South Oxford Street."

"Well, who can complain? Property values go up. Neighborhoods get nicer. I have a place at 103rd near Central Park West. When we moved back from Virginia, it was considered lower Harlem. Now it's the Upper West Side. My apartment is worth three times as much, and it's a lot safer for my family . . ."

"But how do you feel? Suppose you were just some poor black guy on the street, without a pot to piss in?"

"And the white dude comes along, cleans up my building, throws me out, chases me further uptown? I'd be damned mad."

"Homicidal?"

"Who can say? There's lots of pretty angry community groups now: Keep Harlem Black, etcetera."

"And that's what's been bothering you, isn't it?"

"What's *it*?"

"That it could as likely be white rage at blacks getting too close, or black rage at whites getting too close."

"There are a lot more indicators that the guy's white. Even the Catholic stuff. There are black Catholics, but they don't have it shoved down their throats the way you guys did. But the black figures—even the minstrel faces—are not negative. And yet . . ." he paused. Then:

"Like I said, there's a split personality, an ambivalence; and that's what I wanted to base our strategy on."

"Go ahead."

"We should follow what the boys in Quantico call a pro-active approach."

"You've mentioned it before, but run it by me again. Federal jargon tends to lose meaning for me an hour after I've eaten it. Like Chinese food."

"I think this guy is split, confused, ambivalent about something. Whether it's racial or has to do with his mother is irrelevant. So. If we theorize two somewhat distinct elements or personalities in him, we can also theorize that one of them is a lot guiltier than the other. So, first, you get the media to cooperate, beginning with that radio woman he's been calling up. You get the press in general, but particularly her, to suggest the opposite of what she's suggesting now, to promote the idea that we're getting closer and closer to the killer. Make him jumpy. Second, play on the guilty part. Do some sympathetic stories on the victims' families. If they didn't have any, make them up. You can't let the guy off the hook psychologically. You try to put stress on him to make him change his behavior, make a slip. Third, you watch the scenes of crime, in case he makes a return visit. Watch the graves of the victims. These messages and phone calls are early indications anyway that he *wants* to be reached, if not caught. There's the ethical problem, of course, but I don't imagine you're feeling too thin-skinned about that."

"Ethical," coughed Kavanaugh.

"He could commit suicide, say."

"Good riddance," said Kavanaugh.

"He could also step up his activities, get his unfinished business taken care of before his time runs out," DeSales articulated slowly. "If he feels hemmed in."

The three policemen sat in silence for a while.

"There's one more thing's been on my mind," said Allen. "Ever since I sat here with you and that Desmond guy and went over this Carruthers case. And then read the *Times* story on the case this morning."

"Yeh?"

"These people who say they have Carruthers have notified the entire news media that they want the City University to be re-integrated, or *more* integrated, right? They want city statutes to guarantee heterogeneous ethnic populations in neighborhoods, right? They want ghettoes like Brownsville busted up, but they also want housing provided or subsidized for minorities when white middle-class gentrifiers come into a neighborhood and start to take it over. Right?"

"You got it."

"Has it occurred to you that not only do these two crimes seem to focus around the same part of Brooklyn, but that they're almost mirror images of one another—the same issues, but backwards or upside down? It's almost like they're on a collision course."

# CHAPTER 19

THE BEEPER SOUNDED. Megan Moore plugged in the headset, put on the earphones, turned the switch to "Radio." On the two-way, she listened to her producer summarize the message from the police department. When he finished, she pressed the "Talk" button. Her voice was shaky with anger:

"Who the fuck do they think I am? Tokyo Rose? Tell them to shove it. I'm going independent on this. And I won't *stand* for somebody looking over my shoulder."

She switched off the two-way, ignoring the persistent beeping from the studio. She put the Ford into "Drive" and burned rubber pulling out of the NYPD parking zone in front of the morgue. She drove straight ahead for a while, distracted. It was only when she ran the red light and the other cars screeched their brakes in the intersection, horns blowing, that she realized she didn't even know where she was.

She pulled over at a fire hydrant and rubbed her eyes until her left elbow set her own horn screaming. She sat back and sighed heavily. This was her big chance. If she kept an exclusive on this story, and saw it through, she could wave goodbye to the Voice of the Big Apple. She envisioned, sometimes, a TV spot on a network; sometimes, an executive office at one of the affiliates. Perhaps such success, such independent achievement, would break her, once and for all, of the habit of seeking out the series of father-figures she and her analyst talked about so often.

Then the echoes returned of the Assistant Medical Examiner's coarse, indifferent voice telling her bluntly that there was, after the autopsy, nothing recognizable left of Samantha Lawrence for her to see. She had begun to identify with Samantha Lawrence, whose husband had left her stranded in Brooklyn. Then, in lieu of a hands-on encounter with the corpse, she had listened to the M.E. read his report. The words had become flesh in her consciousness; and now her own flesh quivered, as if she had been personally violated. Samantha Lawrence, when lowered from the statue in the Cemetery of the Evergreens, had had receding eyeballs, sunken cheeks, and dried lips; her scalp and the skin on her fingers had shrunk in such a way as to give the untutored eye the impression that the hair and fingernails had continued to grow after death; her back was purplish-black. Worst of all, at least to Megan Moore's sensibility, the dead woman's nipples had been dramatically erect—"outstanding," the goat-faced M.E. had leered. The flesh of the breasts had, like the fingers and scalp, begun to retreat into the dust of mortality by sending out a contradictory message of regeneration.

Megan Moore felt in her own breasts the sort of shooting pain that she sometimes got during her period from the benign cysts the doctors were always threatening to cut out of her.

She could call DeSales and agree to collaborate, or she could go home unattended and wait for "The Creep" to call. She could screw the equipment onto the mouthpiece of the phone and feed him live to the world at large. She would be a star. But a star in a lusterless firmament, for she had trouble imagining that even her home was her own anymore. It was time to find an apartment in Manhattan and move back. Brooklyn seemed very dark indeed.

The man Megan Moore thought of as the Creep heard the water running and emerged from his half-dozing state. He gently lifted the closet door before opening it, so it would not drag noisily on the floor. He padded out into the hallway and listened at the top of the stairs. The water stopped. He could hear the woman humming an old-fashioned tune—maybe it was "You Belong to Me"—and then the rustling of clothes. There was a moment of silence, then he saw an arm throw the outfit she had been wearing for the house-tour into the wicker laundry basket in the hall. Sensing that she had gone into the bathroom, he slipped halfway down the stairs, then to the hall outside her door. He could see her bare feet splayed out on the tile floor, and heard the first tentative drops in the toilet bowl. She was taking a leak. He hesitated a moment, then remembered the locks downstairs. He turned and descended the remaining two flights to the garden floor. With extraordinary quickness for his size, he moved to the garden door at the rear, then the door under the stoop, and upstairs again to the parlor floor where he went to the front door and the deck door. In each case he made sure that the double locks were set and that he had pocketed the safety keys she had left hanging from the side of the frame so that no one could get locked in. Now, no matter what happened, she wasn't going to get out of the house until he wanted her to.

Unless—he allowed the thick-lipped twisted grin to encroach itself upon his features—unless she carried a spare key ring in the shower.

He then heard the gurgling of water in the pipes as she flushed the toilet. As he stepped to the foot of the stairs, the shower was turned on, and more water began to rush through the pipes. Her insulation was lousy.

He felt confident, almost dreamwalking. He had more time than he had expected. So he found the telephone line that led to the box affixed to the back of the building, and cut it with his Swiss Army knife. As an afterthought, he cut the line again near the wall extension in the kitchen, then cut the curling twelve-foot line from the mouthpiece to the dial. This gave him plenty of cord if he needed to tie her up. Slowly, he climbed the stairs to the third floor again.

The brown vinyl curtain was pulled closed, and one of the fluffy towels, a matching brown, was draped over the curtain bar. Steam came from above the bar, and the water pounded mercilessly against the curtain and walls. He took a step toward the tub, the telephone cord looped over his shoulder, the knife open in his hand, and then stopped suddenly.

Something was wrong.

Then he knew what it was. The water was, first of all, too hot; secondly, it was hitting the walls and curtain with too equally distributed a force. There was supposed to be a female human being in there, her body diverting the spray into spatter and spume.

He whirled, and she was behind him in the bedroom, naked, disbelieving, with the dead phone against her ear, a silent scream tugging at the lines around her open mouth.

He was disappointed. He had already framed the image of her dripping wet in the shower, hair plastered over her eyes, flesh blotchy in the steam. Now here she was, dry, almost parched in appearance; part of it had to do with her age. Clearly, she was older than he had imagined, breasts flat and drooping like the African native women in the Frank Buck Bring-'Em-Back-Alive movies he used to see Saturday afternoons at the Loew's on Flatbush Avenue. And the rest of her was sort of pear-shaped. Her crotch-hair was sparse, and cellulite rippled in waves on her upper thighs.

She was no Samantha or Jerry, that was for sure.

She dropped the phone and plunged toward the stairs. She tripped on the oriental throw-rug in the hall, got up again, skidded in panic as she grabbed the banister and spun down the stairs. She showed no inclination to scream. Otherwise he would have pursued her more diligently, gagged her immediately as he had had to gag Jerry, thus making the beginning of a messier job than he wanted. Preservation took attention to detail.

He walked slowly down the stairs, hearing her try, sobbing and choking, the front door and then the deck opening, where she ran her fingernails in futility down the broad expanse of glass. No one could see her; the high stockade fencing that she had probably installed for security and privacy took care of that. Once again he thought of the Frank Buck movies, remembered not only the naked women, but the men with the loincloths, the black boogie-woogies beating drums, their faces painted, a leopard wrestling with a giant snake; and he heard a madder music in his own heart. He decided to take her away then, before she got her voice back, before she managed to mar or disfigure herself falling downstairs or trying to get a weapon for defense.

He caught her against the deck door. He pulled her away and into the parlor, where he propelled her onto the well-stuffed Victorian sofa with the flower patterns. He dug his knee into her chest, and pressed her arms behind her. Her eyes were wide and flecked with fear. He jerked her head up by the hair and then forced the gag into her mouth. There would be no need for an injection; she appeared to have lost all her strength and will. He tied her up neatly and expertly with the cord—a skill he had learned, along with his hypodermic expertise, in the Army. He found a trench coat in a closet and wrapped her in it. He tied a scarf around her head. He carried her, semi-upright, out to the van, having carefully locked up the house. He placed her in the back, propped up on the mattress. Then he got in the front and drove away slowly. He noticed that the Puerto Ricans, the only people remaining on the block now that the sun was going down, had taken no notice of them. They were too busy trying to hit the whiffle ball in the dark. He drove the van down to the place on the harbor between the Army Terminal and the garbage heaps. And parked. Quick-stepping, he walked around the van and stripped the stick-on florist's sign from each side. He checked out the terrain; no one was in sight. Not that it mattered. With the people who came down to this neck of the woods, it was "See no evil, hear no evil."

He climbed back into the van, into the spacious back. He opened two sixteen-ounce Buds, out of the cooler, held one and placed the other near the mattress. The woman's eyes bulged above the gag.

He drank thirstily. It had been a long wait. He lighted a joss stick. He looked into her eyes. Gently, he removed the trench coat and scarf, moving her up to a sitting position, facing him. He untied her, leaving the gag. He spoke to her for the first time:

"Make any noise," he said, "you get the knife. Be quiet and I'll take the choker outa your t'roat and be nice to you. Got it?"

She nodded, almost eagerly. He undid the gag, straightened her hair. Kneeling, he reached into a box and removed four pills. He put two on her naked thigh, and put two in front of where he sat, a couple of feet from her, cross-legged. Her thigh twitched, and the pills slipped off onto the mattress.

"Pick 'em up," he said. She did.

"You're Page, right? Page Zelenik? Owner of the robust brownstone?"

She nodded.

"Well, my name is Robinson. You might not believe it to look at me, but Jackie Robinson—from the Dodgers?—was my fadder."

Something in his tone gave her a voice: "Oh, yes," she squeaked. "I . . . uh . . . believe."

He looked pleased. "Now," he said, "take them two pills. Then wash 'em down with the Bud. Don't worry. I'm taking the same ones, see." He popped them into the back of his mouth and drank heartily from the can. "Now take yours like a good girl, Page, 'cause we're gonna *party*."

Kavanaugh said, "WVBA just called. She's decided to play ball."

DeSales snorted, "It's about time. She's probably so fucking scared her teeth are falling out."

"She's on her way home now. The tail reports that she ran a red light and then sat parked for a while. Guess that's when she made her decision and called in to the station. Anyway, she's agreed to record two short tapes to be played tonight and tomorrow. She can do them at home now and feed them into the station over the phone. The station will be able to run them within a few minutes of her finishing them. So we just dictate, she records, and we're in business. She has two conditions."

"Which?"

"She wants an exclusive. She doesn't want this stuff to go to any other stations. And she wants the boys watching her to keep as far away as possible. She thinks if he spots a tail he won't call. Which will lose her her story."

DeSales nodded his head briefly. He stood leaning on his desk, each hand an arch from middle finger to thumb. "She can have the exclusive for twenty-four hours. Then we're going to have to go mass-media. You can tell her what you want about the tail. The boys will use their discretion, that's all I can say." He stood erect and slapped the heel of his right hand into the palm of the left. "What about the wiretap and the bug?"

"She says go ahead. Just don't let her know about it. And don't let *him* know about it."

"You know what I like about her, Bernie? She thinks of everything; and while she's thinking of everything, she's also thinking that the rest of us aren't."

"So what do we tell her to say?" Kavanaugh took a pencil from the breast pocket of his jacket, sat on the edge of the chair with his knees bent, almost kneeling, put his elbows on the desk, and prepared to write on the yellow legal pad.

DeSales sat also. He leaned back in the chair, put his feet on the desk, his hands behind his head, and closed his eyes.

"Something *pro-active*, right?" He cleared his throat. "Fed bullshit! Look: Allen says we try to either make him feel guilty. Or pressed. Or both. I've got a better idea. The guy's a show-off; he wants to be noticed. He's got a message. The way you fuck up his cool is to make him think nobody—especially Megan Moore—is getting it. The reason he went to her in the first place was because he liked the way she read him. So let's have her say, somehow, she *isn't* reading him. Or . . ." He jumped up: "That's it: she isn't reading him because she doesn't *believe* him. She understands the police have solid evidence that the crimes are the work of two entirely different killers, and the guy who called her on the phone is just a crank who happened to have the shit luck to know that Samantha Lawrence was a woman who disappeared on Lincoln's Birthday. Maybe she should say that our friend the so-called Grim Graveyard Reaper is just a neighborhood busybody who didn't have the guts to squeal that he knew about a crime until it hit the headlines. *Needle* him a bit, too."

Kavanaugh was scribbling hastily. When he finished, he looked it over, then read it aloud back to DeSales. Together they phrased a rough draft of just what Megan Moore should say on the air. When they were finished, Kavanaugh asked: "And you think this'll flush him?"

"Who knows?"

"You think he might go after *her*?"

"I've been thinking about that a lot. I called Allen about it too. He put it in his computer. The FBI has decided that he won't try to hurt her. She's his medium to the outside world. But he'll try to *prove* himself to her. We can *hope* he won't do it by killing again, but by sending her something, some proof that he's who he says he is. And we've got to hope that in doing this he gives himself away, blows his cover. In the meantime . . . Bernie?"

"Yeh?"

"Call your wife and tell her you're gonna be home late.

Maybe very late. We're going down to my old neighborhood. Where we think Carruthers dropped out of sight. I'm beginning to think the boys we have down there aren't looking in the right places. Or for the right things."

Kavanaugh groaned.

Desmond was sitting up in bed, a notepad poised against his knees, a copy of Norman Mailer's *Advertisements for Myself* at his side. He was preparing a lecture for his class on "Urban Counter-cultures After World War II." He was selecting the passages from the essay "The White Negro" that he would read aloud to illustrate Mailer's points, suggesting their prophetic qualities. He copied the lines: "In such places as Greenwich Village, a ménage-à-trois was completed—the bohemian and the juvenile delinquent came face-to-face with the Negro . . . marijuana was the wedding ring . . . And in this wedding of the white and the black it was the Negro who brought the cultural dowry . . ."

Mona, having finished in the bathroom, came into the room and said, "I came back early because I *had* to see you. I wasn't doing what we promised Dr. Gross we'd do. I wasn't telling you how I *felt*. Instead my words came out sounding like an accusation." On the cherrywood mantelpiece over the non-working fireplace, she began to rearrange the books into symmetrical piles. Desmond continued to scrawl: "In such a pass where paranoia is as vital to survival as blood, the Negro has stayed alive and begun to grow by following the need of his body where he could . . ." He looked up.

"I'm glad," he said. "Maybe we can get back to Square One." He wrote on: "So there was a new breed of adventurers, urban adventurers who drifted out at night looking for action with a black man's code to fit their facts. The hipster had absorbed the existentialist synapses of the Negro, and for practical purposes could be considered a white Negro. . . ."

"Well," she said, "are you interested or not?"

"Of course." He realized he had not made any small-talk, asked her any personal questions. "You get any work done up there, at least?"

"The piano's out of tune again." She seemed annoyed with the question. But she gave a diplomatic answer. "Two jingles. One for that new diet cola." She turned to the pictures on the glass-topped table. She held up the picture of Desmond on their honeymoon, sitting at the cafe in Pamplona with three drunken Scotsmen. The four men wore Basque berets and drank Anis from small pony glasses. There were a lot of glasses on the table. It was during San Fermin. Desmond still had his moustache; it would be another year before he shaved it. Mona replaced the picture, brushing off a speck of dust. "Mitch says I should get a big bonus this year. That, *at least,* should please you."

Desmond could tell from the tone that he would do well to stop working. Hurriedly, he closed the book.

"Well?" she demanded.

"Now you sound pissed-off again." He raised an eyebrow rather than his voice. "I thought you were going to say how you *felt*, instead of going for sarcasm."

"Who's sarcastic now?"

"Forget it," he said.

She folded her arms. "I come all the way down here to tell you how I *feel*; I tell you that's what I want to do, and it isn't easy, believe me; and then you change the subject and keep on taking notes."

He dropped the book, notebook, and pen on the floor next to the bed. First he put his arms straight at his sides, but that made him aware that he might appear passive. Or, worse, satirical. So he locked his fingers behind his head, flexed his biceps, and sucked in his stomach. He wore only a pair of slim boxer shorts with red polka dots.

"You're absolutely right," he admitted. "I was lost in a fog. Now, what *did* you want to tell me?"

She stepped into the large closet, switched on the light, and began to undress with her back to him. "My feelings were hurt. I was scared. I felt dismissed. I wanted you to think of *me* first, not your job or Carruthers or any of this crap about the house. I felt *you were shutting me out.*"

She unbuckled the bra as if she were in a hurry, and stepped out of her underpants. Her hips were broader than they once had been, and the dimples on her thighs had deepened, but this seemed to Desmond merely to enhance her potential for carnality. "I'm sorry," he said. "I certainly didn't mean to."

She turned and casually dropped the pink nightgown over her head. "Good. I'm glad to hear it. It sure didn't *feel* that way."

The old mixture of anger and desire began to bring him down. He longed to devour, and be devoured by, the erogenous zones disappearing under the smooth fabric. He felt at the same time that he had been coerced into an admission of guilt. He suppressed a dozen antagonistic remarks that buzzed at the back of his brain like horseflies against a window.

She picked up a book from the top of one of the piles on the mantel. It was a hardcover Latin American novel that had been recommended the week before in the section of the Sunday *Book Review* that appeared beneath the best-seller list. She put the thick volume on the night table, pulled back the covers on her side, fluffed up the pillow, and said, in the ambiguously neutral tone she had perfected for such occasions, "I suppose you'd like to make love."

"Sure."

His response was so inadequate as a representation of how *he* really felt that a kind of deep swoon took him over from within, as if he were being lowered against his will into a well of lonely shadows. So, in order to arrest this nascent impotence, he reached for her. He first caressed the backs of her knees with his hands, kneaded her buttocks, hiked up the nightie, pulled her toward him at the waist, scratched the area beneath her shoulder blades where, she had once said, the relief from itching was almost orgasmic. He rubbed his nose against hers, which was freckled and turned up slightly at the tip, giving her, up close, an appearance of eternal youth. He brought his hands around to her breasts. He wanted to pop them out of the nightdress, pink on pink, and suck them gently. . . .

She pulled back abruptly: "Gimme a break," she protested. "I've been in bed about two seconds and you're already grabbing my tits. Can't you *relax*? Maybe I want to do it at my own pace."

He was mute for a moment. Then he rolled onto his back, breathing. "Okay, fine. Let's do it your way. I'm happy to let you take over some of the initiating."

She was turning on her reading lamp, picking up the book, putting the pillow against the headboard: "I can't *stand* your *controlling* me that way. It's classic passive-aggressive behavior."

Desmond lay silent, moving his lips without really being conscious of it. She turned a couple of pages, then put a hand out, touched his arm. "Look, let's just write this off to tension. It's been a long time. We need a good night's snuggle together. We can do it in the morning. First thing. Whatever you want. I've already put in the diaphragm."

She squeezed his hand, which remained limp for a moment, then squeezed back. She turned a page.

He was speechless, dangling still in the well, somewhere between rage and uncertainty. He could not even bring himself to tell her that he would not be available for lovemaking in the morning because he had to meet Joe Verb in Greenwood Cemetery.

He tried to read Mailer again, unseeing. Mona put out her light. "*Mañana*, sweetie," she whispered.

When he was sure she was asleep, he slipped out of bed, carrying his book with him. In the bathroom, he looked at himself in the mirror, rubbing the place on his nose where his glasses left their mark. He washed down a Valium with a glass of water.

Downstairs, he drank wine for a while, then set the timer

alarm on the new gas range for five A.M. He lay down on the sofa in the parlor, reopening the book.

Mailer had written "The White Negro" in 1957. That was the year Desmond had discovered B. B. King and Muddy Waters. And Jack Kerouac. And marijuana. It was the year he hitchhiked from Pennsylvania to Provincetown, an early stage in an ultimately abortive assault on hipness, and first saw Norman Mailer in person. The sense that his own history somehow paralleled that which was already written down added a driblet of solace to the tide that was washing over him.

He underlined the last lines he read before closing his eyes, taking sleep head on:

> . . . a muted cool religious revival to be sure, but the element which is exciting, disturbing, nightmarish perhaps, is that incompatibles have come to bed, the inner life and the violent life, the orgy and the dream of love, the desire to murder and the desire to create, a dialectical conception of existence with a lust for power, a dark, romantic, and yet undeniably dynamic view of existence for it sees every man and woman as moving individually through each moment of life forward into growth or backward into death.

And the man who had written this was from Brooklyn.

# CHAPTER 20

SHE KNEW THE TAPES were already being played by the station, but she couldn't bring herself to turn on the radio. She had followed DeSales's instructions more or less literally, and she knew she had sounded sullen and insincere. It was not a performance that would win her an Academy Award, or, for that matter, earn her a network spot. So instead of listening to the radio or watching TV or reading a book or dutifully calling her mother in Sarasota, she decided to straighten out her possessions as a prelude to getting out of Brooklyn. At least the situation she found herself in had given her inspiration to move. It was typical that she had come to Brooklyn to accommodate Sam, and that he had managed to get right back to the city while she, who had never wanted to move in the first place, was left holding the bag.

She wandered back and forth between the guest room, which had been Sam's kids' room and now functioned as a study, and her own bedroom. Once she stopped at her dressing-table and applied some Opium perfume to the backs of her ears. You had to smell nice in order to clean house. Finally she found herself compelled to drag from a closet the box that contained what remained of her first, and only, marriage.

As she was dragging it out, she glanced out the window and saw the white van with the telephone-company insignia on the side panels. Most likely DeSales's idea of a clever and misleading way to set up a wiretap and house-bugging system. If the van stayed there much longer, she would be sure. She wondered where her tail was. Her protection. Probably a fire truck double-parked around the corner on Clinton Street. Something subtle like that. She bit her lip. No, her tail was probably the van too. The police couldn't afford to use two entire vehicles on a mere piece of *bait*. Which was what she had begun to feel like.

She skimmed the surface of the box. The old snapshots, which she usually found embarrassing, tonight amused her: the Bermuda shorts, the Charlotte Ford hairdo, the winter vacations at Sun Valley, Brian doing the Twist at the Peppermint Lounge.

That was his name. Brian. Brian Sadleir. They had met while he was at Princeton and she was at Vassar. It seemed perfectly logical that they should marry after the first year in New York. She had done Katie Gibbs and lived at the Barbizon until she found a roommate and a one-bedroom with a sunken living room in a high-rise on East End Avenue. Brian had gone to Wall Street and done well, living not far away from her. Of course it was logical. Brian had the right background. He had money, and would surely have a lot more. He was good-looking in an adolescent sort of way. He looked quite dashing when he went coatless in the dead of winter, wearing only the Princeton Crew orange-and-black scarf around his neck over his tweed jacket and corduroys. He seemed more interested in her than any other guy had ever been. And he was good in bed. At least he had seemed to her in her state of mind at the time to be good in bed. He rammed it in her vigorously, lasted a long time— sometimes *too* long—and rammed it often. She remembered a clear, bright, October Sunday morning when she had gone over to his studio in the East Seventies, by prearrangement, to cook him Eggs Benedict for brunch. He rammed it in her vigorously four times in the next twelve hours between the eggs (the Hollandaise had curdled), the bullshots, the Giants on TV, the martinis, the Jets on TV, the roast beef he proudly cooked himself on a rotisserie grill his mother had given him as a housewarming gift, the beers, the Sunday Night Movie (she was no longer sure now whether it was *High Noon* or *Gunfight at the O.K. Corral*); indeed he was trying to ram it in her a fifth time when he passed out as Norman Mailer debated William F. Buckley, Jr., on "Firing Line."

Shortly thereafter they became engaged, then married. Megan remembered vividly that among the absolute *heap* of wedding presents were seven identical teak ice-buckets from Bloomie's gift shop.

She could laugh about it all now: her utter stupidity. She had solemnly believed that sex consisted entirely of a man doing his vigorous ramming while she performed an untutored bump-and-grind beneath him until he came. She hadn't thought much about coming herself because it had not been entirely clear whether such a thing was possible.

This memory gave her an idea. She stood and stretched her legs. DeSales's stupid white van was still outside. She went down to the kitchen, found some gin and some vermouth and an old cocktail shaker, and made herself some martinis. She even put two olives in the glass, the way Brian used to. She hadn't drunk hard booze in years, and the last martini she had had was on one of those endless suburban Sundays just before she and Brian had split up. They had by that time moved to the modest but tasteful Colonial in Scarsdale. On these Sundays it was considered *de rigueur* to gather together in the house all available Old Buddies from Lawrenceville and Princeton, Farmington and Poughkeepsie, Martell's and the Madison Pub. Even summer people from Southampton, some of whom they barely knew, came up.

She sipped the martini. She had forgotten how clear, cold, and bracing they could be. She found a toothpick and stabbed an olive, biting into it. Laughing, she went back to the refrigerator and found a jar of cocktail onions that she must have been carrying with her since the days in Scarsdale. She was beginning to realize what a pack rat she was. She had certainly not served a cocktail onion, indeed had not even *seen* one served, since Scarsdale. She added two to the remaining olive in the wineglass and drank rather more heartily. Something was wrong: the *glass*! She searched the cupboards until she found some actual *martini* glasses, long-stemmed, conical, which she had also been dragging around with her all these years. Amused, she finished what was in the wineglass, ate the olive and onions, and made herself another in the *proper* glass, after, of course, washing it.

In Scarsdale, Brian had stopped ramming her so vigorously and so often. At the time, this hurt her feelings. She suspected it had something to do with them trying to have a child. One doctor had said Brian's sperm was weak; another had said her vaginal acidity was wiping out the sperm before it could get into the Fallopian tubes or wherever it was that the egg was fertilized. Brian found it easier to live with the acidic-vagina theory. He seemed to hold it against her. He came home on the train later and later, gained weight, bought a Chesterfield at Tripler's for wintry days, began playing a lot of golf and wearing red pants, and in the warmer weather, no socks under his Gucci loafers with the tassels. When he did condescend to make love, he lay heavily on top of her and finished quickly. If he could get it up at all.

But what had she expected? Errol Flynn? Yves Montand? She no longer resented Brian, because she now realized that he had turned out exactly as he was supposed to. It was she who had changed. She had become interested in broadcasting, gotten a job as a newswriter, disdained the red-pants people, and wanted to move back into the city.

Brian was probably at that very moment telling his third wife (reputedly a rich widow with teenaged children of her own) that his first wife, the one on the radio, had an acidic cunt. Brian had moved to Oyster Bay, was making megabucks selling stocks and bonds to red-pants people on the golf course, and had not let up on the martinis. In her mind's eye she could see his sandy hair thinning to nothing on top, his cheeks pudgy and crimson. He was a sure thing for a heart attack by the time he reached fifty.

Just like her father.

The second drink was even better than the first. As she drained the glass, she loaded it with the rest of the cocktail onions. She threw the empty jar into the fireplace, then the glass full of onions after it. They shattered neatly into the ashes. Two bull's-eyes. That was one way to take care of the past.

Then she spied the tape on the Carruthers kidnapping, which, in all the excitement over the Graveyard Grim Reaper, she had forgotten to feed to the station. It was nothing, really, just a rehash of the previous day's indignation with police inaction. In fact, her producer would be unlikely to even run something so soft.

But as she peeped from behind the curtain at the white van she had an idea. It was an impish idea, a childish prank. It was also a perfectly appropriate way to express her scorn for the police and keep them on their toes. She would feed her tape to the station, but she would do it from the Mobile Unit rather than the tapped phone. And while doing so, she would take a little ride.

Back upstairs in one of the closets, she found the black veil and dress that she had worn to her father's funeral her sophomore year at Vassar and had been neurotically clinging to ever since. She undressed and put the dress on hurriedly, struggling a moment as she pulled it over her hips. She found the black low-heeled pumps at the rear of the closet and stepped into them. She set the hat at a perky angle and pulled down the veil. In the mirror she looked like Gale Sondergaard playing the Spider Lady in a Sherlock Holmes movie. She was in disguise.

She turned out all the lights in the duplex and stood silently in the foyer, waiting for the perfect moment to slip away unnoticed. Or, better yet, noticed *too late*. There was no evidence of life or movement in the telephone-company van. She wondered if her protectors were asleep. In a way, she laughed to herself, she was contributing to her own safety, keeping the snoopers on their toes.

She slipped out the door and into the car, which was parked just in front. Without turning on the lights, she started up the engine and eased away from the curb. She turned onto Clinton and drove slowly north, toward Brooklyn Heights. At Pacific Street, she turned on her lights and stood on the accelerator, just beating the red light at Atlantic. She looked into the rearview mirror. First she saw nothing, then the white van peeked from behind two cars that had stopped for the light. It edged into the wrong lane, trying to sneak around after her, but was confronted head-on by an angry horn-blowing Cadillac that had just turned off Atlantic.

She decided to play cat-and-mouse. She dawdled along, making sure her watchers were able to keep her in view. She called the station on the two-way. Her producer sounded outraged: "You're *out*? You're supposed to be waiting by the phone. What if *he* calls?"

"He can try again. I want to feed some tape." She punched in the cassette and hit the switch. At Joralemon Street she turned left, then left again on Henry; at Atlantic she turned right, and then took another right on Hicks, back into the Heights. A perfect zig-zag. The tape, only ninety seconds, had been fed. The producer called on the two-way. She pushed the button. "Where are you?" he wailed. "I've gotta let the cops know."

"They already know, dummy; they're *following* me. Don't you remember? I'm under *surveillance*." She cut him off.

A short while before, and quite nearby, DeSales and Kavanaugh had begun their own zig-zag pattern, working their way south from Butler Street in Boerum Hill, crossing back and forth over the Gowanus Canal. It was a no-man's land, lying between Park Slope and Cobble Hill. They traversed the bridges at Union,

Carroll—where Jerry Jacuzzi had been found—Third, and Ninth streets. The east side of the canal, particularly below Carroll, looked more like a wasteland in New Jersey or L.A. than part of the Big Apple. There was a disused church out of Edward Hopper, and a trailer rental firm called "Hitch City." There were junkyards, industrial spaces littered with tow-motors and pallets; graveyards for defunct buses, postal trucks, sanitation vehicles. At this hour of night the entire area appeared to have been drained of humanity.

"No wonder they call it the Basin," said Kavanaugh. "It feels like we're below sea level and all the water in the harbor is liable to rush in."

"When I was a kid," answered DeSales, "I always felt, whatever direction I went, it was *up*."

On the west side of the canal there was mean residential housing, foothills for Cobble Hill and the Heights.

"Once this was Red Hook," said DeSales, "but now they're calling it Carroll Gardens. Like it?"

At the Smith Street stop of the IND, where they theorized Carruthers had left the F train, DeSales had Kavanaugh let him out of the car and trail him slowly. DeSales walked a block west on Ninth and then up Court Street, stopping in a dozen saloons and Italian Social Clubs. After five or six blocks he cut back toward Smith. Catty-corner from Carroll Park, he disappeared into a row house. For fifteen minutes, Kavanaugh sat in the police car and watched with detached amusement as four young Italian men had a fight on the streetcorner. Each wore jeans and a white strap undershirt. Each had his sideburns shaved off and had combed his black hair straight back from a low forehead to the nape of the neck. Each had apparently sustained at least one injury before the present altercation began. One had a cast on his foot. Another had an arm in a sling. Another had a supportive collar around his neck. The fourth had a large plaster over his eye. Each wore shiny white band-aids on assorted parts of his body. After a while, Kavanaugh realized that the fight was not a formal two-against-two affair, he had assumed at first. It was instead a random free-for-all. Any one of the pugilists appeared to be free to punch or kick or gouge any other one. When DeSales emerged from the house, the one with the cast had tripped and stumbled to the pavement, and the other three had fallen on him like beasts of prey.

DeSales said, "Smart boys. *Cugines.*"

"Must make you proud to be Italian, Frank."

"It does, Bernie, it does. I once saw three Irishmen in your old neighborhood, East Flatbush, having a contest as to which one could punch a brick wall the most times before he busted his hand. This was after the glass-eating contest, of course."

Kavanaugh saw that DeSales was smiling.

"You got something?"

"My aunt Sally does. The guys in the bars and social clubs aren't talking to cops these days. Even *paisanos.* I think we've been too hard on some of their benefactors recently. But Aunt Sally comes through."

"Yeh?"

"She says there are two groups of new people around here. Both weird and undesirable. The first is the brownstoners from Manhattan. They pay too much for the houses; all the landlords are raising the rents; the *salumerias* are calling themselves gourmet shops; even the pizza has deteriorated since they started coming in a few years ago. And, worst, they got no morals; don't even go to church."

"C'mon Frank, you're teasin' me. Who else is new?"

"Nuns."

"Nuns?"

"Nuns. Two of them. One black, one white. What's different about them is they don't always wear their habits. Some days they're Sisters of the Immaculate Heart of Mary, some days the white one is a punk rocker and the colored one is half-naked with her hair braided like a pickaninny. Aunt Sally says she'll take the brownstoners now any old time. She thinks there's gonna be an invasion of hippies from the East Village next. A lot of her friends are talking about moving to Bensonhurst. Or further out."

"These nuns are alone?"

"Good question, Bernie. Aunt Sally isn't exactly sure, but her friend Rosemary says she saw them one day with a little Jewish guy and a very big guy who looked like, and I quote Rosemary now, 'a white nigger.'"

Kavanaugh whistled: "Where do they live?"

"Aunt Sally isn't sure of that either, but she knows it's down further into Red Hook. Rosemary isn't home. Aunt Sally says everyone will be at Mass tommorow, it being Easter and all, and she's sure to find out there." He shrugged his shoulders. "We may as well wait. I can't raise the men to do a house-to-house tonight anyway. If Aunt Sally can't find out in the morning, I'll do it then."

His beeper sounded. He switched on the two-way radio.

"Jesus Christ," he swore, "Caruso and Jackson have lost Megan Moore. Somewhere in the Heights. Let's go."

Megan Moore crossed Joralemon, heading north through the most charming, and expensive, and WASPish blocks of residential housing in Brooklyn. She saw that the van had picked her up again and was now maintaining a respectable distance, about a block behind.

Suddenly she felt tired, tired of playing games. An undercurrent of fear had begun to seep into the buoyancy. The martinis were wearing off. She needed sleep. She opened up the line with the studio again: "Hold on," she said. "I'll let you know what's happening in a minute."

She saw the sign for Grace Court. She felt like a bad little girl who wants to be caught. She was going to catch hell from the cops, and she wanted to get it over with as quickly as possible. She just hoped DeSales wasn't in on this personally. She turned left into Grace Court. That, being a dead end, would bring the merry chase to a sudden halt. The van pulled after her, closed on her as she approached the barrier at the end of the short block that separated the street from a parapet above the Brooklyn-Queens Expressway. She had forgotten how dark a block it was. Unlike most of the Heights, which is composed of four-story row houses and tiny carriage-houses, Grace Court is lined with pre-war apartment buildings, which cast long shadows even in bright daylight. And the streetlight at the end was out. She decided to take the offensive defensive. She braked suddenly, slipped the car into "Park," and jumped out to greet, disarmingly, her angry bodyguards.

And, indeed, at least one of them appeared upset. The driver emerged and moved quickly toward her. She could almost hear his teeth gnashing. As he got closer and her eyes adjusted to the darkness, she had a momentary glimpse of a wild-eyed and most peculiar face. The man, now caught in the blinding headlights from the van, appeared to be blond or even white-haired. His features were distinctly, even exaggeratedly, negroid, but his skin was milky white. As he caught her up in his grasp, she imagined that he was albino, mongoloid, pink-eyed, deformed, but then his hand clamped over her face and she felt quite light, swept away like a feather in a wind. He had beer on his breath.

He carried her to the rear of the van and threw her inside. There was no one else; she was alone with him. She tried to stumble forward, but in one motion he caught the black skirt from behind, ripping it half off, pulled the rear door shut behind him. He loomed over her. She knelt before him, looking up, thinking now that his face resembled that of a prehistoric fish, a picture of which she had been asked to write a spot in-class essay on in Freshman English. His voice, as she expected, was that of the Creep:

"So, *bitch*," he rasped. "Ya said on the radio that ya don't believe me. Here," he lifted her roughly by the left arm, "have a drink before we get on with the evenin'." She tried to shake her head. He pushed her backward, and she realized she was leaning against an old-fashioned Coca-Cola cooler. "Open it up, get a can of what you want, and *drink!*"

Keeping an eye on him, she tentatively pushed back the sliding door on the top of the cooler. She touched the freezing water, and heard the rattle of ice cubes. This was strangely reassuring. He took her by the shoulders, turned her around to face the opening, and flicked on the ceiling bulb. He forced her arm deeper into the water. There was a can of Budweiser floating with the cubes, and, inexplicably, a piece of fabric. Then, from beneath the opaque surface of the water, in the weird half-light, she saw something coming to the surface, like a ghost in a nightmare.

"Grab it."

The pressure of his hand on the back of her neck was incredible. She grabbed, she recoiled as if she had touched an open electrical current. She tried to scream, but the enormous hand seemed to have clamped her windpipe shut. The head of a human being, a woman, a dead woman, a face grotesque and frozen in fear, bobbed to the surface of the water in the cooler, next to the beer can, like a Halloween apple.

"Neighborhood busybody, huh," he hissed. "This'll show you who I am."

Megan Moore lost consciousness.


Sirens wailed as the patrol cars converged, from Atlantic Avenue, from the BQE, from Adams Street near Borough Hall. DeSales, grim, stared into his double espresso inside the café, watching the lights whirling on top of the cars up and down Montague Street.

"You gotta believe us, Lieutenant," said Caruso. "It was really weird. A broad, looked old, came out of the house in a black dress and a veil. Jackson saw her first." Jackson nodded; there was sweat in the depression between his lips and his proud, Ethiopian nose. "But we didn't make a move or anything. Why would somebody we were protecting make a run for it?"

"We were parked across that little plot of grass in front of her house," Jackson added. "We figured our first priority was to get to the house if anyone went after her. On foot, it would have taken about ten seconds to the door. Maybe seventy-five yards."

"It was my fault," said Caruso, who always wore a "Kiss me, I'm Sicilian" button when he worked in plain-clothes. "I parked going the wrong way. We had to do a 'U-ie,' and it was a tight squeeze. By the time we got on Clinton she was gone. She went like a bat outa hell. All we know is she headed north. Up here." His gesture took in all of Montague Street; the glitzy chrome of the café, the bright row of pubs and ethnic restaurants and boutiques.

DeSales sat back. His face twitched: "When this is over, there'll be an investigation. I'll accept the findings of the panel. *Now*, you got the plates, the description of the car?"

Kavanaugh said, "Yeh"; the two detectives across the table nodded.

"You two can stay up all night; I don't give a shit when your shift ends. I want you to drive up and down Brooklyn until you find that car. And, of course, *Ms.* Moore. Tell the siren-heads out there to calm down, go back on their rounds, but to concentrate on the car too. Broadcast it to all the precincts."

"Shall we put together a special force for the Heights?"

"Why? There's no cemeteries, the people call nine-one-one if there's as much as a cat-fight in a back yard, and I'm sure our guy can't afford to live here."

"Check."

"Get going."

He turned to Kavanaugh wearily. "What'll it be, Bernie? Do we do anybody more good by getting some sleep, or by going down to Red Hook—pardon me, Carroll Gardens—and rousting about through the wee hours for our nuns?"

"I gotta go home, Frank. I'd stay on if it would do any good. But it's Easter already and we don't even know if the broad is in trouble. Maybe she just don't want to cooperate. She apparently left that house on her own volition, and the entire N Y P D for the borough is on alert for her. Get up in the morning and be sharp. You got your job for your brains, not for knocking on doors in the middle of the night."

"Sometimes I wonder, Bernie. I give in. See you at nine."

"Ten, Frank. Gotta go to Mass at nine. One of my kids, the one who wants to be like Michael Jackson, is a lily boy."

# CHAPTER 21

DESMOND AWOKE FIVE minutes before the alarm was to go off. He had a headache, and the acidity of the wine lingered unpleasantly on his palate. His ankles were weak.

He also felt stupid. Somehow he had managed to get nothing he'd wanted the night before, and then had compounded the situation by making sure that he would be ill-prepared for the morning as well.

He went back upstairs to shower and dress. In the half-light peeking through the shutters, he could see that Mona was curled up on her side, facing the wall, mouth open. He could not resist going to her. He crawled under the covers and pressed lightly against her. The warmth from her rear radiated into his pelvis and throughout his body. He had one of his infrequent realizations of how much he truly loved her. These epiphanies, as now, inevitably occurred under the most difficult circumstances. And it was not just the enduring physical attraction that informed his emotions. He loved her laugh, her intelligence. The happier early years nourished him; she had supported him through thick and thin, and her loyalty provided a constant underpinning.

And her only demand of him, really, was that he somehow attempt to recalibrate his sexual affections, marry the physical and emotional in himself, so that she could sense that her feelings were being consulted, so that she was given the freedom to get what she wanted.

And he wanted to give it to her. The problem was that what she wanted was neither quantifiable nor concretely communicable.

It was puzzling. He could tell her what *he* wanted, though he seldom did because she seldom asked. He could cite specific positions and activities that pleased him. He could produce pornographic descriptions or pictures that illustrated quite graphically the needs that fed his fantasies. But she could not, or would not, do this. In fact, it somehow offended her that he was capable of such a quantification of the act of love. She relished mystery. She, at the same time that she declared a commitment to giving him sexual pleasure, seemed most determined to flaunt her option to say "No."

But her nay-saying was a tricky issue. He had learned in couples therapy that she, and indeed most sexual partners, would go along with most anything if he overtly and directly stated his need. The problem was that having to *ask* took away the excitement. He wanted sex to just happen, the more at her unsolicited initiation the better. He wanted her to read his mind.

He was becoming aroused. He moved closer to her nakedness, where the nightgown had remained hiked up after his clumsy attempt at seduction the night before. He backed off a bit and moved around, against her thighs and buttocks, praying that she would awake in a heat of passion.

He wanted her desperately, but he could not bring himself to rudely, directly, wake her up and tell her so.

He would give her five minutes to come to on her own, to wiggle her butt with pleasure against him, to turn and press her open mouth on his, while fondling him here and here and here, and then taking him inside her to satiate *her* compelling need for *him*. If she would only do this in the next five minutes, he would stay with her, never shut her out again.

And he would forget completely about Joe Verb and the little suicide mission he had conceived for himself just before the Valium had taken hold and he had drifted off into a troubled sleep.

He thrust himself slowly between her thighs and kissed the back of her neck.

She stirred. She mumbled something, she backed up against him, intensifying the erotic tingle. She purred.

The purr turned into a snore as she flung the sheet aside and rolled onto her back, throwing the limp back of an arm over his neck. She was dead asleep.

He would have to force her to wake up, but he couldn't do it.

He got out of bed and went into the bathroom, where he brushed his teeth, resisted the impulse to masturbate, and took a shower instead.

He headed out to meet Joe Verb.

Yoo-Hoo wore the same cut-off tank-top and short shorts. Birdie, as was her habit on warm evenings at home, sleeping or waking, wore only bikini underpants and her spike earrings. They sat on cushions on the floor of the room where the closet was where they held Carruthers. Yoo-Hoo's legs were sprawled out in front of her, flat, in the shape of a V. Between them lay the nine-millimeter Browning semi-automatic, the silencer mechanism, the plastic bag of Sensimilla and a packet of Zig Zag rolling papers. She licked the glue part of the joint she had just rolled, sucked the neat cylinder from end to end, lighted up, and inhaled deeply, holding it daintily between thumb and index finger aloft about six inches from her right ear, her head thrown back, showing her teeth. When she finally exhaled, no smoke was visible. She handed the joint to Birdie.

Light had begun to break through the grimy window, highlighting the otherworldly orange in Birdie's hair. As she smoked, she held her bunched-up knobby knees to her chest with one arm and wriggled her toes. The nails were painted purple today.

"This is *great* shit," she said.

"The only thing in this bloody country that's improved since I arrived. Really."

"Yeh?" Birdie's eyes had a kind of glazed solemnity, enhanced by the no-nonsense hook in her nose. Yoo-Hoo had once asked her if the nose had given her her name; she said that she couldn't remember. Names, just the same, appeared to be on her mind. As she passed the cigarette back, she squinted behind the trail of smoke, and asked, "Why'd they call you Yoo-Hoo? Like 'Hello' or somethin'? Or what?"

Yoo-Hoo flicked ash into the bowl she had fashioned out of tinfoil. On a paper plate between them were the remains of the food they had eaten while alternating sentry duty during the night: apple cores, peach pits, cans of Tab, banana peels, spicy Arab seeds, a cup of Lo-Cal raspberry yogurt.

"It was with the Weather Underground. We made a movie. I had a thing with one of the grips. He said he'd call me 'Yoo-Hoo' 'cause I was 'sweet and chocolate.'" She beamed.

Birdie knit her brow: "You ever want to go back to England?"

"Listen, sister, ever since I watched the riots in Chicago, '68, on telly over there, I knew I had to be *here*. This is where it's at. I dumped my family in Trinidad, I dumped colonialism in England where they sent me to convent school to be a running dog for the Establishment. . . ."

"But," Birdie persisted, "sometimes things aren't really *together* here, right?"

Yoo-Hoo stood and strode around her in circles. She nodded her head, sagely: "Only really bad times I've had were when we tried to establish some solidarity with the Black Liberation Army. I mean, it was *logical*; we were all fighting the military-industrial complex." She paused, smoked, waved the joint, "But those were some bad dudes, really. Sexists. Treated women as slaves. In bed, especially. 'Course, the white chicks loved it. . . . But those guys were nothing but *criminals*. I mean, you've got to draw the line *some*where."

"Was that when you met Joe?"

"Put it this way. Joe had a house. He let the B L A use it as a hideout. One day he found they were also using it as a heroin factory. Hey, I'm eight miles high. I better not smoke any more." She offered the joint to Birdie, who waved it away. She butted it gently in the tinfoil, and dropped it into the Ziplock bag. "Joe didn't like that one bit—especially the way they used the local *nigra* women at slave wages to cut the stuff. And I wanted out anyway. So we split over here. Joe just left them the house. It wasn't worth bargaining over anyway. Mmm. They were some *bad* dudes. We took some weapons and military shit, what we got around here, and they got a *house* in return. But Joe has lotsa houses, and we needed the hardware to get into some heavy overt political action on our own. Like our friend in there."

She pointed the gun at the closet door. "Pow! Pow! Pow!" She pretended the semi-automatic was recoiling mightily in her hand.

Birdie was thoughtful. "Tyrone's a criminal," she said.

"How do you know?"

"I saw his tattoos once. All his tattoos. Real jailbird stuff. Attica, Riker's."

"You been making it with him?"

Birdie shook her head slowly.

"Thank heavens. You had me worried there for a moment. I can't imagine him doing anything of the sort. . . ."

Birdie was still shaking her head, dreamily. "I saw him coming out of the shower. He got real mad. He's got a *tiny* one, for somebody who's *colored*."

"Who knows what color he is? He's a freak."

"Now, *he*," Birdie nodded toward the closet, "has got a *big* one."

Yoo-Hoo waved the gun again.

Birdie went on: "And he doesn't have no tattoos. I don't like tattoos. My Uncle Sal had a tattoo, a snake with a forked tongue that said 'Korea' on its back."

Yoo-Hoo looked up: "Uncle? I didn't think you had any family."

"This was my last *foster* family, dig? Bensonhurst."

"Or Benson*hoist*, as Tyrone says."

"They was Italians. Name of Grappa. They only took in white kids. Since there ain't many loose white kids around, I was usually the only kid they had."

"Get lots of attention?" Yoo-Hoo had taken on a kind of maternal air.

"Yeh." Birdie shivered a minute. She vigorously scratched her shoulder, then drew her knees up again, covering her boyish figure from the elements. "Lots of attention. When Gina wasn't beatin' up on me, Sal was makin' me jerk him off. He liked me to call him 'Uncle.' It was great."

"You go to school?"

"Off and on. New Utrecht." She pronounced it "Nootrek." "Mostly I played hooky. That's one of the reasons Gina beat the shit outa me."

"You have fun playing hooky?"

Birdie shrugged her shoulders: "You know Gravesend Park? Mostly we hung out there. And in some playgrounds at night. The people . . . it was like around here, except without the brownstone types. Italians, lotsa screaming. The guys . . . the *cugines* . . . they got fancy cars, gold chains, comb their hair a lot, fight a lot, do a lot of uppers and downers."

"But was it fun?"

Birdie thought hard and long. "There was this one playground near my house. Near Eighteenth Avenue and Sixty-Seventh Street. I was fourteen, fifteen? There was about thirty of us. The guys used to deal a lot, so the girls would hold. Especially me. I looked younger than the other ones and I was blond and had blue eyes. Looked innocent." She smiled broadly. Her teeth were remarkably straight, but two were missing.

"Hey, that was fun, and I had a lot of respect. I was the best holder they had. I used to get paid in organic mescaline. I liked that. A lot."

"And that was all?"

"Nah! Now it's comin' back. One of the guys would sell downers to a pillhead. We'd watch the deal. The pillhead would walk over to the water fountain. We'd watch him swallow the pills, and then we'd start to count. One, Two, Three . . . The pillhead would begin to stagger, stumble—we'd still be counting. Eleven, Twelve, like that. Maybe it was Tuinols. There was a lot of them around in those days. Then the guy'd just get to a bench and sit there. Sometimes one of them would just fall out on the blacktop. And we'd finish the countdown, cheerin', y'know. We could tell who was selling the strongest downers by how long it took his customers to crash. The best part was if the guy completely crashed instead of just goin' into a stupor. If he was sitting on the park bench, out cold, the guys—the same guys who sold him the stuff—would nail his clothes to the bench. Sal and Gina used to think I was nuts 'cause I laughed out loud in bed at night. I was really imagining the guy waking up and finding his clothes nailed to the bench." She rocked back and forth, profoundly pleased with the memories.

When she finally looked up, the glaze was off her eyes. They were misty and sparkling: "I want that baby," she said.

"And I want to make my political statement," Yoo-Hoo said. "I'll help."

"Okay, bloody hell, I'll help you. What time is it?" She got up and went to the window, the baubles at the end of her corn-curls jingling. "The sun is up completely," she said. "Joe's selling us out at his great summit-meeting in the cemetery right now. And Tyrone will be covering him. They won't be back for a couple of hours at least. Joe *can* talk." She attached the silencer to the weapon. "You got the key?"

Birdie nodded, rose, stretched, her rib cage starkly prominent, and removed a key from her underpants. She stepped to the closet door. "Joe's gonna be mad."

"So's Tyrone. Fuck 'em."

Yoo-Hoo screwed on the silencer, trained the barrel of the gun on the door: "Let's elicit some *sperm* from Professor Carruthers. And then some *blood.*" She tittered: "When I write the story of my life, that's what I'll call it. *Sperm and Blood.*"

Birdie was eagerly turning the key.

# CHAPTER 22

EASTER MORNING HAD dawned, and the mist hovered thickly over Greenwood Cemetery, obscuring the Gothic spires atop the main gate. Desmond took in only the stone engraving at the entrance, of Christ in the sepulcher, with the inscription, "The Dead Shall Be Raised," before joining the small and motley group that constituted the Sunrise Tour. The guide, a tall, slender, fiftyish woman wearing a tweed hat and sensible shoes, was saying: "There are more than fifty-three cemeteries in the city. Greenwood, at 478 acres, is largest. In fact, there are more people below ground than above in New York. You might say we are a City of the Dead rather than the Living." One of the group guffawed, and the sound became eerie in the heavy air, as if it had drifted on its own out of the murk. The guide had a colleague, a short, bald, red-faced man in sneakers. He added, redundantly, "A necropolis."

Joe Verb was nowhere in sight.

They began to climb a sloping paved road. The guides lingered first with melancholy fondness over the chapel, which was an imitation of Christopher Wren's Thom Tower, Christ Church, Cambridge. It had fallen into disuse. "People just don't bother with the extra service at the cemetery nowadays," lamented the man. He scratched his leg, revealing that he wore high black dress socks with his sneakers. Then they paused again, this time to note proudly the old underground receiving vaults, archways covered with ivy, where in the nineteenth century the bodies of those who died in winter had been hermetically sealed up and preserved until springtime for burial.

"We just didn't have the technology to dig the frozen earth," said the man.

"Still useful," uttered the woman. "A couple of winters ago there was a gravediggers' strike, and the old vaults did quite nicely for the time, thank you very much."

"Why, they kept Charles Pratt in there for *several* years in the 1890s, before the family could concur on a final resting place."

"Charles Pratt," the woman added, "was a crony of John D. Rockefeller. Refined kerosene in Greenpoint. Built Pratt Institute. And those magnificent houses on Clinton Hill? Gives you an idea of the social cachet of Brooklyn a hundred years ago that one of the world's richest men would choose to give each of his sons a choice of locale and house when they were married, and they chose Brooklyn. That area is slowly regentrifying, as I'm sure most of you know."

The man waved a finger, "But the *last* son chose Park Avenue and Sixty-Eighth Street, in Manhattan, for *his* nuptial palace."

"Times change," she sniffed, "and change again." She shrugged her shoulders, and set off uphill with a long no-nonsense stride. Visibility seemed to be reduced at each level of higher ground. In the fog, the parklike greenery of the graveyard was transformed into a dense and ominous magic forest. Crows cawed in the weeping willows. The tombstones scattered on the gloomy slopes stood like shrouds of lost souls. Desmond decided to lag behind. It was possible that Verb was waiting for him to isolate himself from the others so that their rendezvous could be completely private.

The tall woman was recounting a tale of a giant snapping

turtle that reputedly inhabited Sylvan Water, a large pond whose desolate unrippled surface lay below the path on the right. She called back to Desmond: "Don't get too far behind. There are twenty-five miles of twisting narrow roads in here, and, I regret to say, we've lost a number of our clients." The snicker doubled back on itself and then echoed again from the silent water.

They passed mausoleums, catafalques, sarcophagi. One of the latter had been built by a "soda-water king" who had decorated his tomb, before his death, with an entire bestiary. Desmond marveled that he should, at this stage in his life, encounter not only an unfamiliar vocabulary, but an idea associated with dying—this incredible self-conscious, self-aggrandizing memorialization—that he had never really considered before. He wondered what Mona might do with his remains if he should not return. The only conversation about death and burial he could remember having with her in eight years of marriage had been a sneer they had shared over a Catholic friend who insisted that he wanted to be viewed in an open casket at his wake. Desmond suspected that Mona would consider that their social and professional status dictated a cremation with a minimum of fuss. They were, after all, the *new* gentry. He scoured the bushes and marble edifices for some sign of Joe Verb, but got for his trouble only the sense of finding himself at the heart of an unfathomable mystery, the myths of so many religions and periods of history entangled in this mishmash of stony symbolism that the line between the natural and supernatural had become conspicuously opaque.

The fog was holding it together, in a suffocating sort of way. Yet implicit in this intuition was the contradictory suggestion that when the fog lifted, when light penetrated the mystery, they might all shrivel into nothingness, like creatures in a science-fiction film. And the paradox was aggravated by the litany of historical personages resting in Greenwood recited by the guides: Lola Montez, the international courtesan who shocked the Western world with her notorious Spider Dance; William S. Hart, the Hollywood Cowboy; the Roosevelts; Horace Greeley, the publisher, who, contrary to popular opinion, did not say, "Go West, young man"; De Witt Clinton, Samuel Morse, Henry Ward Beecher, Tiffany of Tiffany's. The facts undermined meaning, rather than otherwise. Desmond re-experienced high-school history courses, in which the details tended to run together just as the gravel in a septic field will inevitably turn to sludge.

Nervously, he edged closer to the group.

The chubby man stood before the elaborate tomb of a girl who had died mysteriously at her seventeenth-birthday party well over a hundred years before, wearing a dress, now recreated in stone, decorated with seventeen forget-me-nots. He was holding forth on the overt symbolism of nineteenth-century graveyard statuary. A lamb stood for infant death. A truncated column stood for a vigorous life rudely and unexpectedly terminated. A sphere suggested completeness; with wings, the soul flying to heaven. To Christians of the Victorian era, the ever-present obelisk was synonymous with hope, or aspiration to higher things.

"Of course," he concluded, "we know, as did the Romans, that it looks more like an erect phallus than anything else."

His face got redder. There were a few hearty laughs, but mostly silence. The woman began a dissertation on the enormous burial plot of the Pierreponts, "Brooklyn's first gentrifiers."

Desmond felt a tug at his arm, and Joe Verb, wearing a peaked seaman's cap at a jaunty angle, was standing next to him. "Gentrifiers," said Joe, "means robber barons. Just like today. The Pierreponts made millions developing Brooklyn Heights, then tricked the city into stopping the street plans at Twentieth Street and putting a fence around this area, at the *city's* expense, so they could build a fancy park for *dead* rich people. There were a lot of living poor people who could have used the land for housing instead of dying of cholera on the Lower East Side. . . ."

". . . parkland cemetery trend, initiated at Père-Lachaise in

Paris and Mount Auburn outside Boston, arguably refined to its zenith here at Greenwood," the woman was saying, "can also be seen as an inevitable development of the Romantic Movement and the glorification of nature and individualism. . . ."

"Like Lenin said," Verb seemed to be finishing a thought, begun in the middle, " 'A Marxist is one who *extends* the acceptance of class struggle to the acceptance of *the dictatorship of the proletariat!*' "

Desmond pulled Verb by the arm until they stood, partially obscured from the tour, under a double-flowering cherry tree of great age. Buds were just beginning to peep from the ends of the branches. "I'm beyond abstract analysis, Joe. Cut the bullshit. Where's Carruthers?"

Verb's eyes danced playfully. His gaze, when it fixed itself, seemed to alight at a point just over Desmond's shoulder, as if he were watching for a signal. Desmond realized that Joe was not only his normal, manic, slogan-spouting self: he was more scared than Desmond himself had been. And he was distracted to the point of being perhaps crazier than Desmond had guessed.

"Guarantees," said Joe. "We need things in writing. To release to the media. What's your bottom line? For bargaining? What's the city willing to put up?"

"The city, Joe? What's the city got to do with all of this?"

The tour moved forward onto higher ground, and the two old colleagues from the Urban Institute followed at a safe distance. The haze began to break up, and scenes of the harbor, like isolated pieces of a jigsaw puzzle, drifted into view. The outlines of the skyscrapers of lower Manhattan remained obscure, giant tombstones hovering over the water, megaliths emerging from a dark and undecipherable past. Desmond understood now Verb's eagerness on the phone. Verb thought that the city government or the police had sent Desmond to negotiate officially, if *sub rosa*, with Verb's "army" for Carruthers's safe return.

"Joe," he said, "I'm here on my own. I'm not dealing for the city."

The woman guide interrupted her prepared discourse to observe: "Ah, there's the view. Thank heavens. This is the highest point in the city, and I wouldn't want you to miss it. Imagine a hundred years ago. All you could see from here was farmland to the south and east, and, towards the city, communities of row houses punctuated by churches. Think of the paradox: the architect, Upjohn, who designed the Ruskinian main gate here, also did Trinity Church. Yet later architects have built commercial buildings, higher than mountains such as we stand on, which now surround Trinity Church, obliterating it from the view which was selected so one could look down on it."

Verb was caught in mid-sentence, waving his arm over the hillsides of graves. Inertia carried him to the end: ". . . the *ultimate* bourgeois commercial creation." Then he finally heard what Desmond had said: "What?" he squawked.

"I said I came here on my own, Joe. Ever since Carruthers disappeared, I had an idea you might be in on it. And . . ."

Verb's face fell slowly. Then he brought his teeth back in line, making a chomping sound. He had some trouble swallowing. He clenched his fists but seemed unable to decide in which direction to strike out. Finally he was able to speak:

"You mean the establishment *still* isn't noticing, taking us seriously?" He kicked at the tree in vicious disappointment. "I should have listened to Yoo-Hoo. I'm gonna go back and blow out his fucking brains right now. Dump him on the Brooklyn Heights promenade. Then they'll know we mean business."

"Joe, I have a better idea."

"What?" He looked on the verge of tears. The tour began to move along. Verb looked over Desmond's shoulder again, a hint of panic in his eyes, then walked ahead, keeping pace, with his head down. Desmond put his arm around his shoulders.

"Give it up, Joe. I'll go with you. We release Carruthers. Maybe we can reason with him not to press anything. I know the cop in charge. I'll take you. If you let go now, there will probably only be a suspended sentence. And Joe, I know I forgot you. Too long. But maybe I can make it up. Get you a job . . ."

Verb pushed his hand away. "Are you shitting me? This is a big rap. I'll never walk. And me get a *job*? Are you *shitting* me! After this . . ." He took two quick, long steps downhill, as if ensuring the distance between his own purity and Desmond's decadent offer. He spat: "And what do you think I *am*! You think I'm doing this because I need a *job*. So I can do what you do and schmooze the poor bastards into thinking they're getting a fair deal while you're really setting them up for a fall?"

"There's truth there, Joe. But I'm doing something. Besides, if you feel that way, why pick on an egregious asshole like Carruthers? Neither he nor anybody else ever really pretended that he was going to teach Remedial English. Why not kidnap someone like me, then? I play the role of the concerned patriarchal type, and if you're right, lead people down the garden path. Why aren't I a symbol of Bureaucratic Insensitivity to the Needs of the People, or whatever it is you're trying to destroy? I've even got a gentrified house in Park Slope. I evicted eleven drunken old men so I could live there."

For the first time ever, Desmond saw Joe Verb truly speechless. The tour had gone out of sight, and silently, compliantly, they moved together to catch up.

They turned a corner, and the sky seemed to open up, the panorama of the entire harbor lay before them, and Desmond caught his breath: there was the Statue of Liberty in the center, still greenish-blue but trussed in scaffolding, like Gulliver by the Lilliputians, for the projected clean-up; the Jersey docks; Staten Island, looking rural and undiscovered, still secretive about its urbanization; the tugs, yachts, ferries, and cargo ships; the Wall Street skyline phasing into the working-class façade of commercial Brooklyn as far north as the bridges. All of this presented a spectacle at its heart ineffably banal, as if a kaleidoscope of postcard clichés had been inverted, and all the dramatic tone, the pulse and bustle, the skyline etched in progress, had been reduced to a monotony that suggested that monotony and life itself were a continuum, interchangeable, indistinguishable from one another. . . . No wonder these people in Greenwood had gone to such expense, such chicanery, to preserve their images in marble. . . .

When they stopped, Joe's lips were moving without sound. He kept searching the higher ground behind him with his eyes. He seemed to have found what he wanted. Desmond turned to see what it was. Verb spoke loudly, as if he thought Desmond were deaf, "It won't do, Tim. You'd better get out of here. You're not what we want. . . ."

"Will you excuse us, gentlemen. Your little chat is making it difficult to be heard. . . ." chided the guide.

Desmond pulled Verb aside, turned their faces to the harbor, where their words would be lost in the wind. He saw Verb glance past his ear again nervously, then turn and make a furtive gesture over his own shoulder. The words of the guide wafted more sonorously than ever down to them with the wind: "And here is the tomb of James Gordon Bennett, the rowdy and sensationalistic newspaper publisher who sent Stanley to Africa to find Livingstone in eighteen-sixty—" Her voice faltered; there was a shout, then a kind of whimpering scream. Desmond and Verb, as one, by instinct, began to rush forward. Then they saw the woman strung up on the rusted iron cross, wearing only what appeared to be an ill-fitting brassiere. On the other side of the path, the male guide had gone down on one knee in front of Bennett's tomb, as if he were genuflecting in the direction of the adjoining Madonna. On the headstone itself rested a tape-deck and car radio with the letters "PROPERTY OF WVBA-FM" emblazoned in Da-Glo tape. Then Desmond, standing between the cross and the tomb, noted that it was not a bra but a piece of cloth that had been draped along the crossbars, over the woman's breasts, not unlike the conventional representation of Christ with INRI on a parchment over his head. On the cloth, in red ink, was inscribed: "Go West Young Woman."

The woman guide leaned against a stone: "He got the wrong

one," she gasped. "The wrong publisher. It was Greeley who . . ."

Desmond realized that Verb was no longer beside him. Downhill, toward the harbor, he saw the little man scurry into a copse of bushes. It looked as though he was with someone else, someone very large. Desmond began to run, clumsily at first, but he was wearing his jogging shoes and did three or four miles in the park most mornings, and began to glide as soon as he adjusted to the terrain. Verb turned and saw him coming on, prodded his companion, and they both took off further downhill. The chase became an obstacle course; where there were no tombstones, there were plantings. Some bushes were prickly; some masked the rest of the hillside. Desmond lost his prey. He came to a pond, smaller than the one with the snapping turtle, and caught sight of Verb's cap disappearing further into a tangle of undergrowth. He circled the pond, took a chance and struck out in a more vertical descent, hoping to cut them off further down. He vaulted a sarcophagus whose marble was deteriorating badly on the windward side, and came upon an open mausoleum. Cautiously, he crept up on it, but found within only the remains of a voodoo picnic—several empty bottles of cheap wine, bones, a chicken's head, mounds of ashes, bloodstains spattered about. He charged ahead and emerged on an open slope not far above the main gate. He saw Verb and his friend creeping slowly around the back of the disused chapel. When they were out of sight, he raced over and peered out from behind the corner they had turned.

The larger one produced a key and opened the heavy, creaking door of the nineteenth-century receiving vault. He held the door open and allowed Verb to precede him inside.

At some subliminal level, Desmond realized he had reached a moment of truth. He had come for a purpose, to donate himself to a worthy cause, to subject his psyche to a test by fire; to test, if truth be told, the devotion or commitment or pity of those who were supposed to be close to him. It was an old sacrificial dirge, a dithyramb of self-pity mixed with aggression. He had taken some steps; he had to take at least one more. Looking over his shoulder to make sure he wasn't seen or followed, he sprinted to the vault door, and got his arm in just before it closed. The large pale man with the negroid features allowed the door to open again, staring at him agape, seemingly unable to react to such boldness. Tim Desmond walked into the burial vault, and the chill of the catacomb air raised goose bumps on his skin. The mortuary shelves were stacked atop one another; the ceilings were high. His face framed in flickering candlelight like some malevolent elf, Joe Verb sat at a makeshift table against the far wall. Desmond heard the door shut, with finality, behind him.

Verb put his head in his hands: "Oh, shit, Timmy, now we *are* gonna have to take you with us."

# CHAPTER 23

"Is it up yet?" asked Yoo-Hoo.

Birdie made an unintelligible sound from deep in her throat. She came up for air: "Nope, but he sure is a mouthful."

Fletcher Carruthers III lay on the closet floor, naked, his hands behind his head. "One thing," he declared, glancing up at Yoo-Hoo, "is certain. As long as you insist on pointing that weapon at my head, you are unlikely to achieve your desired result."

Yoo-Hoo spun the pistol in her hand like a movie cowboy, and answered in a contemptuous Western drawl. She was a woman of many voices: "Listen up, pardner, if Birdbrain here hadn't saw that goldarned TV show about the sperm bank for geniuses in California and decided she needed to have a baby by one, you'd be pushin' up daisies already."

"Genius! I'm flattered."

"Don't be. You just happen to be the closest she's likely to get to one."

"Shit!" Birdie snapped her fingers. "I forgot the magazine." She rushed out into the room and returned in a moment with a copy of *Playgirl*. "This is the best I could do on Court Street.

There's some real hunks in here . . . but no hard-ons or hairy assholes. I guess Brooklyn don't have enough faggots yet for the stands to stock the real stuff. Like I seen in the Village: *Buns, Blue Boy, Home of the Whopper.*" She flipped pages until she found the centerfold and then handed the magazine to Carruthers: "C'mon, give it a try. I never did too good in school. I wanna have a smart kid of my own. *Real* smart."

Carruthers appeared momentarily diverted by the slick glossy photos of nude men. Birdie resumed her administration of the various techniques of arousal she had first been taught by Uncle Sal and had then put into general practice with various and sundry *cugines* behind the park benches of Bensonhurst. But still to no avail.

Yoo-Hoo yawned, leaning against the door, pistol drooping slightly in her long fingers: "I'm losing my patience. And this makes me bloody *angry*; it dramatizes the female predicament. We can be raped. He can't. Unless I shove this Browning up his bloody arse. . . ."

"That won't get *me* knocked up," Birdie moaned.

Carruthers delicately laid the magazine aside. He was a surprisingly wiry little man, with a hairy chest and legs. "Pictures do little for me. I prefer live action. Now, if you were to get that big rough lovely friend of yours. Tyrone? I'm sure I would be absolutely throbbing in no time. There would be no difficulty, at the moment of ejaculation, planting the seed in Birdie, if we keep her at the ready. . . ."

"Tyrone would break all of our necks if he knew what we were doing," said Birdie.

"So shut up," snapped Yoo-Hoo. She trained the gun on Carruthers's flaccid organ. "Try playing with yourself for a while."

Carruthers sat up suddenly. Yoo-Hoo's finger tightened on the trigger. Quickly he held up his arms in a gesture of surrender as he propped himself against the wall. "This is preposterous," he said. "And mortifying. Look, can we negotiate?"

"What?"

"Well, *negotiate* may not be the right word. I'm not exactly dealing from strength. I mean *cooperate*. Look, just please don't wave the gun at me and I think I can help you get me in the mood. Then, maybe . . . maybe I can rely on your good will later. Will you listen to my proposal?"

Birdie looked imploringly at Yoo-Hoo.

"Besides," Carruthers went on, "it must be obvious to you by now that I am a complete and total coward. Physically, at any rate. I know that deceiving you or trying to bolt will only increase my chance of suffering a violent death. Or just *pain*. I prefer to throw myself at the mercy of your female sympathies. Which are, I know, both tender *and* strong."

Yoo-Hoo paced to the other end of the closet. It was a relatively large area for a place to hang clothes, about eight feet long by four feet wide. Carruthers and Birdie, both small people in any case, took up only about a third of the space. Her head lay on his thigh. She continued to caress him, but without enthusiasm. Finally, Yoo-Hoo said: "The joke in all this is that you have no choice. I can promise anything and have no obligation, moral or practical, to carry it out. You understand that you are completely at my disposal."

"I certainly do. I don't even mind. I'm putting myself in your hands. It seems safer, because I think the men in your organization are not playing with full decks in any case."

"You're not the only one. Okay, what's your plan?"

"You're attempting to accomplish an experiment in, shall we say, genetic *engineering*, but without an *engineer*. Without a conductor, so to speak."

"Yes?"

"I can be that person, as well as a participant. You see, just as you are politically interested in dominance, I am sexually fascinated, not to say titillated, by the topic. I have done extensive research on it, both in pornographic books and films and in firsthand experience. Indeed, one of my best recent articles is a comparison between dominance techniques in homosexual versus heterosexual pornography, traced from 1860 to 1980. It should appear in the fall in a new journal I am editing, *Erotic Signifiers Quarterly.*"

Birdie looked at him, skeptical. She had never seen a guy get a rod on as a consequence of an intellectual discussion.

"Okay, genius," urged Yoo-Hoo, "you've established your credentials, now let's get down to the nitty-gritty." She looked at her watch. "We've got less than an hour to pull this off safely. If we get caught, someone's head is going to roll."

"I need some leather. These handcuffs won't do." He indicated the manacles he had been held in, and which Birdie had released him from as Yoo-Hoo had first trained the pistol on his head. "Nice long strips of leather, if you can."

"Get Joe's jacket, Birdie. The one that makes him look like something out of Sacco and Vanzetti. He promised me he'd throw it out anyway. Makes people suspicious. And bring a scissors."

Birdie did as instructed. When she returned, Carruthers had her cut the coat into strips. He tied one of these around each of his wrists, rather expertly, in spite of the fact that he had only one hand to work with. "One of the problems was that you released me from my bonds. But I like leather better anyway. I am more easily stimulated while tied up. If it is done properly. Now," he turned to Yoo-Hoo, seeking permission, "we need to fasten a kind of noose or collar around Birdie's neck. May I?"

Yoo-Hoo, for the first time, appeared interested. "As long as I've got the gun on you and you don't make any quick or fancy moves."

Carruthers tied a thick strand around Birdie's neck, fastening it with an elaborate Boy Scout knot. To this knot he attached a long strip that clearly was to function as a leash. "In the bondage shops in the Village," he said, "and even these days among the nominally heterosexual punk-rockers, one can easily find elaborate versions of this simple device, some with spiky collars and the like. But I think excessive gimcrackery suggests a diminishing commitment to the end itself, don't you? And the end, as I'm sure you are aware, is to elicit the maximum sexual response from the complex human psychology which informs dominant-submissive relationships, with leather bondage as both symbol and catalyst."

"Right on," said Yoo-Hoo out of the side of her mouth.

"Does this mean I'm gonna get hurt?" asked Birdie.

"Not to worry," said Carruthers. He pulled the leash left, right, and back, as a test of the pressure points, watching Birdie's head move with each tug on the collar. "Do you get it now, Birdie? You're a slave. I'm the master. But it's only pretend."

"I've seen this shit on the rock videos. All the time. I saw it once on the Muppets, even."

"Now, Yoo-Hoo, here's where you come in. But I'm afraid of the gun. So I don't want you to think I'm pulling a fast one. I need your help, but I also need your confidence that everything is legitimate. First I want Birdie to get down on all fours, like a dog. Or horse. Obviously, for the purpose she desires, I don't want to see *her* front, only her rear, from which perspective she cuts a trim boyish figure in any case."

"Light up that joint," said Birdie. "I need a toke."

"Not a bad idea," concurred Carruthers. "The aphrodisiacal qualities of *cannabis sativa* have aided me a number of times."

Yoo-Hoo dug a half-joint from her shorts pocket, lighted it, smoked some herself, and passed it around, eyeing Carruthers that much more keenly.

"So, Birdie gets down. Good. Buns up. I won't violate you anally, but I'll fantasize to myself that I'm going to. Now, *I* need to be tied up. Crucifixion, by the way, is my favorite position." He held his arms out, leather straps dangling from his wrists. "See," he nodded toward his genitals, "I'm already starting to get a bit perky."

"You want I should run out to the local Catholic church and bring you a cross?"

"That won't be necessary. There are clothes-hooks behind me. See? Just tie as tight a knot as you can to each hook. So you won't have to worry about me getting loose. And"—he looked demure—"because I *like* it that way."

Yoo-Hoo took the joint from Birdie's mouth and stubbed it on the wall. "Turn around, Birdie. Hold the gun on him while I tie him up." Her grin was sadistic. "I read once where cutting down the circulation stimulates the orgasm."

"Right," said Carruthers. "At least two acquaintances of mine were listed as suicides by the police, when in fact they accidentally hanged themselves while practicing that particular form of autoeroticism. Of course, it saved face for the families. The suicide verdict, that is."

"I don't wanna get hung. I don't even wanna come. I just wanna get knocked up," wailed Birdie.

Yoo-Hoo tied triple knots of leather on each hook, then tested the knots and the hook by pulling the thong as hard as she could away from the wall. They held. Then she threaded the other end of the strip through the loops dangling from Carruthers's wrists, pulled it through again, then a third time, fastening the two strands together with a square knot. His arms were spread as if in flight, his wrists firmly anchored to the hooks on the wall. "That should do it," she said. "Not that it matters; I've got you in my sights every second."

"It's good. Tight enough to cut off some of the circulation, but I can still get enough movement to have the sensation of leading Birdie's head on the leash." He clutched the end of the leash in his fist. "Oh, damn!"

"Now what's wrong?"

"I'm too high to get into her. Bring in that bench outside the door, the one you always make me sit on. She can kneel on it."

Yoo-Hoo pulled it in. Birdie climbed onto it on her knees, stuck her buttocks up in the air, and lowered her face onto the wood, showing her neck like an animal signifying submission. Then she backed into him like a truck into a loading platform.

Carruthers did a tentative bump-and-grind against Birdie's backside. He turned down the corners of his mouth with displeasure. "Sorry, you chaps," he said. "Not quite enough." He winked at Yoo-Hoo: "It's a long way from tumescence to Tipperary, eh?"

Yoo-Hoo's hands were on her hips; in the crazy shadows of the closet, her bosom rising under the tank-top, her pelvic bones protruding over the waistband of her shorts, she was more than ever the sensual tropical goddess. Carruthers kept smiling:

"I've *got* it," he said. "It's you. Yoo-Hoo. You're too *much* of a woman. I can appreciate your qualities in the abstract, but, frankly, there's nothing that turns me off so much as swollen breasts and female buns peeking cutely out from their shorts. And I like hairy legs. Yours are like an Indian. Too smooth. You've *got* to cover yourself up."

Yoo-Hoo aimed the pistol between his eyes. Then pointed it, clowning, into her ear. She crossed her eyes: "You're driving me *crazy*. But I promised Birdie. Cover myself with *what?*"

Carruthers contemplated this, eyes closed, as Birdie wiggled against him.

"I saw some military uniforms in the basement," he said finally. "And a gun-belt, with ammunition?"

"Right. Jungle fatigues and weaponry. If we have to fight guerrilla style. Like the Viet Cong."

"*Perfecto*. There's nothing that excites me more than a military man. With a shiny belt and polished brass. The works. I've risked my life for the taste a number of times. Barcelona, Marseille, the bars outside Quantico. Even Key West has some nice rough trade in uniform."

Yoo-Hoo leaned back in resignation: "Birdie, take off the collar, go down to the basement, and get me my combat gear. We'll give him one more chance to get his rocks off. If he doesn't, I'll get them off for him. *Shot* off."

Carruthers had become more erect with each inch of Yoo-Hoo's flesh covered by the camouflage material. When she had pulled the green beret over her forehead, thus removing the last trace of corn-curls, adjusted the gleaming X-shaped bandolier over her chest, and tightened the shiny black belt, he said, "I'm ready if you are. But you'll have to assist me in getting in."

Yoo-Hoo had to steady herself by putting her weight on her

knees at the front of the bench as she leaned across Birdie's back. She dug her left elbow into the girl's rib cage, using it as a platform to keep the pistol steady. With her right hand she hefted Carruthers's elitist, 170-IQ phallus, probing and pulling until it was securely lodged within her revolutionary colleague. She then backed off, but continued to lean forward, knees against the bench, part out of a healthy natural voyeurism and part as a cautionary tactic against any funny business on the part of the hostage.

Carruthers at first made some small tugs on the leather. This caused Birdie's head to move up, then from side to side against Yoo-Hoo's olive-and-tan thighs. It also prompted Birdie to begin to raise and lower herself on him like a carousel pony, causing the desired friction. This went on for some time. Carruthers watched the action of the noose and the gender-free crack between Birdie's cheeks to keep himself up. He also kept an eye on Yoo-Hoo for signs of distraction, while Yoo-Hoo showed an increasing interest in the movement of his hands and of Birdie's rear end.

When he finally detected a loosening of Yoo-Hoo's finger on the trigger, the possibility that he would indeed pull off his scheme successfully moved his level of arousal up a notch. Birdie felt it and began to intensify her movements. Carruthers emitted a deep croak that he hoped would evoke images of total abandon, then shouted, "Here I come!" Birdie, desperate to fill her womb with genius, almost orgasmic at the prospect, let herself go. Her hips began to gyrate wildly, and her bucking managed to throw one of Yoo-Hoo's knees partially off-balance at the bench. Carruthers, taking note, thrust his hips forward as violently as possible, propelling the crown of Birdie's skull into Yoo-Hoo's groin. Yoo-Hoo grunted in pain, reaching for the spot. At this moment Carruthers, as he had planned, released himself from the trick knots on his wrists, which he had prepared to slip at the slightest outward pressure. Yoo-Hoo's knots, of course, were still securely fastened to the hooks, and the hooks to the wall, but his wrists had never been secured. He jerked with both free hands as mightily as he could on the noose around Birdie's neck, almost garroting her, and raising her onto her knees on the bench until she completely covered him from Yoo-Hoo. Using the wall as a base, he put his foot into her backside, pushing her off him and hurtling her into Yoo-Hoo. Her long nails tore at the shining rounds of ammo that had flattened Yoo-Hoo's breasts. There was a snakelike hiss of the silencer, and quantities of Birdie's skin and bone and muscle and innards were splattered on closet walls, a large portion of her back apparently blown off. By this time, however, Carruthers had already ducked, and was scrambling out the door. He turned the key in the lock as Yoo-Hoo struggled to disentangle herself from Birdie's corpse. He switched off the light and hit the floor, doing a low crawl, scraping his palms and his knees on the floor as the silencer hissed again and again and the hail of bullets went over him and crashed into the walls. Yoo-Hoo wailed in fury and frustration.

As soon as he got out of the room, he stumbled to his feet and ran. At the front door he turned the bolt, hesitated, wondering if he should try to cover his body somehow. No. They would be after him. Yoo-Hoo could shoot out the closet lock. Joe and Tyrone might at that very moment be returning from their appointed errands. He needed the police, some sort of public attention, fast. And the fastest way to do it would be to run into the streets of a residential Brooklyn neighborhood on Easter Sunday morning, stark naked.

He opened the door. The air was thick and humid, but fresh. He wrinkled his nose and squinted. He sprinted joyfully in the direction of a church spire.

# CHAPTER 24

LIEUTENANT FRANCIS DESALES, of course, did not go home to get a good night's sleep. He went back to the office and waited for the phone to ring. He had been attracted to Megan Moore, but she gave off distinct danger signals, so he had walked out on her. In retribution, she had neglected to share evidence with him and had, indeed, denounced him on the radio. When he did manage to coerce her cooperation, he had set her up as bait, what someone might see as sitting-duck status. Then his men had allowed her to evade surveillance, and now she was lost. It looked vindictive, not good at all for the Force. It didn't look good for him either. He could imagine what that station of hers would do with it. They would bust his balls. Indefinitely.

And, speaking of balls, he had to admit—if only to himself—that he still had a bit of a yen for her in that direction.

He certainly couldn't foresee sleeping. Until she was found. In whatever shape.

But the phone did not ring, so he got a little compulsive. He began to pore through, to no avail, the files of past unsolved murders, which Maceo Allen had told him not to bother with. He called Aunt Sally, waking her up and getting Rosemary's number. He dialed Rosemary, but there was no answer. At three A.M. Easter morning. Maybe she was away for the weekend. He would probably have to go to the parish church next morning and just buttonhole people. At St. Mary's Star of the Sea, where his mother had received First Communion, been confirmed, and belonged to the sodality, before she married his father and moved across the Gowanus to the other parish, Our Lady of Peace.

So then he wandered around headquarters and rousted every idle cop, assigning nitpicking tasks. It was a cliché, maybe, but the real answer to police work was attention to detail. And the more fastidious he could make this attention on this particular night, the lighter the burden on his conscience would be. He had Daly at the front desk call every station house in Brooklyn to ask again if anyone could remember any similar funny business in cemeteries. Maybe one of the cops had just returned from vacation, or a bender, or had just been in a daze the past few days. Daly, at the same time, could kill two birds with one stone by making sure that each precinct was continuing to press the search for Megan Moore's car.

He found Shultz sleeping in one of the stalls in the men's room, his fat ass on the toilet seat, his feet on his desk chair, his head propped against three pillows with Star Wars covers on the toilet tank. Shultz was the Task Force's Patrolmen's Benevolent Association rep. He was a refugee from marital discord. His wife had thrown him out of their tidy white cottage in Mahopac when she had found, in his glove compartment, part of his legendary collection of pornography. This part happened to be a videotape of Shultz and an unemployed showgirl of Chinese extraction in Vegas during the PBA convention.

The Star Wars pillows, originally intended for holiday overnight visits from grandchildren, were part of what Shultz referred to as "The Settlement." That is, they were among the

linen and toilet items that his wife had hurled after him as he
scurried out of the house to his car on the night of "The
Discovery."

DeSales now sent Shultz, grumbling, down to Red Hook to
see if any cops or informers or perps in the overnight cage had
noticed the nuns and their entourage. Then he harassed Caruso
and Jackson on the two-way for a few minutes. He called
W V B A and abused the girl who answered the phone. He demanded the station-manager's home number, finally got it—
somewhere in Fort Lee—and then decided there was no point
in calling the guy until the morning.

He was getting jumpy. He paced around his desk. He looked
at the maps. Aunt Sally's voice resonated in the back of his
mind. He thought of her moving to Bensonhurst after three
generations of family had lived in the environs of South Brooklyn. That is, after *some* of three generations had *chosen* to stay
there. The ones, like himself, who had assimilated—or alienat-
ed, as the case may be—didn't count. But what about the Aunt
Sallys and Uncle Tonys who wanted to stay in the old neighborhood, keep up the old traditions, outdated and impoverished
though they might be, and were being driven out of what was
once a slum, or blue-collar ghetto, by upscale readers of the
*Times* and *New York Magazine* with their Volvo station wagons
and Montessori schools and natural-childbirth classes and psy-
chotherapy and fish mousses made in one-tenth the time by
food processors? What about the people further out, with even
lesser expectations, who would then be driven, riven, apart by
Aunt Sally and Uncle Tony, who were, after all, reasonably
prosperous and capable of some selectivity and renovation in
their housing? It was a domino theory of urban development.
He began to think about Uncle Tony, who had made the best
living of anyone in his mother's family, or her in-laws', by
commuting to Manhattan each day before dawn to carve up
sides of beef in the wholesale meat market on the Lower West
Side. The experience of visiting Uncle Tony there after his

mother had had to go away, and his father was gone, and he had become Aunt Sally's charge most of the time, seemed to have taken on some deep meaning, was trying to send him a message relevant to his current predicament, to this domino theory, when the phone finally rang. He snatched it up: "DeSales here."

"Saint? You weren't home, so I figured you might be gettin' in some overtime."

"Roz, I told you . . ."

Roz seemed uncharacteristically elated. She interrupted him with a mock falsetto laugh: "I *told* you never call me *at the office.*"

DeSales was not amused: "So why are you doing it?"

"Two reasons: the first legitimizes the call." She became relatively solemn. "I found out something that may help you with that Jerry Jacuzzi case."

"Yeh?"

"Remember nobody knew where she'd spent the day on Christmas Eve? Well, I was talking to a would-be colleague of hers, a pimp in fact, who of course doesn't want to talk to you. He says she was down and out and was begging him to take her into his stable. So he says to her, 'Start tonight.' Christmas Eve is a big night, very big, in the profession, right? All these johns parked out front with the blue spruces in the trunks. She says, 'Fine, but I may be a little late. I have an appointment.' She gives him an address and phone number where she'll be if he needs her early. It's a club—the Restoration Society—where they look at different houses that have been fixed up and then have chitchat over coffee about how to do it. She never showed up. For the pimp."

"Give me the number."

She did. "But I tried to get them this afternoon. There's a recording. Says nobody'll be in until Monday."

"Okay."

"But that's not what I *really* wanted to tell you." Now her voice rose again. "I been calling you at home since I found out."

"I'm real busy, Roz; I got here at least two, maybe four or five homicides, and I'm trying to hold the line on the next one."

"I'm quitting."

"Huh?"

"Quitting. Selling my ass. I got a *job*. A *straight* job."

"So you couldn't tell me, like, next week?"

"You sure can be a prick, Lieutenant. Listen, maybe it isn't sinking in. I get my degree from Hunter in June, right? Well, I went to a jobs conference the other day. I didn't tell you about it when I was over your house 'cause I didn't want to raise any false hopes. At this conference, there was this guy from one of the city agencies. He told me there was a private group in the South Bronx working with delinquent teenage girls there, needed a psychologist, willing to take someone with a B.A. if they went to school at night for the master's. And it had to be a *black woman*. Affirmative action, dig! So I hustled my *sepia* butt up to the South Bronx today and I met with all these rich Fifth Avenue *philanthropists*. And they hired me. On the spot. And Saint, get this, I'm getting *forty grand* a year. They not only needed a *black* woman, they needed her in the upper salary scale to balance the payroll or something, so I make top dollar. It must be as much as you make, right? Of course, it's a drop in income for me, but I own the loft and I can cut back on clothes and taxi fares; I should do just fine. Saint, you're silent. You mean you aren't gonna let *me* take *you* out to dinner? Look, I'll still do what you want, in the hay, like, but . . ."

"I got a call on the other line, Roz. I'll get back to you. After the holiday."

He hung up. There was no call on the other line, and he doubted he'd ever get back to her. There was a good thing lost. Next thing, Roz would want him to take her home to meet his family. He thought of his mother and shoved that away as quickly as he could.

He made a false start with his hand in the direction of the files on the desk. He began to get out of the chair, another unfinished gesture that suggested he was about to continue in his compulsive nitpicking with the night staff. Instead he plopped back into his seat. The prospect of losing both of them, Roz and Megan Moore, in one night, after having lost so much before, when he was a kid and unable to handle it, had taken the wind out of him. He was exhausted. He rose slowly and made his way to the cot that was kept for him in the anteroom. He lay down and closed his eyes and, it seemed later, almost immediately began to dream about Uncle Tony's butcher shop.

In the dream Uncle Tony, who was bald and kept an unlighted cigar in his mouth all day at work, was delivering a lecture about the various cuts of meat, their values and salient qualities: filet, sirloin, eye of the round. Uncle Tony wore a bloodstained apron. He held a side of beef balanced precariously on a butcher block at his side. He asked if there were any questions. DeSales, ten years old, asked, "Where's my mother?" Aunt Sally was there, at his side. She made a series of mute Italian gestures. She shook her limp palm. She made the sign of the horns, index and little fingers sticking out and middle fingers bent into the fist. She rotated her extended index finger in fast circles near her ear. Uncle Tony began to hack wildly at the meat, saying, "I'm goin' for the filet. It's the most expensive cut." Pieces of fat and meat and bone flew off the carcass; aged blood splashed the walls. On one wall was a map of Brooklyn, the same as the one on the wall in the Violence Task Force office. DeSales, feeling very tender and vulnerable, cringed at each reckless amputation, as if he, and Brooklyn, were being torn asunder, devalued. "They're making us eat the cheap cuts," complained Aunt Sally.

DeSales awoke in a sweat. Aunt Sally's image was still with him. He went into the bathroom and found Shultz once again asleep in his stall. He ignored him, splashing cold water on his own face. He retied his tie and combed his hair. He went back out to the map on the wall. The sense that remained from the dream was one of anger, revenge. All over Brooklyn, Aunt Sallys were being driven out, either by blockbusting, which meant ghettoization, or brownstoning, which meant gentrification. He imagined a painful odyssey, a diaspora of the multitude of ethnic groups that had given Brooklyn its identity: from South Brooklyn to Bensonhurst, or Bushwick, or Brownsville, or East New York, or Canarsie. He felt an empathy now with the maniac he was pursuing, a man backed up to the ocean, like the British at Dunkirk. At some point you had to bail out. Or fight back.

He turned to the window and lifted the shade. It was daylight.

Then the phone rang, and all hell broke loose. They had found another woman, another corpse. In Greenwood Cemetery. As yet unidentified. He screamed to have a car waiting for him at the door. He went into the john and shook Shultz awake and told him to get over to St. Mary's Star of the Sea. After he shaved and changed his clothes. He called Aunt Sally and told her to meet Shultz there and to introduce him to the most voluble and sharp-eyed members of the congregation after each of the Easter Masses. He ran down the stairs and leaped into the patrol car. Siren screaming, they sped southward to Greenwood.

Tyrone had wanted to ice the tall dude with the round Peter Prep glasses who had followed him into the vault. Since it was a sure thing he wouldn't get to use the place for business anymore, they might as well dump him in one of the boxes that slid into the wall and leave him there. It would take the fuzz about two days to find the right box. He chuckled to himself. But Joe seemed to have some kind of thing for this guy and said if they just held him for a little while everything would be okay. Joe *knew* things weren't going to be okay, ever again. This was all right with Tyrone, since that was, basically, the way he had intended it to be, but he didn't see why Joe had to get so fucked up in the head about it. Joe was always blowing it out his ass about being underground, about being invisible. Now he could really put it to the test. The way Tyrone figured it, Joe and Yoo-Hoo, whom he didn't really like or trust—you couldn't ever trust one of *them*, even if they were English, sort of—could go as far underground as they chose, get as invisible as they chose. He would take Birdie and make sure she got on her feet somewhere pretty far away. New Jersey, or Staten Island maybe. He didn't want her to go back to the angel-dust creeps in the East Village where he had found her. Birdie deserved a break. She'd been fucked around with the way he and his mother had, and he felt, like, protective about her. They would probably have to move fast. That was one reason he wanted to eliminate this Desmond character. And now, instead, here he was, sort of keeping an arm on Desmond in the back seat of Joe's VW while Joe kept blowing it out his ass about nonviolence and that shit.

The trouble was, Joe always meant what he said, and he'd bailed him out a couple of times, so he owed him, owed him maybe an extra fifteen minutes. For old times' sake. Then he and Birdie would get down to the van maybe and split. When they took Desmond out of the cemetery, by going over the hills on the Prospect Park side, the place was already getting lousy with cops. Still, you had to say this for Desmond. He'd just gone along without making a sound, didn't even try to make a break for it when they had to climb the fence at Twentieth Street and Eighth Avenue and Joe had got his pants caught on one of the iron pickets.

Joe was really pissed off because of the broad, Page Zelenik. He didn't even want to know what kind of person she was, why he had hung her on the cross. He didn't seem to understand that she was, like, a sacrifice to the cause. After all, it was Joe who had first told him about Community Control and how there were Brothers out there who believed that "political power comes out of the barrel of a gun." That was back in the semester he had spent at the Institute for Urban Studies, just after the Divine Light Mission and before Riker's Island, as part of Joe's

ETO program ("Elevate the Oppressed"), and one of the other
dudes in the class had given him the paper with the poem he
had memorized:

ARMY 45 WILL STOP ALL JIVE
BUCKSHOTS WILL DOWN THE COPS
P38 WILL OPEN THE PRISON GATES
CARBINE WILL STOP THE WAR MACHINE
.357 WILL WIN US HEAVEN
AND IF YOU DON'T BELIEVE IN LEAD
YOU ARE ALREADY DEAD

The poet who had written that was pretty good, he thought,
even if you had to mispronounce some of the words to get the
rhyme. His name was Huey P. Newton, Minister of Justice. It
was later on that he noticed that the paper was from the Black
Panthers and was entirely for niggers, and he said something
about this to Joe and Joe told him he had just as much right as a
nigger to feel angry about things like Community Control. Or
something like that.

That had been a long time ago, and then a year or two ago he
had run into Joe again, in front of the Community Bookstore on
Seventh Avenue in Park Slope. Joe was handing out leaflets
against some landlord who was forcing people to move so he
could raise the rents. Tyrone could get into that. And he liked
the way Joe kept harassing the professor- and lawyer-types who
came out of the store with fancy new books and expensive toys
for their kids. And Joe even went in the store and grabbed this
paper they were selling, *The New York Review*, and started
shouting about how such highbrow bullshit wasn't for the *people*, it was for the phonies and liberals from Manhattan who
liked to blow it out their ass at cocktail parties and in lecture
halls. Tyrone could get into that, too. So he had stayed in his
own businesses, but did his overtime hours for Joe, and everything seemed all right until now, where Joe seemed to be kiss-
ing the ass of this guy who looked like one of the people in the
Community Bookstore, and was bad-mouthing *him*, Tyrone, for

getting everything ass-backwards when he had just put into action all of Joe's theories.

Community Bookstore, Community Control. It could really fuck you up getting them straight.

Joe drove up Fourth Avenue in the left lane, only he went slow. Joe was a terrible driver. Then they crossed the Ninth Street bridge and pulled up in front of the house. Joe turned to him and said: "You've ruined the dream, Tyrone. We were finally getting our point made, and you blew it. Why in the *fuck* would you kill anyone? That poor woman!" He turned to Desmond: "We'll have to talk, Tim. I feel responsible for Tyrone. I signed him out of an . . . institution . . . a halfway house a couple of years ago, and I don't know what to do now."

"And Carruthers?" asked Desmond.

"He'll be released. There's no point. I just have a responsibility to the people who have stuck with me. And to Tyrone. I'm beginning to be afraid he never quite understood what I was telling him. I think he read me wrong."

Tyrone knew then that it was Joe who should go next. He was talking about him the way they did in school, and the Army, and the hospital after he walked from Riker's: as if he wasn't there. But he held it in; he took Desmond by the arm and pulled him out of the cramped back seat. Joe opened the door to the house and did his funny All-Business duckwalk inside. Tyrone prodded Desmond. Then he pulled the door shut behind them. As soon as the door was closed, he knew there was something funny going on. There was, first of all, a kind of silence there never was in that house with Birdie and her friend Yoo-Hoo around. There was also a smell. Gunpowder. And the lights were on in the other room, though the fog had completely lifted and the sunlight streamed in the windows front and back. Tyrone rushed forward, elbowing Verb aside. He took the derringer out of his boot. He leaned on the doorjamb of the rear parlor. He saw Birdie lying in the closet; a pool of blood had collected between her spread legs. He checked the house, upstairs and down. It was empty. He found a note pinned on the wall: *T & J— Not my fault. Too heavy a scene to stick around for the last act. Gotta split. Up the Rev, —Y-H.* He heard Verb sobbing in the back room; he went inside and saw Verb leaning over the body and Desmond retching in a corner. Joe looked up at him; his face was twisted out of shape. He said: "You had to kill her, you . . . You must be a *sex* maniac. This is no political misunderstanding. What did you do with Carruthers? You black *bastard.*"

Tyrone had had enough; it was inevitable that this would happen. It had happened everywhere else, sooner or later: Sunset Park, Bushwick, East Flatbush, East New York, all the way to where his mother was still hanging on. He knew in a flash what he would do. He picked up Verb by the throat and began to strangle him. He had never realized before how weak the man he had listened to for so long was; the weakness of Joe's flesh caused him to desist just before he cracked his neck. And then he saw Desmond begin to dash for the door. He dropped Joe, caught Desmond, chopped him on the side of the head, and kicked him in the balls. Desmond didn't go down right away, stronger than he'd expected, so he chopped him again. Joe lay on the floor. There were a number of ways to kill him— the derringer, the icepick, a chop to the windpipe—but he realized, looking at the empty face, that he couldn't kill the guy, because he *knew* him. They went *back* together. And then he thought of Yoo-Hoo and wondered if the bitch and her nigger friends had done this, taken Carruthers for themselves, if she would now try to do something to him, to his mother, and he realized he had to hurry.

"Why'd you do it, Tyrone?" Joe moaned

"Community Control," said Tyrone, without irony. "Power to all the people." Then he kicked Joe in the forehead and watched his eyes roll back. Joe would be out long enough for Tyrone to get away clean. First he picked up Birdie and carried her gently to the couch. He closed her eyelids. He straightened out her legs. He found the hospital gown that Carruthers had been wearing and covered her with it. Poor Birdie. She'd been pushed back and forth across Brooklyn too. In the closet, he found some strips of leather and used these to tie up Desmond, who was just beginning to stir. This guy, he would take with him. An ace in the hole, an assistant to help him make his trip. First he would go home and get some artillery; then he was going to get out of Brooklyn once and for all.

# CHAPTER 25

"THERE WERE THREE of them," said the short, male guide. He pulled the black socks over his calves, one at a time. "One was pretty tall, an Ivy League type, I'd say. There was a smaller guy with him, looked like a weasel, or a muskrat."

"That's not fair," said the woman. "His features were actually quite nice, and he had open, vulnerable eyes. It was the hair."

"But he had a hat on."

"A peaked cap, but the hair stuck out. It looked like it had been heavily greased, but refused to stay down."

"And the Ivy Leaguer?"

"Ordinary. Floppy light brown hair, glasses, corduroys, short-sleeved shirt, running shoes."

"Did you take in all this because you're normally attentive or because they did something to especially attract your attention?"

"Normally attentive," said the male.

"They were talking loudly while we were trying to address the rest of the tour. Stood out," said the woman.

"And the third man?"

"Didn't really *see* him."

"He wasn't actually *with* the tour," said the woman. "But I noticed that there was a man vaguely following us from up the hill for a while. He had a large head and bushy hair. Looked like an aborigine. Couldn't tell how he was dressed."

"And then you saw the body. What happened?"

"First of all, Addison here fainted dead away. The Ivy Leaguer came straight down to the part of the path between the body and Bennett's tomb. The one with the cap came about halfway and then turned and ran toward the fellow who'd been tracking us. They seemed to argue for a moment; then they began to trot off downhill, toward the main gate. Then the Ivy Leaguer saw them disappearing, and he shouted, 'Joe,' and ran after them, rather in a hurry."

"Fainted away or not," said Addison, throwing the woman a spiteful glance and hitching up his sock again, "I saw the body and the sign and all that. What *could* it mean?"

DeSales rolled his eyes. "Looney Tunes," he muttered. He was beyond caring. This one was not going to be solved by reading any more secret codes. They had to get a straight ID and follow up with routine police work. This woman on the cross so far showed no trace of anything resembling a clue. But they did have an ID. At least she wasn't Megan Moore. He looked at the sheet in front of him. Her name was Page Zelenik. Her house had been displayed in a Sunset Park House Tour the day before, and then she had never shown up for the committee celebration that followed. She had been drugged and drowned. She was all wet when found on the cross. He looked around the plush decor of the cemetery's offices, the witnesses on the leather banquettes. He wondered if there was any sense in detaining these guides or any of the other people on the tour, all of whose names had been taken, and none of whom was in the least suspect.

One of the uniformed officers who had been called up from the local precinct knocked on the door and stuck in his head:

" 'Scuse me, Lieutenant. We think we've found something."

"Yeh?" DeSales sorely hoped that it wasn't another message.

The cop stepped cautiously across to the desk. He whispered in DeSales's ear: "There's this receiving vault up next to the chapel? Well, one of the grounds-keepers noticed the door was part open when it's not supposed to be. We looked in. A real fuckin' . . . 'scuse me . . . creeperooni. Like a morgue in a Frankenstein movie. Anyway, it looks like somebody's been spendin' a lotta time in there. There's beer cans, some women's clothing, syringes and shit. . . ."

DeSales got up. "You people are free to go," he announced. "Make sure you check out with the officer at the door." He turned to the cop: "Let's go."

Bernie Kavanaugh came in the room and leaned on the wall. He blew his nose loudly. He was still pissed off about not seeing his budding Michael Jackson perform as a lily boy.

"They found her," he drawled. "Megan Moore."

The tour group paused, fascinated. They weren't about to walk out on a scene straight out of "Hill Street Blues." DeSales felt a kind of sinking in his stomach. He sat down again. He said to the cop: "Get these folks outa here. I'll meet you under the arches in a second."

Kavanaugh waited, looking at his knuckles while they filed out. After the door was closed, he seemed still loath to speak. He began to open his mouth, but then blew his nose again instead. DeSales knew Kavanaugh was teasing him, drawing out the information as a kind of revenge. Finally, he cracked:

"Where, Bernie, *where?*"

"In the trunk of her car." DeSales, waiting for elaboration, drummed his fingers on the desk. Kavanaugh looked up: "On Grace Court. In the Heights. In a tow-away zone about three blocks from where Caruso lost her, what was it? about ten hours ago?"

"Terrific. Score one for New York's Finest." He raised an eyebrow. Slowly. "And she's been taken to the morgue?"

"Oh. Not at all. Didn't I say that first? She's alive, in L I U

Hospital. Mild shock. Some circulation problems from being tied up so tight."

DeSales tried to remain cool. The news that she was alive had brought back the light feeling in his gut that her peculiar combination of body and brains had first elicited from him:

"And she could pick this guy out of a lineup, maybe?"

"Maybe."

"Bernie, you drag this out any longer, and I'm gonna kick your ass down to Bush Terminal. You get a little inconvenienced, and you act like a princess. A fat sweaty Irish princess."

Kavanaugh smiled broadly: "Yeh, she saw him. She also saw our Ms. Zelenik up there." He jerked his head in the direction of the cross opposite the tomb of the man who had sent Stanley to Africa. "In a Coca-Cola cooler, she saw Zelenik, she says. *And . . .*"

"*Bernie!*"

"And she didn't only see the perp. She says she *knows who he is.*"

"You got a name?"

"Nope. She says she'll only tell *you.*"

DeSales looked through the Gothic arches of the window. He could see the spires of the chapel, the green budding hills of the graveyard beyond. There was the receiving vault; there was Megan Moore in the hospital about ten minutes away; closer, even, there was Shultz and Aunt Sally in front of the church in Red Hook—excuse me, Carroll Gardens—maybe at this moment getting the address of the house where he had a feeling all of this had started. For three days, he had been searching for a lead to follow; now there were too many tantalizing directions in which to turn. There was a knock on the door. Shultz came in. He had a black eye, and one sleeve on his jacket was hanging by threads.

"Unbelievable," he said. "Fucking unbelievable. I'm standin' outside that church. Your aunt's in Mass. There's nobody on the street, but the sermon must've started, see, 'cause a lotta the guys come out and stand on the steps of the church. Some of them light up cigarettes; a couple start arguin'; the rest just leans on the railings, right? It's a mix of guys. There's old guineas look like they just got off the boat; there's a couple of uncle-types, *connected*, y'know, got rap-sheets as long as your arm; and there's a buncha these young guys with their sleeves rolled up, the tattoos and the tight pants. Cocks of the walk."

Shultz took a deep breath and sank into one of the heavy wooden straight-backed chairs arranged around the desk. "Anyway, all of a sudden, from around the corner, heading uphill from the canal, comes this little guy sort of half-running, half-plodding along. He's stark naked and he's got about the longest schlong I ever seen on a white man. It's more or less bouncin' from one knee to the other as he huffs and puffs up to the church steps. This seems to really set off the guys on the steps. Maybe their morality is offended. Maybe they're protecting their women in the church. Maybe they can't stand the sight of a schlong bigger than they got. Anyway they tear down after him, and in about two seconds they're beatin' the shit out of him on the sidewalk. I run over and try to break it up. Inside I can hear the priest goin' on about abortion, then the organ starts up. I flash my badge and for that I get this," he pointed to the eye, "and this," he indicated the jacket. "So I pull out my piece and yell a lot, but I don't get their attention until I start shootin' in the air. This also brings a couple of patrol cars, and we finally pull the assailants off this guy. He's out cold; he's heavily bruised, and, get this, he looks to me like this professor got kidnapped. You believe it?"

"I'm afraid I do," said DeSales.

"He talk?" asked Kavanaugh.

"Not so far," answered Shultz. "He's got a mouth fulla loosies and a sore set of nuts and he says he can't remember much of the last few days. Keeps raving about 'stupid undergraduates' and shit like that."

"Where is he?"

"The ambulance took him to Lutheran. Down by the docks."
"Oh, Christ," exclaimed DeSales. "Get him outa there.
Those fuckin' Pakistani residents will lose his memory for him.
Permanently."

Outside Verb's house, Tyrone held Desmond's tethered wrists in
one viselike hand and, with the other, produced a ring of assorted car keys. He selected a black Cadillac at the corner, turned
one key in the trunk lock, then another. The third worked. He
made Desmond climb in and then closed the door over him.
After a few moments Desmond felt, more than heard, the igni-
tion start up, and they pulled away. They drove for a long time.

The trunk was womblike. In spite of sudden stops and starts
and the persistent jostling from potholes, the pain in Desmond's
groin and head had eased and he notched closer to a kind of
reverie. Perhaps it was because he had grown up on a state
highway in Pennsylvania and the midnight rumble of coal
trucks had been his lullaby; perhaps because the dark totality of
his imprisonment had finally relieved him of the need to show a
sense of responsibility for his own, and others', destiny. Here
there was no permanently pending demand that he alter by
positive action the contours of the environment.

He drifted from languor to vigilance. He imagined that they
were covering the whole of Brooklyn. It was not exactly a
Brooklyn he had ever inhabited himself; nor was it wholly fic-
tional. It was instead a montage of concrete images he had
stored away in the receiving vault of his consciousness, now
neatly paced and sequenced to suggest intent. That too gave
comfort. He remembered driving a disabled student home once,
down a block on Fulton Street, deep in Bed-Stuy, with no fewer
than seven storefront churches. Midway in the block Freddie's
Rib House was flanked by The Spiritual Israel Church and Its
Army, and The Good Tidings Gospel Hall.

He remembered more churches, near the original site of Ebbetts Field, now a black housing project. There was an Eglise
de Dieu, a Gethsemane Pentecostal, a First Church of Latter

Rain (with a note on the door: *Cette église est temperament transferé à 1625 Albany Avenue.*).

He remembered the voodoo remains in the mausoleum in Greenwood. It was as though Brooklyn was inhabited with a spiritual force at once exotic and definitive, as though life as he lived it was completely off the point. It was confirmation of the unrest he had felt the night he left Sherry Verb's and careened down Eastern Parkway assailed by creatures and cultures as alien as if he had landed on Mars: Kiddie College, Allah's Office, a synagogue with a psychedelic banner outside proclaiming WE WANT MOSIACH NOW! and footnoted in Hebrew. The Picasso exhibit at the museum and the St. Francis de Sales School for the Deaf near the Plaza seemed, in juxtaposition to what had come before, positively down home.

Desmond wondered if he would ever see DeSales—the cop, not the saint—again. There was something in the guy, some flinty denial at his core, that he both envied and resented. And felt comfortable with.

The Cadillac came to a halt.

Tyrone opened the trunk and pulled him out by the wrists. As his eyes adjusted to the sunlight, he found himself in a different Brooklyn from the dreamworld he had been inhabiting, in fact a different place entirely from anything he had ever conjured up. He was aware of salt air, sailing masts over a horizon of tiny bungalows, streets so narrow and fitfully paved as to suggest a back-street slum in a New England fishing village, a Provincetown on the skids, the other side of the coin from "picturesque." From one house, on the left, a beautiful blond girl-child emerged, wearing only a tattered pink satin nightgown that could have been one of Mona's hand-me-downs.

He realized he had completely forgotten Mona.

The house from which the little girl tiptoed, barefoot—she could have been ten or twelve—was hardly larger than a doll's house. A gull screeched overhead. The house was tarpaper, a shack, so it would have to be called a doll's tarpaper shack. Desmond smelled fish. The little girl stared at them wide-eyed, as Tyrone marched Desmond, still bound in the leather strips, in her direction. As they passed the girl, Tyrone pointed a finger: "Keep your fuckin' mout' shut." "Go fuck yourself," said the little girl, and began to play in a sodden sandbox. All of the houses had small patches of yard with disfigured stuffed animals, broken swings, rusting tools. Some of the larger plots had an old car or a boat, in need of paint, up on blocks. In one windowpane, Desmond saw a sign: "Up the I R A." In another, "White Power." Tyrone led him to a canal lined with more shacks, pleasureboats in slips, then up another lane even narrower and more tawdry than the last. They turned in where a gate swung limply from a picket fence and approached a cottage that was covered half with unpainted splintered clupbourd and half with cheap aluminum siding. In the doorway was a handsome fair-skinned woman with deep blue eyes, a beehive of dyed black hair, a swizzle-stick protruding from over her ear, and heavily painted lips. She took in Desmond, and the leather bindings, as Tyrone pushed him through the door and into a chair. She cooed in a sort of Celtic brogue: "Well, now, if it isn't my dear sonny's brought himself a friend home."

# CHAPTER 26

SOMETIMES, WHEN HE had too many things to tell and too little time to tell them in, Bernie Kavanaugh spoke while looking at the floor, as if he were reading from cue cards on the toes of his cordovans. This required also that he stand still, or move forward at a slow pace. But DeSales was virtually running to the LIU Hospital elevator, and the words literally tumbled from Kavanaugh's mouth:

"They found prints all over the receiving vault. Most of them identical. I sent them out on the wire. We should have an answer before tonight. There was a kind of card table in there, and a lot of empty Bud cans. . . ."

"Did the cemetery people know how he got in?"

"They seemed more embarrassed than surprised. Ever since the end of that strike when they used the vault a lot and had new locks and security etcetera, they just slacked off completely. They took all the stiffs out, and practically anybody could've got a key. The cemetery people don't even remember if they locked the place up. They certainly didn't check it regularly. They were so far behind on everything else from the strike, seems there was a feeling like, uh, who gives a shit about this fucking morgue anymore; we won't use it for another hundred years."

"What was he doing in there? Just stopping off after work for a few frosty lagers?" DeSales pushed the button for Megan Moore's floor. Kavanaugh breathed a little easier now.

"The syringes had knockout drops in them. The clothes are this Samantha Lawrence's. One of the drawers they lay out the stiffs in was broken open and they figure that's where he kept her for the six weeks. M.E. says that with the cold weather we had in February and March it's not surprising she didn't decompose all that much."

"So when the warm weather came, he had to get rid of her."

"Right. And it also happened to be Easter week and it fit in with the general scheme."

"You get an ID on the two guys who ran away from the tour?"

The elevator stopped. The door opened slowly, and DeSales was already leaning in. But there were two pallets on wheels bearing people who looked more dead than alive, manned by Hispanic attendants in soiled white smocks, filling the space. "Next car, man," said one of the attendants haughtily, pushing the "Door Close" button.

"I got the new kid—Caruso's nephew?—I got him to take the pictures the artist drew out to the secretary at the Urban Institute. She lives near Marine Park. She doesn't recognize the guy who showed Megan Moore the stiff in the Coca-Cola cooler. But she does agree that the tall guy looks like Desmond and says that the little guy looks like a political scientist they used to have out there, name of Verb, friend of Desmond's, who got canned, basically, because he didn't get his doctor's degree and because anyway they wanted to make room for Carruthers."

"So there's jealousy thrown in with the politics? You think Desmond was in on this?"

The next elevator was empty, except for a black nurse with harlequin glasses over attractive features. And *massive* hips. DeSales decided that that was what Roz would look like after a few comfortable years in the Poverty Bureaucracy, resting on her laurels. The lighted arrow above the button pointed up. DeSales and Kavanaugh climbed aboard. The doors closed slowly. The elevator started down. DeSales swore. The nurse gave him a dirty look. Kavanaugh, still relieved that the pace had ebbed, shrugged his shoulders and went on, articulating more fully:

"I called Desmond's house. His wife said he was gone when she woke up this morning at eight. He had given no indication that he would be leaving so early. Or at all. In fact, she said something that implied, like, this was one morning that she especially didn't expect him to go *anywhere*."

"Because it was a holiday?"

The elevator stopped in the basement. The fat nurse got off. The two Hispanics wheeled in another moribund body, reeking of anesthetic. DeSales pushed the "Up" button, then 5. One of the orderlies pushed 6.

Kavanaugh leered: "Maybe they had a date. For a little Bingo-Bango." Kavanaugh stared at the orderlies' white jackets for a moment. "Oh, and I almost forgot; in one of the other pigeonholes in the receiving vault? They found Quaaludes. The real thing that druggists can't sell anymore, not the street home-made type."

"How many?"

"You know Mackey? The one who got his ear cut off in that rumble in Williamsburg last year, when he was undercover? Four-poster Irish, but looks like . . ." He nodded surreptitiously at the orderlies.

"Yeh; I know Mackey. What about the Quaaludes?"

"He says there was about a coffinful. Enough to supply every disco from Bay Ridge to Canarsie. That Mackey's a funny guy, y'know? I asked him if it was true these Quaaludes improve your sex life, like they say. Y'know, I first heard about them from Shultz. He claims there was a broad in Honolulu. On *last* year's PBA convention. She took a couple of them and proceeded to ball the *entire* San Francisco contingent, except for the gay ones—maybe say twenty guys in a row, and then she sang, 'I Left My Heart in San Francisco.' Then she said, 'Where's Chicago? I know that song too!'" Kavanaugh was laughing as the door began to open. DeSales made his way around the stretcher and stepped quickly into the hallway, looking at the numbers of the doors. "So, ya know what Mackey says."

"No," said DeSales, still trying to orient himself.

"He says, 'For every guy gets laid because of Quaaludes, there's nineteen spend the evening humping the nearest tree.'" Kavanaugh roared: "Ya like it?"

DeSales found the room. "Terrific," he said over his shoulder. Megan Moore was propped up against a stack of pillows. She looked wan and frightened.

"You wanted to talk to me?" he asked, working to keep the pitch of his voice level. He had not noticed before that she had a slight mole on her chin.

She spoke slowly, but her voice retained its remarkable clarity: "The guy who did this? I think of him as the Creep."

"Right."

"You got the physical description?"

"We're circulating a police artist's sketch now. You and a few other people have helped a lot. But mostly you." DeSales thought to himself that when he tried to sound sympathetic and gentle he probably sounded the way an ordinary person did when ordering, say, a cup of coffee. But she responded with what he had to take as a grateful look. He waited for her to initiate the rest of the conversation.

She found a Kleenex by the side of the bed and blew her nose. She drank some water out of a bent transparent straw sticking out of a glass on her bed table. "I'm actually all right, you know. Just a little shook up. And weak. I never expected to spend a night in a car trunk bound and gagged. Of course there was a great deal of relief because, after I saw the woman's head . . . Wow, I thought I was a goner. Have you ever thought you were as good as dead? You must have it happen, as a Violence cop, all the time. You know what I did? I saw the head. And I felt the Creep's hands closing on my neck, and I started to think about the first time I stayed out all night with a guy. It was the summer after prep school, and I had a job as a waitress in Ocean City. Maryland, not New Jersey. And we slept together on the beach. Not *that* much happened, but I remember him walking me back to my room over the dunes while the sun came up. And here I was, losing consciousness in this lousy van that smelled of incense and beer, thinking about that night and sure I was going to die." She sighed. "So just before you came in the room I was lying here saying to myself: 'Moore, you dope, you have confirmed the underlying theme of every bad sexist routine, that women are silly, romantic creatures to whom nothing means anything, except boyfriends and remembered kisses.' Scarlett O'Hara syndrome."

DeSales smiled. He meant it, but she took the natural lopsidedness of his grin as impatience, and said: "Oh, I know, you're in a *hurry*. The guy who took me into the van I've seen a fair amount of. That's what you came to hear about, isn't it?"

DeSales sat down in the chair near the bed and leaned forward. "Where?"

"First time was last year. Summer, I think. There was a chain of so-called 'Insomnia Clinics' where it turned out they were just *selling* Quaalude prescriptions over the counter. These were written by real doctors, who needed money and had answered newspaper ads. When the police started closing them down, I covered the one on Eighth Avenue in Park Slope. It was a wild scene. Every Friday and Saturday night there were kids lined up around the block waiting to get in. This guy, this Creep, worked there; he was a kind of bouncer, I think, in charge of the door— who got in, who left. He was booked and released, like the rest of them—there were only four or five employees on the premises—because there was a pending legal situation about whether anyone could be arrested for charging someone money for a legally-written sleeping-pill prescription if the person indeed claims to have trouble sleeping. Later they did get indictments against the ringleaders, but I don't know what happened to the guys who worked the clinics."

"You getting this, Bernie?" Kavanaugh stood in the doorway with his notepad.

"Yeah. And they all walked. We didn't need these guys, just wanted the top men. But there'll be a record of the arrests. I'll get it right away," said Kavanaugh.

"If you call W V B A, they can probably give you a date. We have a pretty efficient librarian."

"And you've seen him since?"

"Yes." She blew her nose and sipped from the straw again. "One of the unflattering things you could say about my job is that I'm an ambulance-chaser."

DeSales gave her his legitimate smile again. He wasn't sure whether he was merely smitten with her, lying there, wanly pretty, powerless, cooperative—and good-humored—or if he could just feel in his being the inevitable closing-in on his prey. Probably both. "You could," he nodded his head.

"A number of times there were crime scenes or accident scenes where he would turn up in his ambulance."

"Ambulance?"

"Yes. He had a white van, something like the one he dragged me into last night, but it had a flashing light and a name that was different."

"The name was?"

"How could I forget? 'Brooklyn Dodgers Emergency Service.'"

"You're sure it wasn't a front? He wasn't just a buff who was trying to get himself a front seat at what would be on the six o'clock news?"

"I'm sure. I actually saw him carry victims into the van and drive off."

"We been missing any victims lately, Bernie?" DeSales asked out of the side of his mouth.

Kavanaugh was deadpan now: "Not that I know of, but anything's possible."

"Well, check it out. Right now. The Insomnia Clinic, the Brooklyn Dodgers Emergency Service, the missing victim angle. Wait a minute. Forget the missing victim angle. We got enough crimes to tie up already, and let's stick with what we're already working on. I think we got him, at least an ID, in any case. And he's with these other two guys, one of them maybe Desmond, maybe as a hostage, and maybe the two nuns. Sounds a little messy, from his point of view. I can taste it, Bernie. Get back to headquarters and get things moving."

As Kavanaugh left, DeSales got up and closed the door.

"Two nuns? Desmond?" she asked.

"You'll read all about it in the paper."

"That's not fair. Maybe I just broke your case for you. Look, I'm going to be discharged tonight or tomorrow morning. You promised me an exclusive, and then your men allowed me to be kidnapped practically from under their noses. Give me a break. Let me in the front row when you begin to make the collar."

There was color in her cheeks now, and, in the sunlight streaming from the window, DeSales saw the deep natural auburn tint at the base of her curls. The color underlined her spunkiness. "So," he said, "that's why you'd only talk to *me*."

"A lie. I wanted to see your blue eyes up close one more time." Her own eyes had grown bright and good-humored. "And I wanted to tell you to your face that I didn't mean all that bad stuff I said about you on the air. I'm sort of, I guess, an old maid, you know, and I was a little hurt when you ditched me the other night. 'Hell hath no fury,' and so forth. . . ."

Her left hand was on the coverlet. It was bruised and swollen where the Creep had twisted it forcing it into the cooler. DeSales touched one finger, gingerly. "I was sorry too," he said. "But no front row. You can sit in my back seat. As long as there's no imminent danger."

"Can I bring my tape recorder?"

"Shit," said DeSales. "You're insatiable, aren't you?" But he said it with a begrudging sort of admiration.

Caruso and Jackson were the only two detectives not on desk duty at the Task Force when Aunt Sally called. The people her nephew Frank was looking for were in a house on a little street, hardly more than an alley, near the el at Smith and Ninth streets. Dennett Place. She gave the address. Caruso and Jackson, not having slept in twenty-four hours, were on their way home. And they were in the doghouse for losing Megan Moore. So, dutifully, they tried to reach DeSales by phone, but all they could find out was that he had gone to a hospital—no one knew which one. His beeper appeared not to be working. So, perhaps unbalanced a bit by lack of sleep and fear of demotion, they decided to bend one of the Task Force rules and check the place out themselves. Maybe they would make some kind of strike and redeem themselves, get back in DeSales's good graces. The one thing neither of them needed was a departmental hearing. They found the street easily. It ran for one short block between and parallel to Court and Smith, connecting Luquer to Nelson Street. Caruso and Jackson had each been with the police over ten years, and each had lived in Brooklyn most of his life, but Dennett Place was, to both of them, one decidedly peculiar thoroughfare. It was narrow, the houses were exceptionally small, and each house had a funny little stoop that hugged the front wall; even then the sidewalks were too narrow at the stoops for more than one person to pass. And although it was a pleasant Easter afternoon, there was no sign of life on the street, except for the cactus-filled terrariums and plaster saints in the windows and the confectionary siding on the façades of a couple of the houses on the side closer to Smith. The Gowanus Canal side. The house that Aunt Sally had told them about was on the other side of the street. Paint peeled from its dull red brick, and it gave no sign of recent habitation. There appeared to be no way, without making a big fuss, of approaching the house from any other direction than the front door.

Jackson whispered: "This doesn't seem real. Maybe I've been up too long. I'm hallucinating."

Caruso shook his head. "Italians visit on Easter. What are there? Ten houses here? So they're all visiting relatives on the Island who have bigger houses and can handle the whole family better. The people who live here probably take the pignoli cookies."

The men looked up and down the street again. Jackson, on tiptoe, attempted to peer in the parlor-floor window of the house. The pane was murky, and a torn shade obscured the view. No help. The men looked at one another. Caruso had deep gray pouches under his eyes, and Jackson's were dramatically bloodshot. Caruso yawned: "We're a couple of beauties," he said. "It's now or never."

Simultaneously, they drew their service revolvers. Jackson rang the doorbell three times. "Won't think it's the postman," he muttered. "Always rings twice. Right?" There was no answer. Hesitantly, Caruso reached for the knob. He said:

"You got your mother at home, right? You got three sisters in college. I got a wife and two boys who, if I'm still around, will make it to Fordham. Easy. Why are we doing this?"

"Just keep alert," said Jackson. "We make the collar here, we get a medal; we don't, we'll be back on the street in Brownsville. And we don't have a big chance of living too long there either."

Caruso tried the knob. To his surprise, it turned easily, and the door swung forward in silence. The front parlor was empty. Jackson went up the stairs noiselessly and found three rooms with mattresses on the floor. And a bathroom. Also empty. He came back downstairs to the front hall. Ahead of them was the closed door leading to the rear parlor and kitchen. Each man slid toward it, back against the wall and revolver at the ready. Jackson put an ear to the door. There was a sweeping sound inside, the crinkle of paper, then a man's voice, humming a song that Caruso was later to describe as "kind of a folk song, maybe Peter, Paul and Mary, like 'Blowin' in the Wind.'"

Caruso leaned into the door. It began to give, but stopped after about an inch. There was a feeble hook-and-eye thing latched. The men looked at one another again. They silently recognized that there was really only one question remaining: should they announce themselves or simply kick the door in? Neither could remember which later, but one of them made a precipitate gesture and they both immediately went into action, simultaneously raising a heel and knocking the door open, tearing the hook-and-eye from the aging plaster.

There was a small man, about forty years old, Caucasian, standing in the middle of the floor. At his feet was the body of a young woman, also Caucasian, orange hair. The young woman was partially covered with a kind of hospital gown, but both Caruso and Jackson detected bullet-holes in exposed parts of her naked torso. The walls, they noted, were also riddled with bullet-holes. The man appeared to be sweeping up the room with a broken-handled broom. He was piling the debris on and about the young woman's body, apple cores, seeds, wrappers, dustballs, a bag of what appeared to be marijuana, and, most notably, many paper towels soaked with blood, which had apparently been used to wipe the blood from the room's surfaces. At the man's feet there was also a spray can of Fantastic.

Jackson and Caruso assumed the position, knees bent, pistols pointed with one hand, cradled in the other. Jackson said: "Police. Drop everything. *Freeze.*"

The man indeed dropped the broom, but instead of freezing he reached into the pile on the floor, producing in his right hand a nine-millimeter Browning pistol. He said, tearfully: "Political power comes out of the barrel of a gun," and pointed the thing without conviction in the general direction of Caruso.

Both detectives opened fire, killing the suspect instantly.

# CHAPTER 27

DESALES LOOKED ACROSS the desk at Maceo Allen:

"You were right on the first two counts. Our guy is the age you predicted, and there's no reason, for the time being in any case, to suspect past homicides."

"You got him pegged, then?"

DeSales pushed the sheet of paper at Allen, then began to recite the details from memory: "ID positive. Confirmed by prints and other strong circumstantial stuff. Plus an eyewitness. Name, Tyrone Ward, a.k.a. Lenox Robinson. Born Cumberland Hospital, Brooklyn, June nineteenth, 1949. Illegitimate. Father unknown. Mother, Mary Eileen Ward. Original address for her is on Nineteenth Street in Windsor Terrace, a couple of blocks from the Prospect Park West entrance to Greenwood Cemetery."

"Right near Farrell's," Kavanaugh piped in. "The last real Brooklyn Irish saloon. Still get a glass of beer for thirty-five cents."

"Ward never finished high school. Lots of fights and lots of time in juvenile court. We got addresses on him in Sunset Park, in Bushwick, you name it. He was picked up in the East Vil-

lage—threatening pedestrians while under influence of drugs—
a few years ago, and they put him in Manhattan State. He gave
his mother's address as the Saint George, in Brooklyn
Heights."

"When it had turned into a welfare hotel; now it's gone co-
op. A hundred thousand a room, I heard."

"That's the last known address for her. He has a rap-sheet as
long as your arm: driving a hack without a license, impersonat-
ing a male nurse, running a Quaalude Clinic. Last known occu-
pation: proprietor of Brooklyn Dodgers Emergency Service, a
private ambulance. For which he also didn't have a license,
though he never got busted for it."

"That's how he got into the cemeteries so easy. His van was a
familiar sight. He free-lanced a lot for undertakers, people who
didn't want to pay for a hearse. Even supervised some of the
preparation of gravesites."

Allen made a pyramid with his hands on his ample stomach.
"So, a petty criminal, but a reasonably successful one. Takes a
high degree of organization. Fits with the type. Just has epi-
sodes where the cord snaps, as it were, but all the attendant
business—the disposal of the body, the messages, the covering
of the tracks—is coldly efficient."

"Efficient *and* profitable. The stockpile of drugs he'd accu-
mulated in the receiving vault was worth big bucks on the
street."

"And he seems to have had medical ambitions."

"Maybe. Could have been just that that's where the drugs are
available. But he was at least partially trained. Was in the
Medical Corps in the Army. General discharge."

"Meaning unadaptable. Probably did quite well until someone pushed his button. How'd he get out of Manhattan State?"

"Well, he was already on halfway-house status. You know
the city's great new policy: get the loonies back into their communities as fast as possible. Then he was released from even
that because this guy Verb signed for him." DeSales grimaced,
grinding out his cigarette with a vengeance. "If Caruso and

Jackson hadn't decided to make a 135-pound slab of Swiss cheese out of this Joe Verb, we might be right on Ward's ass."

"So you're having my friend Braithwaite up from Washington to point you in the right direction."

"We need something. The fucking city's converted to a new system—information retrieval, they call it—and the computer happens, naturally, to be down. So we can't get any psychological records on Ward, only what I've told you, and that, we pulled by hand over at the courthouse. Right now the trail is cold."

"Maybe we'll have something when the lab boys get done with the scene-of-crime down in that house in Red Hook. At least there ain't no messages to screw things up." Kavanaugh coughed. He seemed short of breath.

DeSales jumped out of the chair. He crumpled up a sheet of paper and threw it at the wastebasket. "Fuck the crime-of-scene . . ." he shouted. "I mean fucking *scene-of-crime*. That place is such a mess . . . the carnage took god knows how long and could have involved two or three different killers. It could have all been an accident. I'm tired of forensics and—what did Desmond call it?—*hermeneutics*! Give me a good old address, a car registration, a snitch. I need something hard to get my hands on before those two disappear indefinitely."

"You think," asked Allen, "this Desmond is an accomplice?"

"I don't give a shit. I just know he's *with* him. If he's a hostage, an exchange for Carruthers, I don't give a shit. I want Ward, and if we have to shoot through some fucking professor to get him, so be it."

"I hope the room isn't bugged," said Allen mildly, smiling. "The Civilian Review Board might be offended. . . . Anyway, Braithwaite is a good man, but the first thing he's gonna tell you is that the psychological tests, and the shrinks that administer them, are as unreliable as any English professor interpreting a poem."

The house smelled of cats.

There were stains on the faded slipcovers of the sofa.

The only piece of furniture in the room that looked as if it had not come from a junk shop was a massive scratching-post, a five-foot-high pylon covered with shag carpeting and supported by a four-foot-square base. A white cat slept on top of the pillar, a black one on the base. An orange long-hair, so matted as to have no discernible facial features, came out from beneath the sofa crying. He dug his claws into the post, arched his back, and jumped into the woman's lap. The woman said: "Poor baby's hungry. I'll get Tyrone to feed him when he gets back. My poor old legs can barely move anymore. When there are young men around, believe me, I *use* them." She took the swizzle-stick from behind her ear and stirred her drink: "Tyrone makes the best Old Fashioneds," she said "Canadian Club and two cherries. That boy could have been anything—a doctor, a mixologist—but who's to complain about medical supply. It's an up-and-coming field."

Desmond wondered what use he, as one of the young men in question, could be to her, or, for that matter, what role she imagined him playing in the medical-supply trade. Tyrone had tied him to one of the kitchen chairs and then somehow bolted the chair into the living-room wall. Tyrone was obviously handy with ropes and hardware, besides his other talents.

The woman made a toasting gesture in his direction with the full glass and sipped cautiously from the top, not taking her eyes off him.

"Well," she said, "since you're making a prolonged visit, why don't we have a little chat? I suppose you're interested in Tyrone, how he got where he is from his modest upbringing. That's what most of the people who come here want to know about."

"Sure," Desmond nodded.

"Well, to tell the truth, I think he got his ambition out of adversity. You know we've had a terrible time getting away from . . . *them*." Desmond nodded. "They burnt our house in Bushwick. They forced the Jews to buy the Saint George Hotel. You see what I mean? But," she drank deeply this time, "I guess I can't complain . . . now that Tyrone has established me *here*. Shanty Irish, some of them are, but safe. And if one of those colored troublemakers ever came around, they'd skin the sonofabitch alive. Did you see the siding we've begun on the house. . . ? She speared one of the maraschino cherries with the swizzle-stick and sucked it off. She seemed to have lost her train of thought.

She took a Lucky Strike from a pack and lighted it with a heavy metal table-lighter. There were dozens of rings, many overlapping, on the glass top of the coffee table. On the table also was a copy of one of the weekly tabloids Desmond had become acquainted with on supermarket checkout lines. "WILL TEDDY MARRY AGAIN? YES SAYS SEER!" one headline screamed. Another, slightly more understated, said: *"Princess Di and Mr. T: Would You Believe?"*

She pressed her knees together and leaned forward primly. She was back on track. Before she spoke, she exhaled from her nose. "Not that I'm prejudiced. *Far* from it. There just aren't the fine colored *gentlemen* there used to be in Brooklyn. I mean, look at this Mr. T. No education to speak of. But he's a Christian, I believe, and works for charity. So if he puts the meat to Princess Di every now and then, who's to mind? Poor girl, probably never had a chance at a real man before." She finished the drink, tentatively stood, still chewing ice. She took a couple of unsteady steps and leaned over Desmond conspiratorily. She smelled like dead flowers marinated in whiskey. There was a gob of makeup cracking on her nose. "I suppose," she whispered, "that Tyrone has told you that his real father was Jackie Robinson."

Desmond's mind ran an Instant Replay. He was sitting in the apartment in Pennsylvania in the early 1950s watching the World Series on TV. His older brother, the all-state football player, came into the room. "Who do you like?" he asked. "The Dodgers," Desmond replied, frightened by his own temerity. "Nigger-lover," his brother spat, stalking out of the room. On the TV, Jackie Robinson, ebony skin, ivory teeth, was leading off first base. His lips moved rapidly, riding the pitcher. Then he took off for second, legs bowed and pumping. He hit the dirt of the infield carrying his spikes high. The second baseman bobbled the ball. Robinson was safe. He bounced to his feet. He slapped dirt from his uniform. He doffed his cap. The crowd at Ebbetts Field was going wild. The camera scanned the cheap seats in the outfield. Desmond had never seen such a concentration of black faces.

Tyrone was no son of Jackie Robinson. No way.

"Not exactly," he answered, unsure of what she expected.

"Well, *of course* he wasn't. It's the glamor attached to him. Tyrone can't resist it. That's why he uses that other name sometimes. And Tyrone always wanted to be *first* at something. Just like Jackie Robinson was the first colored in the big leagues. But I couldn't *stand* the man. Think I'd be intimate with someone I couldn't stand?"

Desmond heard the door open, Tyrone's heavy step.

"It was Roy Campanella. Campy," she hissed. "His first year up. A real colored gentleman. He was M V P at least twice later. Tyrone is an old Campanella family name." She scuttled back to her seat. Tyrone emerged from the kitchen, covered with oil and grease.

"How's it goin', Mom?" He nodded toward Desmond.

"Marvelous. Your friend is a charming conversationalist, dear. Now," she held the empty glass aloft, "how's about another itty-bitty Old Fashioned, *two* cherries."

"In a minute. We can't move until just before daybreak. I want him to get some shut-eye. Give him a couple of the 'Ludes. My hands are dirty."

From a side table, she brought a bottle and removed two tablets from it. She held them out to Desmond.

"He's tied up, for Chrissakes. Put them in his mouth." She hesitated. Tyrone addressed Desmond directly: "I can shoot you up, buddy, and you'll wake up with a headache you wouldn't believe, or you can take one of these and have a nice restful nap. If one doesn't work, you can do two. They're not gonna hurt you. You know I need you, you're my ticket outa here. And I need you rested to help me."

Desmond opened his mouth. Tyrone's mother put one pill on his tongue, then hesitated, looking for a wash. She found the Canadian Club bottle on a table and held it to his lips. He almost gagged on the fumes. He had never been able to throw back whiskey straight. In Pennsylvania, he had been tall and very skinny and pretty weak. Drinking had been one of the few avenues to a masculine image that appeared open to him. The business of not being able to drink shots-and-beers had worked against him socially; it made it difficult to curry favor with certain of his adolescent peers.

But now he was able to fight off the revulsion. He gulped and swallowed, with difficulty, all the while thinking: "medical supply."

# CHAPTER 28

DR. LIONEL BRAITHWAITE was a tall slender man with a pencil-moustache. His tan Class-A's were crisply pressed. His major's brass and his black shoes were bright with polish. His skin was a shade darker than that of Maceo Allen; he spoke in the lilting accent of his native Virgin Islands. There was an open attaché case on his lap full of file folders, printouts, and official documents.

DeSales took one look into the case and groaned: "With all due respect, Doctor, we're in a big hurry. Give it to us in a nutshell. Please."

Braithwaite smiled. "I've been trying to sort this out with just such a purpose in mind. It's a short flight, however, and the request comes on awfully short notice, so you'll have to bear with me."

"Shoot."

"First you must understand that the people who examined the subject and analyzed the data are no longer in the service and are of course unavailable. So what I'm giving you is necessarily secondhand."

"Of course."

Braithwaite held before him a sheet of yellow legal paper on which he had scribbled notes. He put on a pair of reading half-glasses and peered over the top, first at DeSales, then at Allen, then Kavanaugh. He spoke in a clipped formal manner: "Private Ward first came to the attention of the Army legal authorities in July 1967. He was a medical trainee at Fort Sam Houston, Texas. He had been a model soldier up to that time, excelling particularly in practical training: bandaging, administering hypos, field training. In fact he had been honored by being selected as an ambulance driver, a much desired MOS. His company had been given their first three-day passes a couple of weeks before, and he had apparently visited one of the border towns in Mexico. Nine days after the visit, he reported to sick call with a case of gonorrhea, a not-unusual circumstance among enlisted men in that region. He was given an injection of penicillin and told to report back to duty. Instead he went AWOL. That evening he picked up a prostitute in downtown San Antonio, near the Alamo, took her to dinner at an expensive restaurant and then afterwards for a cruise on one of the sightseeing boats that go up and down the San Antonio River, drifting by the cafés and mariachi bands. At some point in the evening, Ward became enraged, bodily lifted the woman over his head, and threw her into the river. She hit her head on the shallow bottom and almost drowned. She charged Ward with attempted murder."

"What color was this prostitute?" asked Allen.

"Her 'color' was white. Her blood was chiefly Navajo Indian."

"Another half-breed," muttered Allen.

Braithwaite nodded briskly and resumed: "Ward faced court-martial, therefore, on charges of going AWOL and attempted murder. He faced a very long term at Leavenworth. The prosecution had to anticipate that he might be advised to pursue an insanity—or limited-responsibility—defense, so we had him tested before proceeding with the case."

"Did he say why he'd done it?"

"He said, first, that it was an accident, and, second, that it 'needed to be done anyway.'"

"Did he make any attempt to save her after the rage had passed?"

"No. He testified that he couldn't swim. There was, according to Dr. Sezak's notes, no evidence of remorse."

DeSales gave Allen a dirty look: "The tests, Doc, the tests."

"Standard procedure in a case like this is to administer the MMPI and TAT initially . . ."

"You'd better give us a brief overview. It's been a few years."

"The MMPI is the Minnesota Multiphasic Personality Inventory; it consists of 566 true-false questions. The TAT is the Thematic Apperception Test; in it the subject views a series of nineteen pictures and one blank card and is asked to make up a story about each. As a result of these tests, the Army decided not to go ahead with the prosecution. The charges were not so much dismissed as swept under the carpet, if I may be so bold as to make my own inference. Ward was discharged as 'unadaptable.' In short, the Army was washing its hands of him."

"And sending him back to do some *civilian* drowning."

Braithwaite drew a finger across his moustache and raised both eyebrows at Kavanaugh: "Let he who is without sin cast the first stone."

DeSales intervened: "In the long run, we're going to have to know about his motivations and so forth, but at this point I'm wondering whether you can speculate about what kind of behavior we can expect from him right now, in the spot he's in."

Braithwaite tilted back his head and looked at the ceiling. He leafed quickly through the test results. He said: "There are two solid predictions I can make. The results of the MMPI—with true-false questions like, 'My judgment is almost always correct' and 'My father was a good man'—demonstrated that Ward was a very canny individual, almost too canny. Highly organized, but without any evidence of *feeling*, of empathy. This latter quality suggested severe pathological disorders, particularly in juxtaposition to his lack of guilt feelings about the

Indian prostitute. In any case, I'd say that you are dealing here with a man who will not panic, will indeed put into effect a skillfully devised plan of escape. However, this plan could be *too* well-planned to ever work."

"Meaning?"

"Meaning that his disregard for the feelings of others could lead to a disregard for emotional factors that might influence a 'sane' person's decision to act. His plan will emphasize efficiency, timing, mechanical functioning, but will probably disregard the possibility of the intervention of human error.

"Now, the other conclusion that comes to me is from the TAT. The easiest way is to give an example. One of the pictures shows a mother breast-feeding a child. Ward, when pressed, made up the following story, and I quote: 'The mother has dried up. She don't have any milk of her own to feed the baby. And the father of the baby has run off with all the food in the house. So the mother is *tricking* the baby into thinking it'll get to eat by sticking her tit in his mouth. What she really wants to do is shut the kid up. Suffocate him.'" Braithwaite looked over his glasses again. "Now, there is no evidence to the 'normal' eye of any stress in this picture. A healthy individual should be expected to respond with a story about tranquility, mother-love. So we see immediately that Ward has a deep conflict within himself. He feels anger and disappointment in his mother, but he lamely tries to blame the absent father for the mother's inadequacy. Yet the questions on the MMPI concerning mothers were all answered in a positive, upbeat way, as if he had come from an idyllic family situation. Like the one the picture is intended to convey. In any case, both aspects of skewed vision, as it were, focus on the mother, positive and negative. I'm sure he's heading for her right now, if she's available."

DeSales shook his head. "We haven't found her yet. Still checking."

"Wait a minute, Doc," wheezed Kavanaugh. "You just said two things. You said the guy is really pissed-off at his old lady, and you said he'll have a very efficient, rational plan to get away. Now you say that he's gonna run to his mother. That's crazy. Why should he go to her if he hates her? And why should he go to her, an obvious connection we can check on, if he's planned an *efficient* escape?"

Braithwaite raised his index finger: "That's exactly the point. It *is* crazy, in the sense that *he* is. And the heart of the conflict which leads to his acting out is that he feels rage toward the mother, but the rage is unacceptable to him. So he places the blame on others, perhaps even acts violently against other women as surrogates for the mother. If he's as twisted as these tests and his subsequent behavior suggest, he may rationalize his murderous rage by telling himself that it functions to protect the mother. . . ."

"And it does," said Allen.

"Right," Braithwaite winked. "Protects her from *him*." He paused, looking at a printout. "At any rate," he went on without looking up, "he's having it both ways. He thinks he's supposed to feel sorry for and protect the mother because she had the misfortune to become involved in an interracial liaison which left her abandoned and stigmatized, the stigma symbolized by the very face of her son. But he *really* holds the mother responsible for getting him into this in the first place, bringing him with Negro features into a white world where he doesn't belong. To repeat, these are irreconcilable feelings, intense conflict. This makes the psychosis, the paranoia. So his efficient side often is only rational or functional in a totally irrational context. And if, as is quite possible in such a case, the mother herself isn't all there, the situation becomes exacerbated. . . ." Braithwaite snapped shut the briefcase on his lap. He slumped back in the chair. "Find the mother," he said.

The phone rang. DeSales picked it up. He listened, took some notes, said "Thanks," and hung up.

He lighted up and balanced the cigarette in the notch in the ashtray: "Mary Eileen Ward wrote Tyrone a letter last month. Tyrone Ward crumpled it up and left the envelope in the receiving vault at Greenwood. There's a return address on it. How's this grab you, Bernie? Ebony Court?"

"How appropriate," said Allen, out of the side of his mouth.

"Not at all, Frank. I never heard of it."

"Think for a minute. You've been around long enough to know Brooklyn."

"Nobody's ever gonna be around that long."

"Right," DeSales laughed humorlessly. "I read a story once in which a guy said something like, 'You'd have to be so old to know Brooklyn, you'd be *dead*.'" He went to the map, carrying with him the street index. While looking up Ebony Court in the index he traced a meandering line with his finger along the periphery of Kings County, from the Cemetery of the Evergreens on the north over to the coast, down through Canarsie, past Jamaica Bay where it separates the mainland from the Rockaways, through Floyd Bennett Field and Marine Park. His finger came to rest on a peninsular thumb-shaped section between the green marshland of Marine Park and the blue waters of Sheepshead Bay. "It's in Gerritsen."

Kavanaugh whistled. Allen stood at DeSales's shoulder and squinted at the spot where his finger rested. He said: "It's completely out of scale with the rest of the map. The streets and blocks look minuscule. I can't even read the street names."

"Gerritsen," repeated DeSales to himself. "A rat's nest of alleys and dirty creeks. There may be nice people in there, but all we ever see down here is river rats and I R A fugitives. A black stoolie I once had in here told me he'd rather go back to Attica than have to spend a day alone in Gerritsen. That kind of Irish. Huh, Bernie?"

"Used to be, Frank, we couldn't *burn* somebody outa there if the neighbors wanted them to stay. But Tyrone's face can't recommend him too much, and the place is turning around, I hear. Hey, my sister-in-law and her husband just bought one of those new duplexes they're building off Avenue X. And my cousin Eddie says the hottest real-estate tip in town is to get in on that waterfront while the general public still sees it as a shantytown. See, the Hamptons are too crowded; the South Shore got speedboat traffic jams; and Fire Island is either gonna be washed away by the tides, or by AIDS, whichever works faster. People are gonna want to rent or buy in Gerritsen. It's up-and-coming."

"Not for the Wards, I suspect," said DeSales. "Let's get out there and find out."

"I had a last question for Major Braithwaite," said Maceo Allen. "How come Ward was in the Medics?"

"He pleaded nonviolence," said Braithwaite. "Conscientious Objector. They all go in the Medics, if they're convincing enough."

# CHAPTER 29

DE SALES STOOD IN the background as the helmeted S WAT men and the plainclothes terrorist-specialists worked out their plans in the brightly-lit parking lot at Kings Plaza. Gerritsen could indeed be approached overland from only two directions: from Sheepshead Bay (with a corner of Gravesend thrown in) and from Marine Park. This in effect meant that the most viable initial approach was a kind of scissors movement, the pivotal angle being formed by the conjunction of Knapp and Gerritsen avenues at Avenue U. This was a well-illuminated commercial corner, and would serve nicely as a base of operations. But since Ebony Court was deep into the older section of Gerritsen, it was obvious that about one-third of the area of the triangle they were attempting to cover was superfluous. So, at a second stage of penetration, they decided to cut it off a bit closer, at the intersection of Channel Avenue, Avenue Y, and Shell Bank Creek. The Gerritsen Canal, bridgeless, then intersected the neighborhood again, between Gotham Avenue and Bartlett Place, beyond the house on Ebony Court. Since Gerritsen Avenue would be heavily patrolled at this point, Tyrone Ward's maneuverability would be cut down to an eleven- by three-block area with his mother's house roughly in the center, completely cut off. The blocks were tiny, most only wide enough to accommodate a couple of houses, and small ones at that. It wasn't much more than ten acres of land, the size of a country house-lot. Easily manageable for men used to larger, more populated, and trickier projects. But the neighborhood was also dark, ill-lit, and notorious for the elusiveness of its inhabitants.

The captain in charge of SWAT operations began to disperse his men to stations lining Gerritsen and Knapp avenues, and to the more intensely manned inner operations center at the head of Shell Bank Creek. At DeSales's urging, the Shore Patrol, Park Police, and Coast Guard were also alerted. There would be at least three fast boats in the Rockaway Inlet, prepared for untoward happenings, although Maceo Allen, who leaned against a car near DeSales, protested:

"Don't spread yourself too thin. We've got it on record that the guy can't swim. He's a driver, a car- and van-freak. Roust the house as soon as you can. If he manages to make a break, he's going to have to either blast his way through some *heavy* roadblocks or learn to walk on water. Quick."

"Daylight," said DeSales. "Funny things always happen to stakeouts after dark. We'll go in at first light. You already got a squad watching the house?"

"We've surrounded a three-block grid, such as it is," said the captain. "The boys who know the area say we'll tip him or the next-door neighbors off if we go in any closer. If we stay diffuse enough at the center they'll probably think we're dragging for gunrunners without green cards."

"I'm going in with you," said DeSales.

The captain, a beefy uniformed Irishman with twenty-five years in the police after five as an MP in World War II, looked down at the wiry sallow-faced man in the tight-fitting suit and expensive shoes. He watched as DeSales lighted a Benson & Hedges and blew the smoke into the air, his jaw jutting in ready defiance.

The captain shrugged his shoulders: "Technically, you've got the authority here. It's your funeral."

DeSales walked quickly over to the gray Ford, trailing the cigarette in one hand and with the other adjusting the holster with the service revolver. Megan Moore was sleeping behind the wheel. He touched her shoulder. Her eyes popped open, dewy from sleep. The long feminine lashes fluttered. There was now a spot of color in her cheeks. She had signed herself out of the hospital, in spite of the doctor's warnings, and the struggle with the bureaucracy seemed to have speeded her recovery from the shock of the night before.

"We're going in at daybreak," he said. He patted the hood: "You get your car back in one piece?"

She nodded. "Except for the radio and stuff. That's for exhibit at the trial. He left his prints all over it."

"If there *is* a trial. Listen, as far as I'm concerned you can start phoning in the story now. There's a booth on the other end of the lot. We just need a promise that nothing will go on the air until after we go in. After knocking on a hundred doors we finally got somebody to admit they'd seen him around today. He's inside. So we don't want him making a break for it."

"Even if we wanted to, we couldn't. It'll take the producer a couple of hours to cut the tape, and we don't go back on the air until 'Drive Time.' Seven A.M. Nobody listens until then. How about I get them to promise not to run it until eight?"

DeSales calculated to himself.

"You don't believe me?" she asked. "It's easy enough to check out, you know."

He patted her gently on the cheek: "I'm a cynical guy in a cynical job. But I'll believe you anyway. Like I said in the first place, go ahead."

She looked up, clutching the hand that had patted her cheek with her own good hand:

"You going to wear a bulletproof vest?"

"Why?"

"Because I care. Because I've figured out that your whole tough-as-nails street-smart exterior is a lot of bullshit. I want at least a chance to get underneath it."

"What's bullshit?"

"I had you checked on, when I was doing the first pieces, and then I asked a few more questions from the hospital after you left today."

"And?" DeSales's left cheek twitched.

"And I know that your father died at sea when you were a kid and that your mother had a nervous breakdown and you had to be raised by her sisters. That you went to Duke on a scholarship, majored in English, wrote an honors thesis—on the *Romantic Poets*, for God's sake—and were editing the Law Review at Georgetown when your mother was permanently institutionalized and you quit school and got a job as a cop."

DeSales removed his hand from hers and touched her arm as it rested on the open window on the driver's side of the W V B A Mobile Unit. The gesture was not an affectionate one. It was more a coldly-calculated appraisal of the quality of the material at the tips of his fingers. He kept his hand there a long time. He looked straight into her eyes until her lashes fluttered ever so slightly. He turned back to the lot and broke into a trot, heading for the S WAT men who were changing into full battle-gear. As he pulled on the coveralls and the helmet, he was still swearing under his breath.

When Desmond came to, it was to the sound of breaking glass in the kitchen.

"What the fuck you think you're doin'?" Tyrone's voice had the rumble of distant thunder in it.

"What's it look like, you jerk? I'm washin' my hair in the kitchen sink."

"I told you to go to bed and cut out the booze. If the cops come here, I don't want you drunk and runnin' off at the mouth. You may got suds in the sink and a wet head, but you came down to sneak another shot."

"Like hell. This is my house, and I'm your mother. You won't tell me what to do. Especially the likes of *you!*"

Desmond heard scuffling on the floor, then a splash. He strained his head to see in the kitchen door, but could only see the soapy water dripping onto the floor. Then he saw the woman's feet kick out from under her. Then she was choking and sputtering. Then there was another splash and a grotesque gurgling sound, as if someone had put an empty bottle under water. Then he heard her gasp: "You big scumbag, ya coulda drowned me." Her feet were back on the floor.

His loss of control seemed to have rattled Tyrone. His voice was suddenly small. He said, "You needed to get your head cleared. Sometimes I think your brain got holes in it."

Desmond saw her step back and swing. He heard the splat as her hand hit Tyrone's flesh. Then the door slammed. Tyrone had stalked out. He had turned the other cheek. The woman spent a couple more minutes in the kitchen, then sauntered into the living room. She found her pack of Luckies. She lighted one and sat heavily in her chair. At her arm was a heaping ashtray. It looked as though she had smoked a pack during the night. She whistled a moment, craned her neck toward the kitchen, and fished under her chair. She pulled out another bottle of Canadian Club, about three-quarters full. She lifted it to her lips, in the same moment saw that Desmond was awake, then drank deeply, closing her eyes. She smacked her lips and looked at him.

"It's the Irish in him," she said. "He always has had a temper." She put the bottle back under the chair and shivered. Her dunking in the sink had removed most of the makeup, and Desmond saw that her eyebrows were plucked. Her skin was alternately cracked and puffy. The hair hung limply against the outlines of her skull. "It must have come from his father's side. Not *mine!*" She engaged Desmond in direct eye-contact, the sign that she expected a response.

"Of course not," he said.

"My father was a gentleman farmer. In the west. Of Ireland. They drove him to Dublin in the Troubles because the dumb boyos thought that because he was prosperous he was a Protestant. They burned the farm. But he wrote songs for them anyway. *Sinn Fein* songs for the Republicans. They say he was the model for—what's his name, Robert Preston? In *The Informer.* Him and my mother came to New York on their honeymoon a few years later. Liked it; decided to stay. We had a farm back then. Goats. Above Bush Terminal. Before old Robert Moses built the expressway and drove out the nice people down along Third Avenue." She belched.

She checked out the door again. She drank. "The Puerto Ricans took over after they built the expressway. Then, about the same time, I met this handsome Irish sailor at Michel's on Flatbush, where the Dodgers hung out. And I went with him out to the Half-Moon Hotel at Concy Island and we had breakfast in bed and looked out the window over the beach and pretended we could see all the way to Ireland. I didn't mind a bit that he was so darkly-complected. You see the Spanish once invaded Ireland—the aristocratic Spanish, not the Puerto Ricans—and he was descended in part from them. And he had a bit of the Irish gypsy in him too. So you can see where Tyrone gets his looks. And his temper. I never got his name, see, this romantic Irish sailor who spent his life wandering from sea to shining sea, but I knew he was from County Tyrone, and when the baby came along I saw that he was going to look like his daddy so I named him Tyrone after the county." She ground out the cigarette. "One of these days Tyrone and I are going back to Ireland, where my father came from, and go to County Tyrone and find Tyrone's father. Ah, he was a wildman. Tyrone, you see, was a sweet little thing until he had to go to school and the kids noticed he looked different and they teased him, so I went to the school and took care of them. And I went to the parents' houses and took care of *them.*" She looked across at Desmond knowingly. "They didn't like it. They didn't like it one bit."

"What?"

"When I told them that Tyrone was descended from the aristocracy on the one side and from an Academy Award–winner on the other, and that he was too good for them by far. No, they didn't like it." She shook her head. "And they didn't like it either when I told them how gentlemanly the colored on the Dodgers was. Except for Jackie Robinson, of course."

Tyrone came in the back door and entered the living room through the kitchen. He had a pistol in his belt. He began to untie Desmond's legs: "I've got it runnin'. So we're takin' off. Remember, Mom, we weren't here."

"As far as I'm concerned, I never *knew* you. After the way you've *treated* me." She tapped her finger on the arm of the chair and wiggled her foot, the old house-slipper dangling from a painted toe.

DeSales was concerned about the proximity of the canal. All you had to do, from the house on Ebony Court, was cross Gotham Avenue, walk through somebody's back yard, and you could step into any one of six kinds of small boats and head for sea. So he held back two of his own men, who had been deployed to the SWAT unit, and stationed them along Gotham with instructions to make sure none of the powerboats started up in the canal. Then he moved up to the front line, made sure the rifle he had been issued was loaded, and stood outside the quiet house.

There was one dim light burning in a front room. No one had seen Tyrone or his guest since the evening before, when Tyrone had been observed going in and out the back door by a neighbor who hated Mary Ward and assumed Tyrone was her "high yella" boyfriend. Desmond had not been seen since the little girl had watched Tyrone lead him in with his hands tied behind his back. Now, as light began to break to the east, over Marine Park, the captain made a silent motion to the door, and two cops in coveralls stepped up, poised to shoot. DeSales went to the door and raised his fist. He was conscious, in the dawn, of the shifting glint of the barrels of the rifles held by the men who formed a tight circle around the house. He was sorry they had not been able to evacuate more of the nearby places, but it would have compromised the operation.

He knocked.

There was a pause, then a jolly female voice inside called, as if she were expecting dinner guests, "Yes? Who is it?"

"The police," said DeSales.

The door opened. Mary Ward stood before him, somehow at once forlorn and imposing. Now her voice was laden with scorn: "I was expecting you." She pulled her housecoat around her in a grand gesture of modesty, returned to her chair, and began to stir a fresh drink. "You got a warrant?"

"Yes," said DeSales.

She made a sweeping gesture, inviting entry. SWAT men poured through the front door, kicked in the back one. DeSales had a distinct sense that they were even coming in the tiny windows in which cardboard replaced the broken panes. Mary Ward sat in the middle of this whirlwind, solid as a rock in spite of red eyes, an apparent inability to focus, and the undeniable presence of large broken blood vessels on the Roman nose. She looked up at DeSales, the nominal leader of the invasion. A sly grin crossed her face; "My lips are sealed," she intoned. Then she stood up and made her way to the foot of the enclosed staircase, from which aperture one could hear the cops turning the house upside down. She screamed: "Keep your mitts off my intimate apparel, you perverts. Do you know who I am? I know the Dodgers. PeeWee, Carl, even Preacher." Her voice had become hoarse. She returned to her chair and sat. To DeSales, she croaked, "And I was on stage with Jimmy Cagney. Once."

The squad leader entered the room and said, "They're not anywhere in this house."

Desmond held his breath and dropped into the darkness. His feet struck a solid platform and he felt it sway beneath him. He heard the water lapping against the sides. Tyrone's weight made the boat rock again, and then all was silent. Tyrone sat Desmond down in the stern while he cast off and took the oars amidships. Expertly, silently, he pulled the oars through the water. He pulled three times and then allowed the boat to drift from between the two ramshackle piers. They were in the middle of some kind of stream or canal. There were more houses of the sort Tyrone's mother occupied on each side of them. An occasional light flickered, but most of the area still rested in darkness.

Desmond now had no idea where they could be. They might be in New Jersey or Connecticut for all he knew. He had lost track of time in the trunk of the car. Sheepshead Bay, Coney Island, all of the waterways he knew of in Brooklyn were either polluted backwaters in the heart of industrial waste or wide open and commercial fishing and beach centers.

Tyrone pulled the oars again. The rowboat slipped through the water. Desmond had a brief flash of the sculls on the Charles in Cambridge. A Spring weekend. Champagne cocktails for breakfast. Madras jackets everywhere. From the dirty noisy highway in Pennsylvania, to Harvard, to Brooklyn. Now here he was, in danger of losing his life. And he had no idea where he was.

Soon they were crossing a wider body of water. There was a marina to the right, and Tyrone guided the rowboat between two large yachts. A smaller powerboat rode the mildly undulating tide. It had an open deck, with a steering wheel–dashboard component in the center. Desmond found that it also had storage space, because Tyrone's first move was to lift him over the side like a sack of potatoes, open a storage locker, and drop him inside. With his hands still tied behind him, he dropped like a dead weight, striking his shoulder on a hook. The shoulder first seared with pain, then went numb. But he had little time to contemplate his new prison, to perhaps drift back again into the reverie of invisibility, of irresponsibility, because Tyrone, after adjusting some mechanisms and checking the fuel, lifted him, grunting, back on deck. He gestured for him to stand up, which Desmond did with some pain. Then he pushed him back against the obelisk-shaped structure in the center of the boat. Quickly he wound rope around Desmond's torso, then his legs, until he was tightly lashed to the steering console, facing the bow. Tyrone now untied his hands. Desmond felt the pins and needles as the circulation returned, but there was no sense of freedom. It was clear that his captor intended to use him as a shield when he ran past or through the authorities in his attempt to get away. Desmond had been lulled, in the trunk, into a kind of false sense of escape from his guilt-fashioned spotlight. Now he was center-stage. Whatever was to happen, his role in it would be visible to the world at large.

For the first time he felt full-force the meaning of being a hostage.

Tyrone turned over the engine. In the silent dawn, it sounded thunderous, a thousand amplifications of Tyrone's voice when he had yelled before almost drowning his mother in the sink. The motor hesitated, then caught. Tyrone backed the boat out of the slip. Then he eased forward, running without lights, past the houses that screened his mother's house from the waterfront. With the sun rising over them, the houses seemed banal, conventional, even mildly prosperous, with their docks and picnic tables, barbecue grills and plastic lawn furniture; there were Easter bunnies in the windows. Desmond wondered if he had hallucinated the half-naked little girl in the tarpaper shack.

> *Go ask Alice.*
> *I think she'll know*

They passed under a highway bridge and hit open water. Tyrone accelerated. The boat reared back. Wind and spray struck Desmond's face. The salt water splotched his glasses and ran into his eyes. He could have been crying, but he didn't know.

# CHAPTER 30

TYRONE GUNNED THE boat under the Belt Parkway, saw the
Harbor Patrol launch—the twenty-four-footer with the cabin—
did a rapid turnabout back under the highway, and sought ref-
uge behind Mau Mau Island. He dropped anchor in a place
where the '65 Buick that they had towed out and left on the
sandbar one low tide would block the line of vision between
him and the patrol. They didn't move, they hadn't seen him.

"Where are we? Where are we going?" Desmond called
back, craning his neck.

"Ireland," snorted Tyrone. "The Old Sod."

He wondered if he should hit the professor with another
'Lude or two, and decided against it. The prof could shout and
agitate until he was hoarse, and no one would hear. With the
wind and the gulls and the fishing boats going out, you couldn't
hear anything on the water more than ten feet away. As the boat
bobbed back and forth, he kept an eye on the patrol boat, first
the prow, then the stern, and made sure it wasn't moving. He
decided to pop a couple of 'Ludes himself.

Bringing the Buick out onto Mau Mau had been his idea. It
was one of the few times he had ever managed to stand in with

the micks from Gerritsen. Maybe they thought he was some kind of gypsy or something, but they knew then that he was a smart one. He had been working the marina that summer, pumping gas, keeping the boats clean, dealing in tax-deduction forms from the geriatric centers. He would, say, take all the leftover mackerel or bluefish from the catch of one of the fishing or party boats, fish that couldn't be sold on the dock, and take it to the old people's home and they'd sign a blank receipt for a donation of fish. Then he'd write in, say, one hundred pounds of lobster at six dollars a pound, and then he'd sell the receipt for a hundred bucks to some rich dude who was on the books and paying fifty percent taxes. That meant the rich dude got two hundred off his taxes and Tyrone got one hundred in cash, and then he'd borrow one of the boats from the marina— indeed the *Pea-Quod*, on which he was now riding the tide, was one of his favorites because the owner was always so smashed that he didn't use it, didn't even care if it was in the slip—and take some dope and run out to where the Night Warriors were partying on Mau Mau. The Warriors wore combat fatigues, had sheath knives and bandannas and no brains. So one night they had all got blasted and crashed in the sand on Mau Mau and they woke up with the sun and Tyrone had seen the tide lower than it had ever been before and there on Plum Beach some asshole had got his car stuck in the sand and Tyrone had the idea of going back to the marina and getting a winch and towboat and they had pulled the motherfucking Buick across from the beach to the sandbar and then stripped it down pretty good and left it to sit there when the tide came back in. The owner never came to get it. Nobody ever drove it again. Except some of the guys who wanted privacy would get laid in the back seat sometimes out on Mau Mau. That was before the crabs got into the Buick and you could get your dick pinched if you didn't watch yourself.

That had got him some respect. He could always think about getting respect when he was out on the water, because from the water you couldn't see the parts of Brooklyn where he'd been fucked over, you could just see the beaches and the high-rises and the city. The most respect he ever got, or felt, was when he was working the Quaalude Clinic. He wore a white lab-coat and he would check out the dudes at the door. There would be a line stretching all around the block. He would let them in one at a time. They would see the doctor behind the counter and tell him they couldn't sleep at night. The doc would write a scrip for a hundred 'Ludes and they'd pay two hundred cash and then they'd run out the door waving at their friends outside, and Tyrone would say, "Next." What got him off was that he had this terrific ability to do 'Ludes, and drink too, and he'd only feel on top. Like some people got with coke. Just like he was beginning to feel now, riding the swell. And these kids, Italians from Bath Beach, Jews from Sheepshead Bay, the Irish from around Marine Park, would pull up on a Friday or Saturday in their parents' big shiny cars—all ready to disco it up—and maybe they'd have done one 'Lude and they'd be hugging the parking meters to stay on their feet while in the meantime Tyrone had drunk maybe two six-packs of Bud, sixteen-ouncers, and maybe dropped three or four 'Ludes, and he was completely with it. Then he could stand extra tall with the pampered brats. And he was watching the door. He controlled them, and they couldn't control themselves.

He felt a little bit that way about this guy Desmond he had tied to the console.

There was an off-shore fog moving in as the air warmed up in the sunshine, from out at the Rockaways, and he saw the patrol boat pull further into Plum Beach Channel. It came under the Belt, then turned in toward Shell Bank Creek, stationing itself so nobody could get out of Gerritsen.

They were wise.

But not wise enough. He was already *out* of Gerritsen. He started up the engine again and passed under the Belt and was in Rockaway Inlet. Completely out of Brooklyn. There was no evidence of anything like a police boat, so he headed south and then west to go around Breezy Point, and the fog got heavy so the best he could do was sort of run with the edge of the fog, kind of sliding in and out of it. This was good because it meant he was traveling at least in part under cover. It was bad because he could see he wasn't going to get over to Jersey until it burnt off, and that might be too late. The Harbor Patrol and the Park Police and the Coast Guard together had at least ten boats and they could run him down easy. He had to do it now before they figured out that he'd split the way he had.

There were a lot of party boats coming out of Sheepshead Bay, and some hotdoggers were throwing up rooster-tails off the beaches, Manhattan, Brighton, Coney Island, and the fishermen without heavy navigational gear were hanging around the edge of the fog like he was, so he decided he'd better make a run for it now. He'd get lost among all the other small craft, and when they hit the turn into the harbor at Seagate, at the old Potato Patch, he'd have to decide if he could take the *Pea-Quod* on a run across open sea with the fog like a shroud over it, or whether he'd have to go into the city.

In the decision-making, in the euphoria he felt as he by-passed, transcended, the borough of his birth, when Bed-Stuy and Bushwick had fallen out of sight as if into the bowels of the earth, he forgot that it would not be easy to get lost with a six-foot three-inch man strapped to the front of the steering console. He had bracketed Desmond, only allowing him to exist in the eventuality of a confrontation with the police.

Then he would be his shield, part of the necessary equipment. He checked the hatch, and the M-16 was still there.

The thing Desmond found most startling as they lay quietly behind the beer can- and condom-littered sandbar with the automobile carcass was the sense that Brooklyn had disappeared. Out of the corner of his eye, he was vaguely aware of the high rises in Sheepshead Bay, but that seemed insignificant to the land, waterbound. Otherwise, looking back across Brooklyn in the direction of his own house, where Mona was probably rolling over, soft and warm in the pink nightie, there was only the cabled arch of the Verrazano Bridge, and the commercial sky-scrapers of Manhattan. In between, beyond the mean patches of sand and scrub at the shoreline, Brooklyn, the borough of churches and large families and Jackie Robinson and the Mafia and half the Jewish comedians in the world, did not exist. It was as if it had fallen into a hole. A nothingness. How, Desmond thought, would there not be a sense of Crown Heights, of the hills of Prospect Park, of even the Williamsburg Savings Bank from sea level? But it wasn't there.

Then they were moving out again. He had been lulled into a sense of relative comfort in the shelter of the island, but now, as they headed away from the extinct borough, the cold wind pierced his bones, his sore shoulder began to throb again, the salt spray assailed him; the rapid alternations of haze and bright sunshine exacerbated the chill. Tyrone had opened the throttle now, and he felt as if he were being shot out of a cannon.

He suppressed the urge to scream. He could not be heard in any case; even Tyrone would not hear him. His teeth had begun to chatter. He fought to inhibit the descent into a null and featureless terror, for which the disappearance of Brooklyn had become a kind of objective correlative. He too would soon sink into nothingness. So he tried to resurrect each thing that was available to his senses, to nurse it, coddle it, love it in his mind, so he could void himself of all that was personal, because anything personal was synonymous with his own nonexistence.

They were in the ocean now. The swell was greater, the wind had more bite, but the city had begun to reconstitute itself in his erratic vision. There was the Institute at Coney Island, the ever-present parachute jump, a useless rusting eyesore because it was too expensive to repair and also too expensive to tear down. Over the vacant lots, there were projects, reassuring in their ugly functionalism. At the end of Coney Island beach, the sight of Seagate, the idea of it, with its enforced coziness, its hiding behind high fences and armed guards, its neat, freshly-painted houses, the budding vulgar azaleas and tulips, seemed so much more rational, so obviously *necessary*, to a Tim Desmond strapped to a boat heading into nothingness, than it ever had to a T. Desmond, Associate Dean, looking out a window from the vantage point of authority, his face framed by Literary England. He thought of his passivity, his need for Mona to solve his problems, his reliance on the soft chair, the glass of wine, and he knew that there had always been a Seagate deep in his heart, a need for an enclave to protect him from surprise.

A helicopter passed overhead and he remembered that they were, after all, only a few hundred yards from civilization, well within the jurisdiction of conventional authority. There were police, Coast Guard, military. DeSales was in there some-where. He had a chance to be saved.

Almost as if he had read his mind, Tyrone leaned across the center console and shouted into his ear: "See that!" He pointed to a rocky sea wall at the edge of Seagate, next to a red light-house. "That's Suicide Jetty. It's covered at three-quarter tide. Wanna run over it?" Tyrone let go of the wheel, and the boat veered crazily toward shore. Then he reached back and turned them back out again. Once again he released the wheel. They entered a rolling cauldron of dark water, and the boat bobbed like a toy. Tyrone laughed in his face. Desmond saw that being at sea had transformed the man. He had before been merely compulsive and probably paranoid; now he saw something manic, out of control, the psychopath who had murdered the women and littered the gravesites with sardonic signatures.

"I have to piss," Desmond shouted at him, and the wind and spray spat the words back into his face. The boat heeled over one way, then the other. Tyrone had to grip his prisoner's bonds to keep his footing. He edged his way back to the helm, accel-erated again, and they were back in the relative calm of Graves-end Bay.

Tyrone seemed to have subsided into a comparably deliberate and even-headed mood: "Piss all you want," he said. "That's why I left your hands free and didn't put the rope over your fly. Piss on the deck. It ain't my boat."

Desmond set himself to the task. Tyrone spun the wheel

suddenly, pointing them back to open sea, and the urine blew back onto Desmond, soaking his already damp trousers. Tyrone laughed sadistically: "Didn't they teach you in your fancy colleges not to piss into the wind?"

Desmond knew now that he was going to die. At the same time he began to feel sorry for Tyrone. Who would kill him. And now the absolute banality of that section of the Brooklyn coastline seemed to join him in resignation. He was a penny-ante Odysseus, with Toys-'R'-Us and Caesar's Bazaar his Sirens. There was no need even to stuff his ears, for Bath Beach, Bensonhurst, and Bay Ridge lay silent—as well as unhearing—tall, red-brick, intersected by lawns and ballparks, and redolent of lives of unrelieved tedium. First Desmond had watched Brooklyn disappear from sight, an Atlantis of the imagination, and now it rose again as mile upon mile of condominium complacency and bumper-to-bumper commuter cars on the Belt Parkway. No slums, no brownstones, no cemeteries, no gentrifiers. Only an extended ant-colony of workers determined above all never to miss a creature comfort. Desmond envied them, every one.

They passed under the Verrazano.

He looked up, and the bridge seemed to reel in the sky. He had lost his equilibrium. Only the ropes were holding him together.

DeSales stood in the little park next to the Verrazano Bridge overlooking the narrows, watching through his binoculars. Twenty feet below the promenade, water lapped at the retaining wall. Oblivious to the heavy police presence, ordinary Brooklynites jogged and bicycled past on the smooth macadam. An old drunk sat on one of the cement benches. Every few minutes he would gulp from his bottle and hoot derisively at the men in blue. As Kavanaugh came up with the walkie-talkie, DeSales saw the twenty-three-foot Seacraft Center-Console Inboard approach and speed under the bridge, heading for the upper bay. At the helm was the man DeSales took to be Tyrone Ward. It was the first time he had seen him, but one glimpse through the magnifying lenses was enough to assure him that this was someone who had to be done away with. A mad dog. Lashed to the console was his old friend Desmond. DeSales dropped the binoculars, allowing them to hang from the strap around his neck. He put the walkie-talkie to his lips and ear.

"Hold them off," he barked. "Keep the twenty-four-footer as far back as it can handle. I don't want him to panic yet. The sixty-footer's in the mouth of the river?"

"Affirmative," the voice squawked. "Buttermilk Channel, between Governor's Island and South Brooklyn."

"What about the other side?"

"The ferry lanes. We've got two small Coast Guard cruisers hanging on in there."

"Good. I think he's headed for the river or up into the Gowanus Bay. Let's aim for this. When he sees the big launch in the channel and the cabin cruiser behind him, he'll be forced to go into the Gowanus, or to try and head for Staten Island or up the Hudson. You got those fast boats behind Liberty Island?"

"Affirmative. He'll be headed off at the pass."

"So we wait and see."

"The Colombians must be havin' a field day," said Kavanaugh. "All the boats we got to keep them from sneakin' into the harbor with their dope are chasin' our friend."

"Not for long," said DeSales. "He's got about fifteen minutes left in his little expedition. Let's get up to Bush Terminal. We can work him pretty good from there." He turned sharply at the sound of squealing tires behind them. A large black limousine braked abruptly, just short of the bench where the old drunk was sitting. "What the fuck's this?"

"Call me a lawyer," yelled the drunk. "I got whiplash."

"It looks like the mayor." Kavanaugh made no effort to suppress his smirk.

The mayor came out of the limo long legs first. He strode up to DeSales, but their eyes did not meet. He stood at his side facing the water, almost a head taller. His Adam's apple bobbed as he spoke softly, "I was at a bagels-and-lox breakfast in Borough Park," he said. "You know they got a kosher branch of Bloomingdale's there now?"

DeSales did not laugh. The mayor resumed:

"I heard there about this situation. It's happened, uh, very quickly."

"Glad to be of service, Your Honor."

The mayor did not sound particularly pleased. "We've had quite a bit of blood spilled this week, no?"

"Yes."

"You know, if this Professor Desmond has so much as a hair on his head touched, your ass is grass."

"We're doing our best. You want we should treat the Grim Reaper with kid gloves also?"

"Hmm. That's what I wanted to talk to you about. If possible. Actually, yes. I'd like to see him . . . uh . . . preserved."

"Is that an order, Your Honor?"

"It is."

"Why, Your Honor?"

"We're working on a big grant. Millions. Get the federal government to subsidize a major Institute of Abnormal Psychiatry. In Brownsville. Where they've burnt everything down. We want to specialize in serial murder. That's a hot topic now. Did you see the show on Channel Thirteen? Anyway, I can envision this Tyrone whatsisname as a pilot project for our case studies. New York . . . Brooklyn . . . can go to the forefront in the motiveless crime business. Not to mention that we have a chance to rejuvenate a blighted community."

"Yes, Your Honor," said DeSales. He picked up the walkie-talkie again. "Smitty, when you get the *Pea-Quod* closed in for sure, press the guy a little bit. Keep the on-shore operations invisible. Ideally, I'd like to chase him back onto dry land. And get him separated from Desmond. As soon as possible."

The mayor waved a silent farewell from the limo. DeSales headed for his car. They would catch up with Ward and Desmond in a few minutes.

"Jesus," said Kavanaugh, pointing at the rising cloud. "Lookit that. It must be the asphalt plant again."

DeSales closed his eyes and gritted his teeth. "What time is it?"

"Nine A.M."

"What day is it?"

"Monday."

"So what the fuck do we expect? At nine o'clock Monday morning people go back to work. Oh," he cried, "why does the rational thing only happen when it can fuck me up!"

# CHAPTER 31

TYRONE COULD NOT be sure when it came over him, but there it was. He *knew*. They were on his tail, but keeping their distance. If it wasn't for Desmond they probably would have blown him out of the water by now. Perhaps there had been one too many Coast Guard planes. Perhaps it was the sense that he had not seen any of the patrol craft since the mouth of Shell Bank Creek. Maybe one of the gulls had screeched a message in a language that he knew but didn't know he knew. He felt the jumps coming on. He got a cold beer out of the styrofoam cooler and tried to settle back into Quaalude comfort. He'd need to stay calm for this one. Actually, it was all very simple. He had been screwed out of the initial plan to run to Jersey, Asbury Park or Red Bank or something, hotwire a car, and drive to the other van that he kept in the flats. The fog had fucked him up, but, like the Maharaji once said, there's two edges to the same sword. And now he saw the thick billowing cloud coming from Red Hook and he decided to run right into it for cover. An omen. A deliverance. If the fog stayed as thick as it had the day they picked up the Carruthers guy, he could get right into the Gowanus, scuttle the boat and Desmond with it, and take a subway uptown. He could maybe sneak over to the house on Dennett Place and see if Joe had called the cops. Maybe Yoo-Hoo had come back with some of her Liberation Army friends. He had the M-16 now, so he could eat 'em up. Absolutely.

Then he remembered he'd left the good van in the parking lot next to the Army Terminal. But Megan Moore had seen it, and he hadn't had time to take off the phone-company signs, so the cops might be sniffing around; that would be Option Two. It was like with the Buick he got out to Mau Mau, you had to plan and make sure you had the technology. He saw the helicopter with the letters on the side swoop down to check him out; he saw the sneaky little police-boat edge around from behind the ferry and press him from that side. He turned around and saw the twenty-four-footer that had been fucking around off Gerritsen that morning begin to move up. He took out the M-16 and put the wheel on lock. He aimed the rifle, first behind him at the Harbor Patrol boat, then at the Coast Guard cutter heading from the Statue of Liberty. They were still too far away. So he raised the weapon and squeezed off some rounds in the general direction of the helicopter. The chopper did such a fast climb that the downdraft almost turned the *Pea-Quod* belly up. Then they were in the deep fog, silent and womblike. The Bush Terminal piers were ghosts on the right. The bent arm of Erie Basin faded and magnified with the crazy light to the left. He had no idea how much water there was to draw, but he didn't give a shit either. He just pointed the boat where he thought the Gowanus Canal opening was. The Quaaludes had really taken hold and he had this relaxed feeling that nobody could really fuck with him anyway.

It was when he was draining the beer that the prop got fouled and started to make the terrible cranking noise and he remembered somebody telling him once that there wasn't a small-boat prop in the world that could make it into the canal. Because of the garbage just beneath the surface. The water around that part of Brooklyn was as dense as the land. And a lot dirtier.

*Anchor:* Can you hear me, chopper, are you there?

*Co-pilot:* (Sounds of crashing and scrambling) Geronimo! That crazy freak just opened fire on us.

*Anchor:* Any casualties?

*Pilot:* Nope. We were lucky. Megan, you holding up?

*Moore:* Of course. After firing, the alleged killer dropped his gun . . .

*Pilot:* Weapon. It looks like an M-16.

*Moore:* Well, he's dropped it, whatever it is. He's running the boat forward and backward. Like someone stuck in the snow.

*Pilot:* He's fouled the prop.

*Co-pilot:* Where's the cops? They must have him now.

*Moore:* I hear from reliable sources in the department that the police are merely to contain the *Pea-Quod*. They don't want to bring harm to the hostage. But now it looks like he's clear. He's turned away from the Gowanus; he's headed into the Erie Basin. That's just the sort of thing the police are hoping for. The basin can be sealed off in a moment. He'll be surrounded on land, within easy reach of marksmen. He'll be forced to surrender in there. You should see this place. It's like an arm sticking out of Red Hook with the elbow bent. Near the fist is a narrow channel just off the old nineteenth-century piers that look like prisons in a Dickens novel. Especially with the pockets of fog blowing in and out.

Desmond's cheeks were fiery from exposure to the wind and sun. His eyes continued to play tricks on him. Brooklyn had fallen into a hole; had reincarnated itself as a red-brick wall of bourgeois complacency; and then, in the harbor, had begun to take on the lineaments of a scenario for the end of the world. The water teemed with flotsam and jetsam: railroad ties, garbage bags, dead animals, automobile tires, a floating wooden box that resembled a coffin. Yet, as Tyrone ground the gears trying to clear the prop, from time to time Desmond could glimpse in the near distance a paradoxical postcard version of New York maritime life: the financial skyline, the ferryboats, the ocean liners, the tugs, the Statue of Liberty, the garbage scows, the gilded yachts, spinnakers billowing in the breeze. And this was most peculiar because, while the words that framed his thoughts flashed through his consciousness at speed, in fact the scene itself most resembled one of those primitive seventeenth-century prints in the Public Library on Forty-Second Street that represent the harbor as it was discovered by the first colonizers—two-dimensional, flat, without perspective, without movement. A painting. A bad painting, without vitality, without technique.

Tyrone had gotten rid of what was on the prop. He spun the *Pea-Quod*, and, dizzily, Desmond rehearsed again in his mind the options available. The channels up-river and into the Gowanus were thick with fog and debris; above the rusted piers at Bush Terminal Greenwood Cemetery sprawled like the head of some vast and hoary porcupine. In the upper bay, all movement was arrested save the encroachment of the police boats.

Then Tyrone steered them past a hulk of old stone and a line of red, disused shipping-containers. And a solemn sort of peace descended on them. The wind stopped, the air warmed, and, for the first time since dawn had broken over the stripped Buick on the sandbar, Desmond could see typical row houses of Old Brooklyn lining one side of the surrounding waterfront. How comforting, how civilized, how secure they seemed. They were not grand houses, but houses of nicely painted stone, with shops on the ground floor and flowerpots in the upstairs windows. And converging before them were police vans with lights flashing.

Tyrone saw the cops coming out of the vans and filling up the spaces between the piers on Columbia and Beard streets. A kind of light bulb exploded in his head when he saw behind the cops an old red row house that looked just like the one the guy in Bushwick had sold them for no money down and a fifty-year mortgage and had then set on fire, putting them out on the street without a pot to piss in the third night they tried to sleep there, so he could collect the government-sponsored urban-renewal insurance. And, above that, up in the Heights, was the unmistakable outline of the tower of the St. George, where they'd put his mother in with the welfare cruds. He hit the throttle as hard as he could and made it out of the basin about a minute before the Harbor Patrol boat would have closed him in. There was nothing to do now but go over to the Army Terminal and try to get to the van.

Desmond was cold again and then almost immediately began to warm up as they re-crossed Gowanus Bay, this time to Bush Terminal. Tyrone, he felt, had lost whatever control he might have been holding on to. They ran over a floating log and Desmond bit his tongue; then they hit a tire that caromed off one of the hatches. Desmond felt as if the boat were cracking to pieces beneath him. He craned his neck and saw that Tyrone was not even looking up. He was adjusting an ammunition belt in an X pattern across his chest. They passed more stacks of red containers and a sequence of piers of which nothing was left but the rusted, twisted skeletons of the infrastructure. A few tilted dangerously in the wind. There were big cranes outlined against the sky behind them. At one working pier was a supertanker: the *Jala Bala* from Bombay. Tyrone cut the engines, sidled up to the pilings of an empty but still usable pier, and cautiously made a slow progress up to dockside. At first Desmond was puzzled by the sign at the head of the pier: W E HELLENICLINES M E. Then he realized that the pier had obviously once welcomed home military personnel after a war and had been leased to Hellenic Lines when the Army had no more need for it; a careless sign-painter had neglected to paint out the first and last letters of the "Welcome Home."

He wondered what sort of welcome he and Tyrone were about to receive.

Tyrone cut the ropes with the knife he carried in the sheath on his belt, then prodded him in the back with the M-16.

"Climb," he said, indicating the rotting wooden ladder.

*Anchor:* I've got the mayor on the line now. Good morning, Sir.

*Mayor:* Top o' the morning to you.

*Anchor:* Your Honor, we understand that this fog which has disrupted traffic patterns now for two successive workdays, Friday and Monday, is attributable to the city's new asphalt plant?

*Mayor:* I'm afraid we, and Nature, must take all the credit. The heat from the air expelled by the plant encounters the much colder air on the water and . . . uh . . . vaporizes, I think they call it. Unfortunately, it happens to take place near a major traffic center. . . .

*Anchor:* And is at this moment aiding and abetting a mass killer's escape. Why was this not attended to after Friday?

*Mayor:* I contacted the accountable people, but they were in Washington. On city business, of course, and . . .

*Moore:* Sorry to break in on you, Your Honor, but the plant apparently has been turned off, and the in-shore fog is lifting. Tyrone Ward and his hostage, Professor Desmond, can be seen much more clearly now. They've docked near the Old Army Supply Base just south of Bush Terminal . . .

*Pilot:* That's Fifty-Ninth Street and First Avenue, Brooklyn. I landed there after Korea. It's been closed for years. What I don't understand is the fact that the parking lot is filled with cars.

*Co-pilot:* And there are police vehicles as well. And

military vehicles. The place looks wide open.

*Moore:* My secretary just got to me on the two-way, Mel. There's some kind of art show opening this morning.

*Pilot:* An *art* show? In a supply depot? That's the biggest damned building I've ever been in in my life. Can you get a line on this show?

*Moore:* She's reading to me from the paper: Four hundred exhibitors, 125,000 square feet of space . . . theme is "Preparing for War" . . . Minimalism, Neo-Expressionist, Punk! . . . I can see the boat tied up at the dock now, Mel, but Ward and Desmond have disappeared. . . . There's a bank of riflemen setting up along the edges of the lot and around the terminal and dockside.

*Anchor:* This is military or police?

*Moore:* NYPD. SWAT and Violence Task Force. I recognize Lieutenant DeSales. The Saint. He seems in charge. Can't we get a little closer, Artie?

Tyrone kept Desmond in front of him as they scrambled up the platform of the massive building and slid back the heavy old door. They stepped inside and were in pitch darkness. Tyrone prodded Desmond forward with the barrel of the gun, muttering to himself: "What's the parking lot all about? I can't even see my van. What are the fuckers tryin' to do to me? If they try to get me in here there'll be a hundred dead before they reach me. A hundred and one, includin' *you.* This is the biggest emptiest fuckin' place in the world."

The first explosion went off a dozen yards to their left. There was incandescence, a fizzing sound, a thunderous crack, and a burst of white heat. Tyrone trained the M-16 in that direction and fired wildly. Another explosion went off to the right, then overhead. They plunged forward, ran into a wall, crept along it. Desmond was bewildered at first, then canny. He had left his dread back there on the water. His adrenaline began to pump, and he looked for a deeper level of darkness where he could make a run for it.

But instead of darkness, they seemed to have begun to penetrate the heart of an exotic civilization—or, rather, a parody of a civilization.

They entered a dimly-lighted area and watched bunny rabbits being massacred on a video screen. Now there was blood on the floor and another turn in the ever-lightening labyrinth. Tyrone apparently saw the SWAT men first; he opened fire before Desmond could take the whole scene in. The automatic rifle bucked and spat in his hands, the papier mâché models were ripped in two, fell over, jumped crazily in the smoke. Then Tyrone began to run, and he tripped over the dummy lying on the floor next to the wreck of the police car. This was the source of the fake blood. A radio was playing "When Johnny Comes Marching Home"; a mannequin in handcuffs had had his face shattered against the broken windshield. Tyrone fired again at the wax policeman behind the wheel; then they entered the enormous glass-topped atriumlike space at the spine of the terminal, and Tyrone fell almost backward as the fifty-foot-high inflated skeleton bore down on him. He began to fire again, bursting the gigantic balloon at its midsection and neck; there was a *whoosh* as it deflated. It quivered, as if in a windstorm, and then began to fall toward them.

Tyrone turned and ran.

Desmond stood at the edge of the metal docking area, looking down into the disused railroad track where the trains had once picked up the Army material from the ships. He stared dumbly at the group holding the champagne breakfast: businessmen—art dealers perhaps—in suits; arty types with blue hair and paint-stained jeans; the usual SoHo-Tribeca hangers-on, ponces in black shirts, groupie women in earrings, boots, and little else. Only a few had comprehended the reality of Tyrone's M-16. Some, nonchalant, pretended indifference to another violent exhibit. Obviously, the notion of combating violence by displaying it in a graphically disgusting way had already become a cliché in the minds of the more cynical critics. Some applauded politely. The artist who had created the skeleton screamed. Tyrone turned in mid-flight and squeezed the trigger again, fanning the heads of the new avant-garde. Then his firing mechanism balked. He threw down the rifle and disappeared back into the maze of dark tunnels. For a moment Desmond watched with fascination the bizarre Darwinian scramble that had ensued beneath him, along the railroad ties. Then he was pierced again by the pity for his captor he had felt on the boat. He turned his back on the demimonde and drifted into the darkness in Tyrone's wake. He passed a film montage of Dachau, Nagasaki, El Salvador. He was back on the loading platform, in the sunshine, and Tyrone was legging it toward the docks with a team of *real* riflemen crouched behind sandbags taking aim at his retreating figure. There had to be *something* he could do.

DeSales had Tyrone in his sights from the moment the demented white Negro leaped off the platform and headed for the *Pea-Quod*. Instead of shooting, however, he raised his hand to indicate to his men not to fire. In his mind he could still see the mayor's Adam's apple bobbing as he informed him of his plan to use Tyrone as Exhibit A in the transformation of Brownsville from wasteland to Psychiatric Paradise. DeSales had formulated a counter-plan to the mayor's.

He dropped his hand, then led the men slowly down to the pier. He saw Desmond jump off the platform and follow Tyrone.

DeSales sprinted forward, got on one knee, and, as Tyrone got to the rotting ladder and put one leg over the edge, fired. He hit him just where he wanted, in the knee. Tyrone tumbled heavily over, clutched at the splintered wood, and dropped into the water with a silent splash. DeSales stood and strode to the edge, looking down and watching his prey desperately try to grasp the piling, the choppy water covering his face every second or so. Desmond was standing next to him.

"Good Christ," Desmond said. "It looks like he can't swim."

"Right," said DeSales. "He can't. He's an inner-city kid. What do you expect?"

"I was a lifeguard, I'll get him."

Desmond felt two simultaneous tugs. DeSales held his arm on the right, Kavanaugh his shirt on the left.

"Don't take a chance," said Kavanaugh. "You could get hit with a Good Samaritan lawsuit. Save your charity for the Fresh-Air Fund. Then the next Tyrone comes along, maybe he can swim."

"The only thing he's going to do when he lives is cost the taxpayers a lot of money." DeSales now gripped Desmond with both hands. Below them, Tyrone went down once, twice, and was about to go for the third time. His broad nostrils, thick lips, parchment-colored skin, all pleaded silently from the filthy water around the pilings. Then Desmond was sure, among the gulls, the wind, the powerboats, the creaking piers, the shouting of the police from behind, that he actually heard the strong silent Tyrone call for help. It was an infant's cry, heartrending, the cry of the child who turns his cheek when slapped by his mother, embedded in the heavy deep-throated murmur of a grown man.

Desmond broke free and improvised a clumsy somersault. He hit the water hard, losing his breath for a moment. Then he managed to turn himself around, break the surface of slime and loose junk, and grope until he found something firm and muscular. He exerted all the strength he had left pulling Tyrone by his gun-belt to the surface and pressing his face just above the water, into the piling of the pier. A Coast Guard craft had pulled alongside. A suntanned blond boy in uniform threw them a line. Desmond managed to get the rope under Tyrone's arms and fashion a square knot in the middle of his back before he had to let go, clinging to the rotten wood, to keep himself afloat. Tyrone, water pouring out of his mouth like bilge, was hoisted aboard the craft. Then DeSales was at the foot of the ladder, lending Desmond a hand, pushing him up, one rung at a time, by the seat of his pants.

Desmond lay on the dock. The cuffs of DeSales's neatly pressed gray trousers, at his eye-level, were wet. The Bally loafers were ruined.

"Why did you have to be a wiseguy? Now? That poor bastard was better off dead than alive. Now he's going to spend the rest of his life with electric currents attached to his brain. And we're going to have to pay for it."

Kavanaugh kicked at a plank: "In more ways than one."

Desmond rolled over once and spat the residue of the harbor onto the plank. There was something stuck between his teeth. He had been baptized finally as a New Yorker. He thought about Tyrone. He said, "I *heard* him, DeSales. You know how hard it is to *hear* somebody when they need help? Especially in this city? When you do, I figure, you have to *do* something about it."

DeSales did not respond. Desmond saw him remove his shoes and socks, roll up the trousers neatly, and make his way deliberately back to land. To Brooklyn. The Coast Guard cutter, Tyrone aboard, headed north toward Manhattan. Bellevue?

Desmond was alone and soaked to the skin. He supposed at some point he would have to go home.

# EPILOGUE

THE LOFT HAD wraparound views. Downtown, the World Trade Center towered over them. Uptown, the silver spire of the Chrysler Building set a perspective for the myriad lights reflecting in the glass walls of the 1980s skyline. DeSales lay on the waterbed, naked, toying with the remote control for the television that was mounted at the foot of the bed. Roz wandered back from the kitchen, across the two thousand square feet of gleaming white open space. She wore the pale filmy peignoir that so effectively threw into relief her dark, voluptuous being. She carried a bunch of grapes, now and then holding it aloft and easing the fruit between her teeth. As DeSales changed channels, she dropped onto the bed, which now rose and fell beneath them like a gentle sea. The announcer was introducing a new show, an hour-long weekly "news magazine" that the network was touting as a worthy rival for "60 Minutes."

"This the one she's on?" asked Roz, her mouth half-full.

"Yeh, I think it's the second story."

"Mmmm." She caught the juice that had run down her chin in the palm of her hand just before it stained the garment. "You ever make it with her?"

"Mmmm."

The first feature dealt with the President's courting of the Jewish vote. Film of him riding a horse on his ranch was juxtaposed with film of an Israeli politician piloting a tank across the Lebanese border.

DeSales got off the bed, went to his pants, and brought out his wallet. "Here's twenty," he said.

"Just drop it in the jar," answered Roz. She curled herself into a kittenish ball.

"What jar?"

She pointed to a tall glass container on the white-painted wrought-iron garden table near the bed: "*That* jar."

"What's that for?"

"For these installments you're paying. When the jar is full, the merchandise is completely paid for, and you can't take it back. No returns, you gotta keep it. Quite a deal. Considering you got it reduced in the first place anyway."

DeSales dropped the bill in the jar and got back on the bed. Megan Moore's head appeared on the TV. Her makeup set off the long lashes, bright eyes. Her hair had been reddened. Her jewelry gleamed. She smiled. Uncertainly, he thought. She said she wanted to provoke viewers' memories by recalling for them the tragic and senseless cemetery killings of the previous April. The camera switched to a montage of scenes: the statuary and cross after the bodies had been removed, the sheet-covered stretchers being carried to the ambulances, an aerial view of the *Pea-Quod* speeding into Gowanus Bay, the fog, a promotional film of the art exhibit at the Army Terminal, Tyrone being led away in handcuffs by the police. For a split second, DeSales could be seen at the edge of the screen. There was a break for a commercial. Stay-Free Tampons.

DeSales turned to Roz and scoffed: "*Reduced*, huh? Was it a *White* Sale?"

"A Going-Out-of-Business Sale, you sucker!" She picked up a pillow and made an effort to smother him with it. He fended her off. He pulled her down. The bed quivered like so much jelly. She tried to push him back with her feet, but he got into a kneeling position, holding down her legs. He lunged forward and tried to pin her shoulders. She spun away and he came up with the top of the peignoir, ripped.

"That'll cost," she said, her uncovered breasts, so marvelously firm, heaving mightily.

"Fair enough. Just so it doesn't go in the jar. I'm going to keep that jar empty."

On the TV, Megan Moore was saying: ". . . a country menaced by an epidemic of mass murder; many of the accused have been found to be driven by demons inside them rather than by some exterior, conventional motive, like simple greed or lust. . . ."

DeSales and Roz were pressed against one another now, wrestling. The bottom of the nightgown had slipped around her knees, impeding movement. She reached down and, in one quick motion, tore it in two. She wrapped her legs around DeSales, scissoring his buttocks with her powerful dancer's muscles.

"What is this," he protested. "The Layaway Plan?" He couldn't stop giggling. "Wait a minute! I'm putting no money down."

"That's just what I wanted to hear," she whispered, first rolling to his side and then sliding beneath him. They rode the wave together. "Oh, baby, I feel that jar fillin' up right now."

"So," intoned Megan Moore, "this will be the first of an extended series of regular features on our show: 'Serial Killers: Up Close and Personal.' Tonight we will investigate the case of Tyrone Ward, the Graveyard Grim Reaper."

The camera panned over Gerritsen and closed in on the home of Tyrone Ward's mother. The tarpaper had been covered completely with siding now, paid for by the proceeds from the memoirs that had appeared in *The Star,* though it did not quite match the job Tyrone had left unfinished. There were lace curtains in the windows. Then Megan Moore was in the Ward living room with Mary Eileen Ward. Megan Moore pointed out that she was now sitting in the very chair to which Desmond had been tied, and that it remained bolted to the wall. She turned to her interviewee.

"How do you deal with the fact that your son is a mass murderer, Ms. Ward?"

"Alleged," replied Ms. Ward, holding her head high, smoke curling from the Lucky Strike in her mouth. *"Alleged."*

DeSales found the remote control switch between Roz's legs. He broke his pace for a moment, hit the "Off" button with his knee, and set about getting back his rhythm.

"I didn't know he looked like that."

"He doesn't—or rather, he didn't."

Mona Desmond leaned forward on the bed, pulling taut her woolen kneesocks. Desmond put down his paper, fascinated.

Having interviewed Tyrone's mother, Megan Moore had just introduced Fletcher Carruthers iii, the newly-appointed Distinguished Professor at the graduate center of the City University of New York in midtown Manhattan. He sat in a plush book-lined office, overlooking Bryant Park, his fingers on the keys of a new-looking word processor, apparently one of the perquisites of his position. A secretary deposited a pile of mail on his desk and moved quickly out of the picture. Indeed Carruthers himself was barely recognizable. He had shaved not only his moustache but his entire head as well. There was a ring in his ear. Contact lenses had replaced the spectacles. He seemed completely at ease, except that now and again he tugged at the pointy long collar of his black leather motorcycle jacket.

"I guess," said Desmond, "he figures he can get away with anything now. They'll never dare make him teach again."

Megan Moore was asking: "How have you been able to cope emotionally with the stressful period you recently endured, Professor?"

Carruthers opened his palms and smiled broadly, revealing his gleaming new set of teeth: "What's to *cope* with?" he asked.

"Justice has been done." He spread his arms wider, indicating the office.

"God," said Mona, "and to think you have to work ten hours a day on Registration. It isn't fair."

"So," Megan Moore pressed on, "you have no ill-feeling about Brooklyn?"

Carruthers wrinkled his nose. "When I think of Brooklyn, I think of what Gertrude Stein said about Oakland. You know it?"

Megan Moore shook her head.

"Why, my dear, she said: 'There's no *there* there'!" Carruthers's hearty roar segued into a repeat of the Stay-Free commercial.

"I've been thinking," said Mona, "that since I'm now thirty-five, it's about time *we* started thinking about a baby."

"Great," said Desmond, turning off the TV and embracing her. "There's no time like the present."

"Not so fast. It was the commercial that reminded me. I've got my period. *And* I've got a chart downstairs, tells when I'll be most fertile. So start counting the days. Today. Okay?"

Desmond began to speak, then hesitated.

"Listen," she went on. "Remember the Callaways are coming for dinner tomorrow. And you have therapy in the city tomorrow morning, right?"

"Right."

"Could you get me some Dijon mustard?"

"I thought you did the shopping today."

"I did. But you know Brooklyn. Sometimes I think we're still in the nineteenth century."

"Four new gourmet stores open on Seventh Avenue in six months, and you can't find Dijon mustard. They've got Dijon mustard in the supermarket!"

"Oh, sure. But I can only find that regular brand. The one we've been using all these years. Well, it's embarrassing. I read in *Cuisine* the other day that they make it in *Newark*. And that's all they have on Seventh Avenue. I need something really Burgundian, but not gussied up with herbs and wine. See? Maybe you can stop by Dean and DeLuca or Balducci's. God, sometimes I wish we still lived in the Village!"

With this, she switched off her bedside lamp. Desmond followed suit. He tried to make his sixties fantasy return, feel the music, taste the tequila, get high on the past, bring back the Village.

But it was no good. He could hear only the intermittent sounds of his next-door neighbor stripping paint from his cherrywood shutters, punctuated by water dripping from the toilet bowl into a bucket. He would have to spend his free time for the next week memorizing fertility charts—when he wasn't waiting for the plumber—instead of making random ecstatic love. Moreover, it was Registration Week, and half the kids in Brooklyn would be banging on his office door, demanding or begging to be released from some onerous academic obligation.

What he needed was a good old-fashioned hangover, something truly incapacitating, so he could lie in one place and get his priorities resolved. But even that took some effort, getting a hangover.

"So do I," he finally responded to Mona's last remark, but she was already asleep.

GREEN HILLS PUB. LIB. DIST